SHADOWMIRE

A DARK ACADEMIA ROMANTASY

STARWEAVER SERIES
BOOK ONE

REAGHAN QUINN

This book is a work of fiction. Names, characters, places and incidents are the product of the author's imagination or are used fictitiously. Any resemblance to actual events, locales, or persons, living or dead, is entirely coincidental.

Cover art and campus map © by Natalia Junqueira

❀ Formatted with Vellum

To my husband, for trying to tell me I'm a "good girl," and realizing I'm anything but.

Browning Hall
Air Hall
THE MOUNTAIN
Carriage House
Infirmary
Adminis
Build
Logistics Building
Ivy House
Whittaker Library
Ashfen Grove
Caldera
Ga
Whittaker School of Magick

Spanish Steps
Gymnasium
Lakehouse
Mess Hall
Obsidian Sun Commons
The Grotto
Blue Dahlia Commons
Lake Caldrith
Silver Fern Commons
The Cavern

PROLOGUE

The first time water spoke to me, I was four.

A summer storm had passed, leaving puddles still as glass in the gravel driveway. I crouched beside one, tracing loops and swirls through the mirrored surface—until the lines held. Just for a second. As if the water itself was listening. Watching.

My father saw.

He didn't speak. Just lifted me in his arms, carried me inside, and locked the door behind us. I remember him more than the magick—the terror in his eyes, the tremble in his hands, the way he went to every window in our house and drew the curtains shut. There were whispered phone calls that followed. Meetings with strangers who poked and prodded me.

I never forgot that day.

But the magick never forgot me either.

CHAPTER 1

Woe to those who hear the elements' call and deny it—for the longer it is caged, the wilder it returns.

—Elemental Foundations: Theory, Affinity, and the Core Threads of Magick

The iron gates of Whittaker close behind me with a hiss of old magick and metal. Smooth stone walls rise like a fortress around me, veined with runes and shadowed by clouds. My hired car rolls to a stop in front of an old carriage house, its arched roof dusted in moss, horse tack hanging from the walls in neat, forgotten rows, like ghosts from another century.

Woe to those who hear the elements' call and deny it—for the longer it is caged, the wilder it returns

The words are carved into a weathered copper archway above me. A warning or a promise. Maybe both.

I pay the driver after he hands me my bag, a spike of nausea climbing up the back of my throat as I watch the car disappear around the bend.

No turning back now.

I hitch my duffle higher on my shoulder, fingers tightening around the strap, lungs tight. My gaze tracks past the arch to the looming buildings beyond. One breath to steady. Then another. I square my shoulders and cross the threshold that will define the next four years of my life.

I'm not supposed to be here.

Whittaker School of Magick—elite, intimidating, ancient. A place for those who command the elements, not for someone who spent her entire life pretending they don't exist. But this isn't a school for children. They only take the already-made—twenty-two to twenty-five-year-olds, the prime age for arrogance, ambition…

And power.

Because here, magick doesn't ask—it claims. It cracks the sky open and dares you to survive the fall.

My boots strike too loud against the stone pathway. Fear and hope tangle in my chest, a knot pulled tight.

Following the signs to registration, I keep my head down but my eyes open, cataloging every detail—the ward-lines etched into the limestone, the way they catch the light like hairline cracks under ice, the students I pass. They funnel around me in a tide of black boots and dark coats. Eyes watching me as much as I watch them.

I catch myself scanning for a familiar height in the crowd—stupid, reflexive—then clamp down on the instinct like it's a weakness. I glance back at the path I just came from, noting how long it might take me to escape back through the gates. Eight minutes, give or take. Five if I run really, really fast.

I walk through the grounds of the enemy my father warned me about—and pray that the part of me that whispers it belongs here doesn't wake up too fast.

The signs lead me to a metal table behind which stands an austere-looking woman with a too-tight bun and shrewd gray eyes. For a second, they gleam silver in the sunlight, and my breath catches—my past colliding with the present. I'm seeing a different face, different eyes watching me. The kind that always saw too much.

"Name?" she says, voice unamused and irritated.

I realize I've been staring, lost in memory.

I blink once, shaking my head like I'm trying to clear static. "Celeste Farris," I answer. She checks my name off a list before handing me a folder and a key, muttering something about uniforms and directing me toward the gymnasium behind her.

The locker room is a study in utilitarian grace. Rows of brushed-metal lockers line the walls, their surfaces matte and cool to the touch, etched with sigils I don't yet recognize. Some are scuffed, dented—proof of the generations that came before.

Down the center, wooden benches stretch in long rows, the oak worn smooth by countless hands and sweat-slick bodies. To the left, a tiled archway opens into a shower area—soft-gray stone and frosted partitions that offer the bare minimum of privacy. A twisted reminder that even in here, solitude is an illusion. At Whittaker, there's always the chance you're being watched.

An uncomfortable shiver runs through me at the thought, but I shake it off and set my gaze forward. If they're watching, let them. I'm determined to give them nothing to see.

Across from me, a girl finishes changing. I offer a polite smile; she flicks me a single glance before turning away, dismissing me, as though she already knows I'm not like the rest of them. I silently change into my uniform. We're both stripped of individuality now. Just two people dressed in gray.

I hate gray. Almost as much as I hate black.

And yet here I am—voluntarily wrapped in both.

The uniform for all first-year Whittaker students: a gray

button-down shirt, gray pants, and a zippered jacket with a first-year triangle patch. Black socks. Black standard-issue boots. I close the locker with a sharp clang and tuck the key into my back pocket.

At least they let me keep my ring. One small rebellion. The gold bites warm where it presses against my finger, like it remembers the hand that gave it to me. Something twinges in my chest—there and gone, like a string plucked in an empty room. But I've long since learned not to look for ghosts.

I touch the stone without thinking, twisting the band, the metal sliding against skin that has always been one step past tan no matter how much sunscreen my mother would try to lather on me.

Never—not in a thousand years—did I think I'd end up here.

I was always taught that magick was dangerous, corrupting, that it no longer had a soul. My father made sure those warnings were etched into me like scripture. Gods, if he knew where I was right now, he'd come back just to drag me away.

* * *

I SPENT much of my life moving between different embassies and classified postings. My father's work in high-risk negotiations meant we lived like ghosts: untraceable, unrooted, constantly moving through the shadows of power.

Nothing rattled him... except Magicks.

It wasn't hatred, exactly—it was just that he always said, *"When their world begins is when the rest of the world ends."* I never really knew what he meant by that, actually. I used to just think he was paranoid. Now I wonder what he knew that I didn't.

When I started showing signs of an affinity to water at a young age—ripples that answered my laughter, puddles that moved when I touched them—he crushed it without a moment's hesitation. Brutally. Like he was fighting a war I couldn't see.

He told me that trying to draw power would be the death of me. Of us. So I learned to hide it. Ignore it. Bury it so deep I almost believed it was gone.

But magick doesn't stay buried. It waits—quiet and patient—until the world tilts just enough to wake it.

Sometimes, things happen that change your path irrevocably. Sometimes fate just has a sick sense of humor.

The water knew before I did.

August fifteenth was supposed to be just another Saturday. But it was the kind of day that felt wrong from the moment I opened my eyes—a day where the air tasted like metal and ozone, long before the sun broke over the mountain.

A boating accident on the lake, they said.

Sudden. Quiet in its finality. Loud in every other way.

My father always hated the water—always warned me to stay far, far away from it. *"Water remembers,"* he used to say, like it was some kind of boogeyman that would rise from the depths and drag me under if I got too close.

So it was cruel, in the worst way, that it was the lake that took him from us.

I was the one who found him—floating face down in the water, his blue shirt spread around him like a warning. The one with the cuff I'd mended just weeks before. The wind was howling—tearing through trees, lashing the water into ribbons in its wake.

I don't remember entering the lake. Only the shape of him—wrong in all the ways that mattered. Still, in a way nature never is.

My mother saw it all.

Said she knew then. What I was. What I was becoming.

She was the one who told me to apply to Whittaker.

She never said it outright, but I think she was afraid. Afraid of what might happen if I stayed. Afraid of what she saw clawing just beneath my skin. Maybe she thought coming here would help me keep it contained. Or maybe she wanted to finally let the monster inside be free.

Either way—she got what she wanted. Because now I'm here. Dressed in gray and black. Surrounded by Magicks.

Trying to remember who I used to be and figuring out who the hell I might still have the chance to become.

Somewhere in the distance, a bell chimes, loud and resonant, pulling me back to the present. I step out into the corridor, hearing the muted voices of students through heavy oak doors that lead to the gym, their iron hinges creaking as they swing slowly shut with a thud.

Behind me, another door opens with a gust of wind cutting through. I turn to look and catch a flash of black—but they are gone before I can call out, leaving only fragments of words on the breeze.

She's here.

The whisper twists through the air like a thread. And for a heartbeat, I swear the ring on my finger burns cold.

I frown at my hand before looking back toward the empty doorway. Maybe I imagined it? But I'm also standing on the grounds of an ancient school of magick… where nothing is quite what it seems. But then again, *I'm* not quite what I seem either.

For some reason, my father's voice chooses that moment to echo in my head: *Magick will be the end of the world.*

But maybe—

Just maybe—

It might be the beginning of mine.

CHAPTER 2

To study at Whittaker is to step willingly into ancient currents of power. It is impossible to come out unchanged.

—*Whittaker School of Magick Handbook for New Students,* "New Student Orientation"

Boom. The gym doors slam shut as another student barrels through. The sound ricochets down the corridor before being drowned beneath a rising drumbeat of boots and voices. A wave of first-years surge past me, shoulder-to-shoulder, and I'm forced to flatten against the side of the hall to let them through—my back hitting cold rock, trying to make myself small as the stream of bodies funnels toward the double doors. When the last of them disappears, I push off the wall and slip in after them.

Inside the gym, I'm immediately herded into a long, winding line of registration tables—schedules, syllabi, ID badges, room keys, and enough paperwork to make my fingers ache and make me question whether I've just signed away my soul.

My badge says:

Celeste Farris
First Year
Red Squad
Blue Dahlia Commons

THE SPACE I'm standing in stretches two stories high with arched glass windows lining the upper walls, allowing sunlight to pour in and illuminate the floor. I keep glancing at my ring, but it just gleams back at me, gold and jewels sitting innocently where they've always been. No trace of the whisper that slid into my ears earlier, no sign of that cold, needle-fine feeling on my hand.

But the truth is, the feeling of unease started before that moment. From the instant I stepped onto Whittaker's grounds, my body has felt restless. Like something is prowling within its confines, erratic and sharp-edged. It feels like the earth here knows something I don't and is just waiting for the right moment to tell me.

I look up from my hand and take in the rows of bleachers and observation platforms found in every corner of the room—all looking down on the black mats that line the floor in a modular pattern. The Training Room is what the guy who gave me my schedule called it. The mats reek of sweat and something sharper—bleach cut with pine and citrus. It burns through my sinuses, clean and cruel, like punishment disguised as purity.

I see a guy to the left of the room holding a sign saying *Red Squad*, a group of other first-years circling around him. I bite my lip, forcing my feet forward before doubt can root me in place. I count each step like a mantra, keeping my mind from spiraling.

"I think I'm with you," I say, pointing to my badge.

He nods and checks something off his clipboard. "Cadet Magnus Williamson," he says, dipping his head in greeting. "Second-year. Your Red Squad orientation leader."

His short black hair is shaved into sharp zigzags along his scalp like lightning bolts—a rebellious contrast to his otherwise meticulous appearance. His figure is lean, almost delicate, more whipcord than muscle. His shrewd black eyes sweep over me with curiosity—and nothing more.

I step into line behind him and find myself between two girls.

The taller one is intently looking at her schedule and pointing to it, annoyed. "Blue Dahlia Commons is clear across the east ridge, but half our classes are by the quad. Whoever planned campus logistics must enjoy watching us run."

A second girl shrugs before running a hand through her blonde shoulder-length hair, one side shaved close, the longer layers sweeping across her face with streaks of blue hidden underneath. "They probably always give the crappier schedules to the first-years."

The first girl looks up from her schedule, eyeing me thoughtfully before her gaze flicks to my badge. "Hey, I'm Rozsen. You our other squadmate? Looks like you're in the same commons as us." Her voice is low and dry, filled with the heat of someone used to speaking her mind and not caring about the consequences.

I nod, offering a small smile, but before I can answer, the other girl beside her gives me a once-over, slow and deliberate.

She sighs dramatically. "Ugh, she might be too pretty to be friends with us, Roz. Those hazel eyes should come with a warning label." Her mouth quirks. "But I'm liking the *sexy librarian that could commit arson* vibe she's got going on."

I blink, caught off guard, unsure whether to laugh or be offended—but she grins and holds out her hand.

"I'm Elliot," she says, her tone light and teasing.

I reach out and shake her hand, still a little stunned but warming quickly to her chaotic charm.

Rozsen just rolls her eyes. "Don't mind that one. She speaks before she thinks most of the time." She gives Elliot an exasperated shake of her head.

Eight of us in total make up Red Squad—four girls and four guys. Magnus tells us to grab our stuff for a quick campus tour as we head over to the commons to settle in.

The walk through campus feels surreal—every building, every tree-lined path, like walking through a story I should already know. Every step feels like retracing a trail someone carved for me long before I arrived. I still can't shake the feeling that I'm being watched.

I came to Whittaker for answers. To try to understand more about the current running beneath my skin, the magick that clawed its way back into me after my father's death, no longer content with the cage I built.

But I'd be lying if I said it was the only reason I'm here. There's another I don't let myself speak aloud. One with unruly hair and turquoise eyes, and a history I can't quite seem to leave behind, no matter how hard I try.

* * *

After high school, my father moved us to Virginia—a small town, no highways, no fast-food restaurants, a little land for my mom to get as many silkie hens as she wanted. Acreage over politics was her request.

My best friend there was Alissa—and she had an older brother.

He was the kind of beautiful that stole your breath away,

leaving only trouble in its wake. Tall. Confident. And a Magick...

Back then, he was always away at school, so I mostly admired him from afar—or from the numerous photographs strewn about Alissa's house.

But all that changed a few months ago.

I thought it would be a fun summer fling, something reckless before real life began.

Some stories don't feel like they start until you say a name that changes everything. His was Noa.

* * *

MAGNUS IS TALKING but it's not his voice that I hear in my mind. He points to the mess hall on the left, and I remember Noa telling me that the best pancakes are from the chef who always wears a pink hat.

The quad to the right is where most Whittaker gatherings are held.

The Garden Grove to the south is where the earth-wielders practice. Noa's words float in the air like a spell, describing earth Magicks as grounded, steady, and "impossibly stubborn."

I spy a low stone wall surrounding dark beds of soil and rows of herbs and trees. Deep-rooted vines cover shadowed lattice alcoves. Small water channels filter through the walls, providing natural irrigation for the space. *Brilliant,* I think as we pass.

"What the—"

"Make it stop!"

"It wasn't me."

I look back at one of the water channels spouting like a fire hydrant over a group of students as they shout and scramble to get away.

My throat goes dry. Did I—? No. I clamp down on the

thought before it takes root. My squad looks back curiously; a few of the boys snigger. Laughter echoes, but I don't dare glance back again.

We pass by two girls standing by the garden wall. The brunette with bronze skin is staring amusedly at the cascading water, but the tall girl with silver-blonde hair beside her doesn't laugh. Her gaze pins me instead, eyes narrowing like she knows more about what's under my skin than I do.

Willing my thoughts to focus on the trees only, I tighten my grip on my duffle and keep walking.

Magnus takes us by the Caldera: an ancient colosseum carved directly from black volcanic rock down into the ground. Rows of tiered granite benches lead down to an arena—a large oval of smooth obsidian and scorched basalt. Deep channels have been carved into the floor in rune-like patterns, likely remnants of forgotten rituals that this arena once honored. A stage for elemental prowess, and duels. The air around it simmers with residual heat, imbued with the element whose power is displayed there. Fire. *Noa's power,* I think as my heart twists.

Behind the Caldera rises a five-story cream-colored building, its windows framed in dark bronze—giving it a modern edge in contrast to the ancient stone architecture surrounding it. Most likely home to our core academic classes: History, Potions, and Elemental Theory.

Everywhere we walk, my eyes search the grounds for a familiar tall figure with brown hair. But fourth-years are probably off doing things far more important than worrying about first-years' orientation. Plus, *he doesn't even know I'm here.*

Oh gods, what if I see him, and he walks right past me—whole while I'm still haunted? I shudder slightly at the thought.

"You okay?" asks Rozsen.

No.

"Yeah, it's just colder than I'm used to in Virginia," I lie. I curse myself for even thinking about him right now.

We walk in silence for a few minutes, lost in thought… or in my case—memory.

Magnus points out a few more buildings in the distance and spouts off various descriptions of their purposes and uses.

"Green and Silver Squads are in the Silver Fern Commons." He points to an ivy-covered stone manor. "Black and Gold in the Obsidian Sun Commons." He nods to an angular building, modern and brutalist in style. He then points up the hill. "Blue Dahlia Commons—Red and Blue Squads. Your new home away from home."

A three-story Victorian house stands above us, painted a deep dusky blue that seems to change with the light as the clouds pass by. White shutters frame each of the tall, arched windows like delicate lace. Every corner of the white trim is carved with swirls and stars and other arcane sigils I can't place but feel like I'm meant to know.

The house itself leans slightly forward, like a forgotten storybook wedged between spreadsheets. Ivy curls up the wrought-iron railings of a wraparound porch, and ceramic pots filled with porcelain-blue dahlias bask in the afternoon sun.

"Used to be the headmistress's house back in the 1800s," Magnus informs us.

We are ushered inside, away from the chill, into a grand entranceway. Arched doorways open into a parlor and study. Twin staircases curve up in an elegant scroll to a wide landing. The balustrades are made of wood carved into twisted vines.

"Boys' dorms to the left, second floor, girls' on the right. Your room numbers are on your orientation letters."

The scent of rain-damp wood, threaded with lavender, drifts out to greet me as I begin the climb—cool, calming, and alive. Rozsen, Elliot, and a quiet girl named Amelia follow behind me as we head to our shared room.

The door opens into an airy living space painted a soft, stormy gray-blue. A deep comfy-looking sofa faces a white stone hearth where a cozy fire is ready to welcome us. Pale wood cabinets and white marble countertops make up a small kitchen tucked behind a half-wall. The aesthetic is plain but elegant, and looks perfect for late-night studying or long, whispered conversations.

At the far end of the living room, hung with translucent white curtains, stands a large bay window that overlooks a huge glittering lake.

Lake Caldrith.

Known for bone-chilling water, silver catfish, and a mythical monster that's been said to haunt the lake floor and pull in unsuspecting students who don't follow orders. At least that's what Magnus told us, the last part jokingly when we walked by it earlier.

I catch a glimpse of my reflection in the glass, dark strands of hair falling around my face from the hasty ponytail I tied it up in earlier, the gray-and-black uniform a stark contrast to the soft creams and blues of the room.

"I think Rozsen should bunk with you, Farris, and I'll take Amelia," says Elliot, clearly making herself the leader of this decision. She winks at me and says, "Better this way. I've known Rozsen since we were six and I'm more likely to kill her if I sleep next to her. Plus, she snores." She playfully pokes Rozsen in the ribs as she ushers an unprotesting Amelia toward her.

Two doors off of the main living quarters lead into bedrooms—each one designed to hold two double beds, two dressers, and just enough space for books and clothes. I enter the room to the left and quickly choose the bed closest to the window. Soft white linens beckon as I sit down, surveying what will be my new home for the next few years. I spy a door to a private bath off the side of our room. I'm grateful all four of us don't have to share one bathroom.

"Okay, Celeste, it's you and me then," says Rozsen as she enters the room and plops herself down on the other bed. Her long, merlot red–dyed hair sweeps over her dark complexion and bright, inquisitive brown eyes.

The four of us spend the next few hours settling in, putting our rooms in order and tentatively getting to know one another. Rozsen and Elliot come from adjacent towns in California, eighth-generation Magicks the both of them. Rozsen's element is fire, and Elliot's is air. Amelia's element is earth.

"So you must be our water then," says Amelia, looking at me thoughtfully. "They like to try and split the squads into different elements if they can."

I nod carefully. "I'm untrained, though. First-generation Magick." I frown slightly at the thought. "So I'll have a lot to catch up on."

My gaze drifts back over to the bay window, to that expanse of blue, as small waves ripple over the lake's surface. In that moment, I can't help but hope my father was right—that if *water remembers*, it will remember me.

Elliot flops back on the sofa. "First-gen? Gods, you're brave. Don't most first-gens usually flame out by the end of their second year?"

Rozsen glares at her. "What she *means* to say is that you must be really talented if you got into Whittaker as a first-gen. Pretty sure most of us won't be getting through these next four years completely intact." She raises her right arm, and I see the fresh burn mark on the outside of her elbow, angry and raw. "If at all."

She just shrugs like it's nothing. Like dying is just another possible outcome—right alongside graduating.

"Bet your parents were surprised," Elliot says. "I was sixteen when I blew my brother across the room for stealing my favorite hoodie. My dad couldn't have been more proud."

My eyes widen, but Elliot only grins, like this is a completely normal occurrence.

Most Magicks show an affinity to an element at a young age but are unable to fully draw from them until they are older. It's rare for anyone under fifteen to have that kind of power. Something to do with the brain requiring a certain hormone to be triggered around then.

Amelia looks up from where she's sitting. "Rozsen is right. You wouldn't be here if you weren't already exceptional, Celeste. Normal colleges only teach magickal theory and the basics. Whittaker forges mastery—and only takes the best," she adds matter-of-factly.

Rozsen's eyes darken. "Translation? Survive four years of hell, then the government's Service department gets the right to claim you after."

Her words land heavy. I twist my ring as I look back out at the lake.

A knock sounds at the door and Magnus's voice shouts out to meet him in the parlor in thirty minutes.

The eight of us gather in the common room, where two of the guys—Ian and Nate—claim the high-backed purple armchairs. A few of us settle on the navy-blue sofa that faces a fireplace on the far wall. The last two members of our squad, Peter and Sawyer, stand by the large bay window opposite the hearth. Earth and air Magicks; cousins, I believe—they keep close, speaking only to each other.

Magnus steps to the center of the room and walks us through the orientation schedule: the next few days of events, where to find the laundry room and infirmary, the gym and mess hall hours. When he finishes, he takes a moment, letting the silence settle, then looks each of us in the eye, one by one. "This is your new home," he says. "And this squad will be your new family for the next four years." He smiles then—warm, but with weight behind it. "This place will test you. Break you. Take until you think you've got nothing left. But I promise—you won't leave here empty-handed."

New family. The phrase cuts deeper than I expect.

I came here haunted by my father's death—by everything he feared.

But I'm done being the ghost in my own story.

And I can't help but wonder what these halls will strip away from me, and more importantly—what will be left after.

CHAPTER 3

At Whittaker, students advance through four ranks—initiate, cadet, lieutenant, and officer. Each stage demands greater skill, loyalty, and sacrifice. Advancement is earned. The cost can be personal.

—*Whittaker School of Magick Handbook for New Students,* "Ranks and Advancement"

The September morning breaks with a golden hush—late summer clings to the air, but it nips with a quiet warning of the autumn that's coming.

The smell of lavender scones and hot coffee rouses me from sleep, along with the energetic voices of Rozsen and Elliot calling out to wake the rest of us up. Magnus is already waiting downstairs to herd us across campus to collect our assigned textbooks for the year.

At the heart of the ancient academy lies the quad, a broad expanse about the size of two football fields placed side by side.

Towering oaks ring the perimeter, their silver-veined leaves casting patterns of shadow across the lawn.

At the northern edge, raised slightly above the courtyard by a fan of wide, worn steps, stands the stone dais—a broad, imposing platform carved from pale-gray granite and streaked with veins of volcanic black. Generations of headmasters and headmistresses have addressed students from this spot. Visiting dignitaries have offered solemn words.

Rows of long tables form a U shape across the lawn, weighed down by textbooks—towers of them, in every color and thickness, some brand-new, others dog-eared and lovingly annotated. The school is hosting a book sale, along with a buyback and trade event, allowing older students to sell their books to younger ones for discounted prices. Students surge toward the tables in waves—some hunting for bargains, others flipping through pages, trying to find the copies with the fewest underlines and torn corners.

Elliot scans our class list, ticking off required texts with an unexpected sharp focus. She leads us around the tables, pointing out stacks and muttering comments about edition numbers and good deals.

"So, Farris, is it?" My squadmate leans toward me as he smirks. Ian, the fire-wielder. His coppery hair falls wild and tangled, spilling over one side of his face. "Sawyer told me you're a first-gen, no training… Hope you don't sink us." His English accent gives the words a teasing lilt, but it stings too sharply to be harmless. Heat pricks at my cheeks.

Rozsen doesn't hesitate beside me, her voice laced with snark. "Careful, Ian. Last guy who underestimated a water-wielder ended up headfirst in a fountain. Besides"—she shoots me a quick but fierce smile—"pretty sure Farris can handle herself."

Ian lifts his brows, amused, but his amber eyes stay on me a beat longer before sliding away.

The tension in my chest loosens. Embarrassment still lingers, but so too does the unexpected warmth from Rozsen at my side. For the first time since stepping onto Whittaker's grounds, I don't feel completely alone. I smile gratefully at her.

I shuffle back, following behind the rest of my squad as they browse through textbooks and old lecture notes, but my eyes keep drifting—sweeping across the quad again and again.

"Are you looking for someone?" Amelia asks quietly. Her moss-green eyes miss nothing as she tries to follow my line of sight.

I shake my head. "Just trying to get my bearings."

The lie rolls off my tongue easily.

I haven't told anyone about my history with a certain student here—not yet.

Most of the crowd is first-years like us, but I spot a few second- and third-years weaving through the rows. "Where are the fourth-years?" I murmur, tapping my fingers against my thigh, still scanning.

A student manning the potions table glances up. "Some of the fourth-years got deployed to help down south. That hurricane last week wrecked a few towns."

I blink, surprised—I hadn't realized I'd spoken aloud.

He shrugs. "It happens sometimes. Once you're an officer."

He's not even here.

The disappointment hits like a slow wave—thick and heavy with false hope. Because some small, humiliating part of me had been braced for impact the moment I stepped through the gates—like he might be waiting for me. Like fate would intervene and be kinder than it's ever been before.

* * *

THAT NIGHT, my roommates and I curl up around the fireplace

in our dorm, trading stories from home. The things or people we've left behind. What we're most excited to learn.

I don't tell them about my dad, or how I ended up at Whittaker. That pain is still too fresh. Too sharp around the edges.

I do tell them about my mom—how she saw me call the lake this summer, and the rush to get a late application in.

Turns out that Elliot left behind her girlfriend in California—a non-Magick. They decided against trying to stay together due to the school's strict rules on outside communication.

Rozsen left behind three boyfriends, each one with varying promises of love and devotion 'til the end of time.

Amelia and I stay quiet, not giving anything away.

I'm starting to doubt if I even have something to tell.

* * *

THE LAST TIME I saw Noa, we were in his living room. He was waiting for his parents and sister to get home before starting the long drive back to Whittaker. Summer was ending, the emotions between us tangled and threadbare.

He'd already changed into his uniform. I sat tucked into his side on the couch, just breathing him in. Wishing for more time. Wishing the distance wouldn't feel so impossible.

When his parents' car finally pulled up, we both stilled. One last moment.

He kissed me—long, lingering. A kiss full of promise and passion we wouldn't get to act on. Our time was up.

When he pulled away, I could still feel him. A slow burn on my lips. An ache settling deep in my chest. And when I walked him to the car, I had to stop myself from begging him to stay just one more day.

We said goodbye, whispering promises that only hope or fate could keep.

I wonder if he's thought of me the way I think of him.

If he's missed me.

If my dreams of him have slipped into his somehow—the ones where I wake up warm, my skin tingling, the ghost of his touch still lingering.

Like he never really left.

CHAPTER 4

To awaken an affinity is to invite the element to speak through you. Listen well. But be warned—it does not always whisper.

—Theory of Elemental Magick, Vol. I

We arrive at the quad bright and early on Wednesday, the sky stretched wide and watchful overhead.

It's evaluation day.

The central lawn bears the signs of those that have already taken place—a large circle outlined with pale stones, scorched in places, grass cut clean in others.

A staggered row of high-backed chairs has been arranged with exacting precision on the dais. In them, professors sit robed in the academy's dark gray and silver, silent and sharp-eyed, their gazes turned toward the circle ahead. But one chair —far right—is occupied by a figure not like the rest. A man dressed in the black uniform of the Service, stark against the others. His coat bears a single sigil—a gold sun with a spear through it on his shoulder. He sits with disciplined stillness, watching everything, a clipboard in his hands—a list of all the first-year names on the sheet in front of him.

"Since when does the Service attend first-year trials?" Rozsen mutters beside me, eyes narrowed as she crosses her arms in front of her.

"Recruiting early this year, it seems," Elliot adds, looking curiously at the man.

Rozsen huffs under her breath, but says nothing.

Ian leans in slightly from behind, voice low. "Last year, a guy from Black Squad got taken right after his affinity trial."

"What?" Elliot twists around to look at him.

Ian shrugs, eyes still on the trial ring. "Some second-years told me about it. Trial ended, and before he even got feedback, two Service agents walked him off the field. Straight into an unmarked car parked by the western gate."

"What did he do?" Amelia asks, voice cautious.

"No one knows. His name was Hayden. His dorm was cleared out by the end of the week."

"I heard he tried to draw two elements at once," Nate whispers.

"Bullshit," Rozsen says too quickly. "That's impossible anyway."

Nate doesn't answer. Just stares at the circle ahead of us.

My fingers twitch. My palms suddenly feel too warm against my sides.

I glance at the Service officer again. He's still watching. Still not blinking.

Behind the dais, the spires of Whittaker stretch up toward the cloudless blue sky. In front, four stone platforms, waist-high and rectangular, stand in a clean arc, each holding a symbolic representation of the most common elements—simple, ancient, and unmistakable.

Water: a shallow stone basin filled to the top, its surface so smooth it reflects the blue sky above.

Fire: a low iron brazier holding a single candle-sized flame, burning blue at its core, utterly still despite the breeze.

Earth: a flat slab piled with smooth stones and shards of crystal, including amethyst and feldspar—local to Whittaker—laid in a spiral pattern.

Air: a tall, narrow vase of handblown glass, sealed at the base and open at the top, containing a column of softly spinning leaves and petals held in place by invisible currents.

There are other elements, of course, but their magick is rare and not often found among the general population. According to the Whittaker handbook, if a rare affinity *is* found within the student body, the school arranges for a private evaluation.

Blue Squad just finished and Red Squad is up next. A chill breeze chooses this moment to roll in from the bay, rippling the Whittaker banners that hang from the poles flanking the dais.

A tall man with dark hair and shrewd blue eyes appears at the front. "Professor Riven Kael," he says by way of introduction. "I'm running today's evaluations." His expression suggests he collects disappointment the way other men collect medals. "One at a time," he calls. "We'll begin with the standard affinity reaction. Control, not strength. Precision, not power."

Waiting students shift nervously along the sidelines. Near the edge of the tree line, an older man stands half in shadow with his hands clasped behind his back. A ghost of authority in his long coat, he stands silent and still. I try not to stare at him, but I feel his dark eyes pass over me once, sharp and unyielding.

Amelia catches my stare and her eyes widen. "Is that Headmaster Thorne? He doesn't normally watch the affinity trials… does he?" she whispers.

Rozsen nods. "That's definitely him. He looks just like his photo in the handbook. Maybe he heard what a kick-ass squad we have this year and came to watch." A slight smile tips the corner of her lips as she nudges me.

We wait to be called up.

Magnus briefed us this morning, but no amount of preparation could quiet the buzz of nerves now humming through my body.

Elliot is first, bouncing into the circle with all the grace of someone who either doesn't know she is being watched by twelve solemn professors and a Service agent—or doesn't care. Shoulder-length blonde hair frames her face in soft waves, the bold streaks of color catching the morning light. It matches the blue in her eyes, now sparkling with anticipation.

Elliot grins and cracks her knuckles. "Here we go," she says, more to herself than anyone else. Her nails are painted silver, chipped at the edges—short and uneven.

She raises her hands, fingers loose, breath steady.

The air answers immediately.

The leaves inside the suspended current stir faster, swirling in a playful cyclone. The entire column pulses outward with a soft *whoomph*, and wind rushes toward the dais in a gentle circle, tousling the robes of the seated professors, scattering petals, flipping a few pages.

Elliot, still smiling, looks up at them and gives a little bow—half mockery, half delight. "Well, that went *breezily*, don't you think?" she says as she rejoins me on the side of the field.

Rozsen is next. She steps into the circle like she owns it—shoulders squared, brown eyes sharp, the air around her already warmer. She raises her hand, palm open toward the flame basin. The focus is absolute. Fire flares instantly, leaping twice its height in a single breath. It twists upward in a tight spiral, burning hotter, brighter, until the white-hot tip arches toward her like it knows her name. The ground beneath her boots cracks faintly from the heat. Rozsen doesn't flinch, just smirks.

Next is Amelia, who steps into the circle almost apologetically, gaze lowered, hands clasped in front of her. The professors barely look up—until the moment she exhales and touches her fingertips to the ground. There is no flash, no noise. Just a deep, resonant thrum beneath the grass, like something ancient stirring. One of the stones on the platform cracks clean down the center as fine moss blooms along its surface. Amelia looks up, green eyes steady now. The earth listened. She looks relieved.

It's my turn next. I step into the circle with quiet determination, but tension rides my shoulders. The wind catches my hair as I pass the dais, the flickering elements stationed at the four points waiting—watchful. I draw a breath, steady but sharp, and reach toward the water basin.

And... nothing.

I set my feet and try again.

The surface of the basin remains perfectly, frustratingly, still.

A hush spreads over the dais. I hear the faint scrape of a pen, someone making a note.

My pulse kicks into panic. My hand trembles. I try to recall what it felt like in the lake this summer—how the water moved for me. How I called it back.

Nothing.

I hear a flicker of laughter from a group of second-years watching. Ian turns to whisper something to Nate. Rozsen stiffens where she stands beside Elliot. She steps forward just slightly. Toward me.

I bite my lip and lower my hand.

Maybe everything that's happened before this means nothing.

Maybe I don't belong here after all.

My thoughts start to cave inward, fear and doubt spreading, seeping through me—cold and deep. I start to turn away.

But then—

The basin shifts.

The water moves—slowly, like a shy creature coaxed from its den. It swirls, forming a shape in the air, its lines sweeping and graceful, almost like a mirrored flower unfurling, or a figure twisting beneath waves. It faces me, as if it's looking *at* me. *Through* me.

I inhale sharply, turning toward it, raising my left hand once more—

And the water twitches, like a stone being thrown through it, ripples edging outward.

My pulse quickens.

The water surges upward in a spiraling column, not gentle like Elliot's air, but fierce and high, sloshing over the basin's rim and hanging in the air like a suspended wave. Water stretches outward, forming small blades, so thin at their edges that mist bursts outward in a sudden ring, catching light in every droplet. The ground dampens. The temperature drops. It's beautiful—and completely out of control.

My eyes widen. I don't move.

I didn't mean to do that. Not really.

And then I feel it.

A flicker of heat—fire. A tug beneath my feet—earth. A stirring pressure in my lungs—air. The shadows from the tall oaks seem to reach toward me as the sun moves overhead. The scent of scorched metal fills the air. Nothing loud. Nothing certain. Just whispers. Glimpses. Like each element blinked once in my direction. Unnoticeable to anyone but me. At least that's what I hope.

But under the oak tree, the headmaster shifts slightly. His sharp gaze scans the stone platforms before turning back to me. The man in black jots something down before glancing toward the trees where he stands. But Thorne's gaze is now locked on the column of water in front of me.

I let my hand drop, and the water collapses back into the basin with a splash that soaks the stone steps as well as the robes of the front row of professors. I stand still in the circle, breath quiet, heart suddenly too loud.

No one speaks.

A professor in academic gray, her flowing blue dress showing beneath it, sits forward, wiping an errant bead of water off her face, one brow raised. "Definitely water."

I step back without a word—uncertain whether something has gone wrong… or very right.

The silence stretches, eyes on me. Some curious. Others wary.

Either way, I can't shake the feeling that I've caught their attention.

And I don't know if that's a good thing.

* * *

Toward the end of the day, I cross campus at dusk, the sky fading to a soft lavender. I've just picked up pizza from the mess hall for my squad when I see him.

A tall figure in uniform, standing near the eastern gate. The posture. The tilt of his head. The way he's turned, just slightly.

My chest locks as the air tangles in my throat. I pick up my pace and walk toward him, almost calling out—

But when he turns to face me, it isn't him.

Different eyes. Different smile.

I swallow hard. The longing feels foolish. Like I'm conjuring him out of habit, some muscle memory of missing him too much for too long.

Where are you, Noa?

I'm turning to walk back to the commons when I see them—Headmaster Thorne and the Service agent, locked in quiet conversation beside a black car at the far edge of campus.

"She's not ready," Thorne says. His voice is low, but clear enough to reach me. He sounds angry.

I slip into the shadows of the nearest building, unwilling to be caught eavesdropping on what is clearly a private exchange, but the rest is lost to the hum of the engine as the agent steps into the car and drives off.

The warmth of the cardboard boxes in my hands suddenly feels too real, too *normal,* against the cold rising off the stone path. I look out over the campus, ghosts suddenly in every shadow.

I shake my head, trying to clear the feeling of eyes tracking me from every darkened window I pass as I walk back to the commons.

CHAPTER 5

Throughout magickal history, no element has been more prone to dwelling in memory—or vengeance—than water.

—*A History of Magick, Vol. I*

Thursday afternoon finds us walking down a rocky moss-slicked path behind the Blue Dahlia Commons. Lake Caldrith stretches out like a pool of labradorite cradled in the arms of the forest. Dense pines, birches, and maples hug the shoreline, their reflections hazy in the blue-gray water below. Early autumn is just beginning to show at the edges of the leaves—flashes of crimson and gold flickering among the green here and there.

The air is cool, but not cold, with that crisp, clean bite particular to New England this time of year. Mist clings to the far edges of the lake in the mornings, curling along the banks before the sun burns it away by midday.

It is beautiful, yes—but it is the kind of beauty that watches you back.

The grass along the bank of Lake Caldrith waves softly in the breeze as the afternoon sun casts gold over dark waters. The air smells faintly of wet stone and something wilder beneath.

First-year squads gather in a semi-circle around the instructors, six squads in total—Red, Blue, Green, Silver, Gold, and Black—each group buzzing with anticipation of the task ahead. A Whittaker orientation week tradition: the Squad Room Regatta Challenge.

The regatta staging area is set up on the lake's western shore —a broad, gently sloping field dotted with flat river stones and patches of moss. The grass here grows thick and soft underfoot, interrupted by wildflowers and tufts of reeds where the land meets water. Wooden platforms jut out intermittently over the edge, some clearly newer, others faded and warped with age.

"Your assignment," Professor Neris says, pacing before us in her silver-threaded robes, "is to construct a vessel from natural materials and transport it across the lake, using *only* your magick. Creativity, cooperation, and elemental synergy are your only tools. You are all first-years here; therefore we aren't expecting perfection... only fun." Her pale eyes brighten for a heartbeat—just long enough for a soft smile to curve her lips before her original stern demeanor slides neatly back into place. Behind her, the lake glints like a dare. "You have one hour before the regatta begins."

Rozsen cracks her knuckles. "Let's make it float and explode glitter when it wins."

"No explosions," Amelia mutters, already running her fingers through the rich soil at the water's edge. "We'll need a stable base. Clay reinforced with bark, maybe."

"I can help seal the seams," Rozsen adds, her hands warming.

I step closer to the shore, kicking off my shoes and socks while staring into the dark stillness of Lake Caldrith. A breeze stirs my hair. I can feel something in the water—not just coolness, but awareness.

"Elliot, think you can steer it with wind?" Amelia asks.

Elliot is already gathering up floating reeds with threads of air. "Easy. I'll make it glide."

We build fast. It's part engineering, part teamwork, and part elemental creativity. Amelia shapes the hull using a curl of bark with thin slabs of clay to stabilize it, then Rozsen bakes the edges to a firm crisp, sealing the base. Elliot crafts a light breeze for the thin, fluttering sail we made from moss and twigs. I concentrate on trying to balance the water around the edges, forming a gentle current to guide it. My efforts come out choppy at first—uncertain and uneven, the water torn between stillness and storm. But after a few trials and errors, I manage to find a rhythm that makes the water within me hum with begrudging approval.

Our boat looks crude, but elegant. It moves like it belongs here—graceful, as though the lake itself now holds our favor today. We name it the *Water Wasp*.

The boys' boat is a brute of a thing. Peter sculpted the base from branches of pine and hardened mud, while Ian fused the seams with blackened fireglass he made from the combination of his fire and the sand along the shore. Sawyer added wind-blades along the sides—delicate-looking sails that crackle with kinetic air. Nate is running thin rivulets of water through the interior like veins, regulating the structure's buoyancy with eerie precision. It looks less like something meant to float and more like a toy warship someone dared to bring to a school event—impressive, fast, and a little bit fierce.

When the race begins, squads shout, clap, and manipulate their elemental creations across the surface. Some boats topple; others wobble forward awkwardly. Sawyer's wind battles Nate's current, ending with their boat turning sideways and colliding with another team's.

The *Water Wasp* is flying ahead, gliding effortlessly.

"We're winning!" Rozsen whoops.

But halfway to its destination, something happens. The water stills.

I blink once at a shadow slithering below the surface. It coils like a serpent of ink before vanishing.

My gut clenches. I'm unsure if I imagined it.

Without warning, a ripple shoots out beneath our boat. The *Wasp* begins to spin, then it dips. A circular wave pattern that doesn't match any of our efforts begins to form.

"Is that part of the challenge?" Rozsen asks, voice tight.

"Not unless someone's cheating," Amelia mutters, already crouching, her hands pressed to the ground as if willing the surface under the lake to answer.

I step closer to the water, feeling it lap around my feet. It's stirring beneath the surface—but not in rhythm. At least not to *my* rhythm.

My hand trembles outward, and without meaning to, I reach out—just a flick of my fingers. Wanting to soothe the waves. *Settle,* I think.

But the lake jerks in answer. Not forward, not back—*against* me. A ripple snapping toward our boat like a lash.

I feel the pull in my chest before it happens.

"Celeste—what are you doing?" Rozsen yells.

But it's too late. The current I tried to calm rebounds, flipping the boat sideways. A whirlpool opens, not wide, but strong enough to suck the *Water Wasp* under in one horrible, splintering gulp, as though a great unseen hand grabbed it and pulled. One blink, and it's gone.

A gasp goes through the crowd as the instructors and students whisper to each other.

"What the fuck?" Rozsen cusses.

"Did you just drown our boat?" Elliot snaps at me, incredulous.

"I—I was trying to fix it." My voice comes out hoarse. "I

didn't mean to—" I step back, eyes falling to the lake as a cold unease slithers across my skin.

The water at my ankles fizzes, static and strange. A pulse throbs against my hand. I glance down. My ring is glowing, faint but unnaturally bright in the afternoon light.

Then—

A whisper. Not a sound exactly, but something in my mind. A name—not mine. Something older, worn, and wild that echoes in my blood.

And then it's gone. Swallowed by the wind.

My breath catches.

The ripple is still echoing. Not only from whatever I did, but from… something else.

"You didn't just stir the lake, Celeste," Amelia whispers. "You called it." She's looking at me with guarded, curious eyes. Her gaze flicks to the water. Then back to me.

I stand frozen, hands trembling as I lower them. There's a quiet shift in the air—as if something sacred has just been disturbed.

I say nothing.

Something brushed through my magick in the lake, and I can't help but feel like now it knows my name.

And for the first time since I arrived at Whittaker—

I start to think that maybe the danger here might actually be *me*.

CHAPTER 6

Attraction between two molecules is a form of alchemy. With the right conditions—heat, base, balance—reactions may arise far beyond design or intent.

—"Modern Principles of Alchemy and Potions," Dr. S. Davenport, *Journal of Applied Alchemical Sciences*

Friday arrives, and it brings Magnus with it, calling all of us into the Blue Dahlia parlor for an announcement.

"It's customary to give first-years a treat on the last day of orientation. If you haven't heard of Whittaker's famous hot springs, you're in for a surprise. Bring swimwear if you have it; if not, you can wear your gym clothes. After that will be a barbecue and the Whittaker bonfire in the quad to celebrate the start of the new school year."

He gives us ten minutes to get ready before herding us out the door, where our squad spills into a growing tide of other first-years and a handful of other orientation leaders.

We follow the others along a narrow, rocky trail that weaves up the base of the mountain curling protectively around Lake Caldrith. The stone underfoot is cool to the touch and the air grows heavier with each step. Shadows deepen as the path narrows, funneling us toward the mouth of a cave. The mountain here seems to breathe—a steady hum of wind and heat that brushes against my skin like a living pulse.

The Cavern, as it is aptly named, breathes eucalyptus and mint over us, cool and sharp, with sulfur lurking just behind its teeth. There is a dampness and a hiss to the stones from the tunnels of underground hot springs that feed the pools carved into the cave floor. The entrance hall—if you can call it that—is flanked on both sides by two giant natural pools where the water bubbles and steams, creating a curtain of haze and making my skin bead with sweat. There are two smaller pools further down, infused with what must be healing herbs and minerals—their rich and earthy scent reaching out to grab us as we pass. Gold lights shine down from the chamber walls, making the water and mist glow. It is obviously a place of rest, ritual, and retreat.

"First-years are allowed to use the first four pools. Changing rooms and showers are here and here," says Magnus, pointing to two wooden doors on opposite ends of the first cave. "I'll give you guys a tour of the whole place, but just know you won't be allowed to use the private pools or showers in the last chamber until you earn it through rank."

We follow him to another cave entrance toward the back of the main hall. The next cave is all black volcanic stone, veined with shimmers of quartz, amethyst, and feldspar. It is lit with torchlight that catches and scatters the crystals in a kaleidoscope of color.

But what is most striking is the center of the cave, where a turquoise pool sits surrounded by crumbling stone, soft moss draping it in greenery under where the cave opens to the sky above. Pure, unfiltered sunlight shines through, making the pool almost iridescent. Tiny ferns sway along the water's edge while purple and green orchids bloom between the stones like forgotten offerings. A faint circle of runes is carved into the ground below, the primordial symbols glinting softly in the light.

The beauty of the scene before me takes my breath away. And yet... I feel like I've been here before.

"Fresh water from rain and gods know what else this cave system creates; it's been here for hundreds of years, if not longer," Magnus says. "You can occasionally find fish and other creatures living in it, though we've no idea how they end up here."

My fingertips prickle with the knowledge of something buried and ancient as the water in the pool seems to sway in response. Or is that just a trick of the light? I smooth my hands against my leggings to try to still the sensation that's now reached my arms—it feels as if ice water is threading through my veins, so cold it almost burns. I look around at the others, but no one else seems to be as affected by the water as I am. *Strange.* I turn back toward the entrance and the sensation stops.

Beyond the pool, the Cavern splits into two, with the chamber on the left showing a dramatic vaulted ceiling. Deep-red and purple stalagmites and stalactites reach toward each other in a mineral prayer. The chamber on the right hovers with curls of steam that beckon toward us as if to draw us in.

"We call this the Crystal Cavern," Magnus says, gesturing to the cave we are standing in. "The cave on the back left is known as the Amaranth—used for meditation or quiet work. To the right are the private pools and rooms for officers only."

A suspended wooden walkway with spaced-out planks—perfectly aligned to make the ground even—leads the way to the private pools. A boom of laughter echoes from the chamber within as a group of officers emerge at the entrance.

The tallest of them has to duck under the cave wall and is looking down as he enters the Crystal Cavern. A shock of chestnut-brown hair falls over what I know are eyes that are not quite blue, not quite green, but something like sea glass held up to a dusky sky, surrounded by a frame of thick lashes. A small lightning-shaped scar cuts across the corner of his jaw, the white of it shining as the torchlight dances across his face. His eyes flick over to us. My breath hitches when he catches my stare, and his eyes widen in utter shock and surprise. He leans down and whispers something to his companions as they start to walk toward us.

"Cadet, what do we have here?" he says, not taking his eyes off me. The silent and glaring question in them is apparent. His easygoing swagger I know so well is only betrayed by the stiffness in his arms, as if he's trying to contain some emotion he doesn't want to give away.

"Just giving a tour of the Cavern to the first-years, Officer Gallegher," Magnus replies.

He smiles at our group—*that* smile, the cocky but ridiculously endearing smile that I know by heart—and I swear I hear every first-year girl gasp just as I feel every first-year boy try to stand as tall as physically possible.

"Squads, you have the honor of meeting Officer Noa Gallegher. First in his class and the winner of pretty much every Whittaker school challenge ever invented," Magnus says with a hint of awe.

Noa. He's here. Not even ten feet away.

I can hear whispers from my squad and some of the others around me, hurriedly talking all at once. *Everyone* in the magick world has apparently heard of Noa Gallegher. His magick is as deadly as his looks are sinful.

His golden-tan skin peeks through a black muscle tee. I suddenly have the urge to reach for his chest and run my hands down that slick fabric, curling myself around his body like a cat.

Gods, get it together, Farris.

Summer is long over, and a lot has happened since then. At least that's what I try to remind myself.

Noa cocks his head at me and then addresses Magnus. His fingers tap at his sides like he's willing them not to reach forward. "I know first-years don't get to see the private caves until they've earned it, but you have among your group an *old family friend* who I'm *very* surprised to see here in our establishment right now," he says with an intense, pointed look in my direction. "I'd like to keep Initiate Farris for a bit, if that's alright with you, Magnus?"

Magnus looks like he might faint that Noa even knows his name and hurriedly agrees, ushering the rest of the group back toward the Cavern's main entrance.

I don't move from where I stand as the group disperses, sending curious looks in my direction. I'm suddenly hyper-aware of everything around me—the hard stone beneath my feet, the wafts of steam caressing my body, the beads of sweat sliding down my back from the heat I can feel pulsing from behind the next room.

"*Initiate* Farris?" Noa says with a hint of a question as he extends an arm forward, clearly wanting me to follow.

His three companions are other fourth-year officers, as noted by the four tiger stripes on the pentagon patches sewn onto their uniforms. The tall, sandy-haired officer on Noa's left gives him an inquisitive look, but I catch the smirk that follows as he tugs his other two companions toward the front entrance. "Right... Noa, we'll meet you at the commons later?" He looks at me curiously and gives me a wink before disappearing out the front archway with the others.

I follow Noa down the wooden walkway toward the back of the cave, and we enter the next room. The space feels more like the hold of an old ship than a cave. There is a bowed ceiling with torchlight highlighting two dozen polished wood doors on either side, each decorated with a carving representing an element—air, fire, water, earth, and a few others I don't recognize. The air in here is steamy and ridiculously warm, smelling of cedar and citrus. I can hear breezes of overlapping conversations and muffled laughter from the other sides of those doors, as well as the sound of water echoing off what sounds like stone, or maybe wood.

A door on the left opens and two girls walk out just as Noa reaches for my hand, pulling me toward one of the doors on the right—the one marked with a flame carved into the wood. I catch their surprised glances as they see me with him before I'm pulled into the room and the door is shut firmly behind me.

Suddenly, it's just us, the outside world vanishing—just the heat of the cave, the flickering torchlight, and space and time between us.

And then I can't breathe.

Noa pushes me against the door, lips meeting mine in a kiss that is anything but gentle. He's tasting me like he might never get to again, like he's been waiting too long and now there's no room for restraint.

I lose myself in it.

My hands find his arms, then his neck. I run them down the planes of his chest, just like I imagined doing earlier. I reach for the hem of his shirt and tug it over his head in one quick motion. We separate for a single heartbeat before crashing back together—teeth, tongues, hands. I want more. I want less clothing.

I want is all I can think.

Fuck summer. Has this not been what I've thought about for weeks? His face, his lips, his skin. His body on mine. I want his heat to burn away everything that's happened in the past month—the lake, the silence, the loss. Leaving just this moment. Just him.

I reach for the button of his pants, fingers trembling, but he leans in, stopping me. He holds us there until our breathing slows and my heartbeat remembers that it's meant to keep a rhythm.

"Celeste..." His voice breaks off. "What the hell are you doing here?"

He draws back slightly, looking at me as if to confirm I'm not some sort of illusion. His hands find my arms, gripping like he's checking that I'm real, eyes wide with disbelief. He scans me—gaze flicking over my face, my limbs—like he's looking for bruises or signs of coercion. Anything to make this make sense.

"I applied to Whittaker... after my dad died," I say softly. "My mom thought maybe coming here would help. She said my magick had just been waiting to surface." I pause, swallowing. "When she found me—with him, in the lake..." My eyes close as I try to breathe past the knot forming at the back of my throat. "The water was still rippling," I whisper, almost to myself. "Curved around us, like it didn't want to let go." A beat of silence. "She knew then. What I was."

It's *mostly* true. Just not all of it.

Noa stares at me, his face clouded for a beat too long, like he's trying to piece together a puzzle that doesn't quite fit. Sensing the edges of a lie. But then something shifts in him and settles, like he's letting himself feel it.

"I heard about your dad," he says, voice lower now, gentle. "I'm sorry, Cel. I tried to call. They only gave me one, and you weren't home, so I left a message with your mom." His jaw clenches, like he still remembers the helplessness. "But this? You here? At *Whittaker*?" He shakes his head slowly, as if saying it aloud doesn't make it any more believable. "I just... I can't wrap my head around it."

He reaches down to cup my face, just the softest brush of his fingers against my cheek, yet it sends sparks firing down every nerve in my body. He leans down to kiss me, gently this time, like a feather sweeping across my lips, making a shiver curl down my spine even as the heat from the hot spring makes steam coil around us.

Another kiss—this one slow and heated, filled with the promise of starting something he has every intention of finishing. His tongue twists around mine, tasting me as his hands pull me into him and wrap around my waist. His skin is warm and slightly damp, and he backs me slowly toward a stone bench carved into the wall, a pile of fresh white towels lying beside it.

"You have no idea how many times I've thought about you these past weeks," he murmurs, and the way he says it makes something bloom low in my stomach. "What I wanted to say when I saw you again... What I wanted to do..."

I can feel just the kinds of things he's wanting, pressed against me—hard, barely contained.

I hesitate for just a second, suddenly unsure of protocol, or of what I'm doing. "I... I don't know how much time I have before I have to get back to my squad," I say lamely.

He looks at me like I've grown a second head. "Celeste. You show up—at *my* school—after a month of silence, and suddenly you're a Magick?" His voice still lifts with disbelief, but a smile ghosts across his mouth. "And while I'm thrilled about the latter, and even more thrilled about the former..." He takes a step closer, fire sparking behind his eyes. "Excuse me, but fuck your squad. And the school, too, for all I care."

He closes the space between us again.

"I *know* we have a lot to talk about. I know. But right now?" His words brush against my skin; a plea wrapped in heat. "I want you. All of you. And I have no intention of letting anyone else have you. So if you want this—if you want *me*—say the words, Celeste." He pauses. The flames behind his eyes flicker into something quieter. Something deeper. "Please... just tell me you want this too."

The question in his eyes tells me he's talking about more than just this moment. He's talking about him. Me.

Us—unwritten and uncertain.

And fuck, if that's not *exactly* what I want. What I've wanted since the first time he looked at me like I mattered. Since the moment I chose to come here.

But wanting and deserving are different things.

What if the magick changes me into something he doesn't recognize?

My heart clenches, lungs tightening like they're wrapped in wire. I can't stop thinking about the tiny boat on the lake, the water pulling at me like it knew something I didn't. My father's warnings echoing in my head.

Noa's still waiting.

The silence stretches long enough for the steam to curl between us like a veil—blurring the lines of what I am and what I might become. I see the question in his eyes falter, just slightly. Hope and doubt flicker like candlelight between us.

"What if I'm not who you think I am?" I finally whisper.

He exhales hard. A pause. A promise. "Then let me find out," he says gently. "Let me *see* you."

My breath shakes.

My pulse stumbles.

And still—though the word feels far too small for everything it means—I say it anyway.

"*Yes.*"

Suddenly, the space between us feels unbearable. He reaches for me, his lips crashing into mine—desperate, hungry, and I can't get my clothes off fast enough. I tear off my shirt while he unhooks my bra, both falling in a careless heap on the stone floor.

He pushes my leggings down in one swift movement, then pauses once they're around my ankles. Kneeling, he looks up at me from the ground, and something in his gaze stills my breath. He pulls them off, one leg at a time, then leans in and kisses my calf—soft and reverent. Then the inside of my knee. The curve of my thigh. Each press of his mouth is slow, deliberate, burning a trail up my skin until he reaches the heat of me, hidden behind now-damp fabric. He kisses me there, eyes still locked on mine, and my heart skips.

His fingers slide beneath the waistband of my underwear, peeling them down with a quiet patience that only intensifies the need. When they fall away, I'm trembling before him, naked —exposed.

I don't realize my eyes are closed until I feel the heat of him behind me. He steps close, his hands gentle as he brushes my hair over one shoulder. His lips follow, warm and lingering, and I shiver as his body presses against mine. The solid weight of him, the unmistakable hardness—every steel inch of him wrapped around me.

He turns me in one fluid motion and lifts me effortlessly, lowering me onto the warm stone bench. The heat radiates through my spine, grounding me even as I feel like I might float away. Above us, dried eucalyptus hangs from the cave ceiling, perfuming the air with its calming, woodsy scent. But there's nothing calm about what's happening between us.

He lowers himself over me, pressing me into the bench, and it's the most delicious pressure I've ever felt, trapped between his body and warm stone and melting into both. His mouth finds mine again—hungry, thorough—as his hands begin their slow, reverent path down my body, his warm breath following as they move toward my breasts. I gasp when his lips brush against the sensitive skin, first gently tasting and then a quick, sharp scrape of teeth around my nipple, causing me to jump both in surprise and sensation.

As his mouth lingers, his hand inches downward as I arch toward him.

One finger, then two, slide into the heat of me as I move against him. Then he starts coasting over the place I want him to touch me the most, feeling the slickness of my own desire as he mounts a repetitive rhythm over and over again until a heat builds within. The tension winds tighter with every second until I cry out.

Suddenly, a rush of sound comes from behind us.

"Celeste." Noa pulls back suddenly, brows drawn, his tone no longer soft. "Stop."

"What?" I gasp, dazed. My eyes flutter open.

His hand cups the back of my neck—but there's urgency now. Concern. Not for him, for *me*. "You're drawing too much. The water—it's answering your want, not your will."

I look up. The pool behind us is rising, sloshing against the stone with unnatural pull. It's swelling, curling up in a spiral like a wave preparing to crest. Droplets lift like silver daggers.

My breath freezes in my lungs. "I—I didn't mean to—"

"Breathe, Cel." His forehead presses to mine, steady. Stern. "You need to breathe. Or you're going to flood this whole cave."

Panic coils. My chest heaves. I look back at the water as it rushes closer.

"Look at me," he says, voice low and commanding. "Not the water. *Me*."

And I do.

And in that moment—his hands alight with flame.

Not burning, not to destroy, just enough to hold me. His fire wraps around my wrists like golden restraints, anchoring me in place, searing through the chill taking over my spine. Grounding me.

The water hisses—and slows.

It sinks back into the pool, calm once more.

I collapse back against the stone bench, mortified, and turn my face away. "I'm sorry," I whisper.

"Don't be," he says. His words cut through the storm that's gathered in my chest.

He pulls me upright so he can wrap a towel and his arms around me, firm and unyielding. His touch is heat and strength and something steadier than either. I match his breath, the vise-like pressure starting to fade from my veins.

When I glance back behind him, any remaining mist settles back into steam like nothing ever happened. Noa's eyes are still wide—but not with fear. His gaze moves from the water to my face, lingering on the steam curling in the air.

"Gods," he whispers. His arm curves around my shoulders, his other hand gently touching my cheek. "You really are one of us."

And in that moment, something changes between us. Not just lust or longing—but belief. Truth.

"Are you okay?" He's looking at me like I'm made of glass or lightning. Possibly both.

I shake my head—because I don't know how to explain what I'm feeling. I barely understand what I even *am*.

His hand lifts to brush my cheek again before moving down my neck, the edge of his thumb skimming the place where my pulse is still thundering. "I can help you control it," he says quietly. "If you'll let me."

The words are gentle—the offer is anything but.

He watches me closely, something fierce and unwavering in his gaze. "Has that ever happened before?"

I bite my lip and shake my head. "I haven't exactly been in a situation like this since you left this summer."

A grin tugs at the corner of his mouth. "Well, thank the gods for that. I'd hate to have to kill anyone this early in the year."

The tension breaks.

I laugh—soft and shaky, but real. "This was quite the welcome party," I tease as he hands me my underwear and bra, noting—somewhat disappointingly—that he's somehow already fully dressed.

"I would've had flowers and chocolates ready," he says with a lifted brow, "had someone bothered to inform me you were coming." His tone is easy. Light. As if I didn't just nearly drown us both in a surge of magick.

He clears his throat, stepping back slightly as his fingers run through his damp hair.

"I told Magnus I'd give you the full officer's tour," he adds with a smirk. "So, just so I'm not a liar—this particular room is mine. Private hot spring, cold-plunge pool through there, sauna through that door, bathroom over there, and the shower-slash-changing room right here." He gestures around us with mock formality.

"Quite the perk," I say, looking around, "of knowing an officer."

"I believe you meant," he says, eyes locking with mine as he pulls me toward him, "quite the perk of *dating* one." The words are teasing, but beneath them, something steadier hums. Possessive. Real. "I meant what I said, Celeste. I'm in this—all of it. All of me. All of you." His voice is low but unwavering.

All of me. The phrase tilts something inside that I haven't looked at for a long time. Because even now, I can still remember silver eyes that once owned every part of me, even the parts I tried to keep hidden.

Noa tilts his head, searching my face—quiet, intent—like he's reading the truths I'm trying not to show.

His fingers hook gently under my jaw, warm and sure as he tips my chin up. His palm cups the side of my face, thumb brushing the edge of my lower lip—testing the space between us like a question he already knows the answer to. "I don't do half-assed. And I sure as hell don't do trial runs. Not when it comes to you. Not now that you're *here*."

The last word—*here*—lands with weight, like he still doesn't trust it to be real.

"I know, Noa," I say quietly, the words threading between us like breath. I shove the memories of my past behind me once more and lock the door. "And what you asked me earlier? I'm in.

You and me." I reach for the hand by my face, pressing a kiss into his palm before releasing him. "I've been in since the very first second we met."

Something in him softens—then sharpens. He pulls me into another kiss, deep and sure, and for a moment, I think my heart might break open from all the emotions floating through it that I'm not quite ready to name.

When he finally pulls back, there's a crooked smile tugging at the corner of his lips. "Well then," he says, eyes dancing, "I guess we've got a statement to make. First event of the school year and all."

He hands me his jacket, the fabric warm from his body, the rank and elemental patches glinting under the torchlight like a silent threat.

"Clothes on, Initiate," he says, tone switching between playful and practical, though his eyes linger on me. "Or else we'll end up spending the night in here, and *neither* of us will be making it back to our squads."

CHAPTER 7

Romantic attachments among students are neither prohibited nor officially encouraged. However, those who pursue them would do well to remember: at Whittaker, little remains private.

—*Whittaker School of Magick Handbook for New Students*, "Code of Conduct"

Back at Blue Dahlia Commons, I'm showered and dressed in jeans, a fitted top, and leather boots. Thank the gods we get to wear our own clothes for events outside of class. I smile as I grab Noa's jacket to wear, slipping into its warmth as my other squadmates wait by the front door. Rozsen and Elliot are already firing off a thousand questions about him, alternating between teasing and legitimate curiosity, barely giving me a chance to zip up.

First-, second-, and third-years stream out of their dorm rooms, the halls buzzing with conversation as everyone heads toward dinner and the famed Flaming W bonfire. A few whisper as they eye me with a mixture of curiosity and suspicion. A hush follows me like static when I pass.

I feel a glance or two of pure animosity from two third-year girls who come out of a first-floor room. I can just barely hear their low whispers of contempt as they eye the patches on my jacket.

I guess news travels fast…

A group of guys loiter near the stairwell, casting the occasional not-so-subtle look in our direction. One of them breaks away, pushing off the stair rail with the kind of self-assured ease that's definitely practiced. His dirty-blond hair is artfully tousled—messy in the way only someone who checks every mirror can manage.

He saunters up to me, flashing a grin that probably works on most girls. "So this is the famous Celeste everyone's buzzing about."

"Famous is hardly the word I'd use," I reply, matching his tone with a cool smile.

"Noa Gallegher's *old family friend*?" He smirks, the insinuation hanging between us. "Quite the pretty picture the two of you made earlier—him walking you back here with his jacket draped around your shoulders." He lifts a hand, casually brushing two fingers over the fire and fourth-year patches on my left arm. "Dash," he says, offering his hand. "Third-year, Blue Squad." A breeze curls around my wrist—gentle, coaxing—tugging me forward like the air itself is taking his side. "Airwielder," he adds, like it's an afterthought… but the grin that follows is pure confidence.

I take his hand, more curious than impressed. There's a flicker in his eyes when we touch—a dare maybe, and I can't help but feel like I just became a challenge in a game I wasn't aware I was playing.

* * *

I WALK with my squadmates toward the quad, where picnic tables are piled high with food. I grab a bag of chips and a cheeseburger stacked high with extra pickles, then fish a cold Coke from a cooler half buried in ice. We settle in, eating together—easy conversation flowing before the crowd starts to thin around us.

Sawyer is mid-story, hands waving as he launches into an animated retelling of his summer adventures—something about diving and surf. Rozsen and Elliot interrupt constantly, chiming in with half-formed questions and bad guesses, talking over him and each other in equal measure.

Amelia and Peter sit at the far end of the table, their conversation quieter, more private. Ian and Nate have wandered off, chatting up a couple of first-year girls—Green Squad, if I'm guessing right.

I start to tune out, letting the voices blur as I scan the quad. All around the field, other students have staked their claims—blankets stretched across the grass, shoes kicked off, snacks in hand. *Damn.* I didn't think to bring anything to sit on. By the looks of it, neither did the rest of my squad.

We finish our food and begin drifting toward the dais. Dash catches my eye and waves, motioning for Rozsen and me to join him and his friends on their blankets. I start to smile, about to say yes—

But an arm snakes around my waist from behind.

I know who it is before I even look. His scent gives him away. Burnt cedar and mint—sharp, clean—but beneath it, something bolder. A trace of spice. Clove, maybe. Something that burns slow and lingers.

I smile as I look up at the face I've dreamed about countless times over these past few weeks—months, really, or years if you count when I only knew him from Alissa's photos.

Noa kisses me then—right there, in front of everyone. It's not quick, not gentle. It's... consuming. Fire lights every nerve in my body as his mouth devours mine. When he finally pulls back, my pulse is chaos, my grin unstoppable.

"Subtle," I tease, a little breathless. "Very subtle."

"I told you I wouldn't let anyone else have you if you said yes," he growls.

"I remember," I say, my face growing warm as I *remember* more.

"And I don't like to share." He nips at my ear as he narrows his eyes at Dash and his companions. His other arm comes around to hold me in place while he tucks my head under his chin and molds my back into the front of his chest. We both look out over the quad.

Around us, the school breathes to life.

Groups are already forming—some easy and familiar, like puzzle pieces snapping back into place. Some students stretch out across blankets, boots off, limbs tangled or relaxed in comfort. Others stand in loose circles, caught in the rhythm of excitement and laughter at inside jokes only they seem to understand. A few lovers reunite in quiet, stolen touches. I hear music, the beat fast and energetic. Farther off, sharp voices clash —rivals rekindling old tension with half-smiles and narrowed eyes.

And us.

Wrapped in our own quiet bubble. Not yet ready to break the spell—not with talk, or truth, or the past.

Not yet at least.

The night feels stitched together by music and magick—old and new friendships, and the smell of fire and fall in the air.

"I've just got to make one quick announcement before the bonfire starts, but then I'll be back, okay?" he murmurs. His warm breath sends shivers down my spine.

I squeeze his hand and flutter my lashes as I look up at him with mock innocence. "Don't be gone too long. I'd hate to have to replace you so soon."

He kisses me at that and gives my behind a squeeze as he makes his way to the dais. Just in front, a giant W made of straw and branches stands propped in a circle of stones, waiting to burn.

A girl with strawberry-pink hair is holding a microphone, making a welcome speech and going over some beginning-of-term announcements. Then the cheers erupt—hollers and stomps—as Noa steps close to the front.

I smile to myself and shake my head in amusement. Of course. Of course he's the school's golden boy.

All eyes are on him as hands clap his back and students call his name, and by the time he reaches the top of the stairs, the crowd is already his.

His voice rings out—clear, commanding, undeniably magnetic. "Good evening, legends-in-training."

A ripple of laughter runs through the crowd.

"Tonight marks more than the start of another school year—it's a turning point." His gaze sweeps the faces in the crowd, unhurried. "There are forty-eight new students here tonight. And if you've been paying attention, you already know that not all of you will make it to graduation." He pauses then, as if letting that sink in. "Some of you will wash out. Some of you will break. Some of you will learn—too late—that talent isn't the same thing as control."

As if on cue, the water in me slithers under my skin, like an uninvited guest. I clench my hands, willing it to settle.

"But hear me when I say this: for returning students—the mistakes, the losses, the bruises you don't talk about... That wasn't cruelty. It was proof. Proof that you can endure. Proof that what you're building here is worth the cost."

Another pause, letting the crowd settle.

"This year is your chance to define who you are, and who you're becoming. Each of us walked through these gates carrying talent, ambition, and the power to shape not only our own paths—but the future of magick itself." His mouth curves with the hint of a smile. "But true greatness isn't forged alone. It's built in unity. In challenge. In the quiet moments when you choose discipline over ease—when you choose the strength of your squad over your pride."

He finds me in the crowd, and our eyes lock. A real smile breaks through this time, soft and unguarded. For a heartbeat, he forgets himself. Then he clears his throat and straightens.

"So let the Whittaker W burn hot tonight. Celebrate. Then wake up Monday and earn your place."

The crowd erupts into applause, boot stomps, and cheers as Noa stands off to the side of the W below.

Damn, I think. *He's* really *good at this.*

Noa makes a motion with his hands so subtle I would have missed it if I wasn't so attuned to his body.

The W bursts into flames.

It isn't ordinary flame. This is *his* fire—so bright it glows blue at the center. The crowd gasps as flames spiral upward, swirling into shapes: dancers moving with provocative grace, their limbs sculpted in light. Then they shoot up into the sky, bursting into a thousand sparks that rain down on us like falling stars.

It is completely magickal. Mysterious. Hypnotic.

And entirely him.

My father used to say that the first magick didn't rise from the earth at all. It *fell.*

I watch as sparks drift around me like fireflies, lighting even the darkest shadows—and I can't help but think that he was right.

Noa winks at me before walking back over to snag me possessively around the waist with one arm, while the other hand holds a beer a fellow student gave him.

"Impressive," I say, nodding to the Flaming W and the glitter of embers still surrounding us.

"We aim to please," he says as he nuzzles my ear.

The rest of the night dissolves in a blur of faces and firelight. I meet some of Noa's friends, their names already slipping from me like smoke. Shared fragments of stories and drinks are passed around like currency. My squad—Rozsen, Elliot, and the others—bask in the sudden elevation that my dating Noa Gallegher seems to have given us.

Status by association.

Heat by proximity.

Elliot's playing a drinking game involving coins and stones with some fourth-years. Rozsen is lying on a blanket, stargazing with Noa's blond friend we met in the Cavern. I think his name is Finn.

Gods, was that only just today? It feels like more time has passed. Like we've been carried miles and years since sunrise. My thoughts blur like watercolor in rain, everything soft-edged and glowing.

A large hand pulls me close. I lean into it, into him, enjoying the warmth radiating between us. And for the first time in a long time, I feel... content. Even with everything that's happened—the pain, the loss, the unknown—something inside me settles. Like a ship finding harbor after too long at sea.

It's not just because of Noa, though that's part of it. But because of this.

Being here. In this moment. Surrounded by people like me.

I've spent my whole life hiding this part of myself, thinking it was wrong. Dangerous. But this—this feels *real*. Like the start of something I didn't know I'd been waiting for.

Noa's breath dances across my lips before he kisses me. Soft and sure. "Walk you back to your dorm?" he asks, voice low. "Or can I convince you to stay with me tonight?"

I smile against his lips. "Lead the way, *legend*," I whisper, throwing his earlier word back at him.

He laughs softly and begins steering us through the crowd.

We move quietly, hand in hand, until the voices and music fade behind us.

The moon is bright tonight and reflects off the lake to our right. The gentle waves hum as they brush up onto the rocky shore. The silver moonlight makes the water glow like it's lit from beneath.

I get that familiar pulse in my fingertips—my magick, just beneath the surface—awakening in response to the lake's call. Something that's only gotten louder since the squad challenge. The memory of the boat, the way it was pulled under like a warning, sends a shiver down my spine.

I pull closer to Noa, his warmth radiating, chasing the chill away. Whispers from the water glide softly over the lake's mirror-like surface, no longer haunting, but peaceful. Serene.

"It's beautiful," I say, voice hushed.

"Yes, it is," he replies.

But he isn't looking at the lake.

CHAPTER 8

What is revealed in shadowed spaces often holds more power than what is shown in the light.

—"On the Nature of Power and Intimacy," Thera Quinn, Professor of Elemental Ethics at Universitas Arcanum Andina

We walk quietly, both lost in thought. Noa weaves me through a grove of cypress trees, their slender shadows swallowing the moonlight and keeping its secrets... and ours.

We end up in a carefully tended rock garden—smooth obsidian and chalk-white stones forming a path that crunches softly beneath our boots. At the edge of the path rises a one-story Spanish stucco manor, its terracotta roof tiles dulled by time and moonlight. The building juts out from behind a massive, ancient willow tree, its silver-green tendrils swaying lazily in the night breeze. Fairy lights glitter through its branches and trail down to a stone bench beside its base.

As we approach, the front stoop emerges—broad sandstone steps worn smooth by generations of use. Iron lantern sconces flank either side of the arched wooden door. The door itself is thick, old-world style, reinforced with black iron studs and a brass knocker shaped like a lion's head. Beneath our feet, the tilework on the stoop forms a geometric mosaic—faded, but still intricate.

He glances back at me, a soft smile on his lips, then pushes the door open, revealing the warm light spilling out from inside.

Cool citrus and clove smoke with undertones of sandalwood stir in the air as we enter. A sunken living room greets us in what must be the common room of Noa's dormitory—except this looks like no dormitory I've ever seen before.

Moroccan rugs in red ochre, dusty gold, and sapphire blue sit beneath soft, cream-colored sofas, their low backs perfect for storytelling, or *other* things… and my body warms at the thought.

Maroon and royal-blue throw pillows are scattered about in silk and woven textures. A casual chaos of sorts. Soft lighting comes from a large wrought-iron chandelier at the center of a pentagon-shaped ceiling, its glass orbs flickering like candlelight. At the heart of the room stands a striking circular hearth, sunken slightly into the terracotta-tiled floor like a gathering point.

A full bar made with gray smoked glass, easily the most dangerous feature in the house, stands behind an intricately carved cherrywood counter with dark-metal barstools, the legs twisted to look like flames, ready and waiting for patrons.

"Welcome to the Spanish Steps," Noa says as he wraps his arms around me from behind. His hands gently caress up and down my arms, shivers breaking out in the trail that they leave.

He leads me down a hallway where glowing cream candles light up as we pass them. Magick, no doubt. Likely from Noa himself. We come to stand in front of a large arched double door carved with swirls and patterns that remind me of water. He finds his room key and uses it to open the door on the right.

I look around Noa's bedroom, trying to make sense of the space that somehow feels exactly like him—warm, practical, powerful, and just a *little* untouchable.

It's a large room with vaulted ceilings and dark exposed beams stretching overhead like ribs in a cathedral. The walls are a warm, creamy stucco—slightly textured, imperfect in the way old artisan work always is. They glow faintly in the amber light from the wrought-iron sconces on either side of the room. It gives the space the look and feel of some sun-warmed villa—far from the foggy shores of Whittaker.

On one side, a massive walnut desk anchors the room, cluttered with scattered textbooks, crumpled notes, and open journals with half-drawn sigils in the margins. Pens and glass vials roll precariously near the edge, and a bronze task lamp throws pools of warm light over the chaos. A tall polished oak bookcase stands next to it, holding various books and objects, some of which look like weapons as I catch the glint of sharp metal edges and wire-thin points.

In front of us, a wide bay window is cloaked in heavy blackout curtains, but I catch a glimpse of a different rock garden outside—a quieter, more meditative version of the one near the front.

The right of the room rises in a shallow stone platform where a king bed sits like a throne: its arched wood headboard carved with a series of sunbursts and fire sigils. The bedding is layers of creamy linen and thick, cloud-like blankets. It's too neat—too perfect—and I can't help but wonder if this space is always this carefully kept. I suddenly get the uncomfortable feeling that I'm likely not the first girl to be invited here... *but damn if I won't be the last,* I think.

"Make yourself at home," he says, casually tossing his things onto a bench by the door as he empties his pockets—badges and pens, a set of miniature brass weights, and keycards land with a dull tap.

He opens the tall wardrobe near the bed and pulls out a soft charcoal-gray T-shirt and loose drawstring pants. As he strips off his jeans, I catch a glimpse of the sharp lines of his body—all muscle and lean strength—and something tightens low in my stomach.

From the dresser near the head of the bed, he grabs a folded white T-shirt and tosses it to me. "No gray or black for you," he says with a small smile. "I remember."

The words land like a stone in my chest.

I slip into the shirt quickly, turning my back even though it reaches my knees. Even though, hours before, I was completely naked with this man. Still, I feel exposed—like wearing something of his makes everything between us too real, too close.

Noa finishes changing and sits at the edge of the bed, watching me. He doesn't speak, but his eyes trace over me slowly, drinking me in with a quiet intensity that makes my breath catch.

He holds out a hand.

I walk hesitantly toward him, my steps uncertain, and let him pull me between his knees. His hands settle on the backs of my thighs, thumbs moving in soft, soothing circles behind my legs. He looks up at me—*really* looks—and everything stills. His fingers twitch, like he's caught between reverence and desire, restraint and hunger.

He could have me. We both know it.

But he doesn't.

Not yet.

And that, somehow, makes me want him more.

"Cel..." His voice is low, steady—but heavy. "We need to

talk." He exhales slowly, dragging a hand through his hair. "I've been thinking about it all afternoon—after I walked you back to the commons. Not *just* what happened in the Cavern." His tone softens, threaded with self-reproach. He looks up again, finally meeting my eyes. "You, here? At this school? It felt impossible. And then it wasn't. And I guess I just—" He pulls in a breath. "I didn't know how to act. I didn't even give you a second to breathe before pulling you into that room."

He reaches for my hand and gently tugs me down beside him.

"I'm sorry," he murmurs. "I should've let you settle in. Let you find your footing on your own terms." He's staring at the floor now, fingers curled tight around the edge of the bedframe. "And then when you almost lost control… I was still trying to piece it all together." He pauses, jaw tight. "But it's real. *You're* real."

"Noa, I…"

There is so much I want to say.

And even more I know I can't.

Because how do I explain that *I* don't even know what I truly am? That magick isn't just a secret—it's a fracture line inside me. And every time I speak it aloud, the ground seems to shift beneath me.

Suddenly, he stands, the air sparking with tension. "You said yes to me earlier," he says quietly. "But I know you didn't tell me everything."

He doesn't yell. He doesn't need to. It's the restraint that cuts deeper.

"Why didn't you tell me? That you're Magick? How long have you been hiding this—hiding *you*?" He gestures broadly, hands rising in emphasis, as if trying to grasp the weight of what he's just learned and how long he's been kept in the dark. His hands fall to his sides, then lift again in a helpless, frustrated motion. "Did you not trust me? Did you truly not *know*? Was it because of your dad?" His voice softens as he looks at me, eyes flicking back and forth, trying to extract truth from emotion. "What exactly were you afraid of?"

I flinch.

"You said it started at your lake," he goes on, a shadow crossing his face. "But that's *not* how magick works. There are always signs. I mean—gods, we spent practically every waking moment together this summer. I would have thought I'd be the *first* person you told. Knowing who and what I am." His voice rises, more incredulous than angry. There's no venom in it—just disappointment. "I had my suspicions," he admits, his eyes meeting mine again, searching. "And now... *now* everything makes sense." He stops in the middle of the room, again running a hand through his hair. "The questions. How you lit up every time magick came up. How you always dodged swimming. That time at the waterfall—Alissa's bracelet?" He shakes his head. "That wasn't you finding it, I realize that now. You *called* it. And then the shower..."

My cheeks flush instantly.

Gods, the *shower*.

I think about all the things we did in that shower. But there was a moment—when we were wrapped around each other—when the water suddenly spiraled around us in a rush of sputtering torrent. I blamed the plumbing.

But that was a lie.

Noa's gaze is on me again—intense, wounded, and laced with something else. Something like... betrayal.

"If we're really doing this," he says, quieter now as he moves back to the bed, "you and me... then we have to trust each other." He sits beside me, our knees brushing. "No games. No half-truths. I know there are things you're keeping from me—maybe things you felt like you *couldn't* tell me before—but if this is going to work..." He threads his fingers through mine. Warm. Steady. Anchoring. "I need honesty, Celeste. Real honesty."

He gives me a moment. The space to breathe.

"Just—start at the beginning."

Just start at the beginning.

It sounds so simple. Like untangling everything I've buried is as easy as choosing a thread and pulling. But there's nothing simple about the truth. Still, something in his voice... in the way he holds my hand like he's not letting go... makes me want to try.

So I inhale, steady and slow, and I begin.

* * *

I WAS twelve when my magick first manifested. Younger than most other Magicks.

My father's work had brought us to Bulgaria—another embassy, another temporary address. There was a lake near the house we were staying in. I passed by it every day on my way to school. One morning, I saw a boy climb up an old oak tree. A rope swing dangled from one of the limbs, the kind that arced out over the water like something out of a storybook.

The next day, determined, I decided to try it.

I waited until my father was gone—he'd always warned me to stay away from water because I couldn't swim.

I remember looking up at that oak tree, thinking that its shadow was taller than our whole house. The swing was just two rough pieces of wood nailed together—crooked, unstable, like a child had built it. The rope was frayed and twisted. I grabbed it anyway and climbed up the hill to where I had seen the boy jump to move over the water.

And then I jumped.

The first glide out over the water was mesmerizing. I saw the entire lake stretched beneath me, the water a dark gray-blue with streaks of turquoise where the sunlight hit it just right. It felt like flying, like I was soaring over an ocean. But on the second—I heard a snap.

I looked up just in time to see that those frayed and twisted ropes were no longer attached to the sturdy tree, but instead free-falling, along with me, toward the deepest part of the lake.

I remember the water feeling cold as ice. I swear there were whispers as I plunged beneath the surface. And I felt the lake wrap around me, like silk and stone. I remember thinking that this was it, *this was how I'd die*. All my father's warnings flooded back through my mind.

I thought I was drowning, and I didn't even think to try to fight it.

Then—I opened my eyes.

I looked up to realize that I was at the bottom of the lake, completely unharmed. Sandy rocks were strewn about, wilted underwater plants being pulled languidly toward what looked like a spinning vortex of water all around me. The lake churned above me like a tornado—with me at its eye.

I was terrified. What twelve-year-old wouldn't be?

Never mind I remember thinking at that moment, *this is actually how I die.*

But then—I saw a shadow move above me.

A face appeared at the top of the vortex—dark hair, silver-gray eyes, the boy I had seen the day before. The boy on the swing. "Hold on!" he shouted. "Don't move!"

Something dropped toward me—long and black. At first, I thought it was just a rope, but then it shifted, pulsed, moved like it was alive.

Like *shadow*.

"Grab it!" he yelled.

I reached for the rope, and it curled around me protectively, almost like a hug. I was being pulled upwards from the bottom of the lake and out of the vortex. The shadow rope pulled me straight into the arms of that same boy, who started swimming us to shore.

That was how I met Gavrail.

He was two years older than me and was the first person to teach me about magick. About how I could somehow shape water, speak to it, command it. He lived in the house next door and was the son of a Bulgarian general.

His power was shadow. Rare. Coveted. *Dangerous.* He could manipulate any shadow around him, and if none were to be found, he could create them in a rush of dark and shimmering night. He taught me to love magick... and to respect it.

His father was known for finding exceptional Magickteers—what Bulgarians call those with magick in their blood—to use for spying, fighting, and other things behind closed doors that no one talked about.

Gavrail and I spent every possible moment together. At the lake. In the forest. Curled up in his room reading books or playing card games. I had never been around many kids the same age as me before. He was my first real friend. My *best* friend.

We'd spend hours laying out on the sun-warmed boulders by the lake, skipping stones, dreaming out loud. We'd talk about life, our hopes, the future... *our* future.

It was on one of those boulders where he kissed me for the first time. I was thirteen—full of teenage hormones and the awkwardness of youth. I'd just had yet another argument with my dad about magick. I had come to my lake to escape.

Gavrail sat beside me while I cried into his shoulder. He brushed a tear off my cheek and told me to stop crying because he couldn't stand to see me sad.

And then he leaned in and kissed me. My first real kiss.

It would be a couple more years before we did anything beyond kissing. But he was patient. Never made me feel rushed or ashamed.

We'd often spend our afternoons secretly practicing magick—tucked away in a quiet cove along the lake, far from disapproving eyes. Experimenting. Testing. Pushing the boundaries of what we could do. The guilt I felt for betraying my father was matched only by the rush that came with each new discovery, each new skill we mastered.

Together, we discovered we could merge our powers to create something new: a dark, viscous substance made of condensed shadows and water. We used it to catch insects we found high up in the trees or to snare fish beneath the lake's surface. We even learned to shape it into a cocoon—a dome that stopped sound and sight—so that my parents couldn't hear us when he'd sneak into my room at night.

We called it *shadowmire.*

One night, shortly after my sixteenth birthday, he came into my room, frantic. He was leaving. His father had been reassigned to a new post. They were moving immediately. He was shaking as he cupped my face and told me that he would find a way to come back to me.

Then he kissed me—deeply, desperately—and I asked him to stay.

I knew that this might be our last night together. I wanted him to make it a night I would never forget.

I had never made love before, but that is what it was. Full of emotion. Full of sensation. Full of *him.* Full of *me.* Wrapped in our cocoon of shadowmire, we held each other like the sun would never rise.

But when the light started to peek over the horizon—we knew what it meant.

He kissed me one final time, told me he loved me. I could tell there was something more he wanted to say, something else in his eyes—but he swallowed it. Instead, he just told me to be careful, warned me against ever letting anyone know the full power that I carried. That there were things that I needed to know, about my magick, about my family, my father. Things that he would tell me when the time was right.

With one last look of longing, he climbed down from my window—and then he was gone.

I fell back asleep and woke when the sun was high, casting no shadows on the ground. Fitting, I thought, as my heart lay broken in pieces, mourning the shadows that would no longer be next to mine.

I grabbed my bike to hurry over to his estate, to see him one last time, only to find the house already empty, a few servants hastily boxing up what remained of my best friend and his family. I ran to his room to find it completely empty of all the things that had made it my favorite space those past four years, all the things that were Gavrail—his coin collection, his sketchbook, his books, the drawing of me he had framed and hung over his desk—gone. All gone.

All except for a small velvet box.

It sat on his now-empty bed, next to a letter addressed to me.

Celeste,

There's so much I wish I could tell you. But I can't—not yet. Not without putting you in danger. And I hate that. I hate keeping anything from you.

What I can say is this: be careful. Please. There is a kind of power in you that most people can't even begin to understand. It's not only extraordinary—it's dangerous. Not because of what you might do, but because of what others will do to get to it. To get to you. There are people out there who will hunt you for it. Who will try to hurt you for it.

You can't let anyone know—not even the people you think you can trust. I know how that sounds, and I hate asking you to hide a part of yourself—but it's the only way I know how to keep you safe.

You are everything to me. I need you to be okay. To be happy. Even if this life keeps us apart, then let the next one bring us back together. Because you are the ending to every story I know.

I love you. More than I know how to say. It's always been you. It will always be you.

Yours,

Gavrail

INSIDE THE BOX was a ring—two pear-shaped diamonds flanking a large cushion-cut deep-blue sapphire.

There was a note tucked inside: *A belated birthday present.*

The last thing he ever gave me.

That first week, I ran to the mailbox every day, convinced there would be a letter. But days turned to weeks. Weeks to months. Months to years. Nothing.

He was gone. Vanished like his shadows, like smoke after fire.

The boy who taught me how to build forts in the woods and whisper secrets into lakes until the lakes whispered back. The first person to teach me about magick. The first person to teach me about love.

The silence he left behind carved something out of me I've never been able to fill.

Those days in our forest were the last time I ever willingly touched my magick. Between his and my father's warnings, I locked it away once more, caged so carefully I almost forgot how it felt as it pressed against the bars.

Sometimes it stirred. A flicker, a breath against the cage. I always forced it still.

Until the day the cage broke.

That day… The day I found my father's body in the lake. Just a warning of blue against the churning waters as the rain swirled around us, chaotic and charged. I don't even know what

I did. All I know is my mother found us together at the shoreline, me sobbing into his chest as I held him, water spooled out around us in a curved wave. Hovering above us, dripping soft tears from its edges like it was crying too.

* * *

Noa and I talk all through the night.

I tell him about my family. I tell him about Gavrail—the tangled history woven between us. I tell him about how I grew up burying my magick beneath layers of silence because of my father and Gavrail's fear, how hiding it became second nature.

He listens—really listens. He doesn't try to fix it, just pulls me closer, kisses the top of my head, and threads his fingers gently through my hair.

Aside from Gavrail, I have never told another living soul some of the things I now lay bare to Noa. It feels like stepping into sunlight after years underground—freeing, and yet terrifying in its exposure.

But even in that moment of raw honesty, I keep some pieces to myself.

I don't tell him about shadowmire or my ring. I don't tell him how far Gavrail pushed me—or how far I went willingly. I tell him I'm Magick, yes... but not what I am capable of. Not the things we did. Not the things I became.

Some secrets still feel tangled in shadows too deep to reach. Some of them don't feel like my secrets to share. Some of them I still don't understand myself.

But still, I feel lighter than I have in a long time.

And when the first light of sunrise starts to peek over the garden wall, casting the room in soft pink hues, he kisses me. Slowly. Unhurried. And with quiet intention. My hands slide into his hair, my sapphire ring shimmering like mist caught in the light, as he pulls me close.

I can feel every hard line of him through his T-shirt. But he doesn't go further than the kiss. "Sleep, Celeste." A gentle command.

I don't want to, not while I can feel his heat seeping into me through his clothes, but he sees the yawn I try to stifle.

I must fall asleep, because the next thing I remember is waking up, wrapped in his sheets and his arms. He is beautiful like this, especially in sleep—dark lashes soft against perfect cheekbones, his lips curving with the hint of a smile.

Carefully, I slip out from under his arms, wanting to get back to the Blue Dahlia to change and get ready for the day before the rest of the campus wakes up. I get dressed quietly, pressing a kiss to his sleeping lips, and slip out the door.

As I pass through the common room, I hear the door to the right open—and see Rozsen being swept into a kiss by Finn. She laughs and pushes him back into his room, shutting the door in his face. When she turns and catches my eye, we both burst out laughing.

"That was one hell of a night," she says with a crooked smile, looping her arm through mine before dragging us out the front door. Walk of shame be damned.

* * *

I SPEND the weekend practically living in Noa's dorm room. His roommates, Ryan and Finn, acknowledge me with wry smiles and overly polite hellos—equal parts amused and resigned.

Ryan Halloway is all quiet intensity: broad-shouldered, steady-eyed, with a voice that rarely rises above a murmur. Earth magick suits him; he doesn't just wield it—he *is* it. Grounded. Unmoving. Honest to a fault.

Finn Rourke, by contrast, is all free-fall and swagger—lithe, sharp-eyed, and always halfway to a grin that makes you wonder what he's just done or is about to do. There is wind in him, even without his magick. Where Ryan is the rock, Finn is the whirlwind circling it—loud, loyal, and never afraid to stir the air.

Noa is careful with me. Too careful. After what happened in the Cavern—after I nearly drowned us both in my own magick—he's determined to make sure I can control it before we take things further.

So he kisses me. Gods, does he kiss me. Long, heated presses of his mouth that leave me dizzy, touches that linger just long enough to set me shaking—but his magick is always coiled close, ready to smother mine if it flares. His control is iron. Mine is paper-thin.

I slip constantly. Leaning in too far. Letting a kiss stretch into hunger, into teeth, into something he cuts off with a groan and a hand braced against my back as my magick flares uncontrolled around us both.

It's excruciating—having this much of him, feeling the desire and the promise, but never all of him.

One night, I test him on purpose. He steps out of the shower, steam curling around the room. I tell him to leave the water on for me as I step into the heat of him, close enough to touch. I make a show of undressing, dragging the straps of my top slowly down my arms, letting the fabric pool across my chest and stomach, thumbs hooking on the waistband of my pants as I slide them slowly down my legs. His eyes track every motion, the turquoise in them glowing gold at the edges. Once I'm completely naked, I lean up on my toes to kiss him, purposefully brushing against the rigid shape of him beneath his towel.

"Fuck, Celeste." His laugh comes out strangled, a grin tugging at his mouth even as his fists clench at his sides. "You are going to be the death of me."

The worst part? *I want to be.* As long as it means he's finally mine.

He's started teaching me how to ground myself. To keep the

water from answering my emotions instead of my will. But it's painstaking work. Every kiss he draws from me makes my magick stir in ways I'm not ready for—sinks flooding, water pooling, rain slicking down from nowhere. I think about the phrase carved into the Whittaker archway—the one that warns about not heeding the elements' call, *"for the longer it is caged, the wilder it returns."* Because that's what it feels like—a wild thing prowling beneath my skin, ready to lash out at the smallest crack in control. After years of being locked away, it's no longer content to sit silent and secret.

One exercise involves a candle set in the center of a deep bowl. Noa shows me how to use my magick to pour water into the bowl slowly, carefully, until it laps high without drowning the flame. But the higher it rises, the faster my heartbeat climbs, my anxiety spiking, the current inside me surging, nervous and wild.

We practice in his bedroom, the bowl on his desk. The water climbs higher and higher. I feel the exact breath where want becomes will—

And miss it.

The flame sputters with a hiss.

Shit.

"Steady," Noa murmurs, his hand firm over mine as the water quivers, his gold heat caging my tide. "Don't try to fight it, Cel. Guide it."

Smoke curls sharp against my face as the fire goes out, and my chest seizes. Because in my head, it isn't just a candle I've drowned—it's him, smothered by my lack of control.

Right now, I can barely fill the bowl halfway on my own before the flame dies by an errant splash. But I keep practicing. Centering myself. Determined to prove to him that I can do this —even when the temptation of him makes me want to lose control entirely.

To distract me from my failures, Noa takes me to some of his favorite spots around campus: a picnic in a secluded bay by the lake, a hike through the winding trails of the Mirewyn Mountains, a secret party in the lantern-lit clearing of Ashfen Grove. It feels like our own little world—removed, suspended in time.

But by Sunday night the spell breaks and reality creeps in. I slip back to my dorm with Noa's taste still on my mouth and a knot in my stomach—because tomorrow, Whittaker will ask me to prove I belong.

CHAPTER 9

Magick, like history itself, is never static. It evolves with the ambitions of those who wield it.

—A History of Magick, Vol. I

Monday arrives with a bite in the air. Whittaker feels sharpened, like a knife waiting for fresh blood. Around me, the campus buzzes with the bright, nervous energy of a new term.

I should feel intimidated, being around so many Magicks who have been practicing with their element for years. But instead, I just feel… ready.

I put on my uniform and walk with the rest of my squad as we make our way to the tall cream-colored building I saw during orientation. History of Magick is our first class, held on the ground floor of the Logistics building.

The auditorium unfolds in a graceful half-circle, with ten ascending rows of polished wooden chairs, each cushioned in deep-maroon fabric. Light filters in through high arched windows, catching on the soft sheen of the lacquered floors and casting long shadows across the room. At its center, a modest stage rises just high enough to command attention without overpowering the space.

Professor Ella Straits looks like someone who does not like to dabble in theory and only enjoys cold, hard facts. Her short black hair curls just above her shoulders. Thick black-rimmed glasses balance precariously on a too-pointed nose that makes her look more like a hawk than a person. She taps a pen on the podium before directing our attention behind her.

A suspended projection screen loops through the centuries —a living timeline of magickal history counting down in slow, luminous increments.

"Welcome," she says, her voice sharp enough to slice through the remaining whispers, "to your first History of Magick class."

The room quiets instantly.

"Most of what you will learn in this course is common knowledge. The Primordial Shattering—when power first fractured into elemental strains. The classification of the elements. The moment humanity learned to harness those forces in service of society."

Her gaze sweeps the rows—and pins a Blue Squad first-year caught mid-yawn.

The student jerks and tries to cover her mouth with her textbook.

Professor Straits doesn't raise her voice. She simply stops speaking. And somehow that makes it worse.

The silence stretches until it becomes a weight on everyone's tongue.

"Miss...?" Straits says at last, glancing down at her roster.

The girl swallows. "Eva Mitchel. Ma'am."

"Miss Mitchel," Straits says, voice devoid of emotion. "Can you please tell us what year the Shattering is commonly dated?"

Eva freezes. Her eyes flick wildly to the screen, to her notes, to her neighbors—who suddenly become very invested in not knowing her.

"I—" she starts.

Straits taps her pen once. The screen scrolls back to the top, the date hovering there like a trap. Eva has the self-preservation to at least duck her head as her cheeks blaze.

Straits's mouth doesn't change. Not quite a smile. Not quite a frown. "Perhaps, one's time is better spent getting a good night's sleep so that one can actually *pay attention* in class." She raises one thin dark brow at Eva before returning to the lesson in a steady monotone.

She leads us through a quick recap of current magick powers and their somewhat contested histories. The Service, Europe's Krovya, and the smaller foreign organizations that orbit them. The timeline behind her begins to move again.

The screen shows a world map highlighting borders and the crests of old and new kingdoms.

"Eventually, what began as creation became conquest. As nations began recruiting Magicks into their armies and governments, everything shifted. Magick became less about wonder and more about warfare."

Because power always invites appetite. It was something my father used to say. Over dinner. Over the sound of the news on the radio. I know from my own research that this was when competing nations began to build their own schools, their own doctrines, their own agendas.

"The Whittaker School of Magick was founded in 1745 by Headmistress Magdalena Jamison," Straits says. The screen shifts, painting Whittaker's crest in clean lines—a mountain silhouette over a still lake, a single star pinned in the upper left like a secret the sky refuses to keep. "It is also the youngest magick school still in operation."

The image flickers. A school rises behind a wrought-iron gate shaped like two condors.

"The oldest was established in Peru—long before the rise of the Inca Empire."

I glance up at the photo. The stone walls, the open sky—

For a split second, a cool draft seems to brush the back of my neck.

The screen shifts again. A gold dragon sigil coils across black. I can almost believe it's trying to move across the screen, its scales catching the light as it twists. "Then came the highly secretive Xinj Academy in Beijing."

Another crest replaces it—this one severe and angular. "Vikhrostrum Akademiya, in Eastern Europe."

A shiver touches my spine when I look at the mountain peaks that represent the famous war college. Krovya's prized jewel of the Carpathians.

"And finally, the ancient royal academy in Jordan."

My fingers twitch at my sides, like my magick is grasping for something just out of reach. I shift slightly in my seat, brushing off the sensation.

Straits turns back to us, hands clasped behind her back. "For most of recorded history, only four elements were recognized. Does anyone know which four?"

Rozsen's hand goes up. Straits nods once.

"Air, fire, water, and earth," she answers.

"Correct." Straits clicks her pen once more, and the screen changes to artwork depicting a bloody battle. "And in 1792, the First Magick Rebellion occurred. A conflict the non-Magick world prefers to romanticize as the French Revolutionary and Napoleonic Wars."

A murmur runs through the room—hushed and dissatisfied. Somewhere behind me, I hear Peter whisper, "My grandfather calls it *the Slaughtering*—"

Straits's head turns. Just slightly.

The whisper dies in Peter's throat like it's been strangled.

"By World War II," she says, "the Nazis were experimenting

on Magicks. Testing the boundaries of what elemental bodies could endure. It was during that era that the other elements were identified—wood, metal, shadow, and light—long hidden, and perpetually misunderstood."

The screen flickers: black-and-white photographs. Medical charts. Bodies reduced to data.

My stomach tightens.

"Professor, is it true that we have a metal Magick student here at Whittaker?" It's Sawyer who asks the question.

Straits nods. "Yes, and two wood-wielders, and one light Magick." Murmurs go through the auditorium.

But no shadow-wielders, I note. My finger twists the ring on my hand in reflex.

"A hundred years of uneasy peace followed, until the Second Rebellion—a brutal conflict where Magick and non-Magick factions warred openly across borders and ideologies."

My father had a special interest in this particular piece of history. I remember combing through some of the many books I found in his office—texts describing the absolute horrors and atrocities committed in the name of *the good of the world* during that time.

In my peripheral vision, my water bottle trembles—the liquid inside rolling once, barely a ripple, but enough to make my pulse jump. I reach out and curl my fingers around the bottle, willing it to still.

"In the last forty years," Straits continues, "more and more nations have turned their backs on democracy, choosing control instead. And with control came more Magicks—recruited, trained, owned. Bound by loyalty… or fear."

Owned.

The word lodges under my ribs.

Because that's how we got here. To the edge of something vast and violent. A hush before chaos.

I know politics—I grew up in its shadow, at my father's side.

Wars don't erupt overnight. They simmer. They wait. Sometimes for decades. Sometimes for centuries. And sometimes, they wait for the right person to light the match.

The water in my bottle gives a tiny, treacherous shiver—like it recognizes something within me it refuses to name.

* * *

AN HOUR LATER, we climb the stairs, headed to the second floor for Potions—the class I am most excited about.

I majored in organic chemistry at my old university. At twenty-two, I was supposed to be starting a clean, sensible life after graduating last spring—Halcyon Biotech in New York this fall, a cute little West Village apartment with Alissa. Pharmaceutical research was the closest I could get to magick without losing my father's approval. But that was before everything changed last summer. Before Noa. Before the lake. Before magick stopped being theoretical and started being *mine*.

What non-Magicks call medicine or chemistry, Magicks call potions. Both factions usually work together in developing new drugs or compounds for various purposes. Where a chemist sees molecules, a potion-maker sees correspondences. Both transform matter, alter states, even save lives. Two sides of the same coin—science and potionwork, speaking different dialects of the same universal language.

The Potions classroom is sterile and orderly, with gleaming white tables and tall metal stools. Everything in its place. White wood shelves line stone walls, filled with glass jars of various sizes, corked vials, and brass-labeled bottles. Floor-to-ceiling windows let in generous natural light—perfect for observing subtle shifts in color and texture. The air smells like my college chemistry lab back in Virginia: crushed herbs, biting metal, the faint sulfur tang of propane flames. An unexpected pang of nostalgia hits.

I drag Rozsen, Amelia, and Peter to the front table, while Elliot and our other squadmates post up in the back. Elliot mutters about how Potions is "for people who like messes and blowing shit up."

Professor Shim Ching looks like he's been alive since the age of alchemy—small and stooped, with parchment-thin skin and a white beard twisted to a precise point. His voice rumbles like gravel, every word deliberate and heavy, like it comes from somewhere deep beneath the school's foundations. His shrewd dark eyes scan the room—quick to narrow in disapproval, quicker still to gleam with curiosity when something, or someone, interests him.

He is also the first non-Magick I've met at Whittaker.

The class turns out to be fairly basic—disappointing, even. Despite it being my first official Potions course, I covered most of this material during my previous degree. Crushed herbs, flame management, simple neutralizers. I go through the motions, my hands working while my mind drifts, already several steps ahead.

After successfully brewing a Scent Veil potion, used to neutralize odors or to mask the scent of an object or person—"Perfect for sharing bathrooms with squadmates," Professor Ching jokes—he asks if I can stay behind after class.

I walk over to his desk at the front of the room, the pristine surface showing organized rows of jewel-toned vials filled with strange substances. Some glow, some bubble, and one looks and smells suspiciously like wine.

"I've read your transcript and file, Miss Farris. Impressive. Very impressive, as a matter of fact." He twists his beard between his fingers. "You have all the basic knowledge—and even some advanced understanding. More so than your peers." He looks out across the now-empty classroom. "What you lack," he says, fixing me with those sharp eyes, "is elemental knowledge. Understanding how magick *breathes*." He pauses then, eyes searching, measuring. "I'd like to move you into my Advanced Potions course. We meet in Browning Hall, Thursdays at nine o'clock sharp. If you're interested."

I thank him sincerely and gather my things, a quiet flicker of pride warming my chest as I head to rejoin my squad.

* * *

AT LUNCH, I head to the mess hall to meet up with Noa and snag a table with him, Finn, Rozsen, Elliot, and another fourth-year named Mauve—the girl with strawberry-pink hair from the bonfire.

The mess hall at Whittaker is a sprawling, high-ceilinged space filled with the low hum of conversation and the clatter of trays and cutlery. Long metal tables and benches stretch across the polished floor, organized into tidy rows. Light slants through tall rectangular windows, cutting gold ribbons across the floor. A large electric sliding glass door on the west side opens and closes with a soft mechanical hiss as students shuffle in and out between classes. The air smells like garlic and yeast, with undertones of sugar and something fried.

Cafeteria workers in crisp aprons move quickly behind the counters, dishing out trays of hot food with practiced efficiency. Noa's pink-hatted pancake chef is among them, flipping something sweet with an exaggerated flourish. It's just past midday, and the lunch stations are in full swing: a make-your-own sandwich bar with fresh breads and fillings, and a rotating hot line that today features rosemary chicken and garlic mashed potatoes.

Finn is the epitome of politeness and affable charm to Rozsen, who's settled beside him. The two fall into an easy rhythm—light banter, eyes brighter than they should be for people claiming to be just friends. Maybe it's something. Maybe it's not. But either way, it's easy and carefree.

I sit beside Noa, who leans in, his familiar heat curling around me like a second skin.

"You sleep okay?" he asks, voice quiet. Then, closer, with words just for me: "I didn't like waking up without you next to me." His lips brush my temple, and his hand finds my thigh beneath the table—warm, steady, possessive in the gentlest way.

I try but fail to hide the satisfied smile tugging at my lips.

He studies me for a beat, his eyes glinting like he's about to say something more—but Mauve cuts in, giving me a slow once-over.

"So *you're* the girl who walked into Whittaker with Noa Gallegher's jacket and zero self-preservation instincts."

I choke into my glass of water, coughing once before managing to look up at her. Noa's glare is sharp and immediate.

But Mauve just grins, completely unfazed. "Welcome to the circus, Initiate."

The rest of lunch passes in a blur of mashed potatoes, teasing, and bite-sized stories. Rozsen steals my bread roll off my tray and is mid-bite before I even notice it's gone. Elliot bombards Finn with a thousand questions about air magick.

Noa never stops touching me—knuckles brushing mine, hand against my thigh, shoulder against my side. His presence grounds me. Even in the chaos. Especially in it.

When lunch is finished and we get ready to head our separate ways, he pulls me in for a kiss, long and lingering. The kind of kiss that makes our friends look anywhere but at us before Finn finally coughs and mumbles something about getting reamed by Professor Kael if they're late.

The rest of the afternoon is packed with more new faces, syllabus breakdowns, first assignments, and professors who all seem equal parts brilliant and terrifying. I survive—barely. And by the time I finally make it back to the dorms, my head is spinning and I'm not entirely sure all my notes are in English.

Dusk on campus is quiet, lights blooming one by one across

the courtyards like small stars. I sink into my bed beside Rozsen, trading gossip and stories with lighthearted laughter. It reminds me of nights back in Virginia with Alissa, Noa's sister. She was the closest thing I ever had to something like this.

My head aches in the best way—exhausted but buzzing, like I crossed an invisible threshold, and somehow I know there will be no going back.

Sleep comes fast that night. And with it, dreams.

Dreams of dark caves full of shadow, water full of secrets, and wildfire blooming on the horizon.

CHAPTER 10

Strength, speed, and technique matter. But so too do intent, composure, and what you are willing—or unwilling—to risk.

—*Combat Theory I: Foundations of Defense*

I wake in the dark, heart pounding. For a breath, I don't know why—fragments of the dream cling to me, the same one I always have, images slipping away like water through my fingers.

Stars rippling across a surface, fractured in black water.

My reflection staring back at me from the depths—scared, wide-eyed.

A voice, low and coaxing saying: *Come here, Celeste.*

And then a pull. The cold grasp of water dragging me under, the stars breaking apart above.

I shift beneath the covers and feel it.

My bedding is drenched. The sheets cling to my skin, hair damp at the nape of my neck. My shirt is soaked through.

Shit. No. No, no, no.

This hasn't happened in years. But the nightmare is always the same—a black pool of stars, a voice, the cold water pulling me under. And then waking up like this.

Wet. Drenched. Soaked.

I lie still for a moment, breath shallow, as I slowly flex each finger. Each toe. Ankles. Hands. All here. All intact.

I'm still me. Just wet.

Water. Everywhere.

I ease out of bed, careful not to wake Rozsen, whose soft snores break the silence like a tether. She's curled toward the wall, oblivious. I grip the edge of the mattress like it might ground me.

Blankets off. Sheets stripped. My laundry basket thuds against my leg.

5:03 a.m.

It's still dark. Still too early. Plenty of time to wash the evidence and pretend this morning never happened.

But the chill has already sunk in.

Not just the cold. The knowing.

Like something inside me roused while I slept—and slipped loose without permission.

I'm back in my dorm, my bed dry and freshly made, before the rest of my roommates even stir.

* * *

IT'S WEDNESDAY, and we have our first combat class in the Training Room—the same massive gymnasium where orientation and registration were held, now stripped of all banners and ceremony. Learning to defend and fight is not optional at Whittaker; in a world where power is commonly conscripted, ignorance is often the fastest way to die.

Gym uniforms on, we all stand along the edge of one of the many black mats scattered across the floor. A subway tile mosaic of promised pain. Some students are already sparring on the nearby mats, trading jabs, punches, and kicks in what look like rehearsed dances—fluid and deliberate.

Our instructor for the class isn't actually a professor at all, but a fellow student built like a tank, with arms and legs the size of small tree trunks. He introduces himself as Jazz, a fourth-year in Green Squad and an earth-wielder.

He guides us through some combat basics, correcting stances, adjusting form, and letting us practice on the wooden dummies lined up along the wall. It's obvious that Peter and Sawyer are the best fighters in our squad. They move as one, more like brothers than cousins, all instinct and rivalry. Rozsen and Elliot are similar. They've been training together since childhood. Rozsen is quick, hands moving so fast they're almost impossible to track. Elliot fights like the air she commands, effortless and wild, making it difficult to predict her next move.

My stance is uneven; my punches don't land clean. I'm still rattled from this morning's quiet disaster and unwanted show of power. But I keep my focus on the wooden figure in front of me.

In the last twenty minutes of class, Jazz announces that we'll be sparring—pairing with older students if any are free. One by one, my classmates partner off with second- and third-years. The older students guide them through the motions, stepping slowly, offering tips when someone misses an opening or leaves themselves vulnerable.

When it's my turn on the mat, I see a girl approach Jazz and whisper something in his ear. He eyes her suspiciously but nods nevertheless. She smiles at me, but there is nothing kind in it. All teeth and intention.

She's tall, with long, silvery-blonde hair and blue eyes so

dark they're nearly violet. I recognize her from orientation day. She and her friend were the ones by the Garden Grove wall. She's quite stunning, if I'm being honest. And for some reason, I'm immediately on edge.

As soon as I set foot onto the mat, she sweeps my legs out from under me, and I hit the mat with a sharp, flat crack that empties the breath from my lungs.

Okay… so it's going to be like that.

I grit my teeth as I get to my feet and she advances on me without holding back. I take a kick to my shin as she whips around and lands a jab into my kidney, my breath catching in a burning hitch. I attempt to block her, but she's fast, ruthless, and seems to have a vendetta against me even though I'm certain I've never met her before in my life.

I try to send a punch to her right side, but she fakes left and spins behind me, and a kick to my back sends me flying.

Jazz is there in an instant, grabbing her by the arm and yanking her back. "You've made your point, Stella. Are you trying to *kill* the girl?"

She flips her hair, breath barely affected. "Just trying to help," she purrs, then saunters off, laughing with her friends like she didn't just treat me like a training dummy. They speak in low whispers to each other, looking over their shoulders at me. She grabs her jacket off the floor—third-year, with a water patch stitched on the shoulder.

"You okay?" Rozsen asks, reaching a hand out to help me up, her eyes burning holes into the backs of the girls as they walk away from us.

"Yeah," I say, wincing as I rub my side and shin—both of which will likely be black and blue by morning. "But what the hell was that about?"

* * *

Later that night, I'm curled on the sofa at the Spanish Steps, trying to finish my essay on the first one hundred years of magick for Professor Straits. My legs are draped across Noa's lap as he reads from a textbook, lazily marking pages with a highlighter while he sips tea from a mug on the console table. The domesticity of it all makes me smile to myself.

He absently rubs my calf until he presses into a sore spot, drawing a groan from me. He glances up, a brow arched in silent question.

"Ugh, don't ask... Some third-year girl had it out for me during sparring today."

Across the room, Finn and Ryan exchange a look. Finn suddenly finds a speck on the ceiling very interesting, while Ryan retreats into his room with a not-so-subtle mutter.

Noa sets his book aside, brow furrowed. "Let me guess—blonde, blue eyes, angsty?"

"Yes." I squint at him. "Wait... how did you—?"

Finn groans and starts shoving his schoolwork into his bag. "This is your mess, Gallegher. I'm out."

I sit up and narrow my eyes at Noa as a faint flush colors his cheeks. He's looking down at his hands like they've personally betrayed him.

I smack him with my essay. "Noa... what exactly is Finn referring to?"

He winces, sheepish. "I think you just met Stella."

"Stella?"

"My ex."

Ah, I think, sinking back into the cushions.

Well. That explains *a lot* about this morning.

"We were never serious," he says quickly. "On and off for the past two years. But I ended it for good last year. We were completely over before I even met you last summer."

He tries to grab my wrist to pull me closer, but I move away, just out of reach.

"Is she going to be a problem for me?" I ask, eyebrows drawn as I fix a sharp glare in his direction.

He drags a hand through his hair—that nervous tell I've already memorized. "No," he says. Too fast. "I'll talk to her. She won't be a problem."

He successfully snags me by my waist this time and pulls me close. And I let him.

"Cross my heart," he says in earnest as he brushes a kiss against the tip of my nose. "I'm sorry she gave you trouble," he adds, voice dipping lower as his hand starts a slow path up my thigh. "But I can think of a few ways to make it up to you..."

I know this game. I *love* this game. And I'm more than ready after his week of utter torture and grounding lessons.

But we are sitting in the living room. I start to rise, intending to take things somewhere more private, but he catches my hand and tugs me back down. He shifts, pressing his body over mine, making sure I feel every deliberate inch of contact as he settles against me.

I glance toward Finn and Ryan's rooms, both doors firmly closed.

"Relax," he says against my jaw, lips grazing skin. "They're not coming out again tonight."

He leans down to kiss me, taking his time to make sure he tastes every bit of me as he nips softly at the corner of my mouth.

My blood starts to heat, and it has nothing to do with the fire burning beside us in the hearth—or the magick I can sense dancing just under Noa's fingertips. His golden touch is never far, just in case I lose control.

"Have you been practicing your grounding?" he whispers into the hollow of my throat, pausing to kiss me there as he starts to trail lower.

I nod, biting my bottom lip. Inside, I clamp down on my magick like it's a wild animal straining at the leash—secretly threatening it if it so much as tries to move a tendril of water against me.

"I'll stop if it starts to be too much," he says, eyes darkening as his gaze meets mine again.

His hands slide along my waist, circling my stomach, slipping beneath the hem of my shirt. He finds my breast through the fabric of my bra and cups it, thumb brushing over the curve with a possessive tenderness that makes me shiver.

Then he uses his teeth to tug the neckline of my shirt lower, easing down the lace on my bra and exposing me to the cool air and his warm mouth. His tongue flicks my nipple, slow and teasing, while his other hand slips my bra strap from my shoulder, giving him full access.

The push and pull of his mouth, the contrast of heat and pressure—it's intoxicating. I arch into him, breathless, the warmth pooling as I feel a dampness start to gather between my legs.

His hands now move down to my waist and slip under the waistband of the boxer shorts I've taken to borrowing. When his fingers reach the wet heat between my thighs, he lets out a low, satisfied growl that sends a shiver straight through me.

I've had enough of barriers.

I wriggle free of the shorts and my panties, kicking them aside without ceremony. He sheds his shirt in one fluid motion, tossing it to the floor, before climbing back over me with a hunger that makes my breath hitch. His hand finds me again, working slow, deliberate circles against my center that make my spine arch against the cushions. He watches me—watches every shift in my face, every gasp—and when he feels me trembling beneath him, he pauses as if waiting. He glances subtly toward the bar sink, then looks at the mug on the console table behind us. Nothing. Not even a twitch of water magick.

The grin that curves his mouth nearly undoes me.

"I told you," I pant, lips trembling against his jaw. "I've been practicing."

I reach for him, freeing him from his pants, wrapping my hand around the hard length of him. The sheer weight, impossible to ignore. His breath hisses between his teeth as I stroke, slow and steady, marveling at how soft his skin is against my palm.

His thumb presses into that delicate center—just right, *just* enough—while his fingers slide into me, again and again, the intensity building until I'm trembling on the edge. I don't *want* to fall alone. I want to drag him with me.

I reach for him again to guide him toward me. Into me.

But he stops. His hand covers mine, pressing it back to my side. His voice a strangled whisper. "Not yet."

He grinds me deeper into the cushions as the candlelight orbs flicker a glow, casting us in an amber light. His hand finds me again, fingers moving rhythmically against my core.

The pressure fractures into something I can no longer hold back, like glass under heat. I cry out, my whole body drawn tight as release barrels through me.

He doesn't pull away. Instead, he just turns us gently, cradling my back against his chest as we lie there facing the quiet room. He presses a kiss on the curve of my spine just between my shoulder blades.

Without moving me, he grabs a blanket and draws it over us like a shield, the fire in the hearth collapsing into embers. I turn my face up to him, his calloused fingers grasping my chin as he kisses me—slow, reverent.

My peripheral vision catches movement: liquid streaming out in erratic zigzags over the wood surface from the now tipped coffee mug. For a heartbeat, the spill gathers, shimmering, almost star-shaped, before it sinks into the grain.

Well, fuck.

I couldn't hold it. Not completely. And I know that Noa saw it too. That's why he stopped us.

Disappointment clings to me, sharper than the afterglow of the pleasure he just wrought from me.

Guess I still need more practice.

Noa presses another kiss to my shoulder, but I feel the truth sink in like cold water: control isn't mine yet. And until it is, apparently neither is he.

CHAPTER 11

Not all reactions follow known pathways. In rare cases, the interaction of certain substances will yield results no potioneer could fully anticipate.

—"Modern Principles of Alchemy and Potions," Dr. S. Davenport, *Journal of Applied Alchemical Sciences*

On Thursday, a misty rain blankets the campus. The crisp air pebbles my skin as I step outside the Blue Dahlia, the buildings around me blurred into ghostly shapes by the haze. I had grabbed Noa's jacket and an umbrella, but I welcome the rain. I always have. The way it falls. The way it feels. Whispering to me just as it did when I was a child.

I walk toward the northern edge of campus, headed to Advanced Potions with Professor Ching. Browning Hall stands alone, as if the rest of the campus moved on and left it behind—forgotten by time but too stubborn to disappear.

The stone cottage is weathered and moss-covered, more like something from a fairy tale than an official school building. Its sloping thatched roof is silvered with age, making me think of a place where a witch might step out at any moment, brushing flour from her hands and muttering spells under her breath.

Inside the oldest Potions classroom in the school, there is a hum of energy—wild, layered, something alive in and of itself. The air is thick with the mingled scent of chalk dust, scorched thyme, and old parchment. Dried herbs hang in tangled bunches from a crooked rack beside the door. An ancient well, its stones crumbling and its bucket long retired, sits off to the side.

The tables are scarred from generations of flame and failed mixtures, their charred edges evidence of those who came before. Strange shapes hang from the rafters and crowd the shelves—bones, vials, shimmering orbs, and preserved things that were once living that I can't name.

While the Logistics building labs were pristine, sterile, Browning Hall is chaotic—unnerving, and yet beautiful.

Some students have already arrived, clustered around the four large tables. At the front, I spot Finn, his tousled sandy-blond hair damp from the rain. His handsome face and warm brown eyes light up when he sees me. I wave.

He grins as I slide into the seat next to him. "Moving up in the world, are we, Farris?" he teases, nodding toward my Advanced Potions textbook.

I shrug as Professor Ching enters and gives me a polite nod. "The professor asked me to come," I say, a little lamely.

"Beautiful *and* brilliant," Finn says, winking. "Should've known from the way Noa talks about—*oof*—"

A strong hand grips his shoulder, hard. "The way Noa talks about what, exactly?" The air warms instantly around me as Noa appears, one eyebrow raised, standing behind us like an unmovable force.

"Noa! You didn't tell me you were in this class," I say, slightly breathless. *Gods, get a grip, Celeste... How does he always affect me like this?*

"I spoke to admin this morning," he says. "Figured I'd squeeze in one more Potions class before I graduate." He leans down and kisses me, soft and quick. "Class was already full, but Thorne pulled some strings."

Finn just rolls his eyes. "Yeah... because Potions has *always* been a favorite subject of yours," he says sarcastically, with a pointed cough in my direction.

Noa just winks at me, and heat rushes up my neck—hot enough I'm sure it shows—as I try, and fail, to hide my grin.

The rest of the class begins to settle as Mauve joins our table, leaving just one seat empty in the back. Then the door blows open, rain gusting in behind it, and the final student steps through.

Professor Ching barely looks up. "Stella, you're late—as always. Take your seat so we can begin."

My heart sinks as I glance back. Stella is glaring—at me, at Noa. Mostly me.

"Well, *this* is delightfully awkward," Finn murmurs, lounging back with his hands behind his head like he's settling in to watch a show.

Noa jabs him in the ribs, and Finn feigns injury then looks at me apologetically.

"Shit, Cel... I'm sorry," Noa says under his breath. He reaches under the table and squeezes my hand gently. "I didn't know she'd be in this class."

"It's fine," I mumble. Annoyed, but nothing I can do about it.

Professor Ching clears his throat, and the lecture begins.

* * *

MEASURE HERE. Stir there. Mix. Pour. Melt. Boil. Cool.

I lose myself in the rhythm of the classroom.

Potions feels natural to me—like water, like breathing. There's something soothing in the measured steps: the careful weighing, the deliberate stirring, the slow transformation of one thing into another. It's a dance I know instinctively, even without needing to look at a page. My hands always seem to move on their own, confident and precise.

The scents of herbs and minerals rise in delicate waves, curling into the air like incense. Each crackle of heat, each simmer of liquid, pulls me deeper into focus. The classroom, the students, even Noa beside me—it all blurs around the edges until there's only the task and the process.

But the hold on my focus is better than the hold on my magick.

I'm attempting to pour ten measured drops of water into our pyraleaf and ironroot mixture when a flicker of power jumps beneath my skin—unasked for, unformed—and the water in the beaker shivers. Then jumps. For a heartbeat, it almost looks like it's trying to flee. Like it knows something the rest of us don't.

The glass vibrates in my hand like it's alive.

I freeze, heart pounding.

Too late.

The beaker fractures in a clean, startling snap, liquid spilling in a glittering arc across the workstation and into Finn's open notes.

He curses softly, flicking droplets off his paper. "What was that?"

"I didn't... I barely touched it," I say, voice low, trying to steady my breath.

Noa leans in, his warmth cutting through the fog in my chest. He doesn't say anything—he just grabs a spare cloth. Mops up the spill. Collects the pieces of glass and disposes of them. All the while shielding me from the curious glances of Mauve and the looks and sniggers from the back table.

Professor Ching glances over from his desk but doesn't comment—just lifts a single snowy brow and continues writing.

"You're fine," Noa says under his breath. "It was just an accident." The glow from his fingers now rests softly on my knee under the table. Steadying me.

But it wasn't. Not really.

It's the third time this week something has slipped.

The magick inside me is unruly and impatient. Like some part of it is no longer waiting for permission. Like it's done asking if I'm ready.

Today we're making Emberveil—a tricky, dual-purpose tincture. When applied, it creates a thin barrier to prevent burns, but it can also heal skin that's already been damaged. One wrong move and it curdles. Noa keeps a steady hand on me through the rest of the lesson—no more mishaps. Our group works well together, precise and coordinated, our potion turning a soft, perfect amber when we finish.

Noa walks over to the container shelves and leans forward to grab a fresh beaker, just as Stella brushes past him—unnecessarily close. Her fingers graze his wrist, deliberate and dripping with suggestion.

"Careful, Noa," she murmurs, just loud enough for me to hear. "Wouldn't want to break anything that looks so very fragile."

My stomach knots.

"Perhaps you just run too hot for that thing to handle." She gives the beaker a pointed look, then glances back at me with a smug little smirk—like she knows exactly what nerve she's aiming for.

But Noa doesn't flinch. He straightens slowly, eyes sparking like flint against steel as he turns to her. "Some things are meant to hold the heat. You just weren't one of them."

A flicker of something—shock, wounded pride—crosses Stella's face before she recovers with a scoff and a toss of her hair. "Still burning bridges like you burn through beds, I see," she hisses, before turning on her heel and stalking back to her table.

I pretend to focus on measuring out more powdered iron-root, but my pulse is thudding in my ears.

Finn lets out a low whistle. "And this is why I never date water-wielders... Too emotional. The lot of you."

I aim an elbow at his ribs as he chuckles. I shoot him a glare, but I'm still watching Noa out of the corner of my eye.

He sets the beaker down like nothing happened, but his jaw is tight—and when he speaks, it's just for me. "You know nothing she says matters, right?" He reaches out and brushes his thumb over the back of my wrist.

I nod. Even if my pulse is still recovering.

Because I'm not glass. I won't shatter.

And I'm not afraid of fire.

I was made for it.

Professor Ching chooses that moment to inspect our tincture. He lifts the vial to the light, the amber substance catching a glint of flame. A raised brow. A pause. Then a nod. "I knew you'd be up to the task of this class, Miss Farris," he says, a note of pride threading his voice. "Keep up the good work." He offers a curt nod to Noa, Finn, and Mauve before moving on to the next table.

I glance across the room just in time to see Stella scowling down at her team's curdled mess—thick, cloudy, and utterly wrong.

I don't gloat. I don't smile.

But inside, I am deeply, thoroughly satisfied.

CHAPTER 12

Some magick is so rare that it shapes the future more than the past or present.

—Theory of Elemental Magick, Vol. I

The first week of classes is fascinating—and challenging—upending many of my preconceptions about how the world of magick really works.

On Friday, we finally reach the third floor of the Logistics building for our Theory of Elemental Magick class. Rows of sturdy oak desks curve in a semi-circle around a central demonstration podium. Each desk still bears its now-vintage built-in inkwell and a slide-out drawer for notes.

In one corner, a low bookshelf groans under the weight of well-worn tomes—*On the Philosophy of Fire, Waters of the Deep, Earth's Patient Heart, The Breath of Air*—their spines faded from decades of use. Above us, a mobile of carved wooden symbols—an air spiral, a flickering flame, a water droplet, an earthen gemstone—turns ever so slightly, though no breeze stirs the room.

At the podium stands Professor Gideon Barrows. He is a tall man in his late forties or early fifties, with twinkling green eyes and a kindly smile framed by laugh-lined cheeks. His salt-and-pepper hair is neatly cut but perpetually tousled, as if he just ran his fingers through it while working out a problem. He wears a tweed jacket with multicolored elbow patches, a crisp shirt, and well-worn khakis—comfortable and approachable, like the favorite uncle you'd trust to help you ride your first bike. Or give you your first beer.

He begins class by defining the fundamentals. "Every Magick here has the innate ability to manipulate their element—whether to move it, shape it, or redirect it. At your level, being a Whittaker student, you also all have the ability to project your element in directed forms: blasts, waves, spikes, whips… whatever your skill and creativity will allow." He grins, leaning casually on the podium. "Just a friendly tip: if you're planning to impress a date, maybe go with a gentle wave, not a full-power blast. Singed eyebrows rarely lead to second dates."

Polite laughter moves across the classroom.

"You also possess elemental resistance. Fire-wielders burn less easily. Water-wielders can hold their breath longer, and resist cold, underwater. Earth-wielders shrug off blunt force with greater ease. Air-wielders can endure high speeds, crushing wind pressures, even thin oxygen. These resistances vary by individual, but they're your first layer of defense."

He clicks a lever on the podium, and a video of water freezing into solid ice flashes onto the screen behind him.

"State manipulation—heating or freezing your element at will—is a rare skill that takes years of advanced study to achieve. And almost unheard of is full-spectrum mastery: controlling the solid, liquid, and gaseous forms of your element interchangeably."

The room is silent, every student carefully copying down notes.

"And rarer than that"—he lowers his voice conspiratorially—"is *elemental fusion*: merging your element with an object, a tool, or even another Magick to create something entirely new. Only a handful of Magicks in history have ever actually achieved it. It's dangerous and even deadly if not done correctly. It is a lost art. But perhaps lost for a reason."

Wait, what did he just say?

I feel a tide rising inside me, something bolting upright and alert.

Fusion. Merging your element with another.

A lost art.

A dangerous one.

He steps down from the podium and begins to pace slowly in front of us, hands clasped behind his back. "Over the next term, you will learn to sense the subtle currents of your element, to work with its natural tendencies rather than against them. You will practice projection until it becomes second nature, then experiment with defense and resistance drills. If you excel—and show the discipline and respect required—some of you may glimpse state manipulation before graduation." He pauses beneath the symbol mobile, which is casting tiny shadows on the ceiling. "Any questions?"

A barrage of hands rise. And I'm grateful to slink back behind my fellow students as they eagerly discuss theory and ask questions specifically related to their elements.

Meanwhile, my mind is racing. Everything he described—the rarity of certain types of magick, the sheer impossibility of what some wielders can do—is going to make this year more complicated than I thought.

Professor Barrows's words repeat through my mind.

Elemental fusion. A lost art. But perhaps lost for a reason.

I glance down at the sapphire ring on my hand, brushing the

gemstone, feeling a vibration against my skin like the rumble of water rushing underground.

Was that what we did? I silently ask the ghost of the boy I once knew.

Wherever he is, he doesn't answer. But his old warnings echo louder now, each one ringing with a truth I was too young to grasp back then. That there is a kind of magick that shouldn't exist in me, and yet it does.

Something cold coils inside my chest, creeping into every vein until my whole body feels wrong, like something waiting to wake fully. And I can't shake the sense that this place, this school, is watching. Waiting. Whispering, like it knows that whatever I am, it isn't what I've been pretending to be.

CHAPTER 13

Beneath every calm surface lies a current strong enough to drown. Mastery is knowing the depths you stir.

—The Art of Water Magick, Vol. I

It isn't until the second week of school that we finally begin actual lessons in magick.

Aside from our classes in the Logistics building, where we meet as a full cohort, we're now split into groups for Elemental Mastery I. Water-wielders meet at the Lakehouse, fire at the Caldera, earth at the Garden Grove, and air at what is known by students as the Mountain.

The Lakehouse stands with quiet elegance at the northern edge of Lake Caldrith. Crafted from pale stone and smooth river wood painted a soft eggshell-white, it's accented with light-blue shutters and trim, mirroring the colors of the sky and the lake beyond it. The architecture is simple and clean—timeless and calming to the eye. Two stories high with a pitched roof that slopes down gracefully, it has wide-set windows that line both floors, letting in an endless view of the lake.

A large open deck extends from the rear of the house, the cedar planks jutting out over the water, the wood gently weathered by decades of mist and rain. It too offers uninterrupted views of the ever-changing water.

At first glance, it is the perfect image of calmness and serenity. But as I step closer, I can *feel* the power under its stillness. Water, after all, can drown, carve stone, and pull entire ships under without warning.

In the courtyard stands a fountain carved from pale moonstone that glitters faintly in the afternoon sun. The base is a wide, round pool, its edges wrapped in flowering vines. Set into the stone is a brass plaque, worn at the edges as if countless fingers have traced it for comfort. The inscription is simple, but it lands in me like something spoken aloud:

A tide-child is never lost. Return to the beginning—to wonder—and you will find your way home.

I look up to the heart of the fountain, where three mermaids rise from a curling wave of sculpted sea foam. Their long tails coil together, forming the base of the sculpture. Each mermaid faces a different direction—a trinity of elemental wisdom. I find myself drawn to them, taking in their expressions, carved so delicately they seem alive somehow. Their lips brush over words I can't hear but desperately want to know. Whispering of pasts seen and futures unknown.

A bell rings out—low and resonant, like the kind you hear in temple courtyards. It ripples through the air, a single perfect note.

The illusion shatters, and I blink—the fountain is just stone and water again.

I slowly walk past it and into the Lakehouse.

* * *

The class is a mix of first- and second-year water elementals. Twenty of us in total.

Professor Ondine Neris is in her late sixties and carries herself with the grace of still, deep water. Long, white hair flows down her back, her pale skin so smooth it looks almost luminous. But it is her eyes that stand out—so light blue they look nearly translucent. It's almost unnerving. Like she's not from this world but perhaps lives beneath the surface of the lake itself. She wears a flowing dress of layered blue silk with a simple belt made of rope to give it shape. On her left wrist are two ornate seashell bangles, her only adornment.

Long rows of bleached wood desks with matching chairs take up the bottom floor of the house. In front of each student stands two glass cups, one empty and the other full of water.

"We start simple today." Her voice is melodic, like the sound of a river moving over stones. "Move the water from one cup to the other without spilling a drop," she commands. "Second-years, this should be review from last year, but a good way to wake up your magick if you haven't been practicing over summer." Her pale eyes sweep across the classroom as more than a few students look down at their desks. "You may begin."

Okay, I think. *This is easy. Just focus, Celeste.*

Gavrail's face instantly comes to my mind. *"See, it's just like breathing, Cel. The water? It's an extension of you. You and it are the same. See what you want in your mind, then make it happen."*

The water in the cup starts to tremble and a thin stream of it stretches out from the glass, reaching toward the empty one as if in question. Waiting for me.

Okay. Now *move,* I tell it.

Crashes of glass sound all around me as students scramble away from their desks, stepping over broken shards and slipping on the now-spilled water that's pooling across the classroom floor.

A boy in the row behind me was crossing the aisle when my

magick flared. I wince as I watch his heel skid and see him go down—hard. There's a sharp hiss of pain as his palm slices open on a jagged shard of glass. Crimson blooms bright, carried outward by the water in silent streams.

Shit. Not the impression I wanted to make. I casually knock over my glass so that it can join all the others in their sad, broken forms. I feign a look of surprise to Nate on my left so as not to draw attention to myself.

Professor Neris raises a single eyebrow, her expression unreadable. With a flick of her fingers, she calls the scattered water to gracefully sweep up the broken crystal, collecting it all into a waiting bucket at the edge of the room. She calls the injured student forward, inspecting his palm. "It's not too deep. But it will need tending." She waves to the door. "Head to Madame Ching at the infirmary."

The boy cradles his bleeding hand against his chest and slips out of the room, his shoes squeaking on the damp floor. The door shuts with a hollow click. The sound reverberates in me longer than it should.

Professor Neris watches him leave before her eyes focus on me, lingering a heartbeat too long. "We are teaching precision here," she says, her voice cool and crisp. "Not party tricks."

The silence that follows is suffocating. The guilt pools deeper than the spilled water. I glance toward the boy's now-empty seat. *My fault.* The words land heavy in my chest as I send a silent apology his way, but I keep my focus on my desk.

Neris hands out more glasses and pitchers of water. By the end of class, I have mastered the task. The water obeys—smooth, clean, controlled—but my head throbs from the effort of concentrating so hard.

I need to learn better control.

My power is now too tangled in warnings and restraint. With Gavrail, my magick used to be pure instinct and surrender. Now it feels like walking a tightrope over water—one misstep, and I'm drowning. Every moment demands discipline. Precision. It's a constant balancing act—holding the line between focus and flooding, control versus complete and utter chaos.

My father's fears and Gavrail's warnings echo in my head as I leave the classroom.

Professor Neris's pale eyes follow me—too sharply to be merely coincidence. But all I keep seeing is the water I spilled, dragging the blood after it like a trophy it wanted to keep.

CHAPTER 14

Mastery may tame the flame, but never its nature. Sooner or later, all fire consumes.

—Elemental Mastery IV: The Covenant of Fire

The rest of the month goes by uneventfully for the most part, at least by Whittaker standards.

We nearly lost a Black Squad fire-wielder during the third week of classes. His attempt at fire basics backfired—literally—and the blast left his face and hands raw enough that his parents brought him home to recover. A second-year lost three toes in Elemental Dueling after his earth-wielding opponent dropped a boulder on his foot during a counterstrike.

My birthday passes at the end of September—I turn twenty-three, which feels both too old and not old enough for everything I've been through this past year. I haven't told anyone in my squad—or Noa. I'm not big on birthdays and try not to draw attention to it. I celebrate it quietly with a phone call to my mom and an extra dessert from the mess hall that night.

Aside from the expected weekly run-ins with Stella during Potions—where she never misses a chance to roll her eyes or make a passive-aggressive comment about my work—she hasn't challenged me on the sparring mat again. Whether that is her decision or someone else's, I don't know. And I don't care enough to ask.

My control is improving. I can execute nearly every elemental task without flinching now. But I'm careful. I watch the others. Measure myself against them—not too fast, not too much. I've learned how to sand down the edges of my ability so it doesn't cut too deep.

Because I'm quickly learning that attention at Whittaker is like currency, and I can't afford to be expensive.

There was a time before all this when magick came to me as easily as breathing. When wonder was instinct and power wasn't something to fear.

But now... I feel like a firehose learning how to turn on just a trickle. Or a volcano trying to simmer instead of erupt. Every drop feels like a battleground, every pulse a negotiation. It's not just control I need.

It's trust.

In myself. In what I carry.

In the part of me that I've been told to fear—even when I don't say it out loud.

How do you trust the thing you've always been warned might destroy you?

I stare through the window beside my bed, watching the trees ripple in the breeze. The water is quiet tonight, but I can feel it.

Calling.

Remembering.

It wants me to remember too.

And sometimes—I wonder if I was wrong to answer.

Because every time I dam it down, try to suppress what I am,

I pay for it with headaches that start just behind my eyes and grow into a pulsing, full-body pressure by nightfall. Like I'm holding back a storm and cracking at the seams.

Noa is starting to notice. He thinks I'm straining to force my magick out. But the truth is worse.

I'm killing myself trying to hold it all in.

"It's not supposed to come easy," he murmurs. "But it will—little by little. You just started, Cel. Don't hold yourself to the same standard as people who've been wielding for years."

We are sitting propped against the carved headboard of his bed, my back against his chest, nestled in the vee of his legs. Our bodies fit together like pieces long meant to align. His hands massage my temples in slow, soothing circles.

He's not mentioning the short years I practiced in secret with Gavrail, and I don't correct him.

Guilt sits heavy in my throat—lying by omission, letting him believe the wrong version of my learning curve. But I know there is truth to Gavrail's warnings. The inherent risk in letting *anyone* know the depth of the power I am only just beginning to understand.

I've started researching in secret—visits to the Whittaker Library under the guise of studying. Books tucked behind other books. Notes hidden in my room. Passages I mark and copy. Names in news articles I don't recognize but now can't forget. There were Magicks who vanished—Magicks like Hayden, the Black Squad first-year. Some taken. Others found dead with no trace of weapon or cause. No bruises. No blood. Just... gone.

No one could explain it. And no one really tried. It's easier not to ask questions in a world where power is everything and bloodlines hold secrets. But the one thing they all have in common is that they were all different. Powerful. Strong. Capable of magick that didn't fit neatly into anyone else's rules.

* * *

History class doesn't help. It just gives my fears more skeletons—and more names.

We've started diving deeper into the ancestral lines that weave through the schools and politics of magick. Turns out, magick isn't just something you have—it is something you inherit, passed through generations like silver or land or secrets.

When something is inherited, it becomes valuable. And when something is valuable, people want to control it.

The bell's echo hasn't even finished fading before the room exhales—first-years surging toward the aisle like we've been held underwater for an hour and finally allowed to breathe. Chairs scrape. Books snap shut.

Professor Straits remains at the podium, pen still in hand, expression unchanged—as if she hasn't just dismantled half the class's social standings with a single lecture. On the screen behind her, the last slide lingers: a branching diagram of names, crests, and dates, lines knitting together like veins. Fire lines in red. Earth in green. Water in blue so deep it looks black at the edges. All the other ancient lines tracing back to just after the Primordial Shattering.

Magick isn't just something you have—it is something you inherit.

Straits didn't say it like a revelation. She said it like a fact. Like gravity.

I shove my notebook into my bag, the words still knocking around in my skull. Near me, students whisper—not quietly enough to be polite, just enough to feel like knives trying to dig at my past.

"My mom told me we're tied to one of the founding orders," a girl says, half brag, half prayer.

Rozsen looks at her like one would look at a bug you're about to step on. Elliot, on the other hand, looks entertained. "I mean… it explains everything," she says under her breath. "All the egos around here."

I stand, slinging my bag over my shoulder—then freeze when Straits's voice slices through the noise.

"Miss Farris."

My pulse trips. I turn slowly.

Straits is looking down at her roster, like she's already bored before I even answer. "First generation," she says flatly. "Correct?"

Heat pricks my face. "Yes," I manage.

"It isn't unheard of," Straits continues. "Rare. But magick can… appear latent in a bloodline. Usually, it can be tied to some distant relative. The gene hiding dormant until activated."

I merely nod, uncomfortable with the attention. I can feel the other squads watching. My own squad watching.

"Your parents are unaware of any magick lineage?" she asks, tone mild.

"No one that we know of." I try to say it casually, but my face feels tight. Even though it's the truth.

"Interesting." She taps her pen once. "Nevertheless, do not confuse rarity with randomness." She looks me over, eyes sharp. "Magick always has traces. Yours may have a story you don't yet know about." She turns away from me then, effectively dismissing me without another word.

I don't realize I've been holding my breath until I'm out in the corridor with the rest of them—air suddenly too cold, light too bright. The hallway outside the Logistics building is a bottleneck of bodies and voices.

A Blue Squad boy walks backward, talking loudly to his friend. "My dad says the Service keeps registries," he says. "Like —families. Elemental lines. Who's paired with who. Wanting to keep the most powerful family lines together."

"Well, that's… disgusting," Rozsen mutters, loud enough for them to hear. Her jaw is tight.

The boy laughs like she's joking.

She isn't.

Rozsen catches up to me, her voice low. "So that's what this is," she mutters. "Not school. Not training. A racetrack."

"A racetrack?" I echo.

She nods toward the line of students spilling out, clustering immediately into little packs—already sorting each other into categories the way Straits sorted us on the screen.

"We're all just a bunch of glorified prized racehorses," she says. "Whittaker is just a breeding ground for power and privilege."

I follow her gaze to the groups gathered in the hall.

Old blood.

New blood.

Worth something.

Worth nothing.

Elliot bumps my shoulder as she joins us. "Congrats, Celeste. You're a mystery. People love a mystery."

I just shrug and turn to follow my squad down the hall—and stop.

Noa is leaning against the stone just outside one of the classroom doors, like he's been there the whole time.

A few students notice him at the same time I do. The whispers shift. Reorient.

He's in his gym uniform, sleeves shoved up his forearms, dense lines of muscle on display. His brown hair is still a little damp at the edges, like he came straight from training. My stomach tightens the way it always does when I see him. Gods, he looks good. Like a Greek statue someone brought to life. A singular, beautiful point in the chaotic hallway—impossible to miss.

And somehow, seeing him right now—outside a classroom where we just learned about magick and inheritance—makes my heart twist.

His eyes find mine immediately. I take one step toward him, then another.

Noa pushes off the wall, his gaze never leaving mine. "Hey," he says quietly, the corner of his lips tipping up like a secret, giving me something steady to hold on to.

Before I can answer, a Silver Squad girl edges closer to her friend and whispers, not even pretending she doesn't want us to hear, "That's him. Straits mentioned his family name—"

Her friend makes a soft sound, almost awed.

Noa's jaw flexes once. He doesn't look at them. But I feel the shift in him—like a door clicking shut.

I stop in front of him, suddenly hyper-aware of my hands, the way my throat feels too tight.

"You okay?" he asks, voice low.

I try to joke. It comes out thin. "History class is... uplifting."

His mouth twitches, not quite a smile. "Yeah. Straits has that effect."

Two boys from Green Squad drift close, eyes bright. "Hey, Gallegher," one of them calls out, too casual. "Is it true your grandfather was a Service general? That you're, like, pure fire line?"

Noa's jaw tightens. He smiles, but it doesn't reach his eyes. "Is it true you can't mind your own damn business?"

The boy laughs like it's a joke, but he shuffles back into the crowd, away from Noa's stare.

Noa looks at me again, and there's apology there—quiet and immediate—as if he hates that I have to stand in the blast radius of his name. His gaze flicks briefly to the clusters of students forming, the way their eyes keep tracking him—me—like we're items on a ledger.

He leans closer, just enough to make his voice mine. "Ignore them."

I swallow. "Is it true?" I ask, softer. "About... all of it?"

His eyes hold mine for a beat—then drop, like the question lands somewhere tender.

"Governments got involved a long time ago," he says quietly.

He doesn't sound proud. He sounds tired. "They learned how to keep power from leaving. How to make sure the strongest lines stayed where they wanted them. Some families fought it."

His gaze lifts back to me, sharp with something protective. But it flickers—showing something beneath the pointed edges, something like... *shame*.

"Some didn't."

I think of Straits's tone. The cold certainty.

I think of the chart. The lines. The crests.

I glance at Noa's hands and I can almost see it: the magick prowling under his skin, powerful and a little bit wild.

He catches my glance and huffs out something like a laugh. "Don't look at me like that."

"Like what?"

"Like I'm... inevitable." A muscle in his jaw ticks. Discomfort crosses his face. "I don't—" He stops. Swallows. "I don't like being reduced to my bloodline."

"And yet," I say, the words slipping out before I can stop them, "when you wield fire... it makes sense."

His eyes flicker—heat, then something softer.

"You're devastatingly good," I add, quieter, because it's true, and now it feels like a piece of this new puzzle clicking into place. "The kind of good that doesn't come from one person. The kind of good that comes from generations of knowledge encoded into your bones."

His throat works. "Celeste—"

"I'm not judging you," I say quickly. "I just..." I glance down at my hands, at my ring, at the skin Straits stared at like she could read my entire history from it. "I didn't realize how much of this world is... inherited."

Noa's gaze drops to my hands, watching the way I twist the ring on my finger. "It's complicated," he says carefully. "And it makes people stupid."

Across the corridor, two girls whisper and glance at me

again—giving me looks that hold both curiosity and calculation, like I'm a question they want answered.

First generation.

Dormant gene.

Activated.

An anomaly.

I straighten my shoulders, forcing myself to breathe around the attention.

Noa shifts closer—not touching, but there, solid beside me—an unspoken warning to anyone watching.

The hallway starts moving again as more students spill out of classrooms. I fall into step beside Noa, heart pounding. The air suddenly feels sharp around me, needling my skin, charged with something dangerous.

Because if magick is inherited…

Then my blood has a story I don't know yet.

And somewhere in those hidden lines—dormant and waiting—there are secrets someone decided I wasn't allowed to know.

* * *

By dusk, the word *inheritance* still tastes like metal on my tongue—until Noa proves exactly why the world keeps count.

That evening, third- and fourth-year fire-wielders are scheduled to duel at the Caldera, the massive sunken arena carved out of the cliffside I saw on my first day. Noa invited my squad and me to come watch, and we arrive just as the sun begins to dip below the horizon, casting gold and blood-orange light across the stone terraces.

We file into the front row and sit in the growing dark as the arena begins to pulse with light and heat. The air here tastes of ash and anticipation. The Caldera itself seems to speak to the fire it commands. Bright and volatile, always reaching. Always consuming.

Two fourth-years are already engaged in a dazzling duel—fire whirling, shields forming and vanishing in precise rhythm. Footwork matched at every movement like a choreographed dance.

When their match ends, a girl with copper curls named Tasha steps into the ring, fire already dancing at her fingertips. She squares off against a boy I vaguely recognize—Liam, one of Noa's friends.

They bow. And then Tasha attacks.

She is fast. Faster than I expect, slinging arrows of flame in a barrage that lights up the dusk like fireworks. Liam blocks one, dodges two, but a fourth slams into his left arm and sends him to the ground with a strangled shout.

Professor Kael is already moving, a metal tin in his hands. He opens it and dabs something onto the wound. A tincture we made in class not long ago—Emberveil. Liam hisses faintly through clenched teeth as the professor applies it to the wound, sealing it shut.

Tasha stands unbothered, barely acknowledging the professor as Liam is helped from the arena. She looks confident. Smug.

That lasts about ten seconds.

Because then Noa steps into the ring.

And the Caldera *changes*.

The moment his boots hit the arena floor, the air shifts. I can feel it, like the oxygen around us has turned into something heavier, thicker. The crowd goes silent. Even Tasha hesitates.

Then she moves—sending bolts of fire screaming toward him. Noa doesn't even flinch. With one flick of his wrist, he summons a wall of flame that curves around him like a cloak. She throws more bolts, each faster than the last. He dodges with minimal effort, barely moving more than a step at a time. His fire bends and arches with lazy precision, deflecting every attack with grace. His fire forms into something almost solid in his hands.

He's toying with her. And she knows it.

Her expression twists into one of frustration and determination. She shifts tactics and summons a burst of firelight so blinding that the entire front row has to shield our eyes, gasping as our vision turns white. When we blink the light away, she's hurling full-bodied fireballs, huge and erratic, like she's trying to land a single hit just to salvage her pride.

Noa doesn't move. Until suddenly, he does.

And just before he strikes—he catches my eye. Smiles.

And then—

That cocky bastard winks.

He *winks* at me as fireballs scream toward him across the arena.

Before I can even curse under my breath, he throws a lasso of flame with a sharp flick of his arm. It wraps around Tasha's legs and sends her sprawling.

The crowd erupts into cheers.

Tasha pushes herself off the stone floor with shaking arms and walks off the field with what little pride she has left. Noa barely acknowledges her departure. He's already turned to the next duel underway, standing at the arena's edge with a casual tilt to his stance—the epitome of poise and confidence, just another day, for him at least.

He walks up to our row after the final match, and more than a few of my squadmates look up at him in full fan-girl mode as he approaches. Including some of the boys. Rozsen and Ian practically launch themselves at him with a barrage of questions, animated and breathless in their praise. As fire elementals themselves, they clearly see him as some kind of god.

Noa takes it in stride, smiling, listening, answering every question with patience and ease. He is always like this in public

—gracious, charismatic, disarming. But I know better. Beneath the smile is something far more dangerous. Something burning. And damn if I don't want to burn right along with him.

It makes me wonder, though—if I ever let go of the reins, even for a second… what would they see in me? Something to be revered?

Or would I be thought of as a threat? Something to be *handled*? Someone that disappears without a trace like those Magicks before me?

The thought curls around my spine like smoke, unshakable.

Because the truth isn't just that I fear what I can do.

It's that I fear what *they* would do if they ever saw it.

CHAPTER 15

The strongest roots grow in silence. Power beneath the surface is the hardest to uproot.

—Botanical Studies and Applied Herbology, Vol. II

The path to the Blue Dahlia Commons is slick with fallen leaves—amber, rust, and crimson—all damp from last night's rain. October has settled over Whittaker like a second skin, the air heavy with the scent of moss and woodsmoke.

It's Sunday, and my squadmates are draped across the common room furniture, bickering over how best to spend our day off.

Sawyer wants to head to the Cavern hot springs.

Ian tells us that some second-years are having a barbecue at the Silver Fern Commons.

Nate suggests a study group after reminding everyone of tomorrow's History exam.

Rozsen flicks a single glance at me. "Why bother? Celeste

already said we could use her notes. And she's already figured out what the three essay questions will be, based on Professor Straits's hints in class."

"Cel, have I told you how much we love that you're in our squad?" comes Ian's teasing voice.

I laugh, moving my feet off the coffee table where I'm sprawled next to Rozsen. "And here I thought you just kept me around for my sparkling personality."

The rest of the group goes back to arguing about whose ideas are better. Only Amelia is quiet, methodically collecting her gardening tools.

"Heading somewhere?" I ask.

She glances up, surprised I've noticed her, then nods and gestures to the tools bundled in her arms. "The frostbloom thistle are blooming. They have to be harvested before winter, or else they lose potency."

"Can I come?" I ask, intrigued. I've never heard of frostbloom thistle—it's certainly not something that grows in Virginia.

She shrugs, then turns toward the door. I take it as a yes.

We walk in companionable silence. Amelia's soft brown hair is tied in a ponytail, though loose strands keep slipping free, which she keeps tucking behind her ears. Her gaze remains mostly downward, scanning the path like she might discover a rare root or seed tucked between the stones. She moves with the hesitancy of someone used to being overlooked—but there is a quiet strength in her. A grounding, as if she is a part of the earth she communes with.

To the south, past the sandstone path that veers toward the central quad, the low stone wall of Garden Grove comes into view, ivy spilling over its edge like an invitation. We step through an arch of twisted iron, where vines bloom pale lavender and mint green. The air shifts immediately—thicker, fragrant with damp soil and crushed basil.

Rows of raised beds stretch before us, the soil dark and rich. Leafy greens shiver in the breeze, while luminous stalks of flowered herbs bend gently under the weight of their blooms. Small fruit trees, their trunks pale and knotted, frame the edges of the garden, casting dappled shadows across the walkways.

Vines curl thickly along trellises and latticed alcoves, creating shaded spaces—one currently occupied by a pair of students entangled in a kiss. Amelia averts her eyes quickly, cheeks pink with embarrassment.

Thin stone aqueducts no wider than a hand run through the space, carrying cool water from unseen sources. The channels split and rejoin in meandering paths, quietly irrigating the garden. The sound of trickling water echoes softly in the background, a calming pulse. The entire space breathes—ancient and alive.

A cluster of students kneel near a bed of silver sage, their fingers nimble and careful. Near one corner of the grove sits a large greenhouse, its glass fogged and softly glowing from within. Inside, figures move like shadows tending to rarer, more delicate flora.

"This place is amazing," I murmur, mostly to myself. It's wild and cultivated all at once—chaotic, yet harmonious.

At the heart of the grove lies a square training courtyard, its soft sand pale and fine. The earth has been tamped down over the years by generations of feet. It feels like standing inside the memory of something sacred. A place of stillness and strength. The earth waits here. It doesn't yield. It endures.

We pass through the courtyard, and Amelia leads us to a shaded corner beneath a copse of black adder trees. Nestled at their base is a patch of pale blue-violet thistle, the edges of their petals rimmed with a silvery sheen—frostbloom thistle.

"What do you use this for?" I ask, crouching beside her.

"It's used in heat resistance potions," Amelia replies, snipping stems just below the bloom and gently placing them into a cloth-lined basket. "But it can also be combined with silver bark and shadowmint to dull pain and slow bleeding." She glances up at me. "It's also used to amplify magick—especially freezing spells."

"Really? How can a plant do that?" My curiosity flares—part fascination, part potioneer's instinct.

"The wielder has to ingest it in powdered form," she says, returning to her work.

I drop to my knees beside her and follow her lead. She guides me with a soft word here, a quick glance there. We fall into a rhythm, surrounded by the whisper of leaves and the distant babble of water.

The afternoon passes just like that—in the hush of growing things, and the quiet company of someone who understands the strength of silence.

CHAPTER 16

Precision. Discipline. Power with purpose. The Service forges more than soldiers it forges those worthy to command the unseen currents of a changing world.

—Recruitment pamphlet for the Service of Elemental Defense and Reconnaissance

(issued to upper-year Whittaker students, confidential circulation)

The air-wielders are going to duel at the Mountain and students are invited to observe. Elliot and Sawyer make us promise we will meet them there after class.

Professor Straits taps her chalk against the board, drawing a sun with a spear through it.

"Before we move into post-rift treaties, we need to discuss the entity that shaped modern magickal law more than any other—the Service." She says it like it carries weight. Like it's not just a name, but a system. "Formed after the Second Rebellion, the Service began as the Elemental Security Bureau—an agency meant to regulate elemental violence, stabilize rogue wielders, and protect the nation's sacred sites. Over time, it absorbed every independent enforcement branch across all federated territories, both magick and non-magick. Today, its reach extends into almost every facet of life as we know it—military, magitech research and development, weaponry, education, diplomacy." She pauses, letting that list settle over the room. "Whittaker, while not officially under Service jurisdiction, operates under the terms of the Altair Pact—meaning the strongest among you will likely be recruited."

There's a beat of silence.

I know what the pact really means—that even if we're not on the Service's leash, we're still always under their rule.

Rozsen mutters under her breath, just loud enough to be heard, "So... conscription with prettier uniforms?"

A few students snicker.

Professor Straits arches a brow but doesn't correct her. "Some see it that way," she replies. "Some call it duty. Others—control. Regardless, the Service is watching. Always."

"And who watches them?" Rozsen asks, eyes narrowed, crossing her arms in front of her.

Straits doesn't smile, but she doesn't reprimand her either. "A good question, Initiate. And a necessary one. One every government fears, and every student should remember. Every power must be held accountable."

* * *

LATER THAT DAY, Noa and I meet up on campus to walk together to where the duel is to be held. We're halfway across the quad when the sound of polished shoes on stone makes me look up.

"Ah, Officer Gallegher," comes a smooth voice. "Still dazzling your instructors, I trust?"

Headmaster Thorne descends the stairs outside the Administration building, his dark coat flaring behind him like a trailing shadow. Hair that was once blond but is now threaded with silver gives him a distinguished look. His smile is warm, his dark-brown eyes bright at seeing us together.

Noa grins, slowing to a stop beside me. "Doing my best, sir."

"And doing it well," Thorne replies, then turns his gaze on me. "Ms. Farris—Celeste, isn't it? Professor Barrows tells me you are at the top of all your classes. And Professor Neris says that your control continues to improve." He looks over me, gaze landing in a way that makes me instantly uncomfortable with its familiarity. "Water, of course, is notoriously temperamental, especially for newcomers. But according to her, you show remarkable promise."

My throat tightens. "Thank you, sir," I manage.

There's something behind his gaze—curling at the edges. Not unkind. Just… measured, curated.

He nods once, then glances at Noa. "Keep an eye on her. I suspect she'll leave a mark before the year is out." He looks back at me then before flicking his gaze to Noa once more. "Raw talent rarely stays under the surface for long."

The corner of his mouth lifts as his attention drifts between us.

Approval.

Like seeing the two of us together is exactly what he expected.

He smiles at us both, wide and genuine. But something deeper shifts there—a shadow crossing behind his eyes. Then he turns and walks away, the echo of his boots swallowed by the wind.

Noa grins, reaching for my hand and pulling me toward him. "I'm not the only one to notice how amazing you are. He sees it too."

I nod, but a current prickles at the back of my neck. "It's

just... strange. Why would the headmaster be asking my professors about *me?*"

Noa shrugs, flashing me another grin. "Because he's not stupid. He knows potential when he sees it. Don't overthink it."

I smile, but the feeling lingers. The way Thorne said my name—not with care, but like it already belonged to him. Like it's a blank medallion in a case of trophies. Another name on a ledger. Potential to be filed away.

I can't help but wonder what else he sees when he looks at me—not only who I am, but what I might become.

And whether he's already decided exactly what that is.

We keep walking toward the Mountain, a chill breeze in our wake. I glance back. Nothing but empty steps behind me. And yet something presses behind my ribs—like the echo of a gaze that hasn't quite let me go.

* * *

IT'S CALLED THE MOUNTAIN—EVEN though it isn't one—because it's on the highest hill on Whittaker grounds.

At the summit is a ring of granite monoliths—nine in all—carved with glyphs whose magick has been lost to time. They were here long before there was ever a school, standing like jagged fingers reaching toward the sky. Set in a broken arc, they funnel the wind, turning the summit into a throat where every gust is amplified. For it is here that the wind is wildest, whipping through the stones in howls and sighs, never still, never silent.

Just below, crouched against the slope, is the Air Elemental Hall, a stark utilitarian building of pale cement, more bunker than school. Designed to endure rather than impress. There are no trees, no hedges, no sheltering foliage of any kind. Only grass that bends low in submission and rocks that have been bleached by the sun.

This is not a place for comfort.

Like all the other elemental training grounds, this one speaks to its power—invisible, mercurial, and unforgiving.

Professor Caelum Stroud stands at the center of the stone circle. Sharp-eyed, witty, and unpredictable, he is known for changing lesson plans mid-sentence—often mid-thought. His light-brown hair curls slightly in the breeze, and his slim frame is wrapped in flowing, layered robes that shift like cloudbanks with every gust.

Behind him stands Finn, flanked by another student. There is a seriousness on Finn's face I've never seen before—his usual boyish charm replaced by grim determination.

Professor Stroud's voice rings out clear and direct, addressing the small crowd that has gathered. He speaks of the importance of air magick—its complexity, its precision, its role in warfare and reconnaissance. There are no frills, no comforting words for the students about to duel. Just the cold weight of truth. His harsh tone clashes starkly with the typically carefree nature of both Elliot and Finn.

The wind has already begun to stir by the time Finn turns to face his challenger, another fourth-year—Lyrah is her name, I think. She stands tall, arms tense at her sides, pale braid snapping like a banner behind her. She gives a single, silent nod of acknowledgment.

Finn raises a hand, and a tight spiral of wind coils around his fingers. He moves with practiced ease—stance wide, shoulders loose. The air greets him like an old friend. With a sharp throw of his hand, a sudden gust barrels across the field, kicking up pebbles and grass as it goes.

Lyrah doesn't hesitate. With a precise slice of her palm through the air, she sends a razor-thin gust slicing toward him. Their blows collide with a thunderous crack, the force knocking her back several steps.

She recovers quickly, her next move ruthless. Drawing in a

dense, high-altitude current, she slams it toward Finn in a sudden press of cold, low-oxygen air. The students behind him flinch, retreating from the blast as it passes.

Finn grits his teeth, then unleashes a pulse from his chest—a rippling ring of wind that cracks against Lyrah like a shockwave. His eyes narrow as he follows up fast and low, sweeping wind toward her calves and sending her stumbling. Before she can recover, he sweeps his arms wide, lifting himself several feet into the air while a powerful gust throws her clean out of the ring.

The crowd is stunned. Even the air itself seems to pause.

Other duels follow in quick succession—some fierce, some forgettable—but none quite as commanding as watching Finn in his element. The third-year, Dash, has mastered sound manipulation, using the wind to redirect the voices of the crowd to disorient his opponent. It's clever, effective. But still, Finn's display set the standard.

We leave the Mountain in silence. Even Finn.

The weight of our futures clings to us like mist. Intangible still, yet inescapable.

* * *

THAT NIGHT at the Steps with the boys, we end up in a quiet conversation about post-graduation plans. It doesn't surprise me that all three—Noa, Finn, and Ryan—plan to enlist with the Service.

There is a heaviness to their voices, a layer of meaning in their half-mentions and sidelong glances. Things they likely can't say in front of me—just an initiate. Information classified for officers alone. But I've heard the rumors, the things they *don't* or *won't* say on the news. Tensions are rising. Between the Service and Krovya. Between Magicks and non-Magicks in certain parts of the world. China has all but shut their doors to outsiders recently.

Gavrail taught me about Bulgaria's military structure when I was younger, and I've seen enough during diplomatic missions to know that military hierarchies vary by region. Whittaker's, though, is clearly defined: first-years are initiates, second-years become cadets, third-years are lieutenants, and fourth-years, officers.

After graduation, officers can rise to become captains, then commanders, if they join the Service.

At the top—generals.

The thought of being separated from Noa next year makes my heart plummet. But he reassures me, saying officers have plenty of leave, and now that I'm at Whittaker, we would have clearance to communicate more freely.

Still, something unsettles me. A quiet fear, clawing at the edges of my thoughts. Not just about distance. But about change.

About what we are all becoming. Whether we want to or not.

Because we aren't just students. That is becoming more and more clear.

We are being shaped into weapons. Honed and sharpened. Ready to make the world bleed on someone else's orders.

CHAPTER 17

Bloodline is not merely inheritance—it is leverage. Where leverage exists, so does the will to take it.

—Lineage and Law: A History of Elemental Governance

November arrives under moody gray skies, long drizzles, and a chilling mist that clings to every surface. By the time I reach the bottom floor of the Logistics building, my sleeves are damp from brushing past wet stone and my boots squeak against the corridor's polished floor.

The room is already warm with bodies, the air thick with the smell of rain-soaked clothing. A handful of upperclassmen sit scattered through the hall today—Straits's idea of "remediation" after last week's essays proved some people could recite dates but not understand why they matter.

Professor Straits stands at the front, not one to waste time on greetings. She turns to the board and writes three names in sharp, deliberate strokes.

MORVAINE
VIRELLAN
THALRIEN

WE'VE JUST BEGUN our unit on the history of water magick—diving into the ancient bloodlines that fascinate me the most. But it isn't just fascination anymore. It's a tug under my ribs, like the names are hooked to something inside me.

Straits dusts the chalk from her hands. "Today we're discussing the three major water lineages—how they rose, how they held power, and how they fell."

Stella Moreau—the third-year water-wielder, and Noa's ex—is sitting in the front row like she's holding court, her blonde braid laid like a crown around her head. She acts like her attendance in this class is beneath her. The essay peeking out of her bag, bleeding with Straits's red ink, would suggest otherwise.

"The Morvaines never fell. They've always been the most stable of all the water lines," I hear her murmur to the boy sitting next to her. It's well known that Stella has an ancestor with Morvaine blood, a fact she likes to remind everyone of constantly.

Professor Straits's gaze snaps to her. "Miss Moreau," she says, each word clipped, "while I appreciate your enthusiasm for the subject matter, talking out of turn will not be tolerated."

Straits underlines *MORVAINE* once, hard enough to squeal.

"But you are correct. The Morvaines have maintained influence through consolidation—marriage alliances, political footholds, and a keen understanding that bloodline is currency."

She moves to *VIRELLAN*, drawing a clean line beneath it.

"The Virellans are no less entrenched," she continues. "Both Morvaines and Virellans still hold high positions of government—here and abroad—because power likes to protect itself."

My pen scratches across the page as I take notes, but my attention keeps snagging on the last name. The one Straits hasn't touched yet.

THALRIEN.

Straits finally turns, and the chalk taps the board beneath it —once, twice.

"The Thalriens were an ancient and powerful water family—possibly the oldest known. They were famous for a particularly rare form of magick, and they were coveted—"

"—and hunted," someone murmurs. I think it's Nate.

Straits's eyes flick over the class. "Yes. *Hunted* to extinction."

My stomach turns, slow and sick, like I've swallowed river silt.

She frowns as she continues. "Their line was completely wiped out after the Second Rebellion."

Rozsen's hand shoots up, but she doesn't wait to be called on. "Professor," she says thoughtfully, "if a bloodline is wiped out, does that mean whatever magick they possessed is just... gone?"

Straits only nods. "Bloodlines carry not only power, but also knowledge, technique, access. History shows us that people in power repeatedly choose to erase what they cannot control."

Stella's mouth curves as she leans back in her chair. "Or maybe it's just choosing to erase a threat."

"A threat," I echo before I can stop myself, disbelief cracking through my tone. I feel heat climb my neck as heads turn. "You mean children? Families? People who happened to be born from certain bloodlines?"

Stella's voice turns razor-thin. "I mean anyone who thinks they're above the rules."

Her chair scrapes softly as she turns toward me, her eyes gleaming like she's preparing for a duel.

"Besides," she adds, her tone bright, almost bored, "the Thalriens weren't 'hunted.' They rebelled. Twice. They lost. That's what happens when you bite the hand that feeds you."

Something hot and ugly flashes behind my ribs.

Professor Straits's eyes narrow. "Is that your scholarly conclusion, Miss Moreau?" she asks. "That extinction was a fair consequence for rebellion?"

Stella lifts one shoulder delicately. "History isn't fair. It's just... efficient."

The word lands like a slap. It sickens me, what people in power have done to Magicks. What Magicks do to their own kind. My fingers tighten around my pen.

Professor Straits steps closer to the board. With one smooth motion, she draws a circle around *THALRIEN*, sealing the name in chalk like a ward.

"The Thalriens were wiped out after the Second Rebellion," she repeats, voice low. "Not because their magick was immoral. Not because they were monsters. But because the wrong people wanted what they carried, and couldn't tolerate the idea that it might not belong to them. They opposed the Magick–Administration alliance. They believed power must be kept in check. That power begets power—and corruption."

Students shift in their seats as the air around us suddenly gets colder.

Straits's gaze moves over the room, lingering a fraction too long on Stella before returning to the rest of us. "Magick does not excuse genocide," she says. "Extinction should not be the consequence for rebellion. To say otherwise is to lose your grasp on your humanity."

Silence stretches.

I remember my father once telling me that magick in and of itself doesn't start wars—power does. *Magick just makes the body count higher.* I feel like I'm beginning to understand what he meant.

And I hate that understanding feels like stepping closer to an edge in the dark, where the only certainty is the drop.

CHAPTER 18

Magick denied its truth will not fade—it will twist. What is repressed beneath the surface will always seek a way to rise.

—Theory of Elemental Magick, Vol. I

I've taken to sparring with Noa on Sundays in the Training Room. I never want to be caught off guard by Stella, or anyone else, for that matter, again.

What started as an offer has now become ritual. My water bottle goes on the same bench it always does. I retie my braid twice because I learned—early—that loose hair is just another handle for someone to take.

Noa is always there ahead of time. Sometimes he spars with Finn or Ryan before training me. This morning he's alone in the gym, wrapping his knuckles with white tape, neat and methodical, sleeves pushed up to his forearms. When he looks up, his mouth quirks.

"You're late," he says.

I glance at the clock. "I'm three minutes early."

He nods once, completely serious. "Then I'm late."

I laugh, stepping onto the mat, bare feet finding the familiar grit of chalk and rubber. "So what's the plan today? Humiliation before breakfast?"

"Merely correction," he says. "There's a difference."

"Mm-hmm. Well, I've been told trauma builds character."

His gaze flicks over my stance—my feet, my shoulders, my hands—and softens by a fraction. "Not today."

That's the thing about Noa: he's patient. Thorough. Helpful without being overly critical.

At least with me.

He circles once, slow and controlled, eyes tracking every small tell. "Your weight's too far back," he says. "You're bracing for impact."

"Maybe I like bracing."

"But that's not what I asked you to do."

I scowl, but shift my body. Knees loose. Center forward. Ready to move instead of endure.

We go through the warm-up circuit—punch combinations until my shoulders burn, kicks until my hips loosen and my thighs tremble, footwork drills that feel like choreography until Noa steps in and turns it into a lesson in survival. He taps my guard, corrects my angle, makes me repeat it until my body stops negotiating and starts obeying.

He doesn't use his full speed—not unless I get sloppy. He lets me fail where it's safe, and stops me where it isn't. I'm just starting to find the rhythm: breathe, pivot, commit—

He catches my wrist when I feint and twists—not painful, just controlled—and suddenly I'm on my back on the mat before my brain catches up.

The ceiling is glaringly white at this angle. His silhouette above me—calm, precise, infuriating. But I can feel the heat of him through my clothes.

I swallow and decide, as always, to make it worse.

"Well… now that we're here…" I murmur seductively.

His eyes flick toward my mouth.

The gym doors bang open and sunlight slices across the mats.

Rozsen strolls in like she owns the place. She glances at the scene she just walked into before yelling, "Gods, get a room, you two."

Finn walks in behind her, rubbing his shoulder, adding, "They're in a room."

"I'm just teasing. Noa here doesn't even know what flirting is," Rozsen says, eyeing the two of us before giving me a wink. "He'd likely file it under 'unauthorized behavior.'"

I'm still on my back on the mat, but I lift my chin toward Noa. "She thinks you're too much of a rule follower."

Rozsen gasps in mock offense. "Celeste, you weren't supposed to tell him that."

Noa's gaze cuts to them. "If you two are done with the side comments, spar or leave."

Then his expression shutters into professionalism so perfect it makes me want to throw something.

He offers me a hand up.

Killjoy.

I take it anyway, because his grip is warm and steady and it pulls me upright like I weigh nothing. For a heart-beat his thumb brushes my palm—too brief to call intentional.

But it is.

I notice the keycard Rozsen is twirling between two fingers. Finn follows behind her with the expression of a man who has suffered deeply.

I glance at them. "How many is that now?"

Finn holds up a hand like he's tallying his own misery. "Five to one."

Rozsen beams like she's won an Olympic medal.

Noa's mouth twitches, almost a smile. He nods toward the far mat. "You two spar. Keep it clean."

Finn snorts. "Clean? With her?"

Rozsen tosses him the stolen card like she's being generous. He fumbles it, muttering, and follows her toward the mat.

The bickering starts immediately—sarcasm snapping back and forth, familiar as breathing. Despite how those two started off the school year, they've never again spent the night together and instead developed an inseparable friendship based on sarcasm, wit, and how many times they can successfully steal each other's keycards without the other noticing.

It's infuriatingly adorable.

I bring my attention back to Noa—only to find him already watching me. Not my stance. My face.

I hear Finn yelp a second later as Rozsen flips him, his back to the mat, quick and clean.

I bite back a grin. Noa doesn't.

"Focus," he says.

"I am," I lie.

For the next fifteen minutes, the room fills with the sounds of training: feet slapping mats, controlled impacts, Finn's complaints, Rozsen's laughter. Noa keeps me moving, correcting, pushing, keeping me from drifting into my head the way I always do when stress builds.

And it does build.

Essays. Exams. The constant pressure of Whittaker humming under my skin like a second heartbeat.

My mind keeps trying to split itself in two—half on what's in front of me, half on an upcoming Potions exam and bullet points for my political negotiations essay. I spent years trailing behind my father on diplomatic missions; I know the games, but that doesn't mean I can regurgitate them in academic format.

On the fourth round, his palm hits my shoulder harder than before, and I stumble.

"That's the third opening in a row," he says, irritation cutting through his usual calm. "You're not committing to your advances."

"I'm distracted," I admit, breathless. "Midterms."

Rozsen pauses from across the room, raising a brow. "Your… advances?"

Finn snorts. "That explains the tension."

I shoot them both a withering look.

Rozsen's grin says she *absolutely* knows what she's doing.

Finn arches a brow dramatically. "We can leave, if you want. For… educational reasons."

"You guys aren't helping," Noa says instantly. "Just go."

Rozsen laughs. "Is that an order, *Officer* Gallegher?"

Noa mumbles something under his breath. I catch the word *children,* followed by a series of quiet curses

Finn grabs his bag from the floor. "Let's go, Red. It's five to one—but that will be the *last* time you steal my keycard."

Rozsen flashes him a smile that promises nothing but trouble.

They head for the doors, still bickering, still laughing—Finn grumbling about breakfast, Rozsen needling him about his footwork. The door closes behind them with a soft, final click, and the Training Room empties out until it feels cavernous. The air is thick with humidity and the faint scent of sweat and scorched rubber.

It's quiet.

Too quiet.

I exhale and loosen my shoulders. "Look, I'm sorry, Noa. I'm here. I *am* trying."

He turns away toward the weight rack, and I think he'll leave it there—but then he pauses, looking back over his shoulder. His eyes gleam, a dangerous shade of turquoise. "I'll make you a deal," he says, voice low. "You get me on my back just once, and I'll let you do *whatever* you want to me. Right here."

My heart skips like a stone thrown across still water.

"Anything?" I ask, my tone deliberately slow and sultry.

"Anything, Celeste," he says, stepping back onto the mat with a playful smirk tugging at his lips.

"Deal."

I lunge low, going for a leg sweep. He sidesteps easily, damn near laughing as he pivots with the grace of a dancer. We start to circle each other, the tension crackling between us—part combat, part challenge, part something much darker and more delicious.

I feint for his throat; a move he taught me himself. He moves like wildfire—fast and unpredictable. I swear I see smoke ghost through the air in his wake.

"Alright," I mutter. "If we're playing dirty…" I throw both hands forward and send a pair of water tendrils skittering across the mat, pooling slick beneath us.

I rush him, slamming my shoulder into his chest before he catches me mid-motion and spins me like I'm weightless. He holds me steady, his expression somewhere between disbelief and amusement.

"You're using your magick on me?"

"Isn't that the point?" I smirk.

Without giving him a chance to respond, I lash two ribbons of water up from the mat, coiling them around his wrists.

He doesn't even flinch—just lets me press in close, lips brushing his as I whisper, *"Yield."*

He grins wickedly, heat surging between us. Steam bursts from his skin in a hiss where the water touches him, and with one fluid twist, he breaks free—water sizzling into mist as he looks down at me. "Try harder."

Cocky bastard.

I narrow my eyes and pivot my approach. A fresh wave of water coils underfoot, but this time, I direct another current behind him. He doesn't see it coming—the push from behind colliding with the slickness below, and the combined momentum sends him flying toward me so fast that he loses his balance, crashing through my wave in a sputter of insulted fire and steam.

He hits the mat hard, winded, swearing under his breath.

I walk over slowly, straddling him before he can move.

His hands stay planted on the mat, eyes locked on mine like he doesn't trust himself to touch me. Water sloshes around us, soaking into our clothes, glistening on our skin.

I lean in, close enough to kiss but just out of reach. "Still *anything?*" I murmur, my lips at the shell of his ear.

He stills, barely breathing.

Then, wordless, I peel off my soaked shirt and toss it aside. My thin white bra clings to my skin, nearly transparent now. His eyes darken, jaw tense, hands still not moving—but I can feel the restraint vibrating through him.

I don't say another word. I don't have to.

I look toward the gym doors and flick my wrist.

Water answers like it knows me.

A thin ribbon slithers off the mat, gliding up through the air, coiling through the metal handles. It freezes. Not slowly—instantly, with a sharp crack that echoes through the empty room. Frost blooms outward in delicate veins across the doorframe, sealing it shut in a sheet of jagged, glistening ice.

Noa stiffens beneath me. "Celeste," he whispers. It's not a question. It's not even a warning. It's something closer to awe… or fear.

I don't answer. I can't.

Shit.

I wasn't even trying. I wasn't thinking. I shouldn't be able to do that. Not without training. *Not like that.*

A sharp pulse hammers behind my eyes, warning me I've overdrawn, but I push past it.

We'll talk—

Later.

Not now.

I turn back to him, slowly. His eyes are still wide, locked on the door, then flick to me like he doesn't quite know *who* I am.

I shift my focus back to the task at hand—back to him. Distracting him in the best way possible.

I lean down, letting my lips brush his just once before claiming his mouth with a reckless hunger. I kiss him as I move slowly above him. Our soaked clothes cling and slide, friction blooming into fire between us until he finally groans against my throat, the sound rough and low—part warning, part promise.

The door is finally forgotten, along with everything else, as he kisses me back.

The heat of our skin contrasts sharply with the cool dampness of the mat beneath us. I sit him up just enough to grab the hem of his shirt, damp and clinging, sliding it over every muscle as I slip it over his head.

I start to trail slow, calculated kisses down his chest, stopping only when I reach the waistband of his pants. I feel him pulsing hard and hot beneath the fabric, like a fire barely contained.

With deliberate hands, I slip his pants down, freeing him, as I look up at him through my lashes.

He groans as I put the tip of him into my mouth, teasing at first, then tasting him like something forbidden. He's too big to take in fully so I use my tongue to circle his sensitive ridge while using my hand to glide up and down the sides of him.

His hands grip the mat, his knuckles white.

I revel in the pleasure I draw from him, sucking and licking as I move above him. He hits the back of my throat and his hands come up to my face in reflex, fingers tangling in my hair. "Fuck," he whispers, wrecked. "That feels… so… fucking good."

His control slips in fragments—one broken sound at a time —until it's gone completely. His breath begins to quicken and his groans grow more wild, until he finally reaches the point where he can no longer be leashed. I taste the salt of him pooling on my tongue as he shudders beneath me, my name on his lips.

His restraint then snaps like a bowstring. His hand grips my shoulder, flipping me beneath him before I can blink. Fire and fury above me. Water and want below.

My back hits the damp mat with a splash, air rushing from my lungs as he settles over me, all heat and command.

"My turn," he says with gravel in his voice.

He tears off my leggings and underwear and immediately starts with his tongue edging into me. He parts me with his hands—like petals unfolding beneath his touch. His hunger is sharp, as if he's trying to worship and ruin me in the same breath.

His mouth finds me, tongue tracing slow, molten circles around my center, insatiable and precise. Pleasure coils behind my ribs like a rising tide.

"Noa," I gasp, the words anchoring me to the moment even as everything else spirals away.

The master is now the student once again as I submit to him completely.

I break with fury—a tidal wave smashed against jagged rocks, the shock stealing my breath, my voice, my name. My world scatters into liquid and firelight.

He holds me there—anchoring, coaxing—until I drift back into bone and skin.

He moves to lie beside me. Steam still rises over us, wrapping us in our own veil of spent power.

"You really are going to be the death of me one day," he chuckles, hand on his chest as he wills his breathing to slow.

I turn on my side, watching his profile as I smile. "Well, not such a bad way to die," I tease.

He turns to look at me, his fingers brushing my lips, eyes full of emotion—uncertainty, awe, longing, the quiet fear of the unknown and perhaps of wanting something too much. "No," he says softly. "It's not."

* * *

LATER THAT NIGHT, Noa sits on the couch in my room at the Blue Dahlia, elbows on his knees, eyes locked on the fire he coaxed to life in my fireplace. The flames flicker wildly, licking the stone hearth in a rhythm only he controls. The silence stretches between us, awkward, filled with things unsaid.

My roommates are still at the mess hall, which buys me time. Not much, but enough.

I watch him for a moment—shoulders tense, jaw tight—and I know what's on his mind. It's on mine too.

Big girl panties on, I tell myself. *Okay. Here we go.*

I clear my throat and speak before I can talk myself out of it. "Noa, what you saw today. What I did... in the Training Room."

He glances at me, but says nothing. The fire crackles.

"I don't just mean the match," I continue. "I mean the door. After."

His eyes narrow slightly. "You mean when you *froze* it shut?"

I nod.

The silence that follows is strained—uncomfortably so.

"It was... incredible," he says finally. "Most third-years can't pull that off. Hell, not even most fourth-years. I'm impressed." I exhale, relieved—but then he adds, quietly, "But—"

I knew it was coming. And still I hoped that we could end the conversation where it was. A stupid hope.

"But the *way* you did it, Cel. Like it cost you *nothing.* Like you weren't even trying. That's not something you just *learned,* is it?" The accusation falls like ash from his tongue.

I look down at my hands, not knowing what to say.

He sits up straighter, his voice low but edged. "I asked you to be honest with me, remember? From the beginning. And I feel like I'm the only one keeping that promise."

"I didn't mean—"

"Elemental state manipulation is advanced magick, Cel," he cuts in. "Dangerous if not completely controlled. I'm one of only a handful on campus who can do it. And I've trained for years. I'm not angry you did it. It's astounding, the power you showed today. I'm angry that you felt like you had to hide it. Because you've clearly been able to do this for a long time. With no training. No help."

I stand, the pressure too much, and walk to the window. The lake glows silver under the moonlight, calm and distant—so unlike what's building inside me. I try to find the right words. "I was fourteen," I say finally. "And I did have help. Gavrail taught me."

His head snaps toward me, his expression a storm of disbelief. "Fourteen? That's… that's unheard of. I don't think anyone's ever been documented that young." He runs a hand through his hair. "Do you even realize what that means? What you could be capable of?"

His breath stalls. I see it—the moment it all connects. His expression falters, eyes darkening with realization.

"The headaches… They aren't from trying to *force* your magick out. They're from trying to keep it all in. It hurts you… to keep it in," he says quietly as his eyes lock on mine, like the truth stings more than he expected.

I bite my lip and nod, then take a step toward him. "Please. I'm trying—"

But he stands abruptly, the movement sharp, like he's been

burned. "No, Celeste." His voice is trembling with restraint. "You've been lying. *Again.*" He takes a step back, shaking his head, jaw clenched. "First about being a Magick. Now this." His hands curl into fists at his sides. "What else are you keeping from me?"

There it is, in his voice, his posture—the fury, yes, but underneath it: hurt. Deep and raw and clawing its way out.

I hesitate. Just long enough.

He sees it. And the worst part is—he waits. Three whole seconds. No pressure. Just patience. Time holding its breath.

"Celeste," he says, softer now. "Whatever it is—just tell me. I can handle the truth. What I can't handle is lies—or silence."

I want to speak. I almost do. But my mouth stays closed. My heart pounds. And I say nothing.

And that's it—that's the moment it breaks.

He exhales, but it's not relief. "You don't trust me," he whispers, shaking his head. "Even now. After everything." He laughs, bitter and low. "The worst part is, I think I would've forgiven you if you'd just said *something*." His face is stoic now, a quiet mask of betrayal. "I told you—this only works if we're being honest with each other. Really honest."

My chest tightens, aching like something's splintering inside me. "It's not that simple—"

"I gave you a chance," he says, voice flat. "And you chose not to take it."

"Noa, please. Let me explain," I plead. Tears prick the corners of my eyes.

But it's like talking to stone.

"I don't think there's anything left to explain," he says—clipped, cold, like each word is severing something between us. "If you can't be honest with me," he adds, voice cracking just slightly before he steels it again, "at least be honest with yourself. I thought we were in this together. But I guess I was wrong."

The ice in his eyes is far more painful than any fire ever has been.

He grabs his jacket from the hook by the door.

And then he's gone.

The door slams behind him, leaving only the echo and the hollow ache of everything I couldn't say in time.

The silence he leaves behind is louder than his words.

I sink to the floor slowly, knees folding beneath me. This wasn't how I thought this would go. My hands grip the edge of the couch cushion, not for comfort, but just to hold on to something—anything—before the guilt and heartbreak swallow me.

I didn't mean to lie. Not really. But lies don't always wear disguises. Sometimes they sound like protection. Sometimes they sound like survival.

I press the heels of my palms to my eyes, trying to hold it all in—tears, shame, panic. But it leaks through anyway. My breath hitches. My chest feels like it's splitting open. And for a terrifying moment, I don't know if I'm going to scream or sob.

He's gone. And this time, I don't know if he's coming back.

And maybe worse than that...

I don't know if I deserve for him to.

A pop and a hiss draw my attention to the fireplace. The flames in the hearth sputter, then die—leaving only embers and a room gone cold, laced with shadow.

CHAPTER 19

Trust is a tactical asset. Spend it like ammunition—but only when the outcome is worth the recoil.

—Service Field Doctrine 3.7: Squad Cohesion

NOA

My footsteps echo too loudly in the empty hallway of the Blue Dahlia. Each step feels like a betrayal—of myself, of her, of everything I thought we were building. I make it out the front door before the fire in my chest breaks loose. A punch to the wall does nothing but scrape my knuckles.

You walked away from her.

My father would call that discipline. Tactical withdrawal. *Maintain control. Reassess the asset.* But this feels nothing like control. It feels like the exact fucking opposite.

I drag a hand through my hair, breath sharp as frost in my lungs. The night air doesn't cool the heat crawling beneath my skin. I didn't expect perfection. But lies? Secrets? That's not what we were supposed to be built on.

She looked wrecked. And I made it worse.

Gavrail.

The name alone twists my stomach into a knot. Not because of what he is.

Because of what she gave him.

That's the piece that splinters something in me. The idea that she carried all of this inside her—this rare power, this knowledge, this history—and never said a word.

Not when we were alone in the Cavern.

Not when she was curled into me on the couch.

Not when she was in my bed, shaking from the force of her own magick, and I was trying to help. My hands around her waist, my mouth at her ear. My fingers cupping her jaw as I turned her face up to mine.

Look at me. Breathe, Cel. I've got you.

And she did. She looked at me like I was the only real thing in this world. She trusted me enough to fall apart in my arms. But not enough to tell me why.

And maybe that's what stings the most. Not that she had secrets.

But that she didn't trust me with them.

But she trusted *him.*

I think about the way she was with me—warm, soft, *mine* in a way that made me believe I'd earned it. And now I can't stop wondering—

Was any of it real?

Because I sure as hell didn't walk into this halfway. And fuck if that doesn't hurt.

Maybe I was just the version of safe she needed until something stronger came along.

Even just the idea of someone else touching her, of those lips whispering secrets into someone else's ear, makes me almost turn back and demand everything from her right now. Her body. Her fucking soul.

I run through every conversation we've had, looking for a fracture I missed.

A moment where she might have almost told me the truth.

A moment I could've asked the right question and gotten the right answer. An answer that ended with her and me in bed right now. Taking out my anger while buried deep inside of her, instead of out here. Alone.

But I don't turn around.

I stalk across the quad, barely aware of where I'm going until the steps of the Caldera rise beneath my feet. The night air greets me like a dare.

My father built his career on reading people. A commander in the Iron Vanguard, the most decorated non-magick soldier of his generation. He would have told me to walk away. But my mother? My mother would tell me to listen to the fire. To pay attention to where it burns brightest. And fuck if it doesn't become a damn inferno the second I'm around Celeste.

The hairs on the back of my neck lift. Not paranoia—instinct.

I look up. Across the field, Headmaster Thorne is walking the path with Professor Stroud, mid-conversation. Thorne's eyes meet mine. His chin dips once—quiet approval, a check-in without words. But there is a question there as he reads the tension in my frame.

I nod, giving him nothing, before heading down the steps. The two men keep walking.

With a flick of my hand, fire blooms across the oval.

I strip off my shirt and kick away my shoes before stepping into the circle of heat barefoot, sweat already rising along my spine. Then I move—precision strikes, high-impact bursts of flame, rolls, dodges. Anything to burn through the anger. Anything to drown out the sound of her voice:

"Noa, please. Let me explain."

I heard the plea. Saw the pain in her eyes.

And still—I walked.

I don't know if I regret it more because I'm angry… or because I'm terrified that pushing her away might have just been the biggest mistake of my life.

I throw another strike and the flame snaps too hot—white at the core. Heat bites up my forearm, fast enough that it shocks a hiss out of me. *Fuck.* I shake it out, furious with my own slip.

A quiet cough cuts through the heat from somewhere above me.

I turn, ready to snap at whoever's watching—

But there's no one there.

CHAPTER 20

Some substances, once combined, do not part willingly.
—"Modern Principles of Alchemy and Potions," Dr. S. Davenport, *Journal of Applied Alchemical Sciences*

CELESTE

The rest of the month goes by with excruciating mundanity. The gray sky drips rain in cold sheets, with the occasional thunderstorm echoing the tears and ache in my chest that seem to have settled in like a ghost—haunting me.

I've been spending my afternoons with Amelia in the Garden Grove, learning about various plants and minerals. There's something grounding about having the earth beneath my nails, the steady rhythm of pruning and planting, the soft rustle of leaves, the comforting silence of nature. Amelia doesn't try to talk to me about it. She doesn't try to console me in my pain. She just sits with me, letting me feel everything. Occasionally, when I fall back from our gardening with silent tears streaming down my face, she places a soft hand on mine—quiet, steady, enough.

Rozsen and Elliot are the opposite—constantly trying to cheer me up with funny stories and wild anecdotes, meanwhile sending glares Noa's way whenever they see him.

I haven't been sleeping. Because the second I close my eyes, I'm instantly drowning. Sometimes trapped again in a dark cave, looking up at fractured stars as I sink to the bottom of a black pool. The voice that normally coaxes me forward is now mixed with voices from hooded figures that surround me. One sounds like Noa. *Liar. Too much. Not enough.* I wake soaked, my sheets sticking to me. It's never as bad as it was before, but enough that I take to sleeping over a towel, just in case.

Food tastes like dust. I can't stand being around too many people, so I've thrown myself into my studies. A desperate attempt to distract myself from the darkness as I try to keep it at bay.

In Advanced Potions, Noa now sits at the back table—much to Stella's absolute delight and satisfaction. Finn just shrugged when Noa grabbed his stuff and moved. He's taken to pressing his lips into tight lines, his brows always knit together, flickers of hesitation crossing his face—like he wants to speak, like he wants to break the wall of ice between Noa and me and fix it. But he doesn't. He can't. It's not for him to fix what I broke.

One such Thursday, I manage to hide out in the storeroom of Browning Hall until the rest of the class leaves. The small space smells of damp stone and crushed herbs, rows of narrow shelves stacked with jars of powdered roots and strange hazy liquids. The air is close, heavy with remnants of steam from the potion our class just finished brewing.

I'm halfway through sorting some ingredients for Professor Ching when the door shuts with a click.

"Funny, isn't it?" Stella leans against the archway, arms

folded, water patch gleaming faintly on her jacket. "How fast loyalties shift at Whittaker."

I stiffen but keep sorting. I don't owe her a word.

"It bothers you, doesn't it? Noa moving to my table."

Her words are soft, with a hint of what sounds almost like regret, like she knows how and what I'm feeling.

She sighs. "Look, he's back where he belongs. Among his own."

I turn fully now, pulse hammering, fire behind my eyes. "And what, exactly, is that supposed to mean?"

Her smile is tight—but not completely unkind. "It means some of us grew up in this world. We understand it. Our families fought, bled, and served together. His father and mine were in the Iron Vanguard together. His mother and mine were in the same class at Whittaker. The Service has always kept its bloodlines close." She tilts her head, pity heavy in her voice. "Some families just... belong together. And outsiders"—she gestures delicately, as if I'm something fragile—"outsiders are never more than guests at the table."

The words land hard, sharper for the calmness with which she speaks them. Because to her, it's the truth. And for a heartbeat, I almost believe her—that I'll always be standing on the threshold, never inside the circle.

But the water in me surges hot, spilling at the edge of my control. The air shifts. The jars along the wall tremble, glass creaking faintly. A thin stream of liquid seeps from one stopper, sliding down in jagged lines like veins.

Stella's gaze flicks to it. "Careful, Celeste," she whispers. "From one water-wielder to another, you better work on that control before your magick tries to control you instead. Water is known to be... temperamental."

She flicks her wrist, returning the water back to the jar in a single twisting motion before turning without another word, leaving me in the cramped quiet, the jars still trembling, and my own thoughts screaming louder than any words she could have spoken.

* * *

THE RUN-IN with Stella has me replaying her words over and over again in my head. Anger flares whenever I think about it, but it's a welcome change to the heartbreak and sadness that normally accompanies my days.

It's pathetic, maybe, but I keep hoping for an accidental meeting. Some excuse just to see him outside of class. Then the faculty announces the fourth-years will be heading to Fort Wyenth for a week to tour the Service's main training grounds, and my heart sinks.

Sooner or later, we'll have to face each other. Talk. But it feels like fate keeps finding new ways to wedge even more distance between us.

* * *

IN THE LAST week of November, the school announces a week of reprieve. Most students use it to visit nearby Elesmere—a quaint New England village with cozy restaurants and charming little shops that draw visitors year-round.

The fourth-years are still gone. Their one-week stay has turned into two.

I try not to think about it. About what they might be doing. About what Noa is doing.

My emotions don't agree on anything—worry braided with relief, threaded through with a sharp, stupid disappointment that he isn't here.

My squadmates have been buzzing since the break was

announced. Rozsen has made a list of every restaurant she wants to try. Elliot has compiled one for the shops. I can get behind that. After months of enduring Whittaker's constant deluge of gray and black, I need something—anything—to break the monotony.

A few other Blue Dahlia residents make plans to stay with us at the local inn, and we decide to turn it into an adventure.

Maybe that's what I need. A little freedom. A little air. Something different than the shadows and silence of Whittaker.

Elesmere is a charming town tucked into the rolling hills just beyond Whittaker's forested boundaries. Cobblestone streets curve between brick-front shops and limewashed cottages, many of them lovingly preserved for generations. The town square boasts a modest clock tower and fountain, and each storefront bears a hand-painted sign that swings gently in the wind. Passersby move beneath them, bundled in scarves and wool coats.

The Village Inn sits at the edge of the main road—known for its eclectic charm and strong cider. The residents of the Blue Dahlia seem to have taken over the reception lobby, lounging on mismatched velvet chairs and striped chaise lounges. The inn's barkeep is busy with heavy pours and fanciful artisan cocktails. It's the unofficial hangout for Whittaker students when they venture into town.

It is here one afternoon, sitting at the bar with Amelia, that Ian drops onto the stool beside me, copper-red hair in permanent disarray and a scar through his brow—a mishap from a story he likes to tell too often. Nate follows with a coffee and the expression of a man assigned to supervise a hurricane.

I guess that's one silver lining—if it can be called that—of Noa's absence: I've gotten to know the guys in my squad and commons more now that his tall, intimidating shadow isn't always nearby.

Ian came over from England to study at Whittaker. He's quick to laugh, though quicker still to fight, and has a knack for setting even the air on fire.

Nate moves like the water he commands—graceful, quiet, sometimes moody. He's tall, with olive skin and light-brown hair. His gray-blue eyes radiate calm… until they don't. If you get on his bad side, they turn dark gray like a tempest at sea. But where Ian provokes, Nate usually defuses. They've been utterly inseparable since orientation.

"We were gonna head to the bookstore later," Ian says, peering into my glass of orange juice, his hand moving toward it.

I pull it just out of reach. "Get your own."

"Tsk tsk. Sharing builds trust, Farris," he grins.

I let him take a sip.

He coughs like he's been poisoned. "Where is the alcohol? This just tastes like—?"

"Juice?" Nate answers helpfully, not looking up as he adds creamer to his coffee.

"It *is* just juice," I say. "It's not even noon yet." I roll my eyes at Ian while Amelia shakes her head. "Was that you who set the common room curtains on fire last week?" I ask him, changing the subject.

He lifts one scarred eyebrow in mock innocence. "You have no proof of such shenanigans."

Nate finally looks up. "There were witnesses. And scorch marks."

Ian only huffs. "I was actually trying to set Dash's jacket on fire."

Amelia looks aghast. "Why on earth would you do that?"

"He told me my accent was 'cute,'" Ian says, appalled. "In front of Chelsea! It is not cute; it is aggressive and manly and delightfully charming."

Nate takes a sip of his coffee. "I actually was impressed with your restraint that time."

"Thank you. At least someone appreciates it."

"You didn't even aim for his hair," Nate says, deadpan.

I can't help the small laugh that escapes my lips. It feels good to be sitting here with my squadmates. To be talking of anything other than the hole in my chest where my heart used to be.

"Anyway," Ian says, like he didn't just confess to attempted arson, "do you guys wanna come with us? I want to find something for my mum for Parents' Week in April. Something that says *I'm thriving,* not *I'm one incident away from expulsion.*"

Amelia shrugs—which we've all learned by now means "yes."

Fifteen minutes later we spill out into the cold. Ink & Ether is a peculiar little bookstore tucked between a florist and a bakery. Inside, the shelves bow under the weight of obscure arcane tomes, folklore compendiums, and out-of-print novels. Somewhere in the back, incense burns, the smoke curling lazily toward the ceiling.

The shopkeeper, known only as Madame Romari, is a raven-haired woman with eyes like storm glass. She seems to appear beside you just as you're reaching for a book—as if she already knows what you were looking for, even when you don't.

I head toward the elemental theory section, wondering if she carries anything our school library doesn't. The soft clinking of her bangles gives her presence away before I even see her.

"You're looking for something," she says. Her accent is thick and foreign, and it's not a question.

"Yeah… I mean, yes. Just browsing elemental theory. Maybe something specifically on water magick?"

She peers at me—no, *through* me, a feeling that's both eerie and unsettling. "I have something you might like," she says, then turns, expecting me to follow.

We pass through a beaded curtain that rustles softly behind

us as she leads me into what must be her office. The space is small but brimming with secrets. A towering bookcase dominates one wall, lined with ancient tomes—cracked leather spines, handwritten titles in dead languages, and symbols I don't recognize. Her desk is a chaotic arrangement of half-melted candles, stacked parchment, and arcane instruments. Crystals glitter faintly beside chipped ceramic bowls filled with sand, salt, and herbs.

She paces to the bookcase and carefully selects a volume. The cover is a faded, blood-red leather, its binding cracked and delicate.

"It looks a hundred years old," I murmur, almost to myself.

"Older," she corrects gently, without looking at me.

The title is faint but still legible: *Elemental Fusion: The Art and Origin of Convergence.*

My heart lurches. Fear and possibility crash together inside me like opposing tides.

I thank her and quickly purchase the book. As I gather my things, she watches me with dark eyes.

"You are sad," she says quietly. Again, not a question.

I pause.

"He will find his way back to you," she adds, her voice almost too soft to hear.

I look up, startled—and a little uneasy. "Excuse me, but—"

I'm cut off as Amelia and Ian burst through the curtain, arms full of books.

"Look what I found!" Ian grins, holding up a fire magick text. "It mentions my family. My mum's going to love it."

We step out into the crisp air of the main street, bags full of new purchases and sweet treats from the local candy store. The others talk and laugh, but I can't shake the feeling Madame Romari's words left behind.

When my squadmates invite me to join them for drinks at the pub, I decline, citing tiredness. Amelia's green eyes scan my face, missing nothing. "You're sure?" she asks quietly. I nod, forcing a small smile.

As I head back to my room at the inn alone, the book clutched tightly against my chest, the words echo like a whisper I can't unhear.

He will find his way back to you.

I wish I could believe her. But the thing about hope is—it hurts just as much as heartbreak when you've been holding it too long.

* * *

THE INN'S room is tiny but comfortable. Worn plaid comforters in shades of maroon and tan are tucked neatly over two queen beds with dark wood frames, their headboards carved with old-fashioned scrollwork. A small window seat is nestled beneath a paned window, the seat cushions faded to a soft yellow. It overlooks the town square and fountain, where strings of lantern lights sway gently in the evening breeze and the sound of chatter from my classmates at the nearby pub drifts up through the glass. I can hear Rozsen's teasing voice and Elliot's answering laughter.

I curl into the window seat, tucking my legs beneath me, and pull the book from my bag. My fingers brush across its worn leather cover, tracing the etched emblem of a diamond within two opposing triangles, creating an eight-pointed star, before I crack it open.

THE FIRST RECORDED case of elemental fusion dates back to 1590, in Trier, Germany. The mage was an unnamed earth-wielder, a woman later accused of witchcraft and burned at the stake during the infamous Trier witch trials. Her grimoire, discovered years later in the walls of a monastery, detailed the successful convergence of earth and air magick—its pages ripped, but intact.

I SWALLOW hard and turn the page, heart beating faster.

IN 1715, a water Magick named Evric Thalrien reportedly merged water and fire. The resulting surge destroyed Ormacleit Castle in the Western Isles of Scotland. No one survived the blast save for Thalrien himself, though he vanished from history not long after. The castle ruins still stand, blackened stones untouched by moss or time.

THE AIR FEELS COLDER ALL of a sudden, as if the words themselves are drawing energy from the room. I tug the sleeves of my sweater over my hands and keep reading.

AUREN EMBERLAIN, a fire-wielder, recorded successful fusion of fire and air in 1893. Her methods remain the cornerstone of what little is known about elemental fusion today, though her notes suggest the process is inherently volatile.

During the first rebellion, in the infamous Battle of Redmere, Serena Thalrien—water Magick, rebel supporter—merged water with an unidentified essence. Witnesses claim she wiped out over 1,400 soldiers in a single strike, sparing only the rebels she swore to protect. She was captured, tried, sentenced... and then vanished after a mysterious break in the prison walls. Her fusion remains one of the most destructive ever recorded.

Much of what we know of elemental fusion is limited, the greatest known text being from Auren Emberlain herself, describing convergence. Many have tried and failed to recreate the process.

. . .

I CLOSE THE BOOK SLOWLY, my fingers trembling. So much power. So much destruction. And so little understanding. A part of me is thrilled at the possibility… but another part is absolutely terrified. If what Gavrail and I did as children was really *fusion*—then I've already crossed a line I can't uncross.

CHAPTER 21

To command power is not enough. One must know when to unleash it and when to hold it in reserve. When the strike comes, it must be final.

—Vikhrostrum Akademiya Doctrine of Elemental Combat

December arrives, bringing most of the fourth-years back to campus. Everyone except Noa and Finn.

"Special assignment," Ryan mutters one morning behind me, equal parts envy and awe curling through his voice.

Illogical bitterness fills me for a moment, because of course the Service would want to keep Noa and Finn close—to show them exactly what they can expect come graduation. Whittaker's top two students already being recruited, no doubt.

December also brings something else—news that the prestigious European school of magick, Vikhrostrum Akademiya, is sending a delegation of its elite students to spend the semester at Whittaker. But more thrilling than their arrival is the announcement that a series of elemental duels will take place between their finest and ours throughout the term. Headmaster Thorne calls it "an effort to improve foreign relations"—but to the students, it sounds like a challenge.

The first real snow comes the week the delegation is due—light at first, a powdering over roofs and bare branches, then thicker, settling like icing into old grooves in the stone walkways.

I tell myself I don't care.

I tell myself that none of this has anything to do with me.

And that is almost believable—until the faculty unveils a ranking board in the center of the quad, names and numbers flickering constantly as it updates in real time.

And the entire campus starts to hum.

Students crowd it at all hours—I can't cross the quad without getting trapped in the press of bodies, watching names rise and fall like empires of the past. The Training Room stays lit well past midnight. Classes sharpen. Tempers shorten.

Because now, it's not just about being the best.

It's about making the list.

Top five. That's all that matters.

Each student is ranked within their element first—fire against fire, water against water, air against air. Then those rankings collapse into a single class standing.

One list.

The list.

The one that decides who represents Whittaker.

When Vikhrostrum arrives, their first will face ours, second against second, third against third. No substitutions. No second chances. If you're not at the top, you're a spectator and nothing more.

First-years are barred from competing, much to Ian, Nate, and Sawyer's deep and ongoing outrage. They spend the week complaining about it at full volume—and then promptly start an unregulated war of their own, ambushing each other from behind corners with bursts of air and water or badly controlled flames, in what they insist is "training" for next year.

Occasionally, Rozsen and Elliot join them. Amelia, Peter, and I learn to recognize the manic, mischievous glints in their eyes and wisely vacate the areas they are in, not wanting to chance losing an eyebrow or being doused in freezing water.

Noa, of course, takes first in fire and overall.

Finn claims air, ranking second.

Neither announcement comes as a surprise to anyone.

A water-wielder named Luana slides into third place. A second-year, Jin Feng, shocks everyone by having already mastered metal, and lands just behind her. And earth, held by a fourth-year who also happens to be Amelia's mentor, rounds out the top five.

Their names are already being whispered like they've won something. Like they're already legends.

The day the delegates are meant to arrive, Whittaker doesn't feel like a school anymore—it feels like a throat held tight before a scream. Even the sky looks different. Cloudless and sharp, the sort of blue that turns towers and gutter lines into clean, angular cuts against the world.

I'm in the mess hall, organizing my Elemental Theory notes —color-coded, neat, obsessive. Rewriting last week's lecture in my own words, as if rephrasing can be a banner of productivity.

Work. Focus. Anything that isn't—

The room shifts.

Heat passes behind my eyes like a match struck in the dark.

I don't turn.

I don't have to.

I know without looking that Noa is here.

The air *changes* around him—subtle, like the room has suddenly remembered fire exists. A few people glance up automatically. Someone clears their throat. Conversation stutters for half a beat, then surges again, louder, pretending normalcy.

My stomach tightens anyway.

"Finn!" Rozsen jumps up, rushing over. "We didn't know when you two were coming back—or *if* you'd be coming back at all." She punches his arm.

"Ow, and hi. We got back late last night," Finn says, rubbing the spot where she hit him.

I can feel eyes on me, heat flicking over my skin.

I don't look up, forcing my focus to stay on my notes, rewriting the same stupid sentence a second time, but my traitorous hand trembles slightly.

Footsteps echo on the polished floor, heading toward me—

"Officer Gallegher." Headmaster Thorne's voice booms through the hall. The entire room looks up as he enters.

"Sir?"

"You're needed in the Training Room." No explanation.

I glance at Noa from under my lashes as he speaks quietly with the headmaster. It's a mistake.

He looks formidable. Untouchable. *Beautiful.*

He glances back at me one last time before the two of them exit the mess hall together.

My pulse is ricocheting off the walls like it doesn't understand what rhythm is. I swallow the lump that's gathered in my throat.

He's back.

I'm simultaneously relieved and terrified.

By last period, none of the student body is even attempting to pay attention. Elemental Theory is our last class of the day. Professor Barrows is almost through his lecture on dueling when a commotion outside forces him to stop mid-sentence.

"Vikhrostrum—just came through the northern gate!" someone blurts from the hallway.

Everyone lifts their heads in unison. Barrows pauses, chalk frozen in midair. His eyes widen, as though he already knows what's about to happen.

For half a second, the entire classroom holds its breath.

Then the room detonates.

Benches scrape. Pens clatter. Someone actually whoops like they're at a stadium. Ian, two rows over, leans across his desk, eyes bright and feral. A few students surge to the windows, craning for a glimpse.

"Noa's dueling today," Ian whispers, like he's savoring it.

So *that's* what Thorne wanted with him earlier. I sink lower in my seat, my stomach drawing into a tight knot.

"Can't believe they're throwing one of them in the pit with *the fire king* the same day they arrive." Ian's excitement is palpable.

Rozsen's grin is all teeth. "That's not a welcome. That's a threat."

Barrows tries to regain control of the room, but it's almost impossible. Nobody sits properly. Students hover. They vibrate. Barrows takes one look at our faces—wild, buzzing—and dismisses us five minutes early.

As everyone packs up their bags, the whispers start—fast and hungry.

"Don't they all get recruited straight into Krovya after graduation?"

"I heard they only duel to the death."

"Shut up—who do you think will win today?"

"Do you think Noa will—"

The name pricks hot under my skin.

I lower my gaze to my notebook, but the words blur. I can't see the pages anymore. I can only see stone and blood and the Caldera's ancient ring waiting like an open mouth.

Outside the classroom, Whittaker becomes a current.

Students flood the corridors in a roar of footsteps. Coats whip. Boots skid on stone. Someone casts a tiny spiral of wind down the hallway just to watch papers lift like startled birds.

I'm swept along past the windows where the grounds stretch

under the light dusting of snow. Out on the lawn, a few of the visitors move between buildings under escort—dark uniforms, different crests, different postures. Even from a distance they look... sharper. Like the air around them is trained to be obedient.

A cluster of students press against the glass, faces smeared into reflections.

"Is that them?" someone breathes.

"I saw them come through the gate. Gods, they're—"

Her friend squeezes her arm to quiet her as a professor walks past.

But the girl is grinning too hard to stop. "—beautiful."

"Well," her friend hisses, gleeful, "then I'll be happy to help *improve foreign relations* in *any* way I can."

Another girl makes a strangled noise. "Shhh. Someone will hear you."

"Let them," the first girl says, practically giddy. "Let them know Whittaker's been starving all term and they just walked in looking like the main course."

A pair of visiting students pass directly beneath the window. On their shoulders: a black shield stamped with a silver three-peaked mountain—the Vikhrostrum crest. Uncomfortably close to Krovya's in shape, even if the details differ.

Their gazes rake the campus walkways with the casual assessment of predators.

The girl beside me goes quiet. Her smile falters.

And that's when I feel it—under everything, beneath the excitement and the hunger and the spectacle: rivalry.

Not friendly. Not playful.

Real.

Whittaker likes to pretend we are civilized. But the Caldera is older than our rules, and every student here knows it exists for one reason: to remind us what we are when the leash comes off.

As the rest of the student body bounds off toward the Caldera, I turn the other way—toward the second floor of the Logistics building.

Professor Ching is waiting in the doorway, sleeves rolled up, expression tight with purpose. His hair is slightly wild, the way it always is when he's been thinking too hard. I promised that I'd help with a particularly tricky compound today.

Inside, the air is thick with the scents of rosemary, metal, and something sharp like crushed stone. Across the benches, reagents sit arranged like offerings.

Ching gestures me over. "Weldver Salt," he says without preamble. "Restorative. Packed into deep lacerations—seals torn skin as if the wound was never there." He sets a mortar and pestle in front of me like a test. "Grind the matico leaves into a fine powder. And don't waste any." His gaze flicks to the jar, then to my hands. "It took me three months to get this after the supply line in Peru was hit."

"Hit?" I repeat. "Attacked?"

"Rebels." He says it like a nuisance, not a warning. "They took out the train tracks feeding the supply chain." A shrug—dismissive, but his fingers are already measuring, already counting. "Shortages always make people anxious. Particularly when they lead to wounds that continue to bleed."

I start grinding, slow and thorough, until the leaves surrender into green dust. Ching leans in just long enough to inspect, then gives a single nod.

"Good. Now fold in the moonsalt. Slowly."

He pours sangre de grado—dragon's blood resin—with maddening precision, drip by measured drip, until it threads through the salt like liquid starlight—beautiful and unnatural, the way a wound looks just before it closes.

"Now," he says, pushing the bowl toward me. "Water. One thread. Not a wave."

I swallow and lift my hand over the mixture.

Water answers. A fine filament rises from the air itself, drawn from the humidity hanging over the room, so thin it's almost invisible. It touches the salt and the compound brightens, as if the moonsalt has remembered what it was made from.

Ching watches with hawklike focus. "Keep it moving," he murmurs. "If it crystallizes too fast, it'll burn when applied."

My fingers tremble with the effort of being small and precise. *A thread. Not a wave.*

Outside, distant voices swell—shouts and laughter sliding through the window cracks, the campus building toward eruption.

"They're going to tear the Caldera apart for seats," Ching says dryly.

"Are you going?" I ask before I can stop myself.

His mouth quirks. "I've seen enough duels to last three lifetimes. But yes. I'll be there."

He tests the mixture between two fingers. It glitters faintly, cold light kissing his skin.

"Good." He starts pouring the salt into small silver tins.

A sharp clang cuts through the air—the Caldera bell.

Not a polite chime. Not a school bell. An ancient strike of metal that vibrates straight through my bones.

My head snaps up. Ching's gaze meets mine, and for a moment the sternness softens into something like understanding. His eyes narrow—assessing, not unkind.

He reaches past me, grabs my coat hanging on the back of my chair, and shoves it—and a small tin—into my arms. "Go," he says briskly. "Before the good seats are gone and you spend the duel staring at the back of someone's head."

I huff a breathless laugh, grateful and terrified.

His voice drops as he nods at the tin. "Keep that with you. Spectacle has a habit of becoming consequence."

My throat tightens. I nod and tuck the tin into my pocket.

The halls are chaos now—Whittaker pouring toward the

Caldera like a river breaking its banks. Students shoulder past each other, laughing, shouting bets, calling names. A group of first-years are already breathless, faces flushed with the thrill of being allowed into something ancient and dangerous.

Outside, the air bites cold, snow starting to cling to the ground. The path down is a stampede. And in the distance, between bare trees, the stone colosseum plunges into the earth like a circular scar—ancient, blackened by time, waiting.

As I move with the crowd, the tin of Weldver Salt knocks against my thigh with every step. A small, cold reminder.

This isn't just a show.

It never is.

I think of Noa.

And I start to run.

* * *

THE CALDERA IS ALREADY PACKED, every seat and ledge filled with students and professors alike. Excitement hangs in the air —dense and electric, so thick you can almost feel it. At the rim, a video recorder stands at attention, its spear-and-sun emblem spinning. Service magitech: technology powered or enhanced by magick—neutral in theory, never in practice. The operating officer's black uniform gives him away. Another reminder that the Service is watching. Always.

I barely find a place to stand before a torrent of fire sweeps through the center of the arena. Noa—a shock of brown hair, that familiar stance, flame coiling around his arms like lassos of fire. My stomach drops.

His opponent stands with his back to me—the student from Vikhrostrum, tall and lean-muscled, his movements smooth and silent. There is something deliberate about him, the way he carries himself—calm, calculating, deadly. Like someone who doesn't need words to command power.

Noa launches bolt after bolt of fire, but the Vikhrostrum delegate matches him without flinching. One moment the student is stepping back from a particularly vicious arc of fire, and the next he conjures something I thought impossible: two large snakes with the blackest scales slither forward, extinguishing the flames as they strike. At first I think they are actual snakes—some sort of rare creature magick—but then I see how they shift with the light.

As they circle each other, something in the way Noa's opponent moves tugs at me—a nagging sense of familiarity, sharp and insistent. His hair, a dark ash-brown. His stance. His silence. The hair on my neck rises as my unease deepens.

Noa presses forward, whips of fire lashing out, but I can see the sweat beading along his brow. He is working for every inch of ground—and that is new.

Suddenly, a tendril of black snaps around his ankle and yanks him down. In the same instant, the entire arena goes black. Not dim. Utterly, suffocatingly dark. As if someone has smothered the sun behind the mountain peaks.

It is then that I realize. They aren't snakes. They aren't ropes. They are *shadows*.

The Vikhrostrum student is a shadow Magick.

A chill rolls over me. I push forward, trying to get closer to the arena, weaving between panicked students and professors who whisper nervously as the darkness spreads. When it lifts slightly, I catch a glimpse—Noa back on his feet, a ring of fire blazing around them both. He drags the back of his hand across his mouth—rough and dismissive—and his eyes flick to the blood on his knuckles.

Something hardens in his expression.

That bright smear of red makes something hot and unsteady rise behind my ribs.

A muscle in Noa's cheek twitches, and he turns and spits onto the ground before turning back to his opponent. In his hand, a sword of pure flame. A sharp inhale escapes me. That is new too.

He lunges, aiming a deadly strike—but the Vikhrostrum delegate sidesteps with eerie grace and simply snaps his fingers.

The darkness explodes.

Not just the arena this time—the entire Caldera falls into absolute black.

Gasps and cries ring out. A few students scream. The crowd shifts in confusion, voices rising in panic. The shadows press around me like a living thing.

And yet, when they brush against my skin, it feels... like a caress. It isn't fear I feel. It's *memory*. Like something I've always known—something I can almost speak to, the same way I speak to water. The shadows seem to hesitate, like they know me too.

Suddenly, I'm moving.

I surge forward through the dark, stumbling down steps, weaving past bodies I can't see, only to collide—hard—into someone. Solid, familiar. My hands splay against their chest.

And it isn't just someone.

"Gavrail," I whisper.

Hands close around my wrists instantly—instinctive, firm—but he doesn't push me away. He doesn't let go either. For a single breathless moment, neither of us move. His chest rises and falls too fast beneath my palms. Shadow magick clings to my body and the air between us like smoke that doesn't want to dissipate.

And in that flicker of twilight before the shadows recede, I see it—astonishment, raw and unmasked, written across his face like he's seeing a ghost.

His mouth opens as if to speak, but voices shout from around us and a cool mask of practiced indifference slams into place. The controlled version of him returns just as the light does. He lets go like my touch burns.

The rest of the shadows fall away, leaving the arena and the

Caldera bathed once again in the amber light of the setting sun. The screams die, swallowed by stunned silence.

Standing before me is a man who resembles the boy I once knew. He's taller now, broader in the shoulders, still with that wild, ash-brown hair, now damp with sweat. His eyes—those impossible eyes—are still the color of a storm about to break, gray edged with silver, glinting like lightning caught in metal. They currently look almost black as they stare at me.

He takes a step back, his face a perfect shield of infuriating, unreadable stillness. But beneath it, a ripple. Something dark. Deep. And utterly dangerous.

My skin prickles in the chilled evening breeze, breath catching like he's pulled the oxygen from the air—and the space between us with it. He's looking at me. Only me.

"No," Gavrail says, harsh, firm. Almost as if to himself. "Celeste." His voice wraps around my name like a wound reopening. He pauses, the sharp, clipped tone with just a hint of an accent dragging me back to sun-dappled woods, fields of wildflowers, and promises made in the shadows of a cool blue lake.

From the corner of my eye, I see Noa pushing toward us, fury carved into every inch of him. His eyes are ablaze, his jaw clenched tight, every step radiating raw anger. Rushing to protect me or to hurt Gavrail, I'm not sure.

"You can't be here," Gavrail says, the words come out low and grinding, like wheels dragging across stone, his eyes locked on mine. There is command in his tone, and something else. Something dark, fraying at the edges.

Noa reaches us, stepping between us like a shield. "What the fuck was that?" he shouts, the accusation edged in fire. "The duel was between *you and me*—you blacked out the entire school! Are you out of your fucking mind?" His eyes dart back to me, scanning for injury before turning to face me fully. "Celeste, why the hell did you run into the arena?" He steps back, looking for a mark of any kind on me while glaring at Gavrail over his shoulder.

I'm worried he's going to set Gavrail on fire on the spot, or worse. I put a hand on his chest, his heartbeat thudding furiously against my palm as I step toward him.

"I'm fine," I say quickly, keeping my hand there, trying to keep him from erupting. But my voice wavers. "Everyone's fine... That duel... It was..." I glance at Gavrail. "I've never seen anything like it."

Gavrail stands perfectly still, but there is nothing passive about him. He watches Noa like he's calculating every weakness. Every flaw. His eyes flick to where my hand touches Noa and I swear I see him clench his fists tighter, knuckles turning white.

Neither man relaxes. Not even a little.

Behind Gavrail, the rest of the Vikhrostrum students form up, twelve in all, their posture stiff and disciplined. The Whittaker fourth-years instinctively line up behind Noa.

For a breathless moment, it feels like the arena might become a battlefield.

Then: "What a dynamic display of elemental power."

Headmaster Thorne's voice rings out, cutting the tension like a knife.

He claps a hand on each of their shoulders like nothing has happened. "Extremely impressive, both of you. An excellent first match." He then turns to address the crowd, his gaze flicking to the Service recording device for a heartbeat. "We have an incredible dinner prepared in the quad tonight to welcome our *guests*." The last word is pointed, his glance sharp as it lands on Noa in veiled reprimand. "I hope to see you all there. A perfect way to begin the elemental duels—with the two top-ranking students of Whittaker and Vikhrostrum Akademiya."

Applause rings out from the stands. The spell of conflict lifts, and students slowly begin to trickle back toward their dormitories, buzzing with adrenaline and speculation.

"Celeste," Thorne says, turning back to me with a pleasant smile. "Would you be so kind as to escort our Vikhrostrum guests to their dormitory?"

I glance at Noa. His jaw is clenched hard enough to grind bone. He takes a step forward, muscles coiled, eyes still locked on Gavrail.

"Of course, Headmaster," I say, then add quickly, "Just... give me a moment?"

Without waiting for a reply, I tug Noa away from the arena, up to where the stone bleachers begin and the noise of the dispersing crowd starts to fade behind us.

"Abso-fucking-lutely not," Noa snaps, still glaring murderously over my shoulder at the Vikhrostrum students. His voice drops. "I know *exactly* who that is."

"Noa. Look at me... *Look. At. Me.*" I reach up and grab his jaw, forcing his fire-lit gaze to drop to mine, breaking his icy staring contest with Gavrail. "I'll be fine. I need to talk to Gavrail. I promise I'll come find you the second I'm done if you want. *I'll be fine,*" I repeat, and I can't help it—I brush my thumb across the fresh cut on his lip, just once. A whisper of touch, but enough to make him freeze.

Being this close to him...

The silence between us pulses with everything we haven't said—anger, heartbreak, longing—and something in him cracks just enough to let it show. He closes his eyes for just a heartbeat. When they open again, they hold that same storm, but it isn't aimed at me.

He finally softens—just a fraction. Then his arms come around me, pulling me in, turning me away from the arena like he wants to shield me from the weight of every watching eye. "So that's Gavrail," he mutters, raising one sharp eyebrow. "*The* Gavrail?"

I nod.

"Thirty minutes," he says, voice low but laced with fire. "And if you're not at the Steps by then, I'm setting the entire Ivy House on fire."

With that, he casts one final glare in Gavrail's direction before storming off up the steps, Finn and Ryan trailing close behind like loyal shadows.

I watch him go, trying to center myself. *Just breathe,* I tell myself. *In and out. Out and in. Again.*

I finally turn back toward the center of the arena. Gavrail hasn't moved. His eyes are still on me—part predator, part promise, one hundred percent lethal. But something flickers there, waiting just beneath the surface. His expression reassembles itself into that glacial calm he wears like armor, every line of his face smoothing into disciplined stillness. Only the faintest swallow betrays that he recognizes me at all.

With a curt nod to his peers, he steps forward and cocks his head, extending his arm—wordlessly inviting me to lead the way.

* * *

WE WALK in silence for the first ten minutes. His peers fan out slightly behind us, taking in the campus, muttering among themselves in Bulgarian and Russian. A few students gawk at the group from across the path, some of the more brazen Whittaker students tossing catcalls their way.

I hate how I still know his gait. The way he keeps slightly ahead, not enough to lose me, just enough to be the first to intercept any danger that might arise. His eyes never stop moving, tracking every student we pass, every whisper half swallowed by the wind—ingrained in him from a lifetime as a general's son. The others follow like wolves behind an alpha. No words. No orders. Just obedience.

I tell myself to keep walking. To keep breathing. To keep my attention on the path.

But my focus keeps sliding back to him anyway, like a compass needle tugged off course.

I want to grab his hand, to pull him aside. To say the thousand things that are spinning in my mind. Seven years. *Seven years.* Has it really been that long? I want to hate him, to demand an explanation for all those years he left me aching, but all I can think about is the way his shadows used to curl around me, and the way his mouth tasted of secrets and summer storms.

The boy I loved is long gone. This is not the reckless, shadow-drenched teenager who used to steal my breath and whisper promises into the trees. Gone is the softness and gangliness of youth. In its place is a man so jaw-droppingly beautiful it's almost disorienting—like stepping off a ledge in the dark and only realizing a second later that you're falling.

This man is carved from time and sin and something harder. His cheekbones and jaw look chiseled from marble—sharp, a touch severe—yet there's an elegance that is unmistakably *him.* The cut of his uniform hides nothing; it only frames the control, the hardened polish of his form, as if he were built from the very shadows he wields and trained into submission. He doesn't speak. He wears silence like a blade—and when his mouth shifts, it isn't a smile so much as a slight, unreadable curve that makes my stomach dip in a way that has nothing to do with fear.

Where has he been all this time? Why did he not write me? Why did he not come find me like he promised? These questions and more are burning on my tongue when we finally reach the gates of the Ivy House. The three-story manor gleams white and restrained, its columns and clean lines radiating an old, unquestioned authority.

A second-year student is already waiting there, poised and

eager to guide the delegation inside. I hang back, waiting—for what, I'm not sure. Maybe for him to say something. Maybe for him to *see* me.

But instead, Gavrail turns. He bows slightly, thanks me for the walk in a quiet, even tone, and steps through the gate.

I stand frozen, watching him cross the courtyard. The stone under my feet suddenly feels unsteady, like the past is trying to drag me down with it.

He moves past the mermaid fountain at the center of the courtyard, where the water catches the last of the light as it drips down her frozen carved scales. And just before he reaches the stairs—he stops.

My lungs seize as I stare after him, and I stifle a sob.

His hand curls against his side. Shoulders tense. Not turning back, not quite. But I know he feels me watching. The pull between us races up like the tide, like the shadows themselves haven't yet let go.

For a flicker of a second, he tips his head—just barely. Then he keeps going. Vanishing into the house.

And that's it.

I just stand there, the weight of everything we didn't say crashing down all at once. My chest tightens.

My oldest friend, my almost-everything.

This wasn't how it was supposed to go. I imagined this moment in a hundred different ways. Not one of them felt like *this.*

The shadows may have left the arena, but one of them just walked through that door. And he took the last unspoken piece of me with him.

I run.

I run all the way back to the Spanish Steps.

CHAPTER 22

Control is not the absence of desire—it is merely command over it.
—Vikhrostrum Akademiya Doctrine of Elemental Discipline

GAVRAIL

Celeste…

She looks like she belongs somewhere warmer, wilder.

Not here—not the fog-choked lakefront of Whittaker. Not in this circus built for performance and control.

What the hell is she even doing here?

Gone is the girl I once knew, the one who used to race barefoot through the forest, the river-dweller who spoke to lakes like they were old friends. That girl was all softness and summer, untouched by cruelty or war.

But the woman standing in that arena…

She moved like moonlight sculpted by tides. Honed into a weapon by the very forces she once worshipped. Dangerous. Devastating.

There is a quiet confidence in her now—captivating in its grace. The dark waves of her hair, her sun-touched skin, eyes the color of autumn. Gods, her eyes. They are still the same piercing hazel, flickering between gold and green, like they can't decide what part of the world they want to reflect.

And her magick… I *felt* it in the arena before I even saw her. It ran through my veins like a drug I never stopped craving. Fluid and coiled. I could feel it pulsing beneath her skin like water behind a dam. Waiting. Watching.

My shadows knew the second they touched her. They always did. They always will.

Because her touch has been ingrained in my very soul, as if her water is somehow mixed into the blood currently pumping far too fast through my body.

And when I saw her standing there in front of me… *Fuck.* I felt everything I've spent years trying to bury.

She has always been beautiful, but now she is something else entirely.

The flushed curve of her throat when she said my name. That ridiculous Whittaker uniform that clung to her waist and hips like a challenge. Even the rose-petal color of her lips, catching the last of the sunset like temptation wrapped in defiance.

I wanted to pull her to me—to see if she still tasted like summer and fury. See if I could still make her fall apart the way I used to.

But then *he* grabbed her—too familiar, too entitled—and turned her away from the arena like he had the right.

He dared to touch Celeste.

My Celeste.

And the way she leaned into him—

I tasted metal. My shadows flexed at my fingertips, vicious, eager for more blood. I could've made him disappear into the dark with a single thought. I could've—

I clench my fists until nails bite skin.

Fuck. *Not. Mine. Not anymore.* But the lie lodges in my throat like a knife.

The walk to the dormitory was hell. I wanted nothing more than to rip her away from here, wrap her in shadows, and shut the rest of the world out. But instead, I walked in silence, a lifetime of unsaid words and emotions between us.

And when I heard her stifle that small, aching sob as I walked away, it nearly broke through the armor I've spent years perfecting.

I will find her. I will finally tell her the truth—the truth I've kept locked behind every silence and shadow.

All the things I should have said that night, before I disappeared from her life.

All the things I've wanted to say since then, found in the stacks of unsent letters I keep in a small pile in the bottom of my trunk.

Not to ask for forgiveness—

But because she deserves to know. *All of it.*

Even if it drowns us both to say it. Even if it doesn't fix things between us.

Especially if it doesn't.

CHAPTER 23

Elements that fuse do not easily untwine. Even when the fusion ends, the imprint remains.

—Elemental Fusion: The Art and Origin of Convergence

CELESTE

I close Noa's bedroom door behind me and lean back against it, breathless. Noa is in front of me in a heartbeat, hands grabbing my upper arms.

"Did he hurt you? I swear to gods, if he—" But he stops midsentence, catching the tear tracks left on my cheeks as I shake my head.

"No," I breathe. "He wouldn't even talk to me. For fuck's sake, he was my *best friend* for years—and he wouldn't even look at me." I absently twist the sapphire ring on my finger. "I thought I'd never see him again and now he's here and it's like we're complete strangers... like our past never happened..." I look up and see the smudges of dirt, ash, and sweat still coating Noa's face, remnants of the duel. "Oh my gods—Noa! Are *you* okay? That was insane. Watching you…" Words are lost to me. I don't know how to describe everything I'm feeling.

He shrugs slightly, brushing it off. "I'm fine. I was more worried about you—about everyone else. A duel should *never* involve outsiders. People could have gotten hurt…" He trails off, a slight sneer curling his mouth. "But your little *boyfriend* didn't leave a scratch."

I look up into his face, etched with worry, anger, pride, and something deeper. Something fierce and raw. Unshakable.

This. *This* is what I need right now.

I don't think. I reach up and kiss him.

At first, he's still—like kissing a statue. But I press closer, sliding my tongue against the seam of his lips, and he groans.

And the dam breaks.

He moves like wildfire, pressing my back up against the door as he kisses me back with heat, with hunger, with something desperate. A month of unsaid words and buried emotions crash between us, all igniting at once. It's not soft. It's not careful.

Noa lifts me like I weigh nothing and carries me over to the bed, never taking his lips from mine. We kick off our shoes, and our clothes fall away like ash, left in a discarded heap on the wood floor.

When I'm completely naked before him, he looks at me with something close to reverence before pushing me back onto the bed. Then he drops to his knees in front of me, grabbing me with a force that makes me gasp as he pulls me to the edge. He lifts one of my legs over his shoulder, pressing hot kisses to the sensitive skin of my inner thigh, licking, sucking, marking.

Then the other leg is braced on his opposite shoulder, and he looks up at me from between my thighs. The look he gives me is full of smoke and lust and possession as he slowly starts to use his tongue to spread me until he reaches that sensitive node. Slowly, torturously, drawing slow circles until he finds the spot that makes me cry out. He nips at me, playful, wicked, and then dives in like a man starved.

Oh gods... I've missed him. This. Us.

The fire builds fast, too fast—I'm not ready for it—and I'm already unraveling, thread by thread, coming apart at the seams with his name on my lips.

"Please, Noa," I pant.

He knows exactly what I'm asking for. He moves over me, eyes locked on mine. The heavy heat of him between my legs. And this time, there is no holding back. He pushes into me in one solid, hard thrust that knocks the air from my lungs. And gods, the feel of him. Unyielding. Filling me and stretching me to the very edge of what I can take. Our bodies perfectly aligned.

He sets a punishing rhythm—deep, relentless, consuming—our breath spiraling into ragged gasps.

He hooks one of my knees, bending it against my chest to hit an even deeper angle that makes both of us cry out. I shift upward, using the headboard for leverage as he drives into me again and again, each thrust sending sparks across my vision.

The sensation is overwhelming, and I try to anchor myself by gripping the fabric beneath me as the heat builds, trailing up my spine like a slow-burning fuse.

Each thrust steals the breath from my lungs like he's reaching for something buried beneath my skin—where magick and memory blur, where want becomes something holy.

His grip tightens—a flicker of gold at his fingertips—steadying us both as we ride the edge together. His hands leave shivers of warmth in their wake as they glide over my back, my sides, a banked flame, waiting to ignite. My touch changes too: silken, cool, like water poured over fire, flowing over his skin in fluid temptation.

I kiss him again, and the air itself seems to respond, steam rising as the world around us blurs at the edges. He watches me like he's about to come undone.

I reach out, letting my fingers skim his chest, leaving trails of water that drip down, only to evaporate with a hiss as the embers beneath his skin surge forward. He inhales sharply at the sensation, his hands gripping my waist—hot and grounding—as my magick curls around his like a wave wrapping flame.

Every inch where we touch becomes a recipe of alchemy: fire to water, pressure to release, destruction to rejuvenation. Unrelenting. Consuming.

It's as if we're suspended in the eye of a storm entirely of our own making, guided only by trust and desire.

We rise together to the crest of one final wave and come crashing down in a cloud of steam and cool mist—separate, yet utterly entwined.

When it ends, we are breathless. Spent. Completely wrecked in the most perfect way.

We lie there tangled together, only the sound of our slowing breaths echoing off the walls.

* * *

I PULL on jeans from the drawer I once claimed as mine. My things are all still there. Perfectly in place. Untouched. Waiting.

"I love you," he says from behind me.

I turn, smiling. The way he's looking at me… like I might vanish. Like I'm something he dreamed and isn't sure he deserves.

His eyes are full of unsaid things—regret, fear, prayers, hope.

And love. New and fragile.

"I love you too," I whisper as I wrap my arms around his neck and he pulls me in by the waist. He cocks his head as he looks at me, as if trying to decipher the truth of my admission. So I kiss him. I kiss him like a promise, putting the truth of my feelings into that kiss so that when I finally pull away, we're both smiling.

But then a shadow flickers behind his eyes, and his smile falters, like a flame sputtering against the wind. "Cel... about that night—"

The anguish in his voice cuts sharp, slicing between us like broken glass.

"Noa—"

"No. Please. Just—let me get this out." He pulls away and looks down, shoulders tense, as if trying to wrestle stillness from the storm inside him. "I shouldn't have walked away from you. I should've stayed. Let you explain."

Guilt pools in his eyes, heavy and unshakable. I can see him weighing every word—measuring them like something he might still get wrong.

"It took me a week to realize what a monumental idiot I had been," he says quietly. "But then we got shipped out to Fort Wyenth and..." He runs a hand through his hair, looking past me and out the window before his gaze locks back on mine. "Look, I know there are things you aren't telling me—"

I move toward him, heart aching to smooth the pain tightening his jaw, the pain I put there. The pain he still wears like a shield. But he lifts a hand, halting me.

"I *know* there are things you aren't telling me," he repeats, the words rough, scraping his throat. "Maybe there are things you can't tell me. And I'm not asking for that. Not now." He looks up again, his gaze locking with mine—steady, searching. Vulnerable. "What I am asking for," he says slowly, "is that we promise not to lie to each other."

Hope and uncertainty hang between us, a fragile thread.

"Can you promise me that?"

His question reverberates through me, the ripples lapping the edges of old wounds.

I step closer—and this time, he doesn't move away.

I thread my fingers through his, drawing our hands to my chest, pressing them against my heart. Hoping the steady beat lets him see the truth.

"I promise," I whisper.

And I mean it.

* * *

WE FINISH GETTING DRESSED.

Noa goes out to talk to Finn and Ryan while I slip into the bathroom. I put some loose curls in my hair and add a touch of rouge to my lips and cheeks. Tonight matters. Everyone will be there—including visiting dignitaries, officers, and the Vikhrostrum delegation.

When I emerge, the boys turn from the bar.

Finn lets out a low whistle, that ever-present gleam now back in his eyes. "Damn, Farris, you clean up good!"

Noa looks up, eyes narrowing in appreciation. He shoves whatever article he was reading at Finn and strides toward me. "*Mine*," he growls playfully, grabbing me from behind and then reaching for my hand as he kisses me.

When we're ready to leave, Noa lets go of me to open the door just as Finn falls into step beside me and bumps my shoulder with a grin.

"Glad to have you back, Farris," he says, loud enough to be overheard. "This one's been a nightmare without you. Moody as hell, snapped at half the squad. We almost staged an intervention."

Noa doesn't react—just pushes the door open with calm precision—but I catch the flicker in his jaw, the slight pause in his movement.

The door swings shut behind us, the night air crisp with a hint of snow. Finn and Ryan walk ahead, in deep discussion about the new Vikhrostrum students. For a moment, Noa and I walk in silence—our hands brushing, then linking again like it's the most natural thing in the world.

Noa exhales softly beside me, and squeezes my hand in his. As if to remind him that I'm still here—that this is real. His fingers tighten around mine—not possessive, just certain. Like he's anchoring himself to the moment, to me. As we walk toward the quad, I know we're not just finding our way back.

This time, we're moving forward, together.

CHAPTER 24

Not all duels begin with power drawn. Some begin with a nod—and end before a hand is ever raised.

—The Art of Elemental Dueling: Principles of Discipline and Dominance

When we reach the quad, firepits flicker softly, each one ringed with smooth white stones that catch the firelight and glow faintly, a welcome warmth contrasting the frost that lingers in the air.

Overhead, strings of fairy lights crisscross the night sky, casting a golden shimmer across the gathering. In the heart of the space, long tables are draped in crisp white linens and stretched beneath the lights, gold metal chairs neatly arranged on either side. Fire magick further traps the warmth in a dome of heat.

A line of guests—students, professors, and visitors alike—are already gathered at the buffet near the back. The air is thick with the mouthwatering scent of roasted potatoes and herbcrusted tenderloin—garlic, rosemary, and the tang of red wine thread through the space.

We find seats near the center table just as Headmaster Thorne spots Noa and asks to borrow him for introductions to visiting dignitaries and high-ranking Service officers.

Noa leans down, brushing a kiss to my cheek. "I'll be right back," he whispers. His hand brushes my back, stretching out until the last second before he pulls away. Like he can't stand not to be touching me.

Finn settles beside me just as Rozsen saunters over. "Alright, fire sprite," he says, palm out, eyes narrowed.

Rozsen drops his keycard into his hand. Then his pen. Then his watch.

"Sooner or later, those sticky fingers of yours are going to get you in trouble," Finn says in mock reprimand, though the admiration in his voice is impossible to miss.

"You'd have to catch me first." She raises one eyebrow at the utter absurdity of that thought.

He only laughs, and soon they're bickering over pumpkin and buttered rolls, tallying her thefts like gamblers arguing debts. Finn swears he's up to three swipes now, but Rozsen insists he's exaggerating.

Their voices fade into the clatter of goblets and the scrape of cutlery. Not hungry, I slip away to an empty firepit in the far corner, needing a moment to breathe, to process the weight of everything from today. Across the quad, I catch Rozsen's gaze snagging on me, then flicking past my shoulder as if looking for someone.

I know she's waiting to grill me about Gavrail. The scene at the Caldera wasn't exactly private.

I twirl my ring, watching as the firelight dances off the precious stone. Something swirls inside, and for a heartbeat, I get the strangest feeling that something's been caught and held there. The ring feels oddly warm against my skin, even though the night air is cool.

"It suits you," a voice says from behind me.

I freeze as Gavrail steps beside me, clearing his throat. He looks sharp in his uniform—charcoal fabric perfectly tailored, silver commendations gleaming on his lapel. Severe and striking. Everything about him is precise. Deadly. And beautiful. The scent of smoke and leather, threaded with dark amber, curls around me like a dare.

His face still holds that controlled, expressionless mask from the arena. Everywhere except his eyes. "I owe you an apology," he says quickly, voice low, even. But there is tension there—tightly leashed, barely hidden.

I look at him, searching his face as if I can peel away every secret he's holding.

"I wasn't expecting to see you," he continues. "Not at Whittaker. And definitely not in the fighting arena." There's an edge to it, almost like a quiet accusation. Surprise sharpened into judgment. I nearly laugh. "The point is… I acted badly. And I'm sorry."

I nod, half turning away—then stop. *Fuck it.*

"I thought you were dead," I say coldly. "Or kidnapped. Or stranded in the Russian wilderness with no way to contact anyone." My words come out sharp, spiked with venom to hide the broken pieces he left behind those many years ago.

His expression doesn't change, but I see the slight flinch that crosses his face.

Good.

"Because that's the only explanation I could live with for why you never wrote. For why you just disappeared."

He opens his mouth, hesitates, then straightens. "I have no excuses. You trusted me, and I broke that trust." His voice softens just slightly. "There's more to it. A lot I want to explain,

Cel. A lot you deserve to hear. We're both here now. And I want to make it right... if you'll let me."

For a moment, he's just *him*. Not the mask, not the statue. I close my hand into a fist at my side, stopping myself from reaching for him, no matter how much some part of me wants to slide back into the gravity of what we once were to each other.

Maybe it was just a crush to him—schoolgirl affection, fleeting and innocent. But thinking that makes my heart ache.

"I heard about your father," he says. "I'm sorry, Celeste. He was a good man. All he ever wanted was to keep you safe." His tone is gentle, the words falling over me like a shadow on a sunburn. Too soft over something still raw.

He looks like he's about to say more when Rozsen walks up with two glasses of wine, saving me from myself. Her timing is too precise to be chance—as if she felt the static in the air and came to ground it. I'm grateful for the interruption and use it to try to piece my emotions back together.

"Quite the impressive display today," she says, handing me a glass before turning her attention to Gavrail. "I've never met a shadow-wielder before." Her gaze lingers—open, assessing.

"Gavrail," he says in introduction, dipping his head just slightly.

Her eyes flick to me, sharp and quick, then back to him. She smiles at him like she's harmless. "So... how exactly do you and Celeste know each other?"

My hand tightens on the glass as I fight the urge to glare at her. Instead, I just bite the inside of my cheek.

Gavrail's eyes meet mine for a heartbeat before he answers. "Childhood friends," he says, and there's the faintest hint of a smirk—like he knows exactly how thin that answer is.

Rozsen studies us both for a moment too long. "Mm" is all she says. The look she gives me lets me know she's not buying it for a second. But she lets it rest. For now.

And then she's off, leaning in with questions—about his school, his shadows, training routines, sleeping quarters—like she's simply curious, and not building a case to interrogate me with later. As the attention shifts off me, I finally exhale, letting myself listen and finding his words painting captivating images in my mind of the life he has lived since I last saw him.

He answers each question with clipped elegance, but his voice has weight, like every word is chosen deliberately and with care. Gavrail is formal, attentive, disarmingly polite. It's both infuriating and intoxicating.

Something in his voice—certainty, memory, truth—has me rooted in place.

They segue into a discussion about international recruitment, and Gavrail's tone darkens.

"In Europe, they're always preparing for the next war. Magickteers are weapons—sharpened or discarded. At least... that's how my father sees them." He glances at me on the last sentence.

"Your father's in the military?" Rozsen asks.

I answer before he can. "His father is General Neron Kamenov, the highest-ranking"—*and most ruthless*—"general in all of Eastern Europe, and head of Krovya."

They both turn to look at me.

Rozsen's brows shoot up as she lets out a low whistle. "Damn. Bet he's a blast at Christmas parties," she jokes, lightening the mood, and I'm grateful.

I can feel him before I see him—Noa's presence is warm and unmistakable. I wonder if Gavrail can, too, as his body tenses a second before I feel an arm wrap around my shoulder.

"Sorry I took so long," Noa murmurs, lips brushing the curve of my ear. "Looks like you two have been catching up?" His smile is easy, relaxed, but there's a subtle edge to his words and a threat of violence still lurking beneath the surface. "I know we met before the duel," he says to Gavrail, extending a hand, "but I don't think we were properly introduced. I'm Noa Gallegher—Cel's *boyfriend*." He emphasizes the last word. His other arm tightens over me possessively. "And you must be the ghost from her past." His grip hardens just slightly, though his tone stays smooth. "Funny thing about shadows—they only exist when something stronger is casting the light."

I kick him with the back of my heel. Annoyingly, he doesn't even flinch.

Gavrail takes his hand, ignoring the jab—but I catch the flicker across his face before that perfect, impassive mask slides back into place. Unnervingly calm. Tension crackles like a live wire in the air between them. "Your fire is... impressive," Gavrail says at last, voice even. "I've never seen anything quite like it."

Noa tries to suppress a smirk. "Well, if you hadn't blacked out the school, you'd know I was just getting started."

I kick him again—harder. This time, I know he feels it.

Gavrail's eyes sharpen, gleaming with challenge. "Perhaps we'll find a better time to finish that conversation."

The two of them lock eyes, and for a moment, the firepit isn't the only thing throwing heat.

Gavrail turns to me one last time, something tight in his expression. "Excuse me. I need to find my companions."

And with that, he's gone—back into the shadows he commands. And my eyes can't help but try to track him through the moonless dark.

CHAPTER 25

Not all wars are declared
—Vikhrostrum Akademiya Doctrine of Elemental Combat

Rozsen and Elliot corner me a few days later, forcing me to tell them *exactly* what sort of history I have with a certain third-year Vikhrostrum student.

I give them the short version—the one that doesn't make me want to drown my emotions with my own tide: childhood friends and something more. Summers of lakes and dares and secrets whispered into the dark—until he vanished without a word and left me with questions too painful to ask out loud.

Elliot's brows climb. "So let me get this straight," she says slowly, like she's assembling a crime scene. "He sleeps with you and then he just disappears?"

My cheeks burn. I don't answer fast enough, and that's answer enough.

"That bastard," Rozsen snaps, voice going razor-thin. Her hand clenches around the strap of her bag like she needs something to do with her anger. "Want me to light his textbooks on fire?"

A laugh punches out of me—until I realize she's not joking. My face sobers. "Rozsen—no."

She leans in anyway, eyes flinty, protective in a way that makes my chest ache. "I'm serious, Celeste. If he *ever* hurts you again, I'll make it my problem."

Elliot exhales like she's trying not to grin. "I'll provide the alibi."

"You two are insane," I mutter, but my voice softens. Then I set my jaw. "It wasn't like that, and it happened a long time ago now. And besides… I'm no longer his to lose anymore."

But even saying it out loud makes something coil tight and sharp beneath my ribs.

Noa, Ryan, and Finn spend much of their downtime grumbling about the newcomers' brooding presence in their advanced classes. The delegates carry Vikhrostrum like a dark banner across Whittaker. Gavrail most of all. Every glance, every silence, a reminder that I don't know him anymore. That maybe I never did.

"No sense of humor," I overhear Finn mutter, leaning back against the bleachers in the Training Room.

He spent the better part of that morning orchestrating a subtle prank on the Vikhrostrum wind-wielder—positioning himself just behind the practice zone and quietly redirecting the backdrafts of his own wind magick into the path of the delegate's attacks. Each blast meant for the dummy curled back in midair, launching sand and grit into the poor boy's face again and again. It took half an hour before the Vikhrostrum student realized what was happening. He spun on his heel, shouted something furious in Russian, and stormed off the field with the wind still kicking up behind him.

Noa smirks but doesn't comment. Neither do I. There's a quiet understanding between us now, a solidness that feels earned, not assumed. It isn't just routine—though we have one. Lunches together in the mess hall. Potions on Thursdays. Sundays in the Training Room. Then nights curled up on his sofa with textbooks between us—or in his bed, the rest of the world shut out.

After that night at the Steps, when we crossed that final barrier, we learned it was never really about control. It was about trust. In myself. In each other.

Since then, the heat between us hasn't cooled, but it's changed into something refined. Rooted. The burn is constant, but it's also steady—a flame that knows its shape. I smile inwardly, replaying this morning's fire-laced shower, his hands on my hips, the tile wall at my back, his breath against my throat.

It feels natural now—easy—but deeper too. Like we're not just falling; we're choosing. Every day. I don't question his hand when it finds mine beneath the table. He doesn't second-guess my silences.

There's love here, growing between us like ivy—steadfast, entwined, a little wild. I can't imagine the shape of my days without him.

Gavrail, on the other hand, remains distant.

We pass occasionally in the halls of the Logistics building, or I catch him across the mess hall. Sometimes he'll give me a single nod. Other times not even that. And still, each time, my chest tightens like a fist.

The night of the duel he said there were things he wanted to tell me, to explain... but he hasn't tried to talk to me since that night.

Fuck him.

I hate how aware of him I am. The way the air shifts when he enters a room—cooler, sharper, like my skin recognizes him before my eyes do. The way my ears strain for his voice even when he isn't speaking to me.

And worse—how many others notice him too.

He's rarely alone, always flanked by two other Vikhrostrum students: Tsvetan and Teodor.

Tsvetan Dragiev is brooding and silent, tall and broad-shouldered like most of the Vikhrostrum delegation. But where others might carry themselves with arrogance, Tsvetan moves like a weapon sheathed in discipline. His eyes are sharp, the kind that miss nothing. Burn scars cross one cheek and criss-cross over his hands, deep and unforgiving, a story untold etched into skin. He rarely speaks, but when he does, his words are careful, chosen like weapons.

Teo Volkov, on the other hand, is sunlight in human form. Golden-brown hair, warm brown eyes that sparkle with mischief, as handsome as he is infuriatingly charming. Everything about him seems effortless: the way he leans in when he talks to you, the way he tosses out compliments like rose petals—beautiful, fleeting, and without pressure. He flirts shamelessly with me, Rozsen, and half of the school, honestly—but never crosses a line. It's playful, not predatory. Disarming, even. There's an ease to him, a warmth that draws people in before they even realize they've stepped closer.

Rozsen has already fallen for it once or twice—frazzled and hurried mornings caught sneaking out of the Ivy House rooms. Something that clearly annoys Finn, though he's never said a word to her.

The entire Vikhrostrum delegation is striking in their own way. Intimidating. Deadly. You can practically feel the power that drips through their veins when you pass them in the halls. But no one draws more stares than Gavrail—lethal beauty laced with shadow, tall and dark, every line of him cut sharp enough to wound. And then there's the element he wields—shadow itself. Rare. Alluring. Mysterious. Darkness and secrets cling to him like a second skin, drawing you closer in the hopes that you might be able to hear their whispers as they trail after him. The most powerful shadow-wielder of our generation. Maybe even of the last century.

Students can't help but drift toward him in corridors and commons, laughter too loud, voices pitched just for his notice. They pretend not to watch him, but I can feel it—the collective hitch in breath, the way magick hums differently around him, darker, denser. He never encourages their attention. Barely even looks their way. But he doesn't push them off either—and that indifference, that quiet power, only makes him more dangerous. More irritatingly irresistible.

Every time I walk past him, I feel… restless. I find myself clenching my fists so often when I'm near him that my nails have left half-moons in my palms. After History once, we had to pass each other in a crowded narrow hall, shoulders almost brushing. I swear I could feel his shadows pressing against me for a moment, like a secret against my skin, his body turning slightly toward mine—but then he walked past, silent, giving nothing away. The corner of his mouth tipped up just slightly, like some private joke.

I tell myself it's his indifference that infuriates me—that blank mask, that weaponized quiet—but sometimes, when his eyes flick to mine across campus, it feels like more than indifference. Like a storm pressed against glass. Like I'm standing trial for a crime I don't remember committing.

On Thursday, outside the mess hall line, I mutter under my breath before I can stop myself. "Do you ever smile, Gavrail? Or is that beneath you now?"

His silver eyes catch mine. Cool, impassive. He stops close enough that the space between us feels charged. He tilts his head, one corner of his mouth catching—then, quietly, in a low voice I almost don't hear: "Give me a reason to, Zvez."

An amused smirk tugs at his lips. Shadows gather at his shoulders, alive and waiting, and I realize it's not only his magick that listens to him—it's the air, the light, and the part of me that should know better.

He turns away, his childhood nickname for me a slow burn on his tongue, leaving me scorched and unsteady. *Zvez*, short for *Zvezda*—meaning *Star* in Bulgarian.

I watch him walk away, my pulse betraying me—racing for all the wrong reasons, and definitely for the wrong man.

CHAPTER 26

Stay light. Hit hard. Leave them breathless
—Elemental Mastery IV: Command of Wind and Sky

The next duel is set for Monday—the last week of classes before the holidays. Finn will be challenging Tsvetan, the Vikhrostrum fire-wielder.

When the final bell rings, the tide of students surges toward the highest point on campus. The Mountain's wind is already biting with cold, screaming, sharp, and restless. The stone circle looms at the center, monolithic and silent—watching. Waiting. Someone has already cleared the snow from the summit. Pushing it out wide, creating a smooth lip around us—like a tiny amphitheater carved in white. Fire magick warms the edges of the crowd, but it doesn't stop the cold from seeping in.

I stand with my squad at the west end of the circle and my eyes find him instantly.

Gavrail.

He stands across from us, near the dueling boundary line

with his year-mates, dark coat billowing in the afternoon wind. The late sun lights across his face, catching the hard lines of his jaw, the dark stubble shadowing it—a perfect, infuriating contrast to the silver of his eyes. Gods, he looks good, even from here. Untouchable. Dangerous. Entirely *him*.

A group of second-year Whittaker girls stands near, giggling and desperate for his and Teo's attention. I roll my eyes, the urge to make a snowbank fall on top of their heads impossibly tempting at the moment.

His eyes flick my way, just once. The curve of his mouth flickers, almost as if he knows where my thoughts have gone—a ghost of a smirk, gone in an instant before his gaze cuts back to the arena.

Warmth envelops me as Noa steps behind, his strong arms pulling me in while he nuzzles my neck. I lean into him—cedar, mint, clove. His fire is just below the surface of his skin, burning away my irritation and drawing every thought toward him.

I turn as his hands slip inside my coat, smiling as he presses a soft kiss against my lips before turning us back to the field. He keeps one hand inside my coat, moving it through layers of fabric until his hand finds the small of my back, tracing circles against flushed skin. I bite my bottom lip as his hand dips lower, a reminder of just where those fingers and everything else of his claimed me this morning.

A knowing smile curves his mouth as he glances down at me. "You keep biting that lip and we'll miss Finn's duel while I take you for a private tour of the Air Hall below."

"Is that a promise?" I murmur, leaning closer.

He only laughs, the sound rumbling through his chest before he kisses me again—heat curling through me all the way to my toes.

A prickling sensation creeps across my skin, a feeling of being watched. I glance across the field and meet Gavrail's narrowed eyes for just a heartbeat before he looks away. His shadows quiver faintly at his feet as if readying for battle.

Professor Stroud's voice booms, carried on the wind like a loudspeaker, pulling my focus back to the summit. "The second duel is about to begin!"

The crowd surges forward, every gaze drawn to the stone circle.

Finn stands at the center, rolling his shoulders, bouncing lightly on the balls of his feet, cocky grin in place as he faces Tsvetan across the ring. "Ready when you are, firefly," he calls out, twirling a gust of wind between his fingers.

Tsvetan doesn't answer. He just lifts one scarred hand, slow and precise, fire blooming along his palm with a deep, molten glow. Controlled. Focused. No theatrics.

Professor Stroud gives the signal, and the duel begins.

Finn is fast. He launches himself into motion, slicing the air with blasts of wind designed to disorient and harass. Dirt kicks up, elements colliding in midair, heat and chill lashing through the circle.

Tsvetan blasts fireballs, just barely missing Finn's feet, scorching stones in a spiral pattern with unrelenting precision while Finn nimbly weaves around them, sending gusts of slicing wind at angles the fire-wielder can't seem to anticipate. A few wind blasts catch Tsvetan's shoulder, pushing him back a few steps. Finn's smirk is confident. He's fast—too fast. The crowd murmurs in surprise and admiration.

Finn's hands lift, and the air itself begins to tighten. The crowd falls silent as wind magick condenses, compressing the oxygen until Tsvetan's flames sputter and die, snuffed out mid-motion.

Smoke coils low and thick across the ground, curling up Tsvetan's legs like shadows with teeth. A hush spreads—Finn has stolen the very breath from the air.

"Try burning something now," he mutters, eyes gleaming.

And for a time, it looks like he has the upper hand.

A burst of compressed wind slams into Tsvetan, and Finn uses the opening to close in—until Tsvetan smiles.

It isn't a kind smile.

Finn catches it too late. The placement of scorched stones. The subtle shifts in Tsvetan's footwork. A ring of ash tightening like a noose. I see it the moment before it happens.

Tsvetan has been playing chess, not checkers.

A crack sounds as red light spills through thin, spiderwebbing fractures in the stones below them, and the air pulses with sudden heat. The oxygen begins to creep back in, sucked greedily into the vacuum Finn just made.

And just like that—*everything ignites.*

Flames erupt in a spiral pattern from the earth below him that Finn didn't see coming, snaring his path and trapping him mid-stride. Fire coils up around his legs, searing-hot and fast. His wind falters as his panic flares. He tries to leap out with a gust of wind, to twist away—but the fire only surges higher, burning across his legs and pulling him back in like a snare.

There is a sharp, sickening crack as Finn hits the ground hard, smoke curling around him. His left arm lies at an irregular angle at his side. He doesn't cry out, but his eyes squeeze shut in pain.

"Enough!"

Professor Stroud's voice slices through the magick-thick air. The flames die in an instant, as if snuffed out by a god's breath. The silence that follows is worse than the noise.

Rozsen is the first to move. She breaks past the perimeter line without permission, barely seeming to register the shouted protests. Her knees hit the ground beside Finn, frantic. Noa and I are close behind her.

"Finn, hey—hey. Look at me," she murmurs, brushing singed curls from his forehead. Stroud and Professor Neris are down beside him in an instant, taking stock of the damage in clipped, hushed voices.

"I'm fine," he lies through a wince. "Just... dramatic flare. Get it? Flair? Flare?" He tries to smile—then sucks in a breath as Neris's hands find the worst of it. His shoulder sits wrong, arm shaking as he tries to shift. He draws another breath and chokes on a groan. Rozsen tries to roll her eyes at his attempt at humor, but I can see the worry in her face. She goes quiet, staring at his injuries—like if she looks hard enough, she can undo them.

Stroud's gaze flicks over Finn, fast and grim. "Shoulder's dislocated. Possible rib fractures. The burns..." His mouth tightens. "Madame Ching will deal with those."

"I should've seen it," Finn finally mutters, voice hoarse. "He baited me. Played me."

"You don't always have to win, Finn," Rozsen says softly, barely audible over the dying wind.

"Thought I had him," Finn mumbles, voice raw.

Rozsen swallows, reaching for his hand. "You just had the wrong game."

Stroud interrupts. "We need to get him to the infirmary."

"I've got him," Noa says quickly, sliding an arm beneath Finn's shoulders, his eyes daring anyone to argue.

As they help him to his feet, Finn winces, face going shock-white, leaning into Noa as they guide him out of the circle.

Behind us, the arena stays quiet—no cheers, no whistles. Only scorched earth and the ugly truth: these aren't matches. They're lessons.

Whittaker. Vikhrostrum. Different crests, same purpose—to create soldiers.

And maybe one day we won't meet on an arena at all.

Maybe we'll face each other across a battlefield, with no one there to stop the bleeding.

CHAPTER 27

Some holds are meant to subdue. Others are meant to test how long one chooses not to submit.

—Combat Theory I: Foundations of Defense

The Training Room falls silent as the Vikhrostrum delegates file in. The rows of polished wooden bleachers have been pushed back, revealing an elevated platform with a thick tan sparring mat at its center. Radiating out are the black rectangular training mats that have been moved into a pattern like spokes of a wheel.

Whittaker students press in around the perimeter—close, curious, and tense. The collective body heat and tang of iron from the stacked weights in the corner is a sharp contrast to the icy-cold wind tapping at the windows above.

At the front, Headmaster Thorne stands between two Vikhrostrum students: Gavrail and Tsvetan. I swallow, my eyes tracing the way light glances off the lines of his forearms. The silver in his eyes cuts brighter today as he scans the room—restless, searching. For something. Or maybe someone.

Thorne addresses the gathered crowd. "The Vikhrostrum delegates have agreed to a showcase of sorts, to share with us some of their combat training and tactics from their own school. We are honored with the chance to learn from and observe them in action."

The two friends enter the ring and bow to each other. Tsvetan's stance is impossibly still, feet shoulder-width apart, relaxed, eyes hooded. But Gavrail—he looks like he was born for this. Shoulders coiled, ready. A weapon waiting to be drawn. Controlled tension held beneath the sharp planes of muscle. Like shadow folded into flesh. He cracks his neck with slow precision.

No magick, no elements. Just bone, muscle, and lethal intent.

A nod from the headmaster, and they begin.

Tsvetan flicks out the first strike—a lightning-fast jab aimed at Gavrail's ribs. It connects with a hard thud, and Gavrail's shoulders dip on the impact. He inhales sharply, eyes narrowing. But he doesn't fall back.

He breathes in once—slowly.

Then retaliates.

He drops low, sweeping for Tsvetan's feet. Tsvetan dodges, coiling away from the sweep, and a knee slams into Gavrail's side as he rises. A lesser fighter would've stumbled.

But not Gavrail.

He shifts, pivots, and strikes.

The room seems to shrink around them, the scrape of bare feet on canvas loud in the silence, every impact echoing sharp against the walls. He moves so fast it's like trying to capture lightning mid-strike—impossible to see where one move lands before another one begins.

Gavrail comes back with a feint—a straight punch that whistles toward Tsvetan's guard. Tsvetan bites, throwing up a block.

Exactly what Gavrail wants. Gavrail catches him by the forearm and yanks him in close, knee snapping up—too close for Tsvetan to slip—before a devastating hook buries itself in his ribs. The air hisses from Tsvetan's lungs, and his stance finally falters.

The crowd sees brilliance. I see calculation. That faint tightening of his mouth, as if Tsvetan's pain was inevitable. As if Gavrail decided the ending long before it began. If last week's duel proved Tsvetan to be an expert at chess and manipulation, then Gavrail is a grandmaster—knowing precisely how to unmake someone, piece by piece.

Sensing the opening, Gavrail pivots on his lead foot and whips a knife-hand across the side of Tsvetan's head—ear and jawline—so vicious, it sends a hush through the crowd as Tsvetan's head snaps back. His eyes glass over for a heartbeat, then sharpen as he jerks his head side to side, like he's trying to force his vision to steady.

Gavrail steps in, pressing his advantage, strike after strike. Each move looks effortless. He's not reacting—he's directing. Controlling the pace. The space.

A jab to the shoulder. A cross to the chest. A brutal front kick to the gut that caves Tsvetan forward with a raw groan—

—and then Gavrail has him. Wrist trapped, balance stolen. One smooth turn and Tsvetan is airborne for a heartbeat before he slams onto the mat, the impact reverberating through the space. Gavrail follows him down, never letting go.

For a moment, Tsvetan just lies there, sucking air. Gavrail holds the lock until Tsvetan's hand hovers, then taps twice in quick surrender.

Gavrail releases him instantly and rises, breathing evenly, every muscle coiled but relaxed. A body meant for fighting, and winning.

A hush falls, broken by Headmaster Thorne's voice: "Gavrail wins. Well fought."

Whittaker students erupt into cheers. Even the Vikhrostrum delegates allow themselves a quiet nod of respect. Gavrail offers his hand; Tsvetan takes it and pushes to his feet.

It's clear the Vikhrostrum students hold the edge in pure physical combat—their movements executed with military precision, each strike as deadly as it is flawless, showcasing them as weapons honed to perfection.

Headmaster Thorne steps forward. "We will continue with the next challenger—except I have a surprise for my Whittaker students. I've arranged for each Vikhrostrum delegate to now select a *Whittaker* opponent of their own choosing."

A ripple of nervous laughter and eager shouts runs through the crowd as some Whittaker students—pulsing with adrenaline—step up to the ring, offering themselves in challenge.

Thorne gestures. "Tsvetan—choose."

Tsvetan's dark eyes lock on Noa. He inclines his head once. Noa steps forward, jaw set. The crowd parts for him, whispers trailing, but all I see is the controlled fury in his stride. A charged silence. The look in Noa's eye is beyond deadly. Ready to pay back Tsvetan for what he did to Finn at the Mountain.

One by one, each delegate selects an opponent. Jazz grins and bounds off to a black mat, squaring up near the gym doors. The room is now divided up into little rings of combat.

Finally, Gavrail stands up next to Headmaster Thorne. Still. Focused. A blade in its sheath. He scans the crowd again.

Until his eyes lock on mine.

A slow, unmistakable smirk tugs at the corner of his lips. Confident. Inevitable. Like he knew exactly where I'd be standing. "Her," he says, with a slight nod in my direction.

The word slams into me like a strike. My breath catches, a sharp, involuntary sound.

Rozsen's hand finds my shoulder—steadying. "Breathe," she murmurs, eyes flicking toward where Noa disappeared with Tsvetan, as if willing him to come back and put a stop to this.

Hushed whispers from the crowd surround me, some derisive, others hungry for spectacle. I catch Stella's quiet sniggers and hushed insults through the chatter.

My heart hammers as I walk toward him.

Thorne raises his hand. "Celeste is a first-year, and while I'm sure she's talented, her skills will not be up to task."

"I choose *her*," Gavrail says, sharp, clipped, with conviction.

Thorne's gaze sharpens, flicking between us. He studies Gavrail—calculating—then me—curious. For a breathless moment, I think he'll refuse. But then he steps back and nods. "You may accept or decline the challenge, Miss Farris. The decision is yours."

I try to draw in a steadying breath as I stand next to the ring, looking up at Gavrail. He doesn't blink. He doesn't move. But his eyes hold a challenge. He's *daring* me. Like when he dared me to jump off that waterfall when I was thirteen. Or when we took a joy ride in his father's treasured restored Volga on his sixteenth birthday.

My eyes narrow. "I accept." It comes out more growl than speech.

Out of the corner of my eye, I see Thorne smile, like he's just been handed a gift, a spectacle that he's been wanting to see.

Gavrail offers me a hand to pull me up and I take it. His grip is warm, infallible, a tether I don't dare trust. A spark runs from his palm into mine, quick and charged, as if the touch means more than it should. I pull my hand away the instant my feet hit the platform, before the current can root itself deeper.

He waits for me to set my feet before extending a hand to me, two fingers curling toward himself to tell me to begin.

I stand on the mat, shoulders squaring with determination. And then I rush him—remembering Noa's words:

"You're small, Celeste. Use it to your advantage. Strike first and you can dictate the tempo. Your opponent will then be reacting to you,

rather than you *reacting to* them. *You want to get inside their reach to deny them the space they need to build force against you."*

My muscle memory from my Sunday drills with Noa takes over—jab, feint, low kick.

Gavrail shifts only a fraction, deflecting each blow on rigid forearms and solid shoulders. He never strikes. He simply remains immovable—precision in-fucking-carnate.

I pivot and press in again—two quick punches to his guard, a snap kick aimed at his ribs. He absorbs them easily, his feet barely moving. He seems to anticipate every strike, every step, as if he knows exactly what I'm about to do before I do it. His eyes—cool and assessing—narrow a fraction, a small smile on his beautiful face. *Damn him.* My breath quickens. I continue my barrage of punches and kicks against his wall of stone, tiring as I do so, slowly running out of breath.

He's *studying* me. Letting me exhaust myself. Letting me *try*.

My knuckles sting, frustration burning hotter than exertion. Sweat trickles into my eyes, salt stinging as my chest heaves. And still his gaze tracks me, like a judge waiting for the guilty to confess.

I lunge one last time—a desperate overhand punch. Overextended and reckless.

That's when he finally moves.

Gavrail's hand closes on my wrist. His grip is iron, callouses scraping my skin as if he could brand me with touch alone. In a single fluid motion, he twists, pulling me around until my back slams against his chest. The breath punches from my lungs and a startled sound escapes me—a low gasp, half snarl, half something else. His arm is locked around my middle, my pulse thundering in my ears. He has me. I can feel his breath, warm at my neck.

For a heartbeat, the world narrows to the heat between us and the solid weight of him behind me. My body betrays me—

fire flaring where fear should be. And he fucking knows it. *Bastard.*

"Glad to see you're better at this than when we were children," he says quietly into the shell of my ear, his voice dark velvet. "But you still leave your left side open."

And I can feel him. *All* of him. The hard lines of his body against the soft curves of mine. Restraint so potent it crackles.

Anger and something more flares under my skin. I surge again, feinting to stamp his instep and disrupt his stance, driving my heel as hard as I can into the side of his knee. His weight jerks, leg buckling. His knee hits the mat, and for one second, he's down. I twist—

His hand clamps around my waist. The world tilts. The floor rushes up, and he follows me down like a shadow—heavy, relentless—until his hips pin mine, owning my center of gravity, and I'm left staring up at him, breath gone.

He leans down, the corner of his mouth ghosting my ear. "If you wanted me on my knees, Celeste, you could have just asked. You and I both know I'm *perfectly* comfortable in that position when it comes to you."

Oh my fucking gods. Did he seriously just—

I bridge hard, trying to throw him off, but his hold is unrelenting. "Glad to see you're still just as cocky," I hiss through clenched teeth.

"Correct," he says, that infuriating smirk back in place.

Time stretches—muscle memory and emotion colliding—until the clear, sharp sound of a throat clearing cuts through the air.

Noa.

I startle. He's there at the edge of the platform, standing with a winded Tsvetan, who is sporting a blooming black eye and clutching his elbow. Match won, Noa's arms are crossed, eyes dark with warning.

Gavrail releases me. He offers a hand to help me up, giving a slight bow of his head as he does so—mocking or respectful, I can't tell.

I step off the platform and walk to Noa's side. My heart races as adrenaline courses through me. Noa stands next to me but doesn't touch me as he glares at Gavrail from across the ring.

Behind us, Headmaster Thorne raises his hand for silence, ready to call the next match.

I'm flushed in a way that makes my skin feel too tight, too sensitive. I glance up at Noa. His jaw is clenched, posture forcibly relaxed even though the tension in his arms suggests otherwise. I press my hand to his. He glances down—relief and something darker flickering across his face—then turns toward the next challenge.

My skin is still charged with the memory of Gavrail's strength against me, Noa's silent warning echoing in my head. I draw a steadying breath, as if trying to make my traitorous body forget what it's feeling. The biological betrayals I refuse to acknowledge.

I hate that even now, I still seem to know the shape of him.

CHAPTER 28

Some remnants of magick are not lost; they merely change form—into scars, into relics, into reckoning. Waiting to be discovered once more.

—Foundations of Arcanarchaeology, Vol. I

It takes Finn the entire holiday break to recover. All of us take turns visiting him in the infirmary beside the Administration building.

Christmas break at Whittaker is quiet in the way snow makes everything quiet. Headmaster Thorne doesn't do holidays—no campus leave without special permission, no school-hosted parties. Not officially.

Gods help us if anyone tries to celebrate something that isn't a duel or a near-death experience.

I leave my dorm with my mother's voice still in my ear—*I miss you, sweetheart*—and a tightness in my throat. It's my first Christmas without my father, and the guilt of leaving my mother to spend it alone tugs hard enough to make my chest ache.

Noa is waiting at the bottom of the stairs like he belongs there. Like winter can't touch him. It must be some unfair fire-wielder advantage—sun-warm skin in the dead of December, turquoise eyes bright as if he's carrying his own light.

They soften when he sees me. He doesn't ask what my mother said or how I'm feeling. But he knows. Somehow he knows. Instead, he just hooks his hand around mine and squeezes—steady, warm, grounding—then walks with me across the quad like it's the simplest thing in the world to hold me together.

We already exchanged gifts yesterday. I gave him a small box of personally modified potions, salves, and tinctures—for burns, bruises, and whatever stupid heroics he insists on doing. He gave me a signed book by my favorite alchemist and potion master, Dr. Sage Davenport, like he'd reached into my head and pulled out the one thing I didn't realize I needed.

The infirmary is the only place on campus that dares to look like Christmas. The air smells like mint and antiseptic, sharp with sterility, but Madame Nahira Ching—the school nurse, a light Magick, and Professor Ching's wife—has threaded warmth into it anyway. A small pine sits near the front desk, its branches hung with tiny glass charms that catch her magick and scatter it in soft prisms across the walls. Above the beds, an intricate lattice of light magick drifts in slow loops—constellations stitched between gold and silver streamers, gentle as breath.

Rows of crisp white beds stretch wall to wall. A fountain in the corner trickles over smooth stone in a steady cadence that barely muffles the low groans of the injured. Nearly every bed is filled now—the aftermath of the Vikhrostrum "showcase."

Professor Ching's words drift back to me.

Spectacle has a habit of becoming consequence.

Finn is propped up against a mound of pillows like a reluctant prisoner, arm in a sling, ribs wrapped, burns fading from angry red to tender pink. He looks better than he did before.

Rozsen strides in first and drops a paper holiday crown onto his head like she's knighting him.

Finn squints up at her. "If you've come to mock me, at least bring tribute."

"I did." Rozsen produces a wrapped bundle with a flourish. "Stolen bread pudding from the dining hall. Don't ask how."

Ryan follows with two steaming cups. "Hot cocoa," he says, offering one.

Finn eyes the cup suspiciously.

"We didn't poison it," Rozsen says, then tilts her head. "Well… *I* didn't poison it."

Before Finn can respond, she throws herself onto the side of his bed like it belongs to her. Finn makes a pained sound and awkwardly tries to make space that doesn't exist. His gaze flicks to her face, then away—but his mouth betrays him, softening at the corners.

"When do you get to stop playing patient?" Rozsen asks, already raiding the candy stash someone else left on his bedside table.

"I'm not playing," Finn mutters. He jerks his chin toward the sling. "I'm actually injured. In case you couldn't tell."

"You're still annoyingly unavailable for sparring." Rozsen sighs like she's mourning a tragedy. "Ryan's doing his best—good lad—but alas… it's just not the same."

Ryan's brows lift. "Wow. Rude."

Noa's mouth twitches like he's trying not to smile. He sets a tin on Finn's bedside table. "Celeste made you this. Emberveil… with a few of her own modifications."

"I added frostbloom thistle," I say, stepping closer. "And a few things for inflammation. It'll help with swelling and pain on top of healing the burns."

Finn lifts a brow. "I knew we kept you around for a reason."

He smiles then—his first real one. "A brilliant alchemist *and* a water Magick to boot."

Noa's arm loops around my waist immediately, pulling me into his side. "Hands off," he tells Finn, dry as dust. "She's already taken."

Finn snorts. "Only because you saw her first," he teases before looking around at our little half-circle. "So now you're all my handlers?"

"Correct," Rozsen says, patting his crown. "Try not to die out of spite."

Finn groans, but he's still smiling.

I hover at the foot of the bed, watching the bandages, the healing skin, the faint wince on Finn's face when he adjusts his sling. My stomach twists.

It was Tsvetan—Gavrail's friend—who did this. And I watched it happen. I saw the scorched pattern under Finn's feet, saw the trap tightening, and didn't do anything to stop it. The guilt clings to me like the frost that coats the campus every morning—cold, stubborn, impossible to shake.

Noa shifts closer behind me, reading me like he always does now. His hand slides to the small of my back—subtle, protective—and his thumb presses one slow circle through my sweater. When I lean back into him, his chin dips briefly to my temple.

"He's going to be just fine," he murmurs, so low only I can hear.

Rozsen turns bright as poison. "Merry Christmas, Finnian."

Finn squints. "I hate when you call me that. Also—that *tone* means you're ten seconds away from stealing something."

Rozsen smiles. "Already did."

"What?"

She taps his paper crown. "Your dignity."

Finn growls at her, but his eyes are bright.

Above us, Madame Ching's light constellations drift in slow loops, throwing soft gold across Finn's too-white sheets, turning a room made for injuries into something almost gentle. Noa's hand stays warm at my back, steady as a heartbeat, and for a few minutes—cocoa steaming, Rozsen bickering with Finn like it's her religion, the fountain tinkling in the corner—it almost feels like a real Christmas.

* * *

THE TREES on campus are now bare and brittle, their branches often rimmed with snow from the night before. Lake Caldrith's smooth surface is beginning to surrender to winter's grasp. A delicate sheen of ice shimmers across the surface—thin, fragile, not yet solid, but enough to dull the water's usual luster.

Noa and I spend much of our break in the Cavern, warming up in the natural hot springs while enjoying private moments in his officers' quarters in the furthest chamber. At least in here, I know I won't accidentally run into a certain silver-eyed student Which means I can truly relax—or at least pretend to.

The afternoon got away from me today; I lost track of time in the Potions lab before rushing to meet Noa. I pause at the Crystal Cavern pool, taking in the icicles now sparkling above it like crystal daggers. A light dusting of snow glistens over the surface from the open sky above. Oddly, the water here doesn't freeze, nor does the snow just melt into it, but instead hovers like a breath made of stardust, its tiny, perfect flakes catching the light from above and below.

The pool's song tugs at me like it always does—a louder, deeper whisper these days. I step closer, boots crunching on frost, crossing the runed circle that surrounds it. My gaze drifts to the rocks scattered like a crumbling wall just above the waterline on the left.

Something carved into the stones catches the light: three interlaced symbols, half buried in lichen and veined with mineral deposits. I kneel, breath fogging the air, and look closer.

Curious, I tug off my glove and brush away the frost, then peel the moss away from the stones. The carvings are even more beautiful up close—weathered, yes, but still pulsing with some long-buried intention.

The first is chipped and faded but I can just make out a long, curling tail that, on closer inspection, resolves into the hidden silhouette of a mermaid in profile. The shape is familiar somehow.

Beside it is a crescent shape above a spiral of concentric waves, like a moon standing guard over the ocean.

The third is softer: a circular bloom of petals over ripples of lines, as though a water lily steadfastly tied to a lake floor has been impressed into the rock and forever frozen there.

I lean closer, fingertips tracing the shapes carved into the stone. What stories lie hidden here? What history was made only to later be forgotten?

Then I spot it.

A fourth symbol. Half submerged in the water. Almost invisible beneath the thin dusting of snow piled against the edge.

I lean forward, heart quickening, and reach out. My skin brushes the wet stone—just barely—and my fingertip slips into the surface of the pool.

The reaction is instant.

The water jerks back, like a creature startled. Waves ripple out from where I touched it, sharp and concentric, smacking against the carved rocks like a warning.

A jolt shoots up my arm. Cold fire surges through me, sharp enough to steal my breath. I yank my hand back, stumbling slightly. Images fog at the edges of my vision, too fast and fleeting to hold on to: a tall hooded figure. A child. A night sky.

For a second, I swear I see something shimmer beneath the surface—a faint outline, a glimmering symbol just out of reach. Light flaring out to multiple points, like a star…

I clutch my fingers to my chest, heart pounding.

What the fuck was that?

Was it trying to speak to me?

Or did it just push me away?

The pool's surface stills, calm again, as if nothing happened.

Maybe I imagined it. Or maybe I wasn't supposed to touch it.

A place of ancient magick buried deep. I can still feel it, sleeping… perhaps waiting for the right time, or the right *person*.

A soft cough echoes from the chamber behind me. Noa's here.

My gaze lingers on the carving of the mermaid one last time —her tail curling like a question.

I grab my glove from the stone floor and rise, turning toward him. The water is calm now, but the ripple still echoes beneath my skin.

I follow Noa back to where the curling steam beckons—but part of me continues to listen, in case the water has more it wants to say.

CHAPTER 29

Elemental lines, once merged, do not fade. They always recognize each other, awakening when the other draws near.

—Traces in the Tide: Water in Elemental Practice

January comes, and with it, a few new classes are added to the first-year load—Defensive Warding and Shielding, along with Arcanarchaeology. I also signed up for the Botany elective held in the Garden Grove, Amelia having sparked my curiosity about various plants and their uses in potion-making.

Winter is now in full command, blanketing the ground in snow and ice. The cold bites so deep that stepping outside steals the feeling from your face entirely—like the world itself has turned to glass and silence.

With the start of the school session comes the announcement of the third elemental duel. This one takes place in the Grotto in honor of the two challengers, both water Magicks.

The Grotto is a wide cavern filled with shifting pools,

glowing from beneath with bioluminescent light. Voices are swallowed by the immense space, and bridges of slick stone and floating platforms form unstable pathways between the pools. The sound of dripping echoes endlessly, a constant reminder of movement. Everything flows—nothing remains the same.

All the bridges converge onto a single large platform at the center of the cave, its surface paved with white river stones, arranged like a constellation beneath the feet of those who stand there. The water training and dueling grounds whisper of change—fluid, persistent, and endlessly deep. It feels as though the cave sees everything and remembers it all.

Professor Darwyn Ashar stands just off to the side of the platform, cloaked in his usual stillness. His black hair is slicked back with precision, not a strand out of place, and his eyes—an unsettling shade of onyx—scan the crowd with a quiet, shrewd intensity. There is something calculating in his gaze, as though he is always three steps ahead, always measuring. A still surface concealing dangerous currents beneath.

He is known for his rare abilities as a water Magick. He can summon or banish rain at will—anything from a soft drizzle to a torrential downpour. But it is the whispered rumors that make him a figure of hushed reverence. They say he can blood-bind—manipulate the water within living things. With a gesture, he can desiccate a thriving plant into withered stems. And if the whispers are true… he can do far worse to a human body.

The third-year water elemental is ready. Stocky, solid, and grounded, Luana steps onto the central platform with the sharp confidence of a seasoned duelist. Her power coils visibly around her like a tide pulling back before a wave. Across from her stands her challenger, Alezay of Vikhrostrum—tall, almost frail-looking, with moonlight hair cascading down her back and a strange, unsettling stillness to her gray eyes. She stands silent, unmoving. The kind of calm that comes not from peace, but from the disciplined patience of a predator.

A faint hiss echoes through the Grotto as the water between them responds—swirling and quivering at their presence.

Professor Ashar's voice rings out, low and resonant: "Begin."

The clash begins with a furious burst of elemental command. Water explodes from the pools around them in synchronized arcs, colliding with enough force to drench the surrounding bridges and the people who stand on them, watching.

Luana conjures a crashing wave that surges across the platform, but Alezay pivots with lithe grace, splitting the surge with a precise slice of water so thin it shimmers like glass.

Then comes the shift.

Ice javelins form in midair—Luana hurling hers with muscle and force, Alezay crafting thin, razor-like spikes of frost that whistle as they fly. One comes dangerously close to Luana, too close, a trickle of blood dripping down her exposed arm.

The temperature drops sharply inside the Grotto. Their power slowly slips out of duel-control and into something else entirely.

Mist creeps in—unnaturally fast, swirling around ankles and obscuring vision. Alezay lifts both hands and calls the mist upward into a ring of fog, just as Luana responds with a low-sweeping strike of freezing water that cracks stone underfoot.

The spectators step back.

I watch with wide, tense eyes. Their magick—*my* magick—on full display.

Then—out of the corner of my eye—I see it.

Luana's frozen wave snaps mid-arc and breaks. One shard shears free, jagged and wild, spiraling free from the duel. It isn't aimed. It isn't controlled. It screams straight toward Nate—

And he's looking the other way.

I don't think.

I just move.

Water rises instinctively under my feet as I throw my body between the shard and my friend, hands raised. A flash of magick bursts from my palms—but it won't be enough. The shard screams forward, faster than I can conjure.

And then—

Shadow swallows the light.

It doesn't just block the ice.

It *devours* it.

A thick, smoky cocoon blooms in front of me, pulsing like a living heart—dark, viscous, and threaded with something glowing faintly violet and blue. It feels impossibly cold and hot at the same time. My water bends into it like roots into soil. My eyes widen with shock. And… memory…

I turn and see him.

Gavrail—standing at the edge of the mist, one hand outstretched, jaw clenched, shadows pulsing from his fingertips like ink from a bleeding page.

Our eyes meet—and for a heartbeat, something sparks between us. Recognition. Power.

The look he gives me strikes through my spine like lightning. For a single blinding moment, the world narrows only to the seam where our magicks meet. I can't tell where my water ends and his shadows begin. And I can feel him. *Everywhere.*

Then—

Darkness slams down as Gavrail's shadows snap outward, swallowing what we did and sparking panic—shouts, scraping feet, a single scream.

Light bleeds back in as the shadows loosen. The cocoon collapses like smoke sucked into a crack.

The ice is gone.

So is everyone's breath.

The Grotto and its occupants stand in stunned silence.

Noa comes rushing over, eyes wide with panic. "Shit, Cel,

are you okay?" His hands are on my shoulders, gripping a little too tight. "One second there was an ice spear heading straight for you, and the next—everything went dark. It was..."

He trails off, looking past me. His eyes lock on Gavrail. The silence stretches.

"It was you," he says, quieter now. A beat of tension hangs in the air before he adds, "Thank you. For stopping it." The words cost him. I can hear it in the tightness of his throat, see it in the set of his jaw. But he says them anyway.

Gavrail only nods, giving nothing away. Then, without a word, he turns and walks away—his shadows trailing behind him like smoke dissolving in the air.

Noa pulls me into a hug, tucking me against him. I feel the press of his lips at the top of my head, grounding me, reminding me I'm here. That I'm safe. Unharmed.

But I can't stop staring. Past his shoulder. Past the chaos of the dueling platform. Past the soft murmurs of my squad as they rush in, surrounding Nate and me in a ring of concern.

I watch Gavrail's back as he disappears into the dark of the cave.

The echo of what we made together lingers like a second heartbeat beneath my skin.

Gavrail.

There is a quiet menace to him that wasn't there when we were children. And yet... beneath all that, there is still a strange, magnetic pull. Like gravity. Or prophecy.

I didn't look at Gavrail and think *dangerous.*

And when our magicks combined, it felt... *infinite.*

I try to shake the feelings as if I can scatter them like raindrops from a summer storm—sharp, directionless, impossible to gather again. But they don't go away... and right now, I'm not exactly sure I want them to.

CHAPTER 30

When lakes sing, beware—for they echo not the present, but the shadows of the past.

—Waters of the Deep

I find myself seeking the solace of the lake after the duel. Wanting to wrap myself in its calm until my thoughts—and racing heart—finally slow.

My fingers twitch slightly, and from the near-shore water—still unfrozen where the spring feeds in—a thin tendril lifts. It spirals, coiling, blooming into the shape of a tiny horse, its translucent body glowing faintly. It flicks its tail as if it's real, then darts across the surface, followed by another. And another. Soon, a small herd of water-formed horses dance along the lake's edge, their silent gallop soothing something frayed inside me.

"I've always loved watching them dance," comes a dark, velvet voice from behind—smooth, low, steady as ever.

I don't turn. I don't need to see him to feel the pull of his presence. The crisp January air stings my cheeks, already numb from the cold, but the air changes when he's near me—thickening, sharpening to a point of almost pain.

The horses keep their pace for one more heartbeat, then I let my magick dissolve back into ripples. And the second they're gone, I realize I miss them.

A flash of childhood—two kids laughing, determinedly trying to conjure creatures out of water and shadow by a different lake, a different shore. He was always better at it than I was.

I continue to stare out over the expanse of blue that calls to me—the lake surface now flecked with ice, shimmering with late sun. It hums with ancient memory, the soft breath of the winter wind carrying its secrets across it.

"What's it saying?" Gavrail asks softly.

He's closer now—close enough that his warmth breaches the space between us. He smells like shadowed woods at dusk: earthy, resinous, like woodsmoke mixed with amber and warm leather. His winter coat brushes the edge of my sleeve as he comes to stand beside me—brief, deliberate, as if he's testing whether I'll move away.

I don't.

I can feel the heat of him through my clothes. And despite myself—despite everything—it's… comforting.

Unfair.

He knows me too well. Knows that when the world tips sideways, I seek the water. Lakes. Rivers. Oceans. Anywhere the element can whisper me still. The lake sings low today. A song of weight. Of change.

"She's remembering," I murmur. "She always remembers."

Water remembers. The echo of my father's voice drifts through the air.

When I finally turn to him, he's watching me—not demanding, just... waiting. Like he has nowhere else to be. Like he never left.

Gods, he is beautiful. Still. Always. It's infuriating. His silver-gray eyes mirror the lake behind me, flickering with light like waves lit under a full moon. When I look at him, I see history. I see heartbreak. I see the boy who once made me laugh until I couldn't breathe—the same one who vanished without a word.

My arms cross over my chest, an instinctive shield.

He motions to a sun-warmed rock by the water, its edges curved from years of weather. "Care to join me?"

I hesitate, then nod. We walk side by side, boots crunching on frozen sand before we settle on the warm stone edge. The rock's heat sends up wisps of steam as it meets the chilled air and mingles with our breaths. The water breathes in and out against the rock—soft inhalations and exhalations that mirror my slowing pulse.

He breaks the silence first. "Remember when your mom found us trying to fish from our rock using her earrings as hooks?" A slight smile appears on his lips, one edge turned up, causing a single dimple to peek through.

I can't help the small smile that answers. "I remember her being furious that we lost her diamond earring, and having to tell her that a catfish was likely swimming away with it as we spoke."

He chuckles softly—a low, warm rumble that vibrates through me, carrying all the comfort of my childhood in it.

We fall into the rhythm of old stories. Rebuilt swings. The time he pretended to drown just to get me to jump in after him. Hunting for marbles and coins. Sunsets on my porch. His notebook sketches. Laughter and nostalgia follow, soft and genuine.

And for a moment, it's actually easy again. My heart stirs at the comfortable familiarity of it all.

Leaning back, Gavrail tilts his face to the sun, arms behind his head, eyes closed. He looks relaxed—peaceful in a way I haven't seen since we were kids. My heart aches with the memory of that boy.

Then, the shadows shift.

The evergreens above us sway, dark needles drifting in the breeze and casting mottled shapes on the snow-dusted ground. One shadow detaches—moving with purpose. It brushes over the frozen grass, then plucks a hardy winter bloom somehow still standing, roots curled in defiance of the cold. It carries it toward us with gentle, eerie grace. It stops, hovering before me, waiting—like some quiet tribute to resilience.

I sigh and shake my head. "Show-off," I mutter, taking the flower.

The shadow coils around my arms before slinking back to the rock's edge like a cat satisfied with its mischief.

I don't need to look at him to picture the smirk on his face. That arrogant half-smile that used to simultaneously infuriate and undo me.

We lapse into silence again.

He sits up finally, speaking softly. "About earlier. The Grotto."

My chest tightens. He doesn't have to say more. I still feel it, like a velvet bruise beneath my skin. Soft but ruthless in the way it lingers. The moment our magick collided—water and shadow merging not in battle, but in instinct. In protection. In something older than both of us. Something dangerous, familiar, and so seductively powerful that for one single moment I wanted nothing else but to drown in it.

In him.

But I don't say that.

"It wasn't just a shield," I say quietly. "It felt… alive. Like something else."

"Shadowmire," he murmurs. The word lands heavy. Like something old, weighted. "I didn't—" He stops. His gaze cuts toward the lake, then the trees, checking with the shadows to make sure we are alone. "It responded. Not just to me. To you. *Us.*"

The word *us* hangs in the air, suspended between possibility and danger.

He reaches over, plucking a pine needle from my hair with practiced ease. His hand lingers, fingertips grazing my temple, my cheek, before resting against my chin.

Time stops.

His breath stills, and so does mine. The pull is magnetic, inescapable. His eyes drop to my lips as he leans in closer. Heat arcs between us, sharp as a struck chord. Waiting. The moment stretches—intense, fragile, trembling.

I turn my head abruptly and rise.

And the spell breaks.

"I have to go," I say, too quickly. My heart thuds against my ribs like it's trying to escape.

Gavrail doesn't stop me. He just nods slowly, his expression once again shuttered, but his eyes still give him away.

I step off the rock and into the frost-scored sand below, keeping my back to him because I don't trust myself to look at him.

"I'm with Noa," I say, my voice barely above a whisper.

"I know" is all he says. But it sounds like he's swallowing a thousand other words.

I walk away, but the lake sings louder now.

And I don't know if it's remembering for me… or warning me.

CHAPTER 31

There are bonds forged in battle—and others in instinct. The latter are far more dangerous, for they are chosen before the mind can refuse them.

—Discipline of the Blade and the Void, Vikhrostrum required text

GAVRAIL

I watch her for a while, standing at the edge of the half-frozen lake. After the duel at the Grotto, after what happened, I knew where to find her. I always do.

Because some part of me—buried deep beneath all that discipline and distance—still moves in time with her. Whether I want to or not.

I'm calm now, after the adrenaline that pulsed through me in the cave. The fear that took over when that ice dagger flew straight for her throat.

Instinct. Possession. Panic. Call it whatever you want.

I threw my shadows without thinking. A stupid choice. Not the cold, calculated strategy I'm known for. I didn't plan it. I never plan when it comes to her. And that's the fucking problem. She makes me reckless. She makes me want to bleed. And it nearly exposed us both.

And when her water slammed into my dark—when it fused, becoming something else entirely, it was like... something ancient inside me lifted its head and said, *There you are.*

I've slept with women. Bled with men. I've fought until my hands shook and my vision went white. None of that touched what this felt like.

It was *intimate* in a way that made sex look like a fucking handshake. It burned through everything I had locked away. Memories of her. By the lake, in the forest, in my room, on her bed, the night that we...

No. I need to stop thinking of that. It will only get me into trouble. But it plays like a godsdamn broken record in my mind every time my head hits the pillow.

Sharing magick with Celeste awakened something no one else has even brushed. Something deep. Reverberating in my chest, in my very bones.

If I'm being honest, it terrifies me. But not because I can't handle it.

I threw up the wall of shadow to bury the proof. To keep the crowd from seeing what happened. To keep her safe from questions. And for one half-breath I was ready to pull her into my darkness where no one else could find her. Where no one else could touch her. Keep her there until she remembered exactly what we were together.

But *he* got there first.

Noa.

Like a golden fucking fire god.

His hands wrapped around her like she belonged to him.

And her body—her traitorous, perfect body—leaned into him like she thought so too.

Every instinct screamed at me—to tear her from his arms, strip his touch from her skin like it burned.

But I let the moment pass. Barely. My shadows curled at my fingertips, itching to lash out.

Not yours anymore.

But the lie tasted like blood.

Now, though, her posture is tense, lost in thought. I watch the way she shapes the water into a herd of dancing horses, mesmerizing as they gallop across the icy lake. Beautiful. Graceful. Like their maker.

I step out of the shadows beneath the pines. The winter air off the lake is biting, but warmth gathers in my chest. When I speak, my voice only startles her slightly.

"I've always loved watching them dance."

Her magick settles, the horses dissolving back into rippling water.

She doesn't need to look. I know that gaze—lost in the expanse of water, listening to something older than the two of us. I wait, breathing slow, letting the hush return and her magick still before saying anything more.

I step closer, her scent curling into me like rain. Wild jasmine after a storm—fresh, unruly. Vanilla and amber lingering on skin I still remember tasting. And beneath it all, water—cool, clean. A warning. A memory. A pull I've never outrun.

"What's it saying?"

I know the answer before she gives it.

"She's remembering," she murmurs.

I nod. Because water always remembers.

Both curse and fantasy wrapped in one.

She turns toward me then, her dark hair spun gold at the edges in the afternoon sun. The sight of her hits like a gut-punch.

She looks like someone you aren't meant to touch. And like

the last place that ever felt like home.

I nod toward the sun-warmed stone, asking her to join me. She hesitates before nodding and coming to sit on the rock beside me. My shadows stir around me, restless, like wolves readying for a hunt.

I notice she's twisting her ring—*my* ring. The sapphire and diamonds glint like they are part of the ice-flecked lake in front of them. It's something I've watched her do countless times. And I can't help but feel like it's a claim I'm staking. Even if she doesn't know what that ring actually means.

Under my skin, my shadows ripple, and I fucking hate how much I want her. How even now, after she chose him, my body still thinks she's mine.

And if that isn't a fucking liability, I don't know what is.

I try to distract myself and her with memories of us. That time we used her mom's earring to fish. The broken swing we mended. We fall into an old rhythm—story after story tumbling out—because words are safer than looking at her.

Every laugh is a reminder of who she was and who she's become. In the afternoon light, I see both, and my heart fucking burns with the loss and return of her.

I study the way her shoulders finally relax, how her fingers trail the vapor rising from the warm stone below them.

Finally, I break the quiet. "About earlier. The Grotto."

She tenses. I don't need to ask what she's thinking—that flash of shadowmire.

"It felt… alive." Her voice is low, contemplative.

I don't answer right away. I can't tell her how it felt when our magicks merged, what *I* felt. Only that it was something ancient. Something powerful. Something that was and has always only been ours.

The words and world hang between us, heavy with the promise of safety and destruction.

I reach out—plucking a stray pine needle from her hair, my

fingers brushing her temple. Her breathing falters. The gold flecks in her eyes shimmer like sunlight through a field of wildflowers, all the colors melting together—impossibly magnetic. Impossibly her. She stills beneath my hand. Her eyes meet mine —open, raw, infinite.

Every instinct screams at me to close the distance, to claim what's always been there. My whole body leans into the fight—want against control, need against restraint.

For a wild second, I almost do it, ready to taste her there and everywhere else on this damned rock. To hell with the consequences.

But she pulls away, and the moment fractures.

The loss of her skin against mine feels almost violent. Like losing a war I never even got to fight.

She rises and steps off the rock, voice soft. "I'm with Noa."

My jaw ticks. "I know."

But her words land like a blade sliding between my ribs.

I hold my face still, keep my breathing even. I don't even let my damn shadows twitch. Because discipline is a language I'm fluent in.

She walks away, the lake singing loudly behind her. And I let her go. Let her get far enough away from me before I can make a mistake. Before I let the animal within try to remind us both of just how truly I remember how to ruin her, body and soul.

I remain on the rock, shadows lingering around my hand where the bloom I picked for her sits like a quiet show of power. I toss it into the snow without looking. It disappears into the white like it never existed.

My shadows curl at my feet, restless—hungry, like they've scented blood. They want to follow her. Wrap around her and pull her back to us both.

But I don't let them.

I leave the lake behind.

Whittaker's paths are slick with ice now. The air is sharp

enough to cut. Students move in packs, loud with adrenaline, still buzzing from the duel and the delicious lie that this is all for sport.

I let them stare. Let them flinch. Let them look away when their eyes meet mine.

Fear is useful. Respect is optional.

The Ivy House rises ahead—white stone, high windows, a pretty cage. Whittaker loves aesthetically pleasing facades. It hides the rot better.

I slip in through a side door. Teo is leaning in the corridor like he's waiting for something to entertain him. Too bright. Eyes that miss nothing. He lifts a brow when he sees me.

"You look like you got stabbed," he says quietly.

"I'm fine."

He huffs a soft laugh. "That's what people say right before they do something stupid."

I stop, just long enough to make the air between us go cold. "Don't you have someone else to bother?"

Teo's smile flashes, quick, knowing, before he disappears down the hall to his room.

I open my door, locking it behind me. My room is sparse. Military neat. Everything in its place because if I let one thing drift, everything else will follow.

I stand there for a beat, palm on the latch, breathing through the tightness in my chest like it's a wound that refuses to close.

The trunk sits at the foot of my bed.

I don't want to look inside. But I open it anyway. Because I'm an idiot with control issues and a talent for self-inflicted damage.

Uniforms. Weapons. A shadowsteel dagger wrapped in cloth. Everything practical. Everything sharp.

And beneath it—what I keep buried like a sin:

A stack of letters.

Her name is on too many of them.

Some are nothing but torn pages and half-finished sentences written in the hours when I couldn't sleep and my shadows wouldn't stop pacing. But there is one I try not to think about. I'm not sure why he wrote me, only that I'm glad he did before it was too late. It's almost as if he—

Fuck. No.

I won't go there.

I take one of the letters out. The paper is worn where my thumb has rubbed it too many times. Edges soft from being handled and handled again like repetition might turn ink into courage.

I don't open it.

If I open it, I'll read it.

If I read it, I'll remember exactly who I was when I wrote it —a younger version of me, stupid and certain I could keep her safe just by wanting it hard enough.

I shove the letter back into the trunk with the others like it's alive. Like it might crawl out and ruin me. I slam the lid hard enough to make the lock rattle. The sound echoes in the quiet room—final, violent, satisfying.

For a second I stand there, fists clenched, shadows crawling up my wrists like they want permission to tear something apart. The lake is still humming in my bones. And somewhere out there, Celeste is probably walking through the campus with Noa Gallegher's hand in hers—

While my magick still remembers the shape of her.

So do I.

And I don't know how long I can keep pretending that doesn't make her dangerous.

Or that it doesn't make me want to be worse.

CHAPTER 32

The layer in which the thread of magick is woven will ultimately determine how hard it is to untangle.

—Principles of Elemental Fusion and Resonance

CELESTE

In Arcanarchaeology, we are now covering ancient sites and artifacts—shadowsteel that drinks light, stardust that whispers futures, fire-laced blades, metal-magicked rings, water-infused jewels. We've also started on symbolism: sigils, glyphs, runes, and family crests. Remnants of the past that survived long enough to be inherited.

Noa has the Emberlain crest proudly displayed on his bedroom wall—his mother's family crest. A flame encased in a sword hilt. Power wielded with discipline.

Duty above all.

When we get to the water family crests, recognition sparks. I've seen them before. Back in the Cavern.

The three ancient families—Thalrien, Virellan, Morvaine—

stories that must have been carved there long before Whittaker stood.

The guardians of water's primal magick.

Thalrien—a mermaid, symbolizing water's tie to the self: emotion, transformation, and truths uncovered.

Virellan—the moon over the ocean, representing the tides: the unseen exerting will, intuition guiding. A distant moon shaping a restless sea.

Morvaine—a waterlily, still and silent: a symbol of serenity and poise, yet its roots reach deep into the dark. True strength lying in unwavering grace.

It is the Thalrien crest that brings me pause. Memory tugs at the corners of my mind, faded pictures floating like mist over a still lake.

I'm fourteen, looking through my father's study. Searching for unique coins for Gavrail to add to his collection. We have so many from all our travels around the world and I promised I would bring him some.

I search through my father's desk, finding embossed folders, letters, a weighted pen. There is a photo of me as a child, smiling, standing between my mom and him. But no coins.

I tug at the drawer to the left of his desk, but it's locked. I look around quietly. No one to see.

I kneel by the drawer, fingers hovering just above the keyhole, then slowly thread a sliver of my water through, feeling the mechanism, the pins and tumblers. I wait to sense the tension like Gavrail taught me, mapping the pressure. I focus, listening through the water to where the metal meets stubborn resistance, and I twist. Liquid hardens, mimicking a key.

Inside, I find old photographs of people I don't recognize—a woman with an easygoing smile standing beside a lake, and a young boy, no older than three, face half hidden in her skirt. There are strange objects—weighted scales, a silver pin, a gold letter opener that looks more like a knife. Something else catches the light, wrapped in a swath of blue velvet, cast in aged silver-blue metal, resembling a large, ancient coin. Its surface is worn smooth in some places, as if passed through countless hands and generations. A mermaid is engraved in profile, with faint, concentric ripples radiating outward from the center.

I can't help it—I reach out to brush my fingers over the carved surface. The metal is cool, but not inert.

It... breathes.

A low hum stirs in my bones, like distant thunder under water, vibrating through my fingers and sinking into my wrist. My pulse jumps and I drop it like it burns.

I hear a noise through the window from the garden below.

Dad's home.

I fold the fabric back over the object and shut the drawer quickly before quietly leaving the room.

Why did my father have an item with the Thalrien crest on it locked in his desk? A piece of a puzzle tucked back into the corner of my mind for another day.

* * *

I HAVEN'T SEEN Gavrail since the lake. Truth is, I've been avoiding him—taking the back stairs to History, grabbing breakfast to go instead of sitting in the mess hall with my squad.

Irritation doesn't even begin to cover it. I hate that I even know *how* to avoid him, that my stupid brain has memorized his schedule down to the hour.

My heart is Noa's—completely. He is the fire I want to consume me, body and soul. So why the hell do I keep seeing *Gavrail* when I close my eyes? The way his gaze darkened at the lake, the curve of that infuriating, beautiful smirk, the way his breath stilled when mine did. It loops in my head like a curse I can't shake—equal parts longing and disgust.

I decide to drown myself in study instead, hoping the noise of ink and theory will quiet the memory of… whatever that was.

I've been continuing my research on elemental fusion. Professor Barrows from my Theory of Elemental Magick class has been my greatest resource, aside from the book I found at Ink & Ether. He tracked down Auren Emberlain's official tome for me. I ask careful questions, framing them as part of an extra credit project. His kindly eyes and relaxed manner make him easier to trust than the other professors.

Today, I head to his office on the top floor of the Logistics building to return some borrowed books. As I turn the corner, I slow—Barrows's low rumble of a voice carries through the half-open door. I'm not trying to eavesdrop… not really.

But then I hear another voice.

Familiar. Intense. Words perfectly measured and composed.

Gavrail.

I lean slightly, just enough to glimpse inside—and I see him standing across from the professor, carrying books. I can make out a few titles: *Principles of Elemental Fusion and Resonance*, *Convergence of Core Frequencies*… He's asking questions. Not idly. Each one is aimed like an arrow—he's hunting, not learning. His expression is unreadable. That practiced mask he wears around everyone—everyone except me.

My pulse skips.

The door moves. He turns—and nearly collides with me.

The air jolts, static and breath tangling between us as his shadows coil at my waist, steadying me before I can stumble back. A dark, intimate tether.

Instinct flickers through him, then the mask resets, smooth as glass. A faint curve touches his mouth. "Stalking me now?"

He sidesteps in close, shoulder brushing mine. His scent, dangerous and heady, stays on my skin where his shadows touched me as he angles away.

My gaze drops to the books in his arms. "You've been

researching," I say quietly—almost an accusation. Unable to keep the edge from my voice.

That earns an upward twitch of his lips. He shifts the books, choosing his words deliberately. "Celeste," he says, voice low, meant only for me as he glances back toward the door he just exited. "You're not the only one who has questions about fusion."

The way he says my name, like a secret. It tugs at something inside of me—recognition, caution. Alarm bells go off in my head. But I nod, crossing my arms, trying to pretend that his presence *isn't* impossible to ignore. I straighten as if posture alone could keep his gravity from pulling at mine.

"I've been researching too," I admit. Slowly. Warily. Like handing over a weapon.

He nods once, no surprise in his eyes. He already knew. Of course he did.

We stand in the hallway, paused in the hush between secrets and confessions. The silence that follows is loaded. Pressurized.

He speaks first. "What would you think of… combining our efforts?" His eyes meet mine. His tone doesn't waver, but there's something beneath the surface. Not hesitation.

Restraint.

It's more than an offer—it's an olive branch. This isn't just about research. It's about trust. Opening a door he never leaves open for anyone.

I hesitate. "I was heading to the library, actually…"

Silence sinks into the space around us, swallowing a feeling I don't name. He watches me—patient, calculating. A slight cock to his head as his eyes glint with something like curiosity.

"Do you want to come?"

The smile he gives me then is dangerous. Not because it's charming, but because it's the one I know. The old one. Easygoing. Infuriatingly sexy. That one dimple forming. The smile from a time when everything was simpler. The one that always used to undo me.

Annoyingly, I find it still does.

And just like that, the walls shift—not falling, but rearranging. A quiet truce written in old smiles and shared purpose.

* * *

THE WHITTAKER LIBRARY stands at the heart of campus like a relic from a more elegant age—circular and towering, built from ancient stone veined with mineral deposits that shimmer in the sunlight.

Inside, it opens into a grand, layered dome, tiers of shelves spiraling like a nautilus shell. Smaller towers filled with books spread out like the arms of an octopus. The upper floors are dotted with study rooms and alcoves for more private meetings.

The main dome soars overhead, its glass roof a mosaic of clear and sea-blue panes. Sunlight fractures through them in ribbons, dancing across the polished stone floor below. At the center of it all, a circular reading chamber rests beneath the apex—curved benches, bright pillows, and the hush of centuries of knowledge surrounding it.

We find a table in the third ring, halfway between the earth-toned history alcoves and the arcane sciences vault. Gavrail drops his satchel and I pull out my worn red tome from Elesmere.

"I found this in Ink & Ether," I say, laying it gently between us. "It doesn't read like a textbook, exactly. It discusses magick history, but when it speaks of fusion, it makes it sound like it lies somewhere between myth and legend. Or maybe dream and nightmare." I trace the cover, frowning slightly. "The practicality of fusion magick seems to be hidden under warnings and *plenty* of examples of failed attempts."

He opens the book, reading silently for a moment. "Not

hidden, exactly," he murmurs, eyes skimming words like a predator tracking something just out of sight. "Perhaps more... intentionally buried."

My stomach tightens at the sharp focus in his expression; at the way stillness clings to him—deliberate and dangerous. Some part of me wonders what it would be like to have that focus directed solely on me. A pulse stirs low in my body at the thought—but it's not from fear. I instinctively move to put some distance between us and try to ignore the magnetic pull I always feel in his presence.

"Warnings against magick are always meant to disguise, to keep the wrong minds away. Or lure the right ones closer." His eyes flick to me as he says that last sentence, his words cast out like a spell.

He closes the book and runs a hand over the cover, his fingers pausing over the title. Tracking the worn gold letters. *Elemental Fusion: The Art and Origin of Convergence.*

"It looks ancient," he murmurs.

"It is. The author doesn't name themselves, but the way they write—it's personal. Like they lived it. Like they know how fusion doesn't just change your magick. It changes *you.*"

His expression shifts—still unreadable, but tighter at the edges, like a flicker of recognition as he glances at me before looking back at the book. "Can I borrow it?" he asks.

I nod. "I've read it cover to cover three times, and while it mentions things similar to what we've done together..." I pause as my cheeks flush faintly, like our magick merging is intimate somehow. He notices—*of course he does.* "It doesn't touch on what I've done, what you've seen me do..."

He reaches out, brushing my hand—a familiar gesture from a version of us that feels far away, but not forgotten. But there's nothing casual in it. It feels intentional, as though he's reminding me of something I'm actively trying to forget. My pulse skips traitorously, and I see a flicker in his silver eyes.

I move my hand away.

He doesn't touch me again.

We fall into a rhythm of silence. Copying passages, cross-referencing notes, chasing threads into old volumes piled higher and higher between us. Somewhere in the middle of it all, time ceases to exist.

One of the textbooks Gavrail brought contains a passage we keep returning to—an anchor in the storm of theory:

Elemental fusion is the transcendence of boundary between the self and magick. Traditionally, it is defined as the merging of one's affinity with an object, the environment, or another wielder. True fusion is rare. Revered. Feared. It can grant immense power—but can also bear a terrible cost.

Gavrail looks at me, eyes narrowed, before looking down again at the page. "Objects are safe, predictable. That's why they're recorded. Weapons, cloaks, staffs. But wielders"—he taps the margin, voice low—"that's where the text shifts. Not a study on the methods of fusion, but more like a warning. That's why it reads more like prophecy here. They weren't just writing theory. It sounds like they were afraid of it."

"So fusion with another wielder..." I murmur.

He finishes the thought: "Almost myth, according to this book, because of how rare successful fusions are." He's holding Auren Emberlain's text in his hands. He glances at me—unflinching, holding my gaze. "This says it requires absolute trust. Emotional resonance. Total alignment."

I'm too aware of how close we're sitting. How his voice seems to vibrate through me, scattering my pulse with its rhythm.

He continues reading quietly with the precision of someone

not just absorbing but calculating, each word like a knife whose balance he's testing before he decides how best to use it. "Fusion isn't random," he says after a moment, low, thoughtful. "You need three things for it to hold. First—resonance. The intent has to match, heartbeat for heartbeat. Second—compatibility. Some elements may refuse to coexist; they tear each other apart instead of blending. And last—an anchor. Something to bind the fusion in form. Doesn't matter if it's flesh or faith, but without it, everything unravels."

A muscle ticks in his cheek, his eyes distant for a heartbeat. I can almost see the equations moving behind them before he shifts back to the table, the calculations and the danger stitched between every word as he continues reading aloud.

"Every fusion comes at a cost. For a moment, each participant must give part of themselves—memory, breath, power, lifeforce, or pain. Sometimes, what is given cannot be returned. And if a misalignment of two magicks occurs or if the fusion is forced instead of created from free will..."

"The result is madness, collapse, or death," I finish reading, my stomach dropping. A threat. A warning.

He glances up at me, taking in the way my shoulders have tensed. "Every one of these texts talks about magick compatibility being the most important part, but I think they're wrong," he finally says. "The *anchor* is everything. Blood. Body. Emotion. Without it, the fusion unravels. With the wrong anchor, it devours."

"So it's a weapon. Or a curse," I say, looking up from the text.

His eyes catch mine, steady, merciless. "Maybe," he says quietly. "Or maybe it's something greater than any one thing could ever be alone. Trust, resonance, anchoring... It's why *we* worked." His gaze flicks to my ring—*his ring*—before returning to me.

Emotions crowd my mind from the way he's looking at me. Like he isn't just speaking of theory—but of us. The words linger, the knowledge of what we are capable of together echoing between us. No longer innocent from the blood spilled into the pages of the books on the table.

But there's something here. Something close. Like catching the glint of a coin beneath deep water. Elusive—but not impossible.

By the time we pack up, the sun is setting behind the mountains outside the high arched windows. But I don't feel tired. I feel energized. Like I've touched the edge of something lost and long buried.

* * *

THE FOLLOWING WEEK, Gavrail meets me in the library again.

In the spirit of full disclosure, I tell Noa that Gavrail's been helping with my extra credit project. He isn't exactly thrilled—but he doesn't stop me. Gavrail saving me in the Grotto earned him a measure of grudging respect from both Noa and my squad.

Rozsen and Elliot respond by issuing me a formal warning and several unhinged threats of bodily harm if Gavrail so much as twitches a toe out of line.

Across the aisle, they pretend to browse. *Pretend* is generous—Elliot is holding a book upside down, and Rozsen peers over the top of hers like a guard at a prison watchtower. She taps two fingers under her eyes before pointing them at Gavrail like tiny warning daggers.

I bite the inside of my cheek to keep from laughing at their well-intentioned stakeout.

"I think I found something," Gavrail says, dropping a book beside mine. His tone is low but edged with something close to excitement. "In your margins—ink that isn't the author's. A reference to a mythological text. *Tales from the Breath of Stone.* Not in Whittaker's archives. I already checked."

I sit straighter, heart thudding.

"Where did you say you got that book again?" he asks.

"Ink & Ether. Elesmere."

He nods slowly. "Then we need to go back. See if they have anything else like it. Or maybe they know where to find this other book."

Anticipation flares in me, momentarily eclipsing caution. "Let's make a plan."

CHAPTER 33

The study of fire is not in the ferocity of its blaze, but in its control. Only the strongest flame-wielders can allow their magick to touch without destroying. Fire untethered devours; fire guided sanctifies. The difference lies in the hand—and the heart—that wields it.

—Elemental Mastery IV: The Covenant of Fire

February arrives at Whittaker, cold and unforgiving, its often-unpredictable weather torn between heavy winter storms and light, fluffy bluebird days. The lake is now completely frozen over. Footsteps vanish instantly beneath a fresh dusting of snow, only to reappear again as the harsh wind scours the ground with icy teeth.

When the school cancels Friday and Monday classes ahead of a storm rolling in, Noa suggests we escape to Elesmere for the extended weekend. I say yes easily—too easily—because the timing is perfect. Gavrail and I finally have a window to search for the book. And, because the universe has an impeccably ironic sense of timing, it also happens to be Valentine's Day.

Elesmere in winter is a dream painted in frost and candlelight.

Snow clings to every eave and branch like spun sugar, and the trees stand frozen in quiet reverence, their limbs glittering with crystal teardrops from last night's thaw. The cobbled streets are swept clean and dusted in white. Bells tinkle above storefronts—warm, soft notes that dance in the cold air, while fairy lights weave between garlands of pine and gold bells that are strung up around the square. In the center, a frozen fountain glistens beneath an archway of lanterns.

Noa drives Finn, Ryan, and me in his car. Other students take the Whittaker shuttle from campus, the one I took the first time I came here. We arrive around lunchtime, and I spot Ink & Ether's swinging sign—*CLOSED EARLY*, posted in the window. My stomach dips, disappointment rushing in.

Noa brushes my hand like he can feel the tension in me when I point it out. "They always close early on Fridays. Don't worry, Cel, you can go tomorrow morning."

Our room at the Village Inn overlooks the town square—a romantic corner suite with a sloped ceiling, a four-poster bed draped in rich reds and maroons, and an iron hearth glowing with dampened embers. Wisteria vines are carved into the headboard, and a small table near the window is already set with a vase holding a single ivory rose.

"It's not the Ritz or the St. Regis," Noa murmurs against my neck, arms circling my waist from behind, "but I wanted to bring you somewhere that felt a little like home, and a little magick."

I turn toward him as he presses a small velvet box into my palm.

Inside, nestled in midnight velvet, is a gold charm bracelet:

tiny golden seashells, a sapphire wave curling around a single pearl, and at the center—a golden mermaid, her tail arched in a delicate swirl, one diamond eye catching the firelight.

I blink, momentarily stunned. "It's beautiful," I whisper.

"I wanted to give you something… that felt like you," Noa says, his voice quieter now. "Not just your power. But *you*. I thought it would look nice with your ring."

My throat tightens, a knot forming there that I attempt to swallow. Unsure what he would think if he knew who the ring was actually from. I don't even know why I don't tell him. Maybe because it's my past. Maybe because what it represents matters more than who gave it to me—at least, that's what I try to tell myself. Once my most prized possession, now it's also a reminder of what I can survive.

He helps me fasten the bracelet to my wrist, and my heart clenches from the way he's looking at me—with love, reverence, promise… and something hungrier beneath.

The velvet box slips from my fingers, forgotten, as I lean in to claim his mouth.

The kiss is fire—the kind that leaves no room for breath, no space between us but the urgent press of skin on skin. His hands trace my waist, my ribs, the curve of my back, pulling me back toward the bed until I'm straddling him, the world outside—the bells, the drifting snow—vanishing. His hands slide under my sweater, my shirt, dragging them up and over my head.

The afternoon light gilds the shadows that curve over Noa's jaw, his shoulders, the line of muscle that flexes as he holds me in place.

"Noa," I whisper, the word half prayer, half warning as I look into those impossibly blue-green eyes. "I love you."

His grin is all molten heat as his lips find the hollow of my throat, teeth grazing, tongue soothing. I rock against him, heat pooling deep inside me as I feel him—hard, straining against the fabric between us.

Clothes vanish under frantic hands, leaving only my bra and panties—just thin strips of lace against bare skin. He turns us as he lays me back on the bed, climbing over me with a heat that sears and shelters all at once. His body cages mine as his fire magick hums against my skin, like lying beneath a summer sun too close to the earth. I arch into it, craving more, and he answers—pressing, claiming, yet careful, as if I am at once his equal and his undoing.

His lips move slowly, pausing to worship every bit of exposed skin before continuing their downward path, tracing languid kisses on my shoulders, my ribs, my stomach, then back up again.

"I want to try something… if you'll let me." His voice is gravel; his eyes are bright.

I look up at him questioningly.

"Do you trust me?" The way he says it, the way he looks at me, makes heat lick up my spine.

I nod.

Suddenly I feel warmth bloom at the edges of the lace—gentle, precise. Not pain. Not burning. Just a playful flare, like his magick is teasing the fabric apart more than destroying it. The threads loosen into ember-light, disappearing in a whisper of ash that makes me gasp. Leaving me completely naked and at his mercy.

He chuckles at the sound, utterly pleased with himself, a cocky grin on his face as he looks down at his handiwork, eyes dark with desire. He moves lower, positioning his head between my thighs.

I gasp as his mouth finds my center. Maddening fire-laced circles contrast with the cool air of the room, making me cry out against him as his strong hands pin my hips to the bed. I come apart under his mouth, trembling and weightless, my hands finding their way into his chestnut-dark hair.

I tug him up and he moves to kiss me again, and I taste myself on him. I can't wait anymore.

"I need you, Noa. Please," I pant between breaths.

His eyes blink gold at the edges as he holds my gaze while moving to guide himself into me. He enters in one deep thrust, filling me until I cry out, clutching at his shoulders. The world narrows to the slide of his body against mine. Each movement is deliberate, deeper, harder, until I'm arching up to meet him, desperate for more, greedy for the way he makes me burn.

The hearth surges, flames clawing high as his pace quickens, wild now, sweat beading along his temples. His hand finds mine, pinning it above my head, fingers laced tight. The other grips my hip, anchoring me as his mouth claims first one breast and the other, teeth and tongue tugging until my back bows off the sheets.

I shatter once more with him still inside me, heat exploding outward like wildfire, every nerve lit. He follows on the next thrust, groaning my name into the hollow of my neck, hips jerking as his magick bursts uncontrolled. The fire blazes white-hot, then collapses into glowing embers, the room hazy with heat and smoke.

He falls back on the bed as he pulls me onto his chest, breath ragged, heart still thundering beneath my cheek. For a long moment, neither of us speak. The rise and fall of his breathing steadies me, a lullaby against the muffled wind outside. His hand strokes absently over my hair, over the bracelet now glittering on my wrist, and the world feels quiet, safe, whole, while I lie there in his arms.

I've only ever felt like this once before. The memory slips in uninvited—silver eyes in the dark, the taste of shadow and skin. I press closer to Noa, as if his heat could chase the ghosts away.

He shifts beneath me as he glances at the now-banked fire with a crooked grin. "Maybe I'm the one who needs grounding lessons."

I laugh, kissing him.

The inn creaks around us, old wood settling. Snow starts to fall softly against the windows, turning to water the instant it presses against the heated glass.

CHAPTER 34

One misplaced drop in a Corazon potion may not ruin the brew, but it will stir the heart's blood toward places best left untouched.
—"Emotional Elixirs and Consequence," Dr. S. Davenport, *Journal of Applied Alchemical Sciences*

Elesmere is full of familiar faces this weekend. Students from Whittaker trickle in, eager to escape campus for candlelit cafés and slow strolls through the frosted town before the storm hits.

Gavrail is also staying at the Village Inn, sharing a room with Tsvetan and Teo. They wander the streets in their long black coats, lingering outside chocolate shops and other stores like foreign princes half melting into local legend.

We make plans to meet tomorrow morning to search for the book.

This evening, Noa has made reservations at the Old Venetian—a beautiful Italian restaurant with marbled pillars and linen-covered tables set beneath low-burning chandeliers. Two white stone fireplaces blaze warmth across the space.

We're being led to a booth tucked into a cozy corner when I glance across the room—and freeze.

I see Gavrail sitting at a small table near the fire.

With *Stella*.

She's laughing too loudly, perched far too close, her manicured hand resting on Gavrail's arm like it belongs there. Her lips are stained a rich berry red, her hair pulled into a perfect knot. She looks like a page torn from a winter fashion spread.

Gavrail sits across from her, his posture too still, carved from stone, his expression impassive. And maddeningly, he isn't pulling away from her.

Jealousy rises in me like a flash flood—intense, sharp, and entirely unwelcome. My fingers tighten around Noa's hand, as if grounding myself in him will make it go away.

We pass by them, and I pull closer to Noa. My eyes go hot and tight. I blink once—twice—until I'm steady again, holding a smile in place like a shield.

Noa stiffens ever so slightly.

Gavrail glances up, his eyes catching mine like a spark in dry grass. Silver flares in the candlelight. For a heartbeat, the mask slips—something jagged and unguarded behind it. "Celeste," he says, voice careful. But I hear what's buried there: pressure. He shifts slightly in his seat. "I didn't expect to see you here tonight."

"I could say the same." My tone is light, overly bright. "I hear this is a popular restaurant."

Stella gives a smile like a cat spotting prey. "We wanted to see the town in the snow—so charming, don't you think?" Her nails drift down Gavrail's sleeve, a gesture polished and deliberate. "It's just so romantic."

He doesn't flinch. Doesn't move. But the stillness is too

sharp. The kind that makes you wonder if it's patience… or restraint.

My stomach twists.

Noa clears his throat as he pulls me closer to him. "We were just heading to our table."

Gavrail says nothing. Only his shadow shifts—the faintest ripple across the floor.

"Oh, stay," Stella purrs, gesturing to the empty seats beside them. "We don't bite."

I give her a brittle smile. "Another time. Enjoy your meal."

At our table, I find myself turning into someone else—laughing too loudly, telling stories that don't matter, touching Noa's hand too often. Bright conversation. Too many teeth. A puppet on a stage, giving a performance.

I hate Gavrail for making me feel this way, but I hate myself more for letting him.

I order dessert I don't want. Wine I don't need. Coffee I'll never finish.

The waiter approaches with our check before setting down two slim flutes, the liquid inside a soft blush pink that seems to glow in the candlelight. "On the house for Valentine's Day," he explains. "A Corazon cordial—rose, hawthorn, cassia."

I've read about Corazon. Not a potion, exactly—closer to a charm in liquid form. Said to stir the blood, to coax the heart closer to whatever it already leans toward. Dragging hidden things to the surface like a tide pulling secrets from the deep. Half folklore, half alchemy.

Noa clinks his glass lightly against mine, and drinks without hesitation. I only wet my lips, tasting sweetness edged with spice, my eyes drawn, unwillingly, across the room. Stella is drinking hers. I wait, throat tight, watching to see if Gavrail drinks his. It stays untouched on his table. His gaze flicks toward me just once, catching my stare before I look away.

We stay until the last of the patrons disappear into the winter night, Stella and Gavrail among them.

As they get up to leave, Gavrail gives me a small nod—barely there.

But it feels like someone pressing on a bruise I forgot I even had, a small ache I don't let anyone see.

* * *

LATER, as Noa and I walk back beneath the stars, I pull my coat tighter around myself to protect from the chill that isn't just in the air. The tension between us feels heavier than the snow.

"That was stupid," I finally mutter, my voice small, brittle around the edges.

Noa glances sideways at me, but he doesn't say anything. His silence presses down on me harder than his words ever could.

I close my eyes for a moment before opening them again as I exhale. "*I* was stupid."

I stop then, my breath puffing out in the cold air, a cloud that dissipates too quickly to make any difference. I want to speak, to explain, but the words catch in my throat. I swallow, trying to push past the lump forming there, but it doesn't work.

"I..." I begin, my voice trailing off. I drop my eyes to the ground, avoiding his.

Shame crawls up my neck, hot and suffocating. I should've known better. I should've—

"I didn't know seeing him with her would make me feel like that," I say at last. "I didn't know I'd still feel something like that. I'm sorry, Noa."

I feel the heat of his gaze on me, but I can't bring myself to look at him just yet.

He exhales slowly, the sound soft, almost like a sigh of relief. He stops and turns to face me, his gaze flicking to my hand just once before meeting my eyes. "Cel, whatever you once were to each other—I don't care. Because I *know* what you are to me."

And there it is, the trust in his eyes that both breaks and makes me at the same time. Because this… this is *real*.

I want to say more, but instead, he takes my hand in his—impossibly warm against the cold—and I hold on. Not out of performance this time, but honesty. Because jealousy is the cruel twin of love—both born from wanting what burns too bright to truly see.

We walk the rest of the way back to the inn, the lanterns throwing soft gold across the snow.

Inside our room, Noa's thumb grazes the sapphire ring on my knuckle. He inhales—then looks up. "It's his, isn't it?"

My breath leaves me in a slow, painful spill. I don't deny it. I can't.

"Yes," I answer. But the word seems too small for the silence it fills.

His mouth tightens, then he nods once, like he's making a choice. "I meant what I said earlier. You are allowed to have a past." His voice lowers. "I only care about your future—because I have every intention of being in it."

He pulls me to him, and I let myself just look at him. The eyes and fire that steady my soul, no matter the storm that brews outside these walls. The way he looks at me—unyielding, certain. I reach up and pull his mouth to mine.

Because the future he sees so vivid and clear… I want to see it too.

* * *

THE NEXT MORNING, Noa is off on an adventure with Ryan and Finn—likely headed toward Elesmere's cliffside tavern or the heated ice gardens just past the town border. I meet Gavrail outside Ink & Ether, the sign swinging gently in the wind like it's waiting for us. There's an awkward second when our eyes meet—something unsaid hovering between us. I look away first.

He doesn't mention Stella. And I don't ask.

Inside, the scent of old parchment, sandalwood, and winter cedar fills the cozy shop. Madame Romari nods at us from behind the counter without a word, her gaze sharp and otherworldly, as if she already knows why we've come.

After Gavrail asks for help, she leads us to the hushed rows of mythology, gold bangles clinking at her wrist. Every book in this section is an artifact from the past, every title a whisper of secrets, culture, and storytelling. Gavrail and I wander down the aisle, still searching for the truth that began to unravel itself in the waters and shadows of the Grotto.

"I've heard of the book you seek," Madame Romari says, her foreign accent thick, the syllables slow and rich like honey stirred with herbs. Her fingers slide through the stacks of books, moving with practiced ease, as if she knows every spine and page by heart. "Alas, I do not carry a copy. Many of the myths it speaks of are European in nature." Her mouth curves, not quite a smile. "If you want a trail, you'll have to follow the old ones. Berlin maybe. There is a library there." She lifts a shoulder, bangles chiming. "Or perhaps what you seek will find you instead." Her eyes meet mine for a heartbeat, dark and knowing.

My shoulders slump. The book isn't here.

I glance at Gavrail, expecting a shared moment of defeat. But instead, he brushes my hand lightly with his—barely a graze. Intentional. Something like static flickers in the air between us. Then he steps back, shuttering whatever just came loose from that impossible control he wields like a weapon. He heads outside without a word, the bell above the door chiming softly behind him.

Madame Romari watches him go, her eyes never leaving him. "I told you he'd find his way back to you," she says, her voice quieter now, as though the words hold weight beyond what they seem.

"Excuse me?" I ask, confused, though my gut tightens at the subtle implication, following her gaze to where it's still focused.

I pause, a sudden chill running over me as I realize *who* she meant. My breath catches, and the hairs on my arms rise, prickling with the intensity of something unspoken. A shiver creeps down my spine as I nod to her in farewell before stepping out into the bite of the winter air.

CHAPTER 35

Heat will always seek a vessel. And flame will always seek something to burn.

—Elemental Mastery IV: The Covenant of Fire

Back on campus on Monday, the winter storm is well underway. Thick sheets of snow slant sideways under slicing wind, turning the stone paths and towers into a blur of white and shadow.

After the way I behaved in Elesmere, I'm desperate to make up for it, even though Noa never mentioned it again. I convince him to wait out the worst of the storm with me inside the Cavern, then drag him to his private quarters to thaw out our frozen skin.

Once inside the fire-carved door, we hang our coats on the hooks jutting out from the stone walls, the fabric stiff where snow has melted and refrozen along the seams. Our hats, scarves, and thick winter gloves are laid out to dry while we indulge.

Noa changes quickly and heads for the steam room, towel wrapped loosely around his hips. I slip off my clothes by the stone bench in the corner and hold up my swimsuit, studying it for a long beat. A slow smirk curves my lips—and I set the suit back on the bench and step barefoot toward the pool at the back of the chamber. The warm water envelops me as I slip in, completely naked.

The private hot-spring pool is neatly carved into the rock, about six feet across, its stone walls gently curving up where you can lean back. There's a small stone staircase at the front, leading down into the water. Built-in benches line the sides, the dark stones polished smooth by centuries of use. Steam rises where the hot spring meets the cool cave air, drifting up past simple iron rings holding lanterns in carved wall niches.

I settle myself on one of the benches while I wait for Noa. The warm water eases over my skin, sinking into every frozen inch of me. My muscles loosen one by one, tension unwinding until I'm boneless, floating—soft and slack, like wax warmed in the sun.

I hear the door open as Noa exits the sauna. Sweat clings to his body, dripping down his chest and pooling at the sharp grooves of his lower abdomen, just above the towel—those vee-cut lines that draw the eye to what I am already wickedly picturing below.

I arch back, resting my head on the stone edge of the pool, my breasts rising above the water as Noa's gaze drops—then lingers—at the peaks of exposed flesh, my nipples hardened as they react to the cold cave air.

His eyes darken with lust and delight at the sight of me there watching him. Waiting for him.

Slowly, he lets the towel fall from his hips, and I can see just how much he already wants me.

He walks over to the pool and steps down the stone steps,

standing over me. He sinks down into the water, drifting so that his body hovers over mine.

"Hi," he says, his smile tipping to the side as he finds my neck with his lips.

I arch back, enjoying the shiver of pleasure it gives me as he nibbles and sucks at the skin below my ear. His hands move lánguidly in the warm water, touching, kneading, massaging. Feeling the slickness between my thighs through the heat.

I reach for him, my fingers wrapping around the thick length of him, stroking slowly, from base to tip. Each movement draws a breathless gasp from his throat, the kind that makes my pulse stutter. His breathing grows harsh, every inhale tight with restraint. I guide him to sit, straddling him as the steam curls around us like smoke.

I lower myself onto him, letting my weight sink down inch by inch with a sharp inhale. His lips part beneath mine as I kiss him—deep, claiming, and then biting down just enough to draw a growl from his throat. I feel... *everything*—the stretch of him filling me, the scrape where my teeth meet his lips, the wet heat between us amplified by the water soaking our skin. His hands clutch my hips, grounding us, while mine slide into his hair, tugging him deeper into the kiss, deeper into me.

I move slowly, savoring the way his breath catches—his agony delicious and just shy of unbearable. I pick up speed, watching for the moment his breathing shifts, the edge of unraveling—then I stop. I kiss him instead. His mouth. His neck. My hands glide down his chest, mapping muscle and bone, until his breath slows again... and I start over.

I take him to the brink twice more, keeping him teetering on that ledge until his control finally snaps.

I can feel the fire before I see it, sparking from his fingertips, sending streaks of impossibly warm water right *there*, alternating the pressure like an extension of his fingers—push, pull, warm, hot—again and again as I ride him.

It's too much.

I drag my hands through the water as it spirals around us, a shallow whirlpool stirred by our magick and movement. Noa's flames heat the surface until steam rises, misting the air, forming a glowing cloud overhead.

Our bodies slide together, slick and seamless, his hands on my hips, lifting me in time with each thrust. The vortex spins faster. The air thickens. Then his real hands—strong and sure—find the aching center of me as I ride him. The contrast of his heat against the cool air makes me cry out as I arch against him.

Above us, the cloud pulses. The pressure in the room shifts—air destabilizing, crackling with something ancient. Our magicks—fire and water—aren't fighting. They're *fusing.*

The pressure inside us builds, rising higher and higher until it can no longer hold.

And then—I break, a wave shattering against a cliff, relentless and consuming.

Light flashes within the cloud above us—brief, brilliant sparks blooming like shooting stars across a night sky.

Oh my gods. I look up.

We've created a storm.

Noa lifts me and slams into me one last time before throwing his head back against the stone ledge, falling over the edge, his eyes closed. We're lost in each other. Lost in this moment. Our bodies are covered in steam and mist as the hot water of the pool laps back around us, wrapping us in its warmth.

We remain tangled, pulses thrumming in time—with each other, and with every flicker of lightning above. He sinks back against the step, exhaling hard, and turns me in his arms until I'm curled on his lap, facing the storm. I'm completely spent. The storm we created *took* as much as it gave. Maybe more.

We watch it together—silent, breathless—as the cloud begins to fade, the air still crackling with electricity. My skin tingles with it. Every nerve sings. Even my blood feels different, thick and slow as it moves through my veins.

I look back and find his eyes already on mine—wide, dark, filled with awe. And something else. Something like fear.

He realizes as well as I do that we've just created something far beyond normal magick. Something older. Wilder.

This wasn't just passion, or lust, or even love—

This was power.

Fusion.

And it was *ours.*

CHAPTER 36

To pull one thread is to risk unraveling the whole.
—Tapestries of Power: A Study of Magickal Bloodlines and Lineage

I feel scattered after what happened in the Cavern, even two days later. It's like pieces of me are still floating in the steam of that cave. My body is whole, but my magick is stretched thin and humming with aftershock. What we did—it changed something. It marked us. And for the first time, I realize that Noa is now just as entangled in my secrets as Gavrail.

I turn the thought over and over, torn between truth and safety, love and protection, knowledge and trust, and something deeper—something I can't name that feels ingrained in my very bones.

Because secrets are heavy. They cost you. And once spoken, they can't be unspoken.

But Noa deserves the truth. The real one. And the truth is—I *want* him to know me. All of me. The shadows and the storms.

The worry I carry. The fear I try to swallow. Even the parts I still don't fully understand myself.

I don't dare tell Gavrail what I'm considering—I already know he'll try to stop me. The risk. The danger. Letting anyone else see what I am. But it's not just the two of us anymore. It's the three of us. And Gavrail doesn't get to be the only one who decides what risks are worth taking.

I walk into Noa's bedroom and find him studying at his desk, books and papers spread out around him haphazardly. He's leaning over, lips pressed against the end of a pen, knuckles tapping against the smooth wood surface.

"I need to show you something," I say as I shut his door behind me and cross to the center of the room.

Noa looks me up and down, a slow smirk tugging at his lips. "Cel, anything you want to *show* me, I'm always ready for," he says, voice low, eyes gleaming with that familiar seductive tilt.

I take a step back.

Noa stops, a brow arching in silent question. He studies me now, cocking his head in that way he does before a duel—calculating, trying to read the terrain before he moves.

"If I show you this… you have to promise me that it stays between us."

"Okay…" There's hesitation. He hears the weight behind my words. And we both know—Noa doesn't do well with secrets. *We* don't do well with secrets. They've tried to break us before.

"No—I need you to promise me. This… this is important."

He stands up from his chair and leans back against his desk, hands at the edge behind him. The teasing slips away. His voice softens. "Cel, I promise. You can trust me. You can *always* trust me." He looks at me—through me—before nodding just once. "Show me."

I cross the room to the slightly raised platform in the back, my steps slower now, heavy with uncertainty. I stand beside his bed. And suddenly—I'm terrified. Terrified of what he might think. Of what this will mean. Terrified that, once again, there's something I've hidden. Something I've kept from him.

He steps toward me, concern etched on his face.

I take a deep, shuddering breath, trying to calm the riot of my heart.

Just breathe, Celeste.

Except it's Gavrail's voice that flashes in my head at that moment.

I close my eyes, and just like I did ten years ago, the first time it happened, I let my thoughts slow... let the water within me rise and take hold. I feel my body begin to soften—my edges blurring. Mist under sunlight.

Until I am no longer flesh and bone, but a thousand glistening droplets suspended in midair.

They hover, holding the shape of me—a shimmering echo, translucent and fluid. Light refracts through me, casting ribbons of color across the room. In this moment, I exist somewhere between seen and unseen.

Noa stumbles back.

His stance shifts in an instant—shoulders squared, feet braced, muscles taut like a coiled spring. Ready to defend. He's not seeing me. He's seeing something unknown. Something impossible. Something that shouldn't exist. Instinct overriding recognition.

Because he's right. *I shouldn't exist.*

But I do.

His chest rises and falls in sharp breaths, his eyes wide, searching. "You... You're... Celeste?" The name chokes out of him like a prayer—like a curse. As if saying it aloud might anchor him, might make sense of what he just witnessed. But even he doesn't believe it. Not yet.

I begin pulling myself back together. Every droplet is drawn inward, cells aligning, my form returning. It's slow, and it costs me. Like it always does. I feel drained. Hollowed out. Just a little... *less.*

He stares at me, panic in his eyes. Worry. But also—curiosity. Awe.

I finally speak again, my words slow and measured. "You know that I'm capable of elemental fusion. That *we* are. But this... this is something different. I've been able to do this since I was a child."

I pause, the past a pathway leading me to the present. And suddenly I'm thirteen again—pine needles under my feet, cold air in my lungs, Gavrail's voice counting by an old oak tree.

"One... two... three..."

I run away to hide, desperate to win this time. Not the boulder—too obvious. Not the orchard—he always finds me there. I panic. Not fast enough. Not clever enough. Then I see the old hunter's blind—just two crumbling walls and a thatched roof. I run barefoot across the forest floor, heart pounding.

"Ten!" Gavrail calls out.

I duck into the blind, splinters scratching my arms.

His footsteps draw closer. "Celeeeessste..."

He's close, and I smile, thinking I might be able to scare him if I jump out. "Boo!" I shout.

He turns toward me and stumbles backward.

"Celeste, your skin... You... Your body..." He sounds horrified as he points at me with a shaking hand.

I look down to see what he's pointing at. But I see nothing but droplets of water. And I start to scream.

"I've been researching—*we've* been researching, Gavrail and I, trying to find answers. Any answers." The words tumble out of me faster than I mean them to, but I don't dare stop. Not now. "But as far as I know, it's never been documented before—a Magick actually being able to *become* their element."

His expression is a perfect storm of fear and wonder—like he's watching something impossible yet undeniably extraordinary unfold before him. Disbelief melts into something deeper. "This is..." He runs a hand through his hair, breathless. "Shit, Cel... This is incredible. Why would you hide this? Why would you *want* to?" Then he pauses, stepping toward me slowly, eyes soft and steady—like I'm something fragile and wild that might vanish. "*You* are incredible, Celeste. There's nothing you could ever show me that would change how I see you," he says quietly, reaching for me.

The way he's looking at me mends something inside me I didn't know was broken.

"Thank you." His hand is at my waist, the other arm pulling me closer, his voice low and reverent. "For trusting me with this. For telling me."

There's a knock at the bedroom door.

"We're busy!" Noa growls at the interruption.

The knock comes again—more persistent this time, impatient.

Noa exhales hard through his nose. "Just... stay here, Cel. I'll tell them to go away."

He strides to the door, and I don't miss the way his posture changes—protective, edged—before he wrenches it open. "Finn, go awa—"

He stops.

Gavrail stands on the threshold, glaring back at him.

The tension is immediate.

Gavrail's storm-gray eyes lock on Noa with barely disguised disdain. "Is this a bad time?" he says, his voice sharp enough to draw blood, slicing through the air. "I'm looking for Cel—" He looks past Noa, sees me, and whatever expression I wear makes something crack in his composure. He barges in without waiting for an invitation.

His eyes flick between us—the remnants of Noa's shock, the guilt painted on my face, the shimmer of my magick still in the air—and his face falls.

"You told him?" The words are laced with betrayal, bitter and rumbling with unseen thunder. His voice is low, but I see it in his eyes—anger. And there, right behind his lethal gaze, a flicker of fear. Not for himself. But for me.

Noa stiffens. The air crackles between them like static.

And then Gavrail moves.

He slams Noa into the wall, forearm pressing hard across his throat. The impact echoes, shaking books loose from the shelf.

"If you tell a soul—if you betray her—if she ends up on someone else's leash because of you," he snarls, eyes brimming with restrained fury, "I will fucking end you."

The shadows in the room start to stretch toward them.

"Gavrail, stop! This was *my* choice!" I shout, throwing myself between them, hands on both chests, trying to pry them apart.

Noa yanks Gavrail's arm down—but I see his other hand twitch, fire blooming over his knuckles.

"No—Noa! Gavrail! Stop, please!" My voice cracks, raw and desperate.

This isn't how I imagined it would happen—the two men I've loved, past and present, now both knowing what I've kept hidden for so long. On the brink of killing each other.

I thought telling Noa would feel like a release. A weight lifted. But instead, panic coils tight in my chest and fear floods in like water with no drain, the magick I've spent already weakening me.

Tears sting the corners of my eyes.

I start to collapse between them.

Both men reach for me. Tension still rides their frames like a second skin, but once Noa's arms are around me, holding me up, Gavrail steps back. His eyes shift between concern for me and violence toward the arms that are daring to touch me.

It's Gavrail who speaks first. His eyes flick to Noa for a heartbeat. "If he betrays you, if he puts you in danger—"

"He won't," I interrupt.

"I won't," Noa echoes, quiet but steady. "Celeste isn't just someone I care about—she's *everything* to me. Why would I ever hurt her or betray her trust?" His arm curls around me protectively, drawing me close. His body is still taut with tension. He doesn't look away from Gavrail. "If you ask me," he says, voice rising, "it's you who's betrayed her from the beginning."

Gavrail stiffens.

"This kind of power… Gods, do you even understand what she is?" Noa's voice shakes—not with fear, but with awe. "Becoming water itself. Not just bending it. Not just wielding it. Invisible. Unstoppable. No one's ever seen anything like it. It's… *fucking extraordinary.*"

"And dangerous," Gavrail snaps, voice low and gritted.

"But *you* have been the voice in her ear, in her mind, from the start. Telling her to hide it. To hide *her*. Stifle *her—*" Noa's accusations are sharp, his disdain bitter.

Gavrail interrupts, his voice laced with ice so cold it could freeze the very room. "What do you think her professors would say? What would someone like my father do if he knew what she was capable of? Someone who could go through any door. Any wall. Vanish. Shape light itself."

He looks at me then, his gaze heavy with the truth.

"They'd turn her into a weapon. A spy. Something loyal *only* to them. She'd be taken from *everything* she loves." His jaw clenches. "You think I just disappeared? That I left without a word for no reason? I've seen what my father does to Magicks he thinks he owns. Why the fuck do you think I stayed away?"

"Gavrail…" His name breaks from my lips before I can stop it—fragile, exposed. I step toward him.

The truth hits all at once, jagged and fast, like shrapnel finding its mark.

"You… That's—that's why you never wrote." It comes out strangled, more breath than words. My thoughts scatter like rain on glass, everything I thought I once knew.

He nods once, eyes still locked on Noa. "I was trying to protect you," he says finally, voice cracking—just barely. "I'm *always* trying to protect you." He's shaking—hands curled into fists at his sides, jaw locked. The calm mask he wears so well is gone. "I left so no one could use me to get to you." He steps closer, and I hate how the air between us bends, like it belongs to him. He draws in a breath, stealing my own.

I can see him, trying to pull it all back—the years of fear, of worry, of walking a line too fine to hold. Torn between keeping my secrets and keeping me safe.

His shoulders slump finally, as if the weight of his choices is pressing down like a physical burden. "I thought distance would shield you. That silence would be enough. But it just built walls between us—walls I can't seem to fully tear down." His eyes meet mine—anger, bitterness, grief, all radiating so deep it's impossible to look away. So rare in its exposure that my breath freezes in my chest. "I was trying to protect you . . . but maybe all I did was leave you alone in the dark."

A silence drops, thick and absolute.

Then—

"Your father, Cel… He knew. He knew everything. He was a water-wielder, like you. He made me promise to protect you—from people like my father. People who would twist your power with promises of love and purpose, only to use you." He flicks his gaze to Noa for just a second, the implication sharp.

My thoughts stumble. My heart pounds.

"My father?" I breathe.

"His real name wasn't Thomas Farris," Gavrail says. "It was Selric Thalrien."

The name slams into me like a cold wave.

Thalrien.

Professor Straits's voice echoes in my memory: *The Thalriens were an ancient, powerful water family—possibly the oldest known—famous for a rare form of magick… coveted…*

Hunted to extinction.

"His parents, your grandparents, were murdered when he was just a kid," Gavrail continues quietly. "He was sent into hiding. Homeschooled. Years later, he met a woman—Valarie Normandy—and they had a son. Orren."

He swallows once, almost imperceptible, steeling himself against the truth he's kept from me all these years.

"One night, while your father was away, Magicks broke into their home. When he returned, Valarie and Orren were gone. No bodies. No traces. Just… gone." His voice breaks. "That's why he hid your power. Why he never let you near water. He was terrified it would awaken something he couldn't protect you from."

I can't speak. Can't breathe.

Gavrail continues, softer now. "Thalriens have been hunted for centuries for what they believed. For the kind of power you hold. Your father saw it in you. He lived every day worried he'd come home to find you gone too." He pauses then, searching my eyes. "I found out he was a Thalrien about a year or two after we met. My father knew. I overheard him talking late one night —I was practicing my shadow magick, hiding in his office."

A flash of regret crosses his face before he starts again.

"The night I learned we were moving, I ran to your house. I was going to tell you everything, say goodbye, but your dad was in the garden." His look is hesitant, laced with ghosts and the truth of our past. "He said he was glad my family was leaving… but that he'd miss me. He said he knew I was a good kid—and maybe I'd grow into a better man than the one who raised me." He exhales. "As I turned to head upstairs to you, he said, 'I know.' I looked back. He was staring at me. He said he knew about the lake. About the shadows. About you discovering your magick."

He meets my eyes again.

"He told me he trusted me to keep your secret. To keep you

safe. And he made me promise never to contact you again." He almost chokes on the words. "I gave him my word. Even though it broke me. Even though I knew it might break you too."

Tears fall freely down my cheeks now, silent and burning. Images crash into me, one after another, everything unraveling. Fragments of memories, dragged from the shadows of my mind.

My father's voice. His hands guiding mine away from the lake.

Whispered warnings. Locked drawers. The faint blue crest hidden in velvet, shaped like a mermaid.

Gavrail's eyes the night he left me. Gavrail and me. Noa.

Water that always seemed to know me better than I knew myself—guiding me, pulling me, hiding me.

It was always there. Waiting.

And I never saw it.

Water remembers.

My ribs feel too tight. My skin too thin. Like the room has shrunk around me and the air has turned to glass, jagged and sharp, slicing through me with each inhale.

The weight of it all—secrets, lies, love, loss—presses down on my chest like a tide I can't outrun.

My hands tremble. I can't breathe.

"I... I need a moment," I whisper. The words are barely mine.

Noa takes a step forward, reaching for me, but I step back, flinching like his touch might burn.

"No, please. Just... I need some time to think."

Panic floods me—fast, bright, and blinding.

I grab my coat and bag with shaking hands and bolt for the door. The scent of Noa's cologne clings to the collar of my jacket. I want to breathe in the familiarity of it. I want to remember it.

But all I feel is the salt on my lips. The burn in my throat.

The cold night air hitting my skin as I run.

I don't look back.

Revelations crash over me, heavy and relentless. Every breath is a battle.

Everything feels like it's unraveling—my past, my present, my power, the people I thought I could trust.

And worst of all... I asked for this. I opened the door.

Now I have to decide what to do with everything that's come spilling through.

CHAPTER 37

Institutions do not protect people. They protect themselves—with people.

—Elements and Empires. A Study of Modern Magickal Governance

GAVRAIL

We both stand in silence, staring at the door she just fled through. The echoes of her footsteps have faded, but the air remains charged with everything she left behind—tears, truth, and the taste of something broken and raw.

I finally speak, each word honed like a blade. "If you really love her like she says you do… then prove it. Protect her. Keep her safe. And above all, keep your fucking mouth shut."

Noa doesn't blink. Doesn't flinch. His hands stay loose at his sides, but his shoulders lock—braced for impact.

I pause, just enough to betray the fracture beneath. Because the thought of her—the fury and dare in her eyes, that stubborn tilt of her mouth when she said this was *her choice*, to tell him, to trust him—hits me like a hook under the ribs. I clench my jaw until it aches, forcing the feeling back down where it belongs.

I exhale, my shoulders flexing once before I forcibly relax them. "You think I don't know what she's carrying? I've kept it hidden longer than you've even known she existed. You've seen just a glimpse of her power, and you're already out of your depth."

I step forward, my tone sharpening like a weapon drawn against stone.

"If her ability is discovered, they will come for her. You know I'm right. Just by being here—by being *her*—she's already compromised. She's not a rumor. She's not some myth. She's proof. And they will want to *own* her." The words taste like metal in my mouth. "And when the Service comes knocking—because they will—I need to know you'll be at her side. Not just standing there. But fighting."

Noa's jaw tightens. He meets my stare head-on. "Why are you so sure they're the enemy?" he asks, measured. "What if her power is exactly what we need to end this war before it even begins?"

I let out a quiet, bitter laugh. Shadows bleed closer from the corners of the room. "Which war?" I ask, voice clipped. "Which war, Noa? Yours… or mine?"

Silence stretches between us like a fault line. My eyes narrow.

Noa hesitates, then says evenly, "The Service exists to protect magick. To serve peace. I believe that."

I look at him, through him. Disappointment flickering behind my eyes. "You still think the Service is honorable?" My voice cuts like glass. "You think a system that registers elementals, tracks them, classifies their usefulness—rewards the powerful and buries the dangerous—is something sacred?"

"I think it's flawed," Noa says carefully, "but it's trying to protect people. Trying to stop chaos from reigning."

"I was raised by a man who built a system just like yours—and I've seen what he does to the people he 'needs.'" I shake my head. "I've seen what he does to people like Celeste—people who don't fit into categories, who threaten their balance. You think she'll be their weapon?" I ask, more growl than words. "No? Then they'll dismantle her. Hollow her out. Erase her, sanctify the remains, and call it progress."

For a second I see a locked door, hear my father's voice—calm and pleased—saying the word *necessary*.

"You don't understand. You still think this is about good versus evil. Light and dark. But it's not. You don't know what it feels like to watch people become collateral damage. Locked away or burned because they don't—or won't—fit the mold." My hand twitches—like I want to punch a wall or break something just to feel it.

Noa doesn't respond. Not right away. Then, with quiet conviction: "Regardless of sides, you think hiding her will save her?"

"I know hiding her is the only reason she's still free." The words come out sharp. Because they're the truth.

"No," Noa says softly. "Hiding her isn't helping. It's hurting her. You don't see the way she burns herself out every day trying to be something she's not. She's terrified of herself. She's drowning in her own skin."

That lands. My shoulders tense, then sag—just slightly.

Noa pauses, then says, "But if anyone can help her—if anyone *should*—it's us." He looks toward the door again. "What if we trained her? Quietly. No exposure. On her terms. Give her a chance to understand what she is before anyone else defines it for her."

A beat.

I turn toward the window. Outside, the last remnants of snow cling to the edges of a rock garden below, half-melted and slushing under a weak sun. The scent of thawing earth hangs in the air—a change on the horizon.

My voice is quieter now, distant. "I've made too many choices for her already. I told myself it was protection. But it was control." My throat works, swallowing hard. "I won't do it again. This choice—this one—has to be hers."

I glance back at Noa, and for a fleeting moment, there is something like a truce between us.

"I'll stand by whatever she decides. Even if it means watching her walk a path that leaves us on opposite sides."

Noa holds my gaze, unblinking. "Then let's hope it doesn't come to that. Because if she becomes the line between us..." His eyes darken. "I won't be the one to walk away."

We both go quiet, staring out into a world just beginning to stir again—branches still bare, but roots shifting beneath the frost.

Because spring is coming.

And war, like the thaw, is inevitable.

CHAPTER 38

When a magick lineage is erased, the element it's tied to keeps record.

—Principles of Arcanarchaeology: Resonant Sites

CELESTE

I somehow find myself at the Lakehouse, staring at that expanse of blue that's just starting to shake off winter's cold fingers.

Once again I'm drawn to the fountain in the courtyard. Three mermaids, all facing different directions.

The first holds a tilted vase, from which a stream of water pours in a graceful arc—endless, steady. Her hair flows like kelp, wild and soft, the very image of calm and continuity.

The second wears a coral hood that shadows her smiling face, her fingers wrapped around a mirror so dark it seems to swallow light. Water trickles from its edges, as if secrets themselves could weep.

The third is turned toward where the sun rises, her features fierce and resolute. In her cupped hands, a flame dances atop a shell, encircled by falling water—a contradiction held in perfect balance.

I stare at them, caught in the pull of their silent myth. Three mermaids, three facets of the arcane, and something more—something *personal.*

Water, shadow, fire.

Me and Gavrail. Me and Noa. Me and myself.

A breeze lifts fine spray from the fountain so that it kisses my cheeks, cold as a warning. And for a moment, I'm not just Celeste. I'm all of them—the girl, the heir, the echo of something older, something I'm only just beginning to grasp, to feel. To understand.

A trinity not unlike the sculpture: flowing and fierce, luminous and hidden, entwined in ways I haven't yet dared name.

For a breathless moment, I feel the world narrow to moonstone and water, to the subtle weight of meaning carved into silence.

When their world begins is when the rest of the world ends. The ghosts of my father's words echo around me in the breeze.

He was a Thalrien. *I am a Thalrien.* Possibly the last one left in this world.

Water remembers.

I should have known. And part of me feels like maybe I always have.

It wasn't the world of magick he was warning me about. It was the ones who took so much from him—from both of us. The ones who tried to control him, to use him. And killed when others refused to fall into line.

I remember our fights. How he'd rage when I got too close to magick. When I asked too many questions.

"The ones who look to rewrite the rules are never written into them!" he once yelled. I thought it was bitterness. Now I know it was fear.

And truth.

I thought he was referring to all Magicks. But he was talking about the ones who killed his parents, the ones who took his family. The ones I realize he was terrified would one day take me too.

I think back to the day I found him in the lake, my body curled around his, holding him in the shallow waters of the shoreline, his lips blue, his body cold.

I almost forgot the reason I went out to look at the lake in the first place, but I felt it—the call, the pull toward the water, as if my very blood were being drawn to him and to the water in which he lay. Now I knew why.

Coveted. Hunted.

A sudden surge flows within me. A truth flickering in the depths of the lake.

My father's death may not have been an accident.

And I am no longer hiding.

I am a Thalrien.

And if they took him from me—*I will make them fucking pay.*

CHAPTER 39

The weight of legacy is not in what we inherit, but in what we choose to carry on.

—The War of Unbinding: The Second Rebellion

Gavrail finds me in the library, tucked away at our usual table beneath the stained-glass dome. A stack of books towers beside me: *Bloodlines of the Arcane; Tapestries of Power: A Study of Magickal Bloodlines and Lineage; Blood and Sigils: The Heraldry and Seals of Ancient Magickal Houses.*

"Studying, I see," comes his cool voice behind me.

I look up. His presence shifts the air, as it always does. The library houses a grateful silence when words are too much or not enough.

"I wanted to find books that had more specific information about my family line," I say finally, running my finger along the margin of a page. "But they all seem to be checked out."

He says nothing, just steps forward and reaches into his messenger bag, pulling out three worn volumes. *Bloodlines of the*

Deep. The House Thalrien. The War of Unbinding: The Second Rebellion.

"I checked these out in January," he says softly. "I figured you'd come looking for answers. Eventually."

My hand moves to the second book. The crest is embossed in silver—a mermaid in profile, ringed by faint ripples—etched deep into the navy leather. The weight of it sends a pang of recognition through my chest.

"Thank you," I say, quiet but sincere. My emotions war beneath my skin. I'm still angry, still hurt, that he withheld the truth all these years. But the feelings are complicated, knowing he was following my father's wishes, even though they went against his own.

The gesture of the books cracks something open. He knew, but he was trying to make it right, in his own way.

I look up at him. "Did you know Whittaker was founded here because of a sacred water site?"

Gavrail tilts his head, a small smile touching his lips. "You've been paying attention in Arcanarchaeology."

I nod. We just started touching on sacred sites of magick and ritual in class. But it makes sense that Whittaker would house one. The Vikhrostrum Mountains that curl around the academy house the Heart of the Mountain, an ancient earth magick site. La Rinconada, in the Peruvian Andes where the Universitas Arcanum Andina is located, holds the sacred Wind Temple dedicated to air magick. The Heart of Light is in Jordan, where the School of First Light was founded. We're supposed to start sacred fire sites next week. Now every fact feels personal, like the world has been quietly rearranging itself around me this whole time.

He slides into the chair across from me, fingers steepled. There is something restrained in his posture—guarded. Controlled. Always infuriatingly controlled.

But his eyes—gods, his eyes aren't.

"Cel..." he begins, voice low. "I want to explain—"

"I don't like what you did, Gavrail," I interrupt. "Keeping me in the dark all these years... but I understand *why* you did it. You thought you were protecting me. Keeping me safe. And I get it, I truly do."

A pause. I meet his eyes. His jaw tightens, but he says nothing.

"And if our roles were reversed, I probably would've done the same," I finish quietly.

He holds my gaze. "But..."

"But," I say, my breath catching slightly, "I don't want to hide anymore. I'm tired of pretending to be something I'm not. I want to know what I am. What I'm capable of."

There is silence between us, electric and still.

"Noa wants us to train you," Gavrail says finally, the words deliberate. Measured. He watches my face intently while he waits for a response.

"Train me?" I blink. "And you're okay with that?"

"Not in public," he says quickly, glancing around as if even the library walls have ears. "It's still too risky. Until we know what revealing the truth might mean—for you, and for everyone around you. Until we know what we're even dealing with. What it might cost."

Excitement surges in my chest. Like the crest of a wave I didn't realize I was riding.

I lean forward. "When do we start?"

CHAPTER 40

Some fusions steady the heart. Some break it. Pay attention to which is which, lest you find yourself without one entirely.

—*The Codex of Convergence*, Auren Emberlain

Noa chooses a secluded bay on the far side of Lake Caldrith for our training grounds. Tucked behind a screen of red maples—each branch tipped with tiny pink buds—the bay feels untouched. Private. A secret hidden in plain sight.

The trail in is more mud than path, the thawing earth soft and slick under our boots. The lake lies before us like a pewter mirror, broken only by the occasional ripple of a cold March breeze. Along the shore, stubborn patches of snow give way to damp, sandy stones.

Spring whispers its arrival everywhere: crocuses' bright-green tips thrusting through dark soil, the air filled with the scent of wet bark and moss. The buzzing of insects that now stir beneath fallen leaves. Still, the air has a bite to it when the wind cuts through, the edge of winter's last grip on the land.

The bay is perfect, its uneven terrain lending a wild, natural edge to every drill. Noa clearly knew this when he brought us here, and Gavrail, after a moment's calculation, agrees.

It's uncomfortable at first, the two of them working together. Disagreements over theory and training methods. Glares cutting sharper than any weapon between them. Occasionally fists will clench, a fight only seconds away from erupting.

And yet—

They hold it together.

Again and again, they put their differences aside.

For me. The shared thread connecting them.

Noa begins with the fundamentals: elemental manipulation, then state manipulation. Shaping water as liquid, solid, and vapor—freezing the shore's edges into glass, turning ice to mist, condensing steam back into droplets, and back to ice—in ever-faster succession. Precision. Control. Speed.

Then Gavrail takes over.

He doesn't teach, not in the way Noa does. He tests. Pushes. Dares.

Gavrail teaches me to draw moisture from the air, from the damp grass underfoot, then from the birch trunks behind the boulders at the bay's edge.

"Draw it from the trees," he says, voice low and cool as the water I summon. "If you want to control the water, then control all of it. Even what wants to stay hidden."

IT BREAKS me to see the fragile shoots wilt or fresh spring blossoms shrivel and fall, and even more so to watch the once-majestic tree trunks turn gray, bark cracking. My stomach twists every time.

"Undo it," he says, unmoved. "If you break it, fix it. That's how you learn."

So I do. I learn to reverse it—pouring life back into the plants until buds pinken, leaves unfurl, trunks gleam with restored sap. Each time, watching life return, I feel a deep sense of satisfaction. Some small piece of me heals at being able to fix what was once broken. Even if I was the one to break it.

On Tuesdays, Gavrail and I meet alone. We start refining shadowmire, changing its consistency, shaping it in ways we haven't tried before. We discover ways to stabilize it beyond its initial formation, suspending it in specially runed vials Gavrail stole from the Potions lab. He begins to collect the variations: thick, thin, slow-moving, fast-acting—bottles of liquid shadow stored like forbidden secrets, locked behind a hidden panel in his bedroom at the Ivy House.

He watches me closely when we work. Not just my magick—me. The way I breathe. The way I move. How fast I react. Sometimes there is a flicker in his gaze—curiosity and calculation and something more. He makes sure he never pushes me beyond what could break me, but also takes me right to the edge. Just like he did when we were children.

Thursdays are for maelflare—the name I give to Noa's and my shared magick. Noa and I practice at the bay, chasing the storm we first summoned together. At first, our attempts sputter—clouds forming without thunder, mist without lightning. Maelflare depends entirely on our emotions, on being in sync. It is volatile, elusive. Unlike shadowmire, which pulses just beneath the surface—always ready, always waiting—maelflare has to be coaxed, sparked, trusted. But when it comes... it is devastating.

Fridays, we train together. The focus shifts to dueling techniques, battle stances, and field strategy. Noa and Gavrail spar with each other as often as they train me.

Noa's fire evolves. He learns to channel it into plasma—a writhing serpent of molten energy that devours everything in its path. But his most remarkable feat comes after watching me refine my freezing techniques: learning to forge freeze-fire, a pale-blue flame that forms unbreakable chains. They don't burn in the way his normal fire does, but they hold. And once they lock around you—there is no escape.

Gavrail, meanwhile, has mastered shadowbinding: the ability to anchor someone's shadow to them and use it to restrict or control their movement. He begins shadowstepping too—vanishing and reappearing between slants of light like a phantom. Noa hates it. It makes Gavrail nearly impossible to pin down in combat, Noa's fire striking nothing but empty air again and again.

By month's end, the bay is both practice and proving ground, where I've discovered just how deeply my power and I are intertwined.

In trying to uncover more about how I can fuse my magick into my own body—not just wield it, but *become it*—we've stumbled onto something no known text has named. Noa calls it *elemental embodiment,* though no such term exists in the current canon of magicks.

As far as we know, Magicks have fused their elements to tools or artifacts—flaming swords, cloaks of smoke, obsidian armor made from the earth's own bones. Even elemental fusion, like maelflare or shadowmire, is rare but recorded. But this... this is different.

This is me.

Me, transforming into an element and being rebuilt by it again and again.

We test its boundaries, its limitations. I can shift any object I'm touching as long as it isn't alive—clothing, weapons, paper, even food. It all disappears with me in my elemental form before being pulled molecule by molecule back to solid matter.

But every time I return to flesh, I feel... less.

At first, it's just fatigue. A headache. A pull behind the eyes. Then it starts to change—bone-deep exhaustion, memories that shimmer at the edges like ripples, small pieces of thought I have to chase down to hold on to.

But I keep going. I don't tell them. I can't. Not when we are so close to breaking through, to understanding, to becoming something more than the world of magick allows.

Elemental embodiment, elemental fusion—each exacting a different toll. Some worse than others... until even I can't ignore the difference.

When Gavrail and I fuse, shadowmire feels energizing. Steady. Dense. Like something ancient and quietly alive. It tethers us, leaving us humming, synchronized.

But with Noa... maelflare is chaos. It's beautiful. Uncontrollable. Igniting and consuming everything around it—and sometimes, it feels like it consumes me too.

Shadowmire is a drumbeat, steady and low.

Maelflare is a strike of lightning.

Shadowmire tethers me.

Maelflare tears me loose.

And in the quiet moments after the storm fades and the mist burns off the water's surface, I often catch Noa watching me.

He doesn't ask. Not yet. But his fingers linger longer on my wrist, checking my pulse. His gaze drifts to my temples when I rub them. He's noticing.

I just don't want him to *know* what he's noticing.

But when his eyes follow me... When he pulls me close...

It's like he's trying to see what's left. Like he's worried I'm already slipping through his fingers, one drop at a time.

CHAPTER 41

Peace is a season, not a certainty
—The War of Unbinding: The Second Rebellion

The end of March brings with it the announcement of the fourth elemental duel, set to take place in the quad that has been transformed into an impromptu stone stadium.

Between classes, training with Noa and Gavrail, and our relentless search for answers about my lineage, elemental fusion, and any trace of embodiment in historical record—by the time my head hits the pillow at night, I am already past exhaustion. I barely remember falling asleep most evenings.

Noa never says it, but I know he worries I'm burning too hot. Stretching too thin.

Still, he doesn't stop me.

Some nights, I dream of him kissing me awake, slow and golden. But more often, I wake to find him already curled around me—his body a furnace, breath soft against my neck, one arm pinning me with sleepy possessiveness—and I kiss him awake instead: mouth hot, hands eager, the kind of kiss that dares him to catch up. His fingers slide beneath the sheets, teasing my body awake with a fire to match his own.

It never lasts long enough—just enough time to burn, to take and be taken, before the world pulls us apart again. But in those stolen moments, between sleep and sunrise—before responsibility claws us back—I'm not a Thalrien. Not a mystery. Not a weapon in training.

I'm just *his*.

Gavrail and Teo sometimes join us for meals in the mess hall now—never announced, never invited, just… there, sliding onto the end of our table like they've always been there. It's a strange, unexpected truce, forged somewhere between clenched teeth and shared bruises now that Noa and Gavrail have taken to training me together at the bay—two rival storms learning the shape of each other's violence, building something grudging and wordless that isn't friendship, exactly, but also isn't hatred anymore.

The first time it happens, Rozsen's gaze cuts between them —wary but faintly amused. "Well… if the fire king says you're housebroken, I guess I'll allow it."

Gavrail's mouth twitches. "How very generous."

She casts a glance at me as if to ask, *Are you okay with this?*

I give the slightest shrug before returning to my meal.

Gavrail doesn't perform. He doesn't charm. The rest of my squad, aside from Rozsen, tries not to stare. They fail. Because even when he just sits there—charcoal uniform, quiet posture—the entire hall rearranges itself around the fact that he exists. Like everyone's instincts know the same thing at once: that he holds the kind of power you don't provoke unless you're ready to bleed.

Teo and Rozsen have stopped pretending that their flirting is merely for fun. Rozsen's boot nudges his under the table like a private joke. Teo's hand lingers at her back a second too long when they stand. Finn, meanwhile, floats from table to table like a social butterfly with a death wish—always laughing with the newest person in his orbit, always leaving behind a trail of smirks and scandalized whispers in his wake.

The duel is scheduled for this Friday. My squad and I walk to the quad together and find seats at the top of the stadium, carved from stone by Whittaker's earth Magicks.

At the center of the arena below, second-year Jin Feng stands with her chin high, bronze cuffs gleaming in the afternoon light, metallic threads winding up her forearms like living veins. Across from her, Teo flashes a lazy grin, arms loose at his sides, acting like he's about to hit a beach party instead of a duel.

"Ladies first," he calls, sweeping into a half-bow.

Jin doesn't smile. She just nods, then lifts her hands.

At first, it's clean—calculated. She calls twin daggers of polished steel into the air, spinning them with mindless precision.

Teo responds by lifting a slab of stone from the earth with casual ease, molding it into a curved shield. He makes a show of yawning behind it.

Laughter ripples through the crowd. Rozsen snorts. Finn, standing near the edge, doesn't react.

Jin's eyes narrow.

The second round is sharper. Her blades dart in quick succession, slicing the air with a thin, lethal whistle. Teo deflects them with rising columns of rock, sidestepping with a dancer's grace, and when he grins again, it's clear he's enjoying himself.

"You're quick," he says, "but not faster than me."

The third strike comes without warning.

Jin hurls a spear of jagged metal—not steel, but something darker, denser, forged from deep veins of iron beneath the school. It punches through Teo's shield like paper, nearly catching his shoulder. He stumbles back, off-balance for the first time.

Gone is the easy grin.

The crowd grows silent.

Jin's eyes flash, and with a flick of her wrist, a fan of needles bursts from her cuffs in a silver swarm. Teo slams his palms to the ground, raising a wall of obsidian so fast it cracks under the force.

When the dust settles, Jin is already forming another weapon, long and thin—a whip of wire. She sends it into the air as she pulls spikes of iron from the earth, each one shooting up from beneath his feet, caging him in. The distraction is enough to be able to send her lasso of death around his neck like a snake, squeezing it tight with a clench of her fist.

Professors are moving now—Stroud, Kael, even Headmaster Thorne stepping onto the field, magick at the ready.

The wire whip lashes into Teo's throat, strangling him, blood dripping down as the stone shield he's called forth to encase his throat desperately tries to stop it.

"Stand down!" Stroud's voice booms.

But Jin stands over Teo, determined, watching as the wire cuts deeper and deeper into his neck.

And then it all freezes.

Wind howls as Professor Stroud steps forward, eyes sharp as a knife's edge. With a single flick of his wrist, a gale-force burst slams into Jin, sending her skidding back across the dueling arena. She braces, but the wind coils around her, tight as chains, locking her arms into place. Her body jerks, suspended in the air like a puppet caught mid-strike.

Before she can even blink, Kael strides in from the edge of the quad. His palm ignites with a low, burning roar. Flames snake outward in a controlled stream, striking the length of Jin's metal whip. The searing heat warps and melts it instantly, droplets of liquefied steel hissing as they hit the stone beneath them.

Jin is bound. Disarmed. Held still by wind and fire.

The crowd stares—shocked into silence.

The duel is over.

Teo is finally able to draw a breath, letting out a sharp exhale, chest heaving. Blood drips in pools around him as others rush toward him to try to help.

Jin doesn't blink. Doesn't look sorry.

Tension spills over the watching crowd like a flood. Gavrail pushes through to Teo's side, but Rozsen gets there first, using her jacket to try to stop the flow of blood. She murmurs something to him that I can't hear, but I see the fear in her eyes.

"I think she broke my favorite rock shield," Teo jokes weakly, then catches Rozsen's eye. "But your concern makes it all worth it."

Rozsen rolls her eyes, but her fingers linger on his cheek a moment longer than they need to. Finn watches from across the quad, stone-faced, unmoving.

As Jin disappears into the crowd, flanked by professors and still trembling with restrained fury, I realize something that sinks in my gut like a stone:

These duels aren't just about strength.

They're echoes—of old wars. Of buried grudges. Of legacies none of us asked for, but all of us carry.

Jin wasn't just fighting Teo. She was fighting a past she couldn't outrun.

And maybe... she wanted him to bleed for it.

It's only later that Gavrail tells me why, and the knowledge settles under my skin like a splinter I can't pull out: Jin's parents were recruited into Krovya when she was just a little girl. She was raised by her grandmother while her parents disappeared into missions and silence. Years without a visit. Years without a choice. Krovya keeps its Magickteers on a tight leash—and their families learn to live with the scars it leaves behind.

CHAPTER 42

Not all come to watch. Some come to weave.

—Magicks and Power: The Political Structures of the Elemental World

With April's arrival, Whittaker becomes a flurry of activity, preparing for Parents' Week—the time of year when the esteemed parents of the student body descend upon campus, filling the air with polished smiles and eager greetings. The quad fills with students who look like they've never had to sprint for a bell in their lives. Faculty appear in pressed robes. Even the wards along the outer gates hum a little brighter, like the school is trying to impress.

I tell myself I'm fine. But when I'm waiting at the carriage house and the line of arriving cars begins to crawl through the gates, my palms are damp and my heartbeat feels too loud in my chest.

This is the first time my mother will get to see my world. The world that swallowed me whole the moment I stepped into Whittaker's halls.

A black town car pulls up near the curb, tires crunching gravel.

The back door opens.

For a moment, she's only a silhouette—then she steps out into the thin April sun and the entire campus seems to shift, like spring itself decided to take human form and walk across Whittaker's gray stone.

"Mom," I breathe.

Rosalind Farris turns, and her face lights up with a brilliant smile. Her dark-brown hair is pulled into a loose knot at the nape of her neck. She moves like rain—unhurried, inevitable, carrying a calm that makes everything around her slow down.

Her eyes meet mine. Green like a forest after a storm. And something in my chest gives, the tension snapping like a cord I didn't realize I'd been holding all year.

"Celeste," she says, and my name sounds like a prayer in her mouth.

I don't walk. I lunge.

She drops her bag without caring where it lands and catches me with both arms, pulling me in so hard I lose my balance for a second. I can smell hand soap and lavender and something warm that has nothing to do with magick and everything to do with home. Her hands are on my hair, my shoulders, my back—like she's counting bones to make sure none are missing.

"Oh, sweetheart," she whispers, voice shaking. "Look at you."

My throat closes instantly. The words I meant to say—*I'm sorry* and *I missed you* and *I didn't mean to leave you alone*—pile up behind my teeth until all I can manage is "Hi."

She laughs, small and breathless, and presses a kiss to my forehead the way she used to when I was small enough to fit under her chin without trying.

"I've been dying to see you," she murmurs. "I hate that it's taken this long."

Guilt slides in like a knife—sharp and familiar.

She pulls back just enough to look at me properly. Her gaze travels over my face, the faint shadows under my eyes, the way my posture has changed—straighter, stance steadier.

Her mouth tightens for a heartbeat. Then she lifts her hand and cups my cheek, thumb brushing the corner of my mouth like she's smoothing away something that isn't there.

"You look... different," she says softly. "In a good way. Coming here was the right choice, right? You're happy?"

My eyes sting. I blink hard, annoyed at myself, at my own emotions. "Yes. I'm fine," I say automatically.

Her brows lift—Rosalind Farris, patron saint of calling bullshit with kindness—and she gives me that look that says she hears what I won't say and is choosing not to press.

Instead she exhales, steadying. "Show me," she says, voice brightening with effort. "Show me everything."

I nod, swallowing. I am excited—nervous, but excited—to show my mother around. To let her see everything I've learned. To introduce her to my friends and show her the pieces of my life she hasn't yet been able to be a part of.

I reach for her bag, and she swats my hand away. "Absolutely not. I'm your mother, not a porcelain doll."

I only laugh and take her hand in mine.

We pass under the archway where ivy is just beginning to bud, pale green against stone. Mom's gaze sweeps over everything: the buildings, the banners, the students moving in clusters, the faint shimmer of wards in the air—if you know where to look. She's trying to take it all in, and I can almost see her mind catching on details and filing them away—the same way she used to memorize the names of my classmates after one brief mention.

"You weren't exaggerating," she murmurs.

"I never exaggerate," I deadpan.

She sighs, just once. "I wish your father could have seen all this."

That lands like a punch I don't know how to take. My grip tightens around her fingers. For a second I can't breathe.

She squeezes my hand once—gentle, wordless. *I know.*

We make it to the center of the quad, now returned to its original state. The stone stadium is no more. Picnic tables have been set up for the visiting parents. Other families are already settling in—jokes and laughter rising, a few tears slipping loose.

Mom turns in a slow circle, then looks at me again. "You've been here all this time," she says quietly. "And I couldn't even picture it."

My chest squeezes. "I… I'm sorry. I should have written more, or called—"

She interrupts me, her expression softening. "Oh, please, honey. I know you've been busy."

I'm about to say something—something honest, something ugly—when I feel a distinct shift in temperature that happens only when a certain person steps into my orbit.

My mother stiffens beside me in a way so subtle no one else would notice.

"I don't believe it. Is that…?"

I follow her gaze.

Gavrail is crossing the quad toward us in his Vikhrostrum uniform—charcoal and silver, crisp lines, the kind of tailoring that makes him look like a weapon. His coat is open despite the bite still in the April air, as if cold is beneath his notice.

He stops a few paces away, posture perfect.

His eyes lock on mine first. Silver-flecked. A storm caged.

Then his gaze moves to my mother.

Something flickers in him. Whatever mask he was wearing shifts. Not gone, exactly. But… softened at the edges.

"Mrs. Farris," he says, and his voice is gentler than I expect. He inclines his head with formal respect, but there's something underneath it—something like *affection.*

My mother stares for a beat too long.

Then her face breaks.

"Gavrail," she says, like she can't decide whether to laugh or cry. "You are *alive*."

His mouth twitches. "Last I checked."

"Oh, don't you get clever with me," she snaps—fond, fierce—and then she's moving. She releases my hand and strides right up to him like she owns the space between them.

Gavrail's posture shifts a fraction—braced, ready for impact, unsure what to expect.

She grabs him. Both arms. Full force. A hug that is not polite or careful, but ferocious and maternal and—*how dare you disappear from our lives and stand here like you didn't crush us with the weight of it.*

I freeze. Because Gavrail… doesn't.

He exhales slowly—and his arms come around her without hesitation. One hand spreads across her back, holding her, and for a heartbeat he looks startlingly young, even though he towers over her now.

Then my mother squeezes harder.

"Rosalind—" he starts, voice heavy.

She tightens her grip like she's trying to compress seven years into one breath. "Do not 'Rosalind' me. Do you have any idea what you put Celeste through? Me through?"

Heat flares in my face. "Mom—"

She lifts one hand without letting go of him, like she's swatting my protest away. "No. I get to say it. I've been saving it."

Gavrail's eyes flick to me again—quick, warning, apologetic, and maybe with a tiny thread of shame.

My mother pulls back just enough to look at him. Her hands slide up to his shoulders, gripping the uniform fabric like it's the only thing keeping him in place.

"You look…" She frowns, eyes scanning his face, the hard edges, the discipline carved into his expression. "You look like your father."

His jaw tightens. I can see him choosing words the way he chooses strikes.

"I'm sorry," he says carefully. "It's inexcusable—the way I disappeared..."

She waves her hand as if chasing away an insect. "It doesn't matter. You are here *now*." Tears well in the corners of her eyes, threatening to spill any second. And it's hard to tell who she's more excited to see—her own daughter or my childhood best friend.

"You've grown," she says, softer now as she looks up at him. "And my goodness, are you handsome. Celeste—isn't he handsome?"

A corner of his mouth lifts. Just barely. "Oh... Celeste here has a lot of thoughts about me these days, but I'm not sure 'handsome' is one of them."

He's right, of course. *Beautiful. Intimidating. Infuriating.* Take your pick.

He smirks as if he knows exactly what I'm thinking, and then there it is—that one dimple. The one that always appeared when he was standing on my front steps back in Bulgaria with mud on his jeans and mischief in his eyes. The one that belongs to summers and secrets.

Mom makes a noise—half laugh, half sob. "Gods, you're still incorrigible."

"Absolutely," he agrees, utterly straight-faced.

She pats his cheek affectionately—then looks over her shoulder at me. Her eyes are too knowing. Too sharp. Too *mother*.

She narrows them slightly, not fooled for a second. But she doesn't push—not here, in front of him, in the quad with everyone watching. Instead she draws herself up, smoothing her coat like she's reassembling her composure.

"Well," she says briskly, "since you two seem intent on giving me heart failure—and since my daughter *neglected* to mention you were here—I expect the both of you to show me around campus this week." She looks at Gavrail again, and her voice softens at the edges. "If you have time, of course. I'd love to hear what you've been up to."

Something shifts in his expression—gratitude, maybe. Or regret.

"Of course," he says simply.

My mother nods once, satisfied, then loops her arm through his like she's reclaiming him for herself.

As we start walking, I glance back before I can stop myself. And it makes funny things happen to my heart to watch the always cool, composed Gavrail chat with my mother like no time has passed, giving her a smile that shows off that one ridiculous dimple—the one usually only reserved for me.

* * *

THE FIRST NIGHT OF PARENTS' Week, the school hosts a welcome barbecue in the quad. The event is a warm, bustling affair meant to ease the transition between Whittaker's rigorous world and the families peering in from the outside.

The picnic tables are bedecked in the flowers and ferns of spring. A guitarist strums mellow tunes from the dais. The air carries hints of lemon zest, fresh herbs, and something buttery baking. Students and parents wander about with sparkling spritzes and lavender lemonades in hand, catching up like no time has passed at all.

Rozsen's parents came all the way out from California. Elemental healers, the both of them. They make it very clear that they find Whittaker... distasteful. Rozsen jokes that they raised her on herbal tea and anti-establishment ideals—autonomy over allegiance, intuition over institution. "Rules are for people too afraid to trust their own power," her dad whispers conspiratorially to me as Rozsen rolls her eyes.

Elliot's mom sits next to them. Her curly blonde hair and sharp blue eyes give her a startling resemblance to her daughter. She's already deep into a debate on government overreach with Rozsen's parents.

Amelia shyly introduces Peter and his parents to her dad, who made the trip from Vermont. All of the earth Magicks are drawn together at the far side of the quad.

Ian's mother proudly shows everyone around them the book he bought her at Ink & Ether, and she's as loud and vivacious as her son. She's unofficially adopted Nate, since his parents couldn't make it from Canada for the week. Sawyer's parents couldn't make it either—some surf trip in the Maldives, he says with a shrug.

As we settle into our plates—herb-roasted chicken, spring pea risotto, honey-glazed carrots, and warm rosemary rolls—Headmaster Thorne approaches the dais. A light clinking of glass brings the quad to attention.

"Parents, guests, and students," he begins, "welcome to Whittaker. This week is yours—to explore, to ask questions, to see what your remarkable children have built and become."

He continues, describing upcoming demonstrations and lectures, tours and special events. When he finishes, he steps down, moving among the tables, offering polite nods and handshakes as he passes familiar students and their families.

Then, to my surprise, my mother reaches out a hand. "Evander!" she calls, standing to greet him.

He stops. For a moment, something flickers behind his eyes. Then, the perfect smile returns, polished and unyielding. "Rosalind," he replies smoothly. "So nice to see you again."

Again?

They slip into an easy conversation. I watch them closely—the subtle familiarity, the warmth in her voice, the way he inclines his head. Something about it feels off. Comfortable. *Too* comfortable.

My eyes narrow before a commotion draws my gaze across the quad, landing on Noa's parents speaking with none other than General Silas Vaylor—the highest-ranking general of the magick faction of the Service. His attendance alone elevates the entire evening, a silent nod to Whittaker's prestige and the promise of its students. His dark hair is threaded with silver. He's older, but not softened by it. His ice-blue eyes are cool and clear enough to make you want to believe that only truth lives there.

Vaylor is what the Service has sold to the world: magick made handsome, efficient, and loyal. And yet, beneath the cordial smile and sophistication, there is something too still about him—too unpredictable, like a serpent dressed in silk. His presence commands respect and obedience, the quiet dominance of a man long accustomed to control.

It's only then that I notice pairs of Service officers at each corner of the quad as well as a few scattered through the crowd.

Across the field, Noa catches my eye. One eyebrow raises in my direction as he tips his chin at me. I smile and wave back, then feel Gavrail's presence before I see him.

"What is he doing here?" he mutters, suddenly beside me. His voice is low and sharp as ice, his gaze not moving from Vaylor's back. A predatory stillness settles over him as he watches the group of soldiers in black.

Thorne eventually peels away from my mother, just as she starts launching into another meandering anecdote. He nods toward General Vaylor, and I watch as his polished mask reassembles itself in full.

I turn back to my mother. "I didn't know you knew Headmaster Thorne."

"Oh, my goodness, yes!" she chirps, voice like honey, softened by the glasses of wine Gavrail charmed out of a server for her earlier. "He's been a friend of the family for years. He knew your father well—from their college days, I believe."

I freeze. "My father?"

She clucks her tongue. "Your father didn't always hate Magicks, Celeste."

I try to mask my shock. Funny, I think, that Thorne never *once* mentioned knowing my dad.

"He was actually the one who encouraged me to have you apply to Whittaker," she adds.

I turn to look at her, surprise jolting through me. Beside me, Gavrail's expression darkens, all trace of charm gone. A muscle in his jaw ticks, but he doesn't speak.

Before I can press her further, a familiar presence approaches.

Noa and his parents walk over. His father folds me into a crushing bear hug, and his mother kisses my cheek before pulling me in close. I haven't seen them since last summer, since Noa left for Whittaker. Since before my dad passed. Somehow that's both forever ago and only yesterday.

"Celeste! We couldn't be more proud of you and how much you've accomplished in such a short time!" his mother gushes.

I flick a questioning look toward Noa, searching for confirmation. His expression remains carefully blank, but I understand. He hasn't told them about my past. They still believe my powers only recently manifested.

His mother sits beside me, looping her arm through mine like we're old friends as she greets my mother. She tells us about Alissa's new job, her boyfriend Greg, and their future plans like nothing about the world has changed since last summer.

Blake Gallegher stands nearby, tall and powerful, the kind of man who makes other people step back. His hair, like Noa's, is a chestnut brown, streaked with silver at his temples, his presence quiet but undeniably warm. A retired commander of the non-magick faction of the Service, the prestigious Iron Vanguard, he exudes silent strength and discipline.

Noa's mother, by contrast, is tiny and fiery, with amber eyes and strawberry-blonde hair—the spitting image of her daughter Alissa. Brigid Gallegher practically sparks with energy, never short on opinions or opportunities to poke fun at the men in her family. She is the true flame in the family, her maiden name Emberlain—one of the original founding fire families. The same Emberlain whose textbook on fusion we've been studying. I want to ask her about her family, but now is not the time for history lessons.

My mother rises to pull Noa into a warm embrace, and the two of them start chatting as he charms her—and the rest of the table—in the way only he can.

Dinner passes in laughter and nostalgia, all of us catching up on what we've missed in each other's lives. My mom lost two of her favorite silkie hens to foxes but now has two horses named Starla and Paul. I smile as I watch her win over my friends with her stories and ever-present warmth. The comfort of it all makes my eyes prickle with tears as I move in closer, laying my head on her shoulder. Gods, I've missed her.

Gavrail turns to Noa. "What business does General Vaylor have here?" His tone is clipped, short, almost accusatory.

Noa's father answers for him. "He's trying to recruit Noa for his own unit come summer," he says, unmistakable pride in his voice as he looks at his son.

Gavrail's eyes darken, his body tensing, as he looks out over the quad at the general—the black of his uniform cutting and sharp, the awards of service dripping from his lapel denoting decades of missions and wars, stories not spoken of, or perhaps too classified to know.

My mother lets out a delicate yawn. Gavrail rises smoothly to his feet, asking if he can escort her back to her room for the night—years of manners ingrained in him by his father, ever the gentleman. The parents who didn't book accommodation in the nearby town of Elesmere were offered rooms at the Ivy House, my mother along with them.

She smiles at Gavrail with something close to adoration, placing a hand on his cheek. "Bless you, boy. It's been too long since I've seen that handsome face."

He inclines his head and bows with charming ease, just enough to distract from the way his shoulders hold tension beneath the easy smile. He then leads her away, leaving me with Noa and his parents under a starlit sky.

I watch them go, and something primal stirs inside me. A sense of protection… but not for my mother.

For him.

The kind of man who doesn't let anyone close unless he wants them there. And even then—only on his terms.

"Do you know what your plans are after graduation, Celeste?" Noa's mother asks. Her question is laced with an unmistakable sense of expectation. To the Galleghers, the Service isn't just a path—it is an honor, a duty one owes to their country.

"I'm not sure," I say honestly. The truth is, I haven't dared to imagine that far ahead.

Noa reaches for my hand under the table. "She's only a first-year, Mom," he says lightly. "There's still plenty of time to decide—and as long as that future has room for me in it, I don't care what she does."

His arm curls around the back of my chair, easy and sure. But I catch the glance his parents exchange, the small grin on Blake's face. The quiet approval. A shared understanding.

They see everything. So much like Noa, I think.

* * *

THE NEXT DAY brings the campus tour, where our parents are invited into our classrooms, given the rare chance to witness the inner workings of Whittaker—and, by extension, our lives.

My mother is immediately taken with Professor Barrows.

She hangs on his every word, her curiosity lighting up as he speaks about the interplay of ley lines and mineral resonance. I realize then—somewhat sheepishly—that I've never actually asked what type of elemental he is. I know he wields, of course, but haven't thought to find out which element.

Earth, it turns out. And suddenly, everything about him makes sense. He has the patience of stone worn smooth by time, his presence grounding and solid as the earth beneath his feet. Like mulch pressed into a garden bed, he is cultivating, nurturing, and known for helping things grow.

"Actually, Celeste here is one of my prized students," I hear him say, and my heart flutters with a kind of startled pride. "She's been working on a fascinating extra credit project about elemental fusion. I'm eager to see how it turns out."

My mother beams at me, clearly impressed, as he leads her through the classroom with gentle authority, gesturing toward charts and diagrams. I stand just behind them, a strange warmth blooming in my chest.

* * *

THE FOLLOWING EVENING, a formal dinner is planned in honor of officers and their families—a high-society affair, from what I've heard. Only the top-tier students are invited, along with handpicked guests.

I'm still brushing off the lingering bits of powdered root and dried petals clinging to my pants from the day's Botany lesson when Noa comes bursting into the Blue Dahlia common room, still in his gym clothes. His cheeks are flushed from the run and something brighter, light catching the fine sheen of sweat along his collarbone. His gray shirt clings to him, pulled tight over his chest and shoulders, every line of muscle defined beneath the fabric. There's a lazy heat in his gaze, a post-run glow that makes him look both wrecked and alive, like the world hasn't quite caught up to his pulse yet.

Gods, how does he look this good after a run? I'd probably look like a drowned rat.

"Guess what," he says, holding up a thick ivory invitation like a golden ticket. "You're going."

"I'm what?"

He grins. "To the dinner. You, me. Black tie, fancy food, full parade of fire and formality."

I raise a brow, still skeptical. "And I'm invited because...?"

He steps closer, the invitation now dangling between two fingers as if he's offering me a secret. "Because Headmaster Thorne said I could bring a guest," he says, then—smirking—"and General Vaylor told me to bring my *stunningly beautiful* girlfriend." The look he gives me is all fire and trouble.

The headmaster's name snags in my chest. I haven't told Noa yet about my father and Thorne's friendship—or the role Thorne played in getting me here.

Noa's arm hooks my waist and he dips me low. "Guess we better find you something to wear to the ball, Cinderella." His breath skims my lips. "But first..." His voice drops, rough velvet. "You're going to take me upstairs and into your shower so I can make sure to get you *thoroughly* dirty before we both get clean."

The hunger in his eyes ignites something low in me—and if swooning were a reasonable option, I'd have done it on principle alone.

CHAPTER 43

A lover's gaze or a general's command can often move the same pieces across the board.

—A History of Elemental Conflict: The Magickal Wars and Rebellions of the Last Millennium

I didn't bring anything formal enough for the dinner to Whittaker, but Amelia insists I borrow a gown of hers. Apparently, earth-wielders host a few formal gatherings throughout the year that warrant more than just jeans and a cute top.

I'm stunned when she hands me a gown of deep green silk—the kind of green that feels both lush and dangerous, like it was pulled straight from the heart of a forest. Delicate embroidery climbs the sheer fabric: leaves and pale-gold blossoms that shimmer as they spill down the gathered bodice and skirt like sunlight through a canopy.

Two velvet ribbons are tied into bows around my upper

arms, leaving my shoulders bare. The bodice is snug and regal, cut daringly low in the back—an invitation of skin—before giving way to a shimmering skirt that moves like windswept petals.

Rozsen does my hair in soft waves that fall down my back, pinning one side back with a gold barrette shaped like a crescent leaf. Elliot takes over my makeup: ruby lips and a dusting of bronze and gold shimmer across my eyelids, subtle but striking. It's a full squad effort.

When I finally look in the mirror, I don't recognize myself.

I look… transformed. Like something ancient. Magick-born. Like someone who can command storms or calm oceans with a glance.

And for a moment, I let myself believe it.

That maybe—just for tonight—I can be all of it. Without fear. Without hiding.

Someone worthy of the name Thalrien.

A knock sounds at our suite door.

Rozsen's eyes light with mischief. "That'll be him."

Elliot sweeps past us and cracks the door open just enough to peek. "No kidnapping without a signed form."

Noa's voice comes through the narrow gap, warm with amusement. "I'll risk it."

Elliot opens the door wider as she grins. And Noa steps inside.

For half a second, my brain blanks. Not because I haven't seen him in uniform—of course I have—but because this isn't the daily version of it. This is the formal cut, crisp and sharp, dark fabric fitted to his shoulders like it's been tailored with intent. His fire insignia and rank patches gleam cleanly against the sleeve. His hair is combed just enough to look effortless, and the turquoise of his eyes lights bright against the dark.

He stops mid-step. Just… stops.

All the easy swagger drains out of him like someone pulled the plug. His throat works as his jaw tightens.

For a rare, perfect moment, Noa Gallegher looks like he forgot how to breathe.

"Hi," I manage, because my mouth has forgotten everything else.

His eyes drop—slowly—to the velvet ribbons at my arms, to the gold blossoms stitched down the bodice, to the way the skirt pools around my feet like something alive. Then they lift again, focusing on my face with a heat that makes my skin prickle.

"Celeste," he says, and my name sounds different in his mouth tonight. Lower. Rougher. Like he's tasting it.

He crosses the room in three strides, and I watch Amelia and Rozsen immediately turn into statues of exaggerated innocence.

Noa stops in front of me, close enough that I can feel the warmth of him before he even touches me. "You look..." He blinks, as if searching for a word to explain whatever it is he's feeling.

"Like I'm about to drown under a wave of Service etiquette?" I offer.

A laugh breaks out of him—short, real—then his gaze sharpens again. His fingers brush my upper arm, feather-light, where the velvet ribbon is tied. His touch lingers just long enough to feel like a claim.

"No," he murmurs. "You look... beautiful." A beat. "You *are* beautiful."

Something warm blooms behind my ribs.

Elliot makes a choked noise. "Alright," she announces, clapping once. "We've done our civic duty. You two can have your fairytale night. But if you ruin her lipstick..." She narrows her eyes as she taps Noa smartly in the chest with her finger. "I will hunt you down and hurt you."

I laugh, but Noa's gaze dips briefly to my mouth—like the

thought crosses his mind, like he can picture it, vividly—and something dark and hungry flashes there before he reins it in.

"No promises," he whispers before holding out his arm to me. "Ready, Miss Farris?"

I hook my arm through his, letting myself feel the heat and steadiness of him.

"Ready, Mr. Gallegher."

* * *

THE DINNER IS HELD in the ballroom of the Ivy House—a place I've never set foot in until tonight.

Marble floors veined with gold gleam beneath the soft glow of crystal chandeliers. Tall, stately pillars guide us toward a vast room with ceilings that soar, three times taller than they are wide. Banquet tables are arranged with military precision, leaving an open space in front for dancing, and a raised platform to the left cradles the podium. Next to that, tucked beneath a gilded arch, a string quartet sits poised, their black attire sharp against the pale marble floors. Servants in immaculate white jackets line the walls, silver trays in hand, poised to begin service as we take our seats.

Headmaster Thorne steps up to the podium, ready to deliver one of his signature speeches, but before he can speak, the ballroom doors open with a slow and deliberate creak.

Six Krovya soldiers stand in formation beneath the arch, Gavrail and several Vikhrostrum students behind them, all dressed in their ceremonial uniforms—stately, polished, severe. But it is the man beside Gavrail who turns the air electric.

General Neron Kamenov.

Gavrail's father.

My spine straightens of its own accord. And suddenly I'm twelve years old again. Nervous and terrified to be caught dripping wet in his living room after Gavrail saved me from the lake.

A hush falls like frost over the room as a servant quietly guides them to a table near the front, adjacent to where General Vaylor and his officers are already seated.

Thorne clears his throat, waiting for attention to return to him. When it does, he smiles, steady and composed. "We are deeply honored tonight by a visit from General Kamenov," he says smoothly. "Of course, it is no surprise that he should find his way here, as we've had the privilege of hosting his son, Gavrail, at Whittaker this past year."

Whispers rise like phantoms around the room. A beat, then polite applause as eyes flick to the two striking men sitting beside each other.

"This evening is meant to honor our fourth-year students—the most accomplished class we've seen in decades. Their discipline, their skill, and their perseverance are a beacon of what lies ahead. The future is in good hands."

Louder applause now, from students and parents alike.

His gaze sweeps the room—then lands on Noa, pride softening the sharp lines of his expression. "And in a fortuitous turn of events," Thorne continues, "I am pleased to announce that one of our most exceptional students—top-ranking across all categories—Officer Noa Gallegher has officially been recruited by General Vaylor to join his elite Echo Squad immediately following graduation."

A rush of applause breaks like a wave. Cheers. Foot stomps. Finn and Ryan's "Oorah!" louder than the rest. But underneath it all, my blood goes strangely still. Because suddenly his future belongs to everyone in this room—and no longer just to us.

Noa grins. I look up at him in surprise as he leans in and squeezes my hand.

"It just happened. I didn't get the chance to tell you yet."

Well, that makes *two* things we now need to talk about.

* * *

THE DINNER IS SPECTACULAR—HONEY-DIPPED burrata on crostinis, lobster bisque served in demitasse cups, iced platters of oysters arranged in elegant spirals. A salad so delicate it looks like edible art. Then the entrées—black cod decadently marinated, buttered crab legs cracked open with silver picks, filet mignon drizzled in black truffle demi-glace. Every plate is a masterpiece, every bite divine.

We eat. We drink. Toast after toast is raised in Noa's honor—his courage, his brilliance, his future. Laughter rings like music, pride gleaming in his parents' eyes, and even Noa looks lighter, brighter, caught in the warmth of a room built to celebrate him.

And all I can do is smile through the tightening in my chest. I feel like a shadow at the edge of the light, clapping for a joy that I can't fully hold. Because beneath the champagne sparkle and silver applause, I know the truth no one is saying—he's leaving. We only have a month left, maybe two, and I'm not ready to let him go.

* * *

ONCE DINNER ENDS, the officers and families begin to mingle near tall side tables, the soft strains of the string quartet weaving through the room like silk.

Noa and his parents are quickly swept into a steady tide of guests—officers, officials, Whittaker professors—each offering congratulations and praise, each speaking of his future like it's already written in the stars.

I'm stepping back from the crowd, the room blurring at the edges, when a throat clears quietly behind me.

I turn. And my breath catches.

Gavrail is there, like a storm caught mid-breath. Not standing so much as claiming the space—black dress uniform carved to him, silver trim catching candlelight like a blade being drawn. Everything about him is restraint. Control so tight it feels almost violent.

His ash-brown hair is immaculately disheveled. A shadow of dark stubble frames the sharp line of his jaw. Every detail of him feels intentional—cut from shadow and steel, a body sculpted for war or worship, or both in equal measure.

But his eyes—his eyes are the tell.

They roam over me, possessive in a way I don't have words for. He looks at me like I'm something he wasn't expecting to see and hasn't yet figured out how to look away from.

It's the look that catches me off guard.

"Celeste," he says, voice low. He closes the distance with measured steps, each one deliberate, as if he's walking into enemy territory and daring anyone to object. He stops close enough that my magick stirs unbidden, responding to the shadows at my feet.

His gaze drops—slowly—to my hand.

To my ring.

A muscle feathers in his cheek.

He reaches for me, taking my hand with infuriating courtesy. A bow that reads like obedience—until he lifts my fingers to his mouth and presses a kiss to my knuckles.

His thumb slides over the ring—*his ring*—firm, unhurried. For a heartbeat, I swear it hums under his touch, faint and alive, like it recognizes him.

His eyes stay on me. Only me.

"You shouldn't be walking around looking like this, Zvez." His voice is calm; his eyes are anything but. "You'll start a war you don't intend to."

The way he's looking at me makes heat crawl up my spine. Like he can see every freckle, every mark, every scar *beneath* the gown.

Something catches in my throat. My heart races, erratic and

helpless, and I hate that he can do that, that he can make my body respond to him with the slightest look or touch. His mouth twitches. A shadow of a smile. That one dimple flickering into existence.

And then it's gone. The air grows impossibly tighter in an instant as a tall figure steps beside him.

General Kamenov is granite hidden within a marble exterior. Commanding. Beautiful in a cruel, unyielding way that leaves no trace of warmth. His features are Gavrail's, but colder. Stripped of softness and emotion.

Gavrail's home was one where children were neither seen nor heard. Most of my memories of his father are of his silent, judging presence... or of him scolding Gavrail in a low, lethal voice after we'd been caught doing something we shouldn't.

"Celeste," he says smoothly. "What an extraordinary surprise."

The look he gives me tells me that it's not. My lips tighten, and cold prickles at the base of my spine.

"Gavrail *neglected* to mention that you were a student here as well." His words weigh more than they should. An accusation.

I see Gavrail's jaw tick as he glances from his father to me, instinctively putting himself between us.

"Gavrail," the general says, not taking his eyes off me, "why don't you ask Celeste to dance?"

Not a question. A directive.

Gavrail's nod is clipped. Dutiful. But when he reaches for my hand, his fingers close around mine like he's claiming—not obeying.

Without a word, he draws me onto the marble floor as the string quartet shifts into something nuanced and lilting. It drifts over the ballroom like fog, coaxing couples into motion in a slow, obedient tide. And around us, the room subtly recalibrates: laughter thinning, conversations stuttering, heads turning as people sense something dangerous moving among them.

Gavrail's hand finds the small of my back. Heat bleeds through the silk where his palm rests, a brand laid down with courtly precision. His other hand closes over mine, fingers firm, unyielding.

He doesn't speak as he guides me through the first steps—smooth, effortless, like he was born knowing how to move people where he wants them. But there's something under the calm. A thread pulled too tight. A tether humming with strain.

His thumb drags once over my knuckle, a quiet, proprietary stroke. His mouth brushes close to my ear and a shiver runs through me.

"Why are you trembling, Zvez?" he asks, voice low. Barely a sound.

I turn my head, daring to meet his eyes.

It's a mistake.

He holds the stare, unflinching. There's no concern there. No softness. There is calculation: the same patient brutality he carries into a duel, the same cold certainty that makes people step aside without being asked. He's watching me like he's cycling through outcomes he's already measured... and choosing the one that hurts the most. But there's something else too—something like *recognition*.

The glint in his eyes isn't cruel.

It's *hungry*.

His mouth twitches—not quite a smile, but close—as he spins me outward with a flick of his wrist, then snaps me back into him before I can catch my balance. The air leaves my lungs in a small, involuntary laugh—startled and breathy.

His hold tightens a fraction. The mask he wears so well falters for a second.

Our bodies fit with a familiarity sharpened by absence. Too close. Too perfect. My traitorous pulse races.

His breath skims my cheek. "That laugh," he says, voice hushed, almost a confession, "has found its way into my dreams more times than I care to admit."

The music swells.

He dips me low—and for a heartbeat my world becomes his hand at my back, his arm like iron, the ceiling spinning into a chandeliered blur. When he lifts me again, he keeps me close, as if letting go isn't an option. And I can feel it then—the gravity between us. Inescapable and bone-deep.

"Do you remember," he murmurs, "watching the dancers from my father's study?"

I laugh again, younger versions of us at the edge of memory, like ghosts dancing beside us. "Of course," I say, the corner of my lips tipping up.

"You were always barefoot," he says. "You kept stepping on my feet." There's a bite to his words—fondness folded into something darker. Ownership sharpened to a point.

"You said I was the worst dancer you'd ever seen," I breathe, trying to laugh it off.

"You were," he says, the vibration of his lips against my hair. "But you were *mine*."

The words don't land with nostalgia. They land with weight. Not a possession spoken loudly, but a seal, pressed permanently into the space between us.

The silence that follows isn't empty. It's packed tight—full of things neither of us should say.

My breath hitches.

The ballroom spins around us—blurred gowns, candlelight, polite applause. But it's not part of us. Not anymore.

We're not dancing. We're circling something. Something dangerous.

I press my hand to his chest, feeling the steady beat under uniform and bone. His pulse drags mine with his—over the edge of some unseen ledge until we're both falling.

"Gavrail..." I whisper, my voice too soft. Too real. A warning and a plea braided into one. Wanting to stay in this moment. Wanting to run from it.

I realize only then that we've stopped moving.

He doesn't let go. Not right away.

His hands remain where they are as his gaze drops to my mouth—and the air between us is suddenly knife-thin, one wrong breath and we will both be cut. Left to bleed out on the marble floor.

Then, slowly—deliberately, like turning his back on a fire he still wants to burn in—he eases his grip.

He releases me. I step away, not daring to look back.

But I feel him anyway—a shadow stitched to mine.

Like gravity I'm not sure I can ever escape.

* * *

MY HEART IS STILL HAMMERING beneath my ribs, the chandeliers blurring as I slip past the ballroom doors, leaving behind silk, music... and the memory of the boy who used to spin me around through the shadows.

But just before I cross the threshold, I feel it—

A flicker at the edge of instinct.

Two gazes. Heavy, assessing.

General Vaylor watches from one side of the ballroom, his posture unyielding, drink untouched in his hand. He's silent and poised as his gaze flicks between me and Gavrail, then between me and Noa, tracking every movement with his sharp, calculating blue eyes.

Directly across the room from him stands General Kamenov, one hand folded neatly behind his back. He doesn't blink. His diplomatic smile hasn't moved since the moment I stepped away with his son.

Opposite ends of the room.

Same silence.

I don't look back, but the pull of their attention feels like threads hooked into my spine. The weight lingers—like warning. Like a reckoning already in motion.

And I wonder, suddenly, which of them sees the threat—and which sees the weapon.

I don't stay to find out.

CHAPTER 44

The oldest bonds are forged in blood—not all remain intact.
—Tapestries of Power: A Study of Magickal Bloodlines and Lineage

I find Noa already seated in Advanced Potions, his voice rising above the gentle clatter of glassware and Professor Ching's gravelly instructions. He and Finn are recapping the dinner like it was some exhilarating sporting match—laughing, mimicking guests with theatrical flair.

Noa turns to me as I sit down. "Where did you go last night? You slipped out early."

"I was tired," I reply simply. "Had some last-minute cramming to do for my conflicts and rebellions exam."

It isn't a lie. The moment I got back to my room, I opened my textbooks and let history drown out the present—names of uprisings and treaties pushing away the memory of silver eyes and thoughts I don't let rise to the surface.

Noa's expression softens. His voice lowers, nearly lost beneath Professor Ching's demonstration of boiling nettleweed.

"I'm sorry I left you alone. My parents had me meeting half the delegation. I didn't know Thorne would make the announcement in public like that."

"It's fine, Noa," I murmur, leaning forward to kiss him—soft, quick. "I had a great time. Thank you for inviting me."

He squeezes my hand, a smile on his lips, eyes still bright from yesterday's events.

* * *

I MEET my mom for lunch in the afternoon, grabbing takeout from the mess hall to have a picnic in the spring bloom the campus finds itself in.

The quad is livelier now—students lingering longer after class, coats unbuttoned, laughter echoing as tension briefly gives way to the spring air. The temperature is crisp but no longer biting, carrying with it the scents of magnolia and crushed clover. Rain comes on quick some days, misty showers that leave the paths slick and the rooftops shining. Umbrellas flick open with practiced ease, though a few water-wielders stroll bare-headed, content to let the drizzle slide over them.

We head to the Lakehouse, where they've set up an awning and picnic tables across the back deck, perfect for meals or study dates overlooking the view. Crocuses bloom along the lake path, and the willows sway with fresh green tips, their branches dipping low in the breeze. The air carries warmth now—subtle but sure—rising off the water of the lake as birds return to the trees overhead.

My mom sits across from me, and Gavrail next to her after she insisted he join us. He's quiet, polite. He hasn't looked at me once. We keep things light—weather, classes, the latest Whittaker gossip. Neither of us mentions the night before. Both of us are content to let the ghosts of our pasts stay there, for the moment.

Eventually, I ask, careful not to put too much behind it: "Mom… did Dad ever talk about his past much? Before you met?"

She pauses, smile faltering. "Your father was never much of a talker, Celeste. But yes… he had a past, like we all do." Her voice softens as her eyes go distant—heavy with the weight of memory, dark and full of sorrow, the look she has whenever she thinks about Dad.

I press further. "When did he meet Headmaster Thorne?"

She frowns, thoughtful. "Your father and Evander were close before I ever met him. They were old schoolmates and worked together for the government, right after college, I believe. Something to do with Magick-tracing, I think. There was some special case Thorne kept in touch about, even after they stopped working together. Something to do with a Magick and her child who disappeared. I can't for the life of me remember their names. But I always assumed it was a long-lost relative of your dad. And now, seeing you—your water magick—I wonder if that's how you inherited it."

For a second, the lake sounds too loud in my ears—every lap of water rings like a warning.

"Yeah… maybe." The lie unsettles me but I don't say more.

"They lost touch for a while, though, soon after we were married. Life happens, as you know." She waves a hand casually in the air. "But he came to your father's memorial. He was incredibly helpful. Told me he'd take care of your application personally." She beams at me at that. "And look at you now. Thriving. Magick. Gosh, I'm so proud of you, honey."

Something isn't sitting right. Gavrail leans back in his chair, arms crossed. I can tell he thinks so too. He shifts beside her, subtly. But I can see the slight tightening of his jaw.

I hesitate before asking, "Was Dad ever married before?"

Her expression hardens. "Heavens, why would you ask that?" she snaps, then reins herself in. "I would *know* if your father had another life before us, Celeste." Her eyes are stern, like she's scolding a child version of me from my past.

Gavrail catches my eye, giving me a barely perceptible shake of his head.

So she doesn't know about Dad, then.

The warning in Gavrail's eyes is clear—the less she knows, the safer she is. And suddenly, I'm starting to realize the delicate line that Gavrail has had to walk all these years. The intricate contradictions that occur between protection and lies when it comes to the people you love.

The conversation turns back to midterms and projects due, Professor Barrows's essay on the ethical limits of elemental state manipulation. My mom asks Gavrail about his classes, his friends, then politely asks after his father, who leaves tomorrow.

"Oh, Gavrail, that reminds me." She reaches into her bag. "A package was delivered to me this morning. From your mother."

Gavrail freezes. I see it—the tensing of his shoulders, the flicker of something sharp behind his eyes.

"I was sorry to hear about your parents' divorce," she continues gently. "Your mother wrote the loveliest note. Said she was happy you and Celeste were at the same school and together again after all this time. She mentioned she hasn't heard from you in years."

Gavrail stays silent.

My mother, undeterred, presses on. Her eyes fix on him, pain and heartbreak at the thought of a mother and son estranged. "I don't know what came between you two, but she's your mother, Gavrail. That bond matters. Nothing is worth losing that." She reaches across the table to squeeze his hand, as if warmth alone could heal the wounds left behind by years of silence. "Minka Senkova was always a complicated woman," she says. "But she loves you. That I know." She hands him the package—a rectangle wrapped in plain brown paper. Her eyes are curious. "Strange that she sent it to me instead of directly to you."

Gavrail takes the package carefully, as if it might cut him. He opens it slowly, tearing off the brown wrapping paper. It's a book, spine cracked and cover faded with age. His fingers trace the edge as he looks at the title:

Tales from the Breath of Stone.

I try to hide my gasp of surprise. Gavrail glances at me, eyes wide with warning and something else.

How did she know?

My skin prickles like I've stepped into cold water fully clothed.

I look between the book, Gavrail, and my mother—still sipping tea, lost in the gentle lie of a perfect afternoon.

I realize now how secrets make ghosts of the people we love.

And I wonder how many more haunt the edges of this school.

CHAPTER 45

Myth is never merely myth. In every legend, the pulse of history beats.

—A History of Magick, Vol. I

Parents' Week comes to a close with hugs and handshakes, teary smiles and gentle touches. My mother and I both cry as we say our goodbyes. Noa's parents make me promise to visit them in Virginia when I'm home for the summer holidays. My mother *demands* that Gavrail come stay with us for part of it.

Once the excitement of visitors is over, Gavrail and I pore over every word of *Tales from the Breath of Stone*. The book is full of haunting stories wrapped in mythology—witches and warlords, dragons and mermaids, kings who bargain with the elements and lovers who don't survive their devotion. The stories are beautiful in the way storms are beautiful: awe-inducing, inevitable, and always threatening to end in ruin.

Gavrail lent me the book, hoping one of us might find something the other doesn't—Noa having now been roped into helping us with our research.

I sit cross-legged on the rug in my suite's common room, the ancient book open in front of me. Noa lounges on the couch behind me, one arm draped along the backrest, his hand idly resting at my shoulder. The fire crackles low in the hearth, casting shifting light over the worn leather cover. *Tales from the Breath of Stone* smells like dust and smoke and something older still—pages yellowed and soft at the corners, as though they've been turned by generations of hands.

I trace my fingers along the inked title of the chapter: "The Twins' Unraveling." The script shimmers faintly in the firelight.

"This one's clearly about elemental fusion, Magick to Magick. It's a warning, I think, about when it doesn't go right." I begin to read aloud:

There were once two mages—sisters born under the same moon, but to different elements.

One wielded water, the other sunlight.

They believed their bond made them unstoppable.

In defiance of the old codes, they attempted the Rite of Convergence, seeking to fuse their powers into something no world had seen before: frozen light, solar radiance encased in stillness, a perfect weapon for truth—or destruction.

But they forgot the first law of fusion: balance.

One craved control, the other chaos.

When their magick met, it did not blend—it battled.

Their bodies unraveled into streaks of frost and solar flare, and the mountain where they stood shattered from within, creating a cliff over which a torrent of frozen water now forever screams into the void below.

And the sisters' voices, they say, can still be heard—arguing in endless echo, forever frozen in time.

I FLIP TO ANOTHER CHAPTER, carefully skimming through the pages. "This one doesn't say embodiment outright," I murmur, "but I think this poem is referring to it." I start to read again.

THERE ONCE LIVED A TIDE-BORN DAUGHTER,
born where rivers meet the sea.
She fell in love with a fisherman,
but with a love that could never be.
For he was land and she was water,
forever destined to be apart.
Her grief was so vast, it made the sea swell with tears,
nothing able to heal her broken heart.
She fractured into droplets,
dissolving into mist,
the rain now carrying her whispers,
every storm now holds her kiss.
Moving as one with the current,
ships vanishing beneath her wails,
her tempests destroying everything,
a lesson when love does not prevail.

I FINISH THE PAGE QUIETLY.

Noa leans forward, elbows on his knees. "It says she dissolved into mist. That sounds similar to what you can do."

I don't answer right away. My pulse flickers. "She didn't return to her body," I finally say. "Can that happen?"

Noa's gaze drops to the book. "Myths hide truth in plain sight," he says slowly. A beat. "But yes—if this refers to embodiment, it reads like there is a point of no return." He frowns, glancing down at the next page. "Here's another: 'The Heart Beneath the Mountain,'" he says, his voice cautious now.

IT IS SAID that where the mists coil through forests of iron and peaks of stone, where the bones of the earth rise to touch the stars—there, Sarn of the Iron Vale buried his heart.

A warrior born of mountain blood and battle cry. He feared no man, no beast. Only Time. For Time is the one enemy no sword can slay.

He wandered into the deep places of the world—beneath roots thick with forgotten magick, past rivers that ran black with memory—until he found a hollow, where the bones of the mountain meet the breath of the world.

There, he tore his heart from his chest and buried it beneath the stone, believing that without it, Time could never find him.

And for a while, it was so.

When he returned to his people, he was invulnerable—but changed. Skin hard as granite, so thick that no blade could pierce him. Eyes that no longer reflected light. A voice that echoed as if spoken from within a cave. Each step he took cracked the stone beneath him.

He was becoming too much earth, and not enough man. Soon, his blood thickened to shale. His breath turned to dust.

At last, afraid of what he had become, he traveled to the mountain, seeking to reclaim his buried heart.

But the earth does not return what it was freely given.

He collapsed beside his heart, his limbs crumbling like ancient cliffs.

His body broke into six—six shards scattered, all reaching toward each other, and toward the heart they now protect.

And deep in the eldest range, his heart still waits—forever beating, sealed beneath the mountain, guarded by the blood of stone and earth's black memory. The cliffs still echo with his name.

A warning and a promise:
Immortality always comes with a cost.

"SARN," Noa mutters. "Sounds like a tragic idiot."

I glance at him. "You don't think it's real?"

"I think it's a metaphor disguised as warning. You want to become unbreakable? Immortal? Fine. But you're not coming back as you once were." Before I can answer, Noa leans casually against the armrest, one hand absentmindedly stroking my back. "I found another one," he says. "'The Flame That Devoured a Crown.'"

I look up as he begins reading:

VIRELDA, the flame-born princess, was born not to rule—but to burn. The Heart of Fire sang to her, its call rising in her blood as her elemental power grew beyond all bounds.

When her form became flame, neither wall nor will could contain her, and her people despaired, then conspired. It is said that they lured her through an old stone tunnel beneath the southern mountain, where earth meets sea and fire breathes from the deep. There, beneath the peak that never sleeps, she found the origin of fire itself—an eternal flame that held her close. Because flame remembers its own. And what it claims, it claims forever. When she discovered her people's treachery, she devoured them, until nothing remained in the cavern and tunnel but blood and ash.

She stands within the heart's flame still, bound and burning, her hunger and vengeance endless. And it is told: should the eternal flame ever call to another, they too must face her fire—or be forever lost to it.

THE FIRE HISSES softly as if listening, smoke curling toward the ceiling.

"Hm." He frowns, thumbing through the next page. "This one's… torn." He angles the book toward the firelight. The parchment edge is streaked, not simply ripped, as if something tried to drown the words it carried. Ink has bled in strange constellations—half remembered, half erased.

He reads slowly, his voice low. "*When the heavens ruled from above and the elements from below… something ancient returned to the world. And where the stars fell, a child was found.*"

A chill moves through me.

He pauses, searching. "*Starlight lived within her eyes, and from her hands, magick flowed in endless—*"

His voice falters as he scans for what remains.

"*… an impossible choice.*"

Then he turns the page gently—and the rest is gone. Just more water-stained pages.

He studies the top margin, jaw tightening. "The title isn't fully legible. Just 'ST—' and then it's missing."

The ink bleeds outward, as though the word itself tried to escape the page.

The air in the room seems to thin.

Only one faint line of the myth remains, pressed into the bottom margin like an afterthought. The words shimmer when the firelight hits them as he reads it aloud.

"*The world saved by what it could not keep.*"

For a moment, neither of us move.

It feels less like a myth and more like a warning.

Noa exhales. "Someone ripped this out on purpose," he murmurs. "You can see the tear—too clean to be an accident."

My pulse stirs, uneasy. "Why?"

"Either someone didn't like the story…" He looks up, gaze locking on mine. "Or didn't want anyone else to read it."

I tell myself it's just a story, another myth swallowed by time. But as the fire pops sharply in the hearth, something deep in my chest responds, like a memory that isn't mine, waking.

I reach over to close the book slowly, my fingers lingering on the cover.

This isn't a book of happy endings.

"Tell me again how embodiment is supposed to be a gift?"

Noa stares at the fire, watching as a log breaks from the flame at its center. "It's not a gift. It's a... transformation."

"It sounds like a curse," I say. "To become what you wield is to be ruled by it."

Noa looks down, thoughtful but serious. "I know what fire wants. It doesn't stop. It only consumes."

A silence settles over us.

"So what does that make me?" I ask quietly. "Water remembers everything. If I become ruled by it... what if I remember so much that I forget myself?"

Noa's voice softens. "If you forget yourself—even if you forget me—I'll find you. And I'll remind you who you are." He leans down to kiss me, soft and tender, his lips warm and full as I kiss him back.

The fire crackles, but we don't speak again. Words are no longer needed for what we are both wanting. A reminder of life, of self.

I stand and take his hand, leading him toward my bedroom, silently thanking Teo for asking Roz out again tonight. Inside, I walk over to my bedside table to take out a carefully wrapped package in gold paper.

His eyebrows rise in surprise, a hint of a smile tugging at the corner of his mouth. "What's this?"

"Happy birthday, Noa." I smile at the look of surprise on his face. "Finn told me. I wanted to do something... just for you."

He sits on the bed, unwrapping the package carefully. Inside is a small silver charm—meant to be sewn into a uniform, tucked somewhere private, where no one else will ever see. It's a mermaid in profile, hair flowing, one sapphire eye catching the moonlight through the window. *Me.*

"So I can be with you," I whisper, "even when I can't."

Outside the window, rain begins to fall—slow, steady, and silent as memory.

"It's perfect." He traces the outline of the charm with his fingertip. Then he looks up at me suddenly. "I don't even know when your birthday is."

I laugh softly. "End of September. I'm not big on birthdays, so I didn't really tell anyone."

He reaches out and pulls me toward him, his hand warm around mine. "I promise next year, we'll celebrate."

Next year.

The words land like both a gift and a plea.

He kisses me. Feather light. Deliberate.

We take our time. Not the usual fire and heat between us—something quieter. An anchor to each other in the rising tide of change.

He undresses me slowly, like he's savoring every piece of me. And I do the same.

We stand at the foot of my bed, before he lifts me, laying me down with reverence.

The rain taps against the glass as he kisses me like he has all the time in the world. His eyes say what neither of us wants to acknowledge.

He's leaving.

The Service. Graduation.

The distance that's already started.

Tears sting my eyes. He kisses them away, his face betraying the quiet war within him. Worry for me. For himself.

The weight of us is drawn deeper—toward some darker part of a lake we can't yet see.

He follows the trail of my tears with his lips, murmuring soft comforts to chase the thoughts away. He kisses my cheeks, my lips, my chin, my neck… lower still, worshipping me like he's trying to memorize the way I feel beneath his mouth, his skin. His warm hands glide down my body as if I'm made of silk.

I gasp as I feel his fingers slide into me at the same time his tongue circles my breast. The heat of him is a balm against the chill lacing the air.

The rain now drips silently down my window, like the tears he kissed away.

He moves up to kiss me again, his fingers still moving with a gentle rhythm that makes me moan against his mouth.

The wave begins to build—rising, cresting.

"Noa... please," I beg.

He nods and moves between my thighs, his hard length pressing against me, moving so agonizingly slow that I stop breathing for a moment.

He eases into me, his hand cupping my jaw, thumb brushing my cheek as he watches me with unwavering focus.

"I love you," he whispers, a breath away.

I say it back—not just with words, but with my body. My soul.

I take what I can. Give what I can. We move like that—slow, then faster. Deep, then deeper still.

We make love through the night, finding our release, returning to each other again and again. Both chasing the chance of forever we are afraid might not come.

In between, there is laughter. Soft teasing. Stories of his childhood and mine. Lives we've lived. Lives we only dare to dream of. We speak of the change pressing in around us—his future bound in flame and oath, mine unraveling with every tide.

I tell him the truth I barely admit to myself: that I'm afraid I'll be swallowed by the water. That I'll become current and memory, lost to drown in something ancient, vast and merciless.

At that, he grips my chin and turns me to face him. "You

could drown the stars and wipe the sky clean… and I'd still find you. Still love you. Even in the dark."

I kiss him again, long and lingering.

And when the dawn breaks, sparkling on the crystals the rain left behind, we drift to sleep, wrapped in each other's arms.

Because, for a little while, we still have this.

Because tomorrow is not today.

CHAPTER 46

The fiercest storms are not born from skies, but from within.
—"The Tempest of the Hollow King," from *Tales from the Breath of Stone*

The final duel of the year is to be held in the Garden Grove—between Whittaker's fourth-year earth-wielder Beatrice and the Vikhrostrum wind master, Vihar.

The Garden Grove doesn't seem like a place meant for violence. It is a place that smells of crushed basil and spring blooms, not blood and fury. The courtyard at its heart has been cleared: sand freshly raked, vines pulled back. The air feels alive with expectation. Professors line the perimeter. Even the fruit trees and insects that would normally buzz around us fall silent.

Beatrice stands at the center, bare feet planted in the soft earth. Her curls are pulled into a loose knot, her sleeves rolled to the elbows. Nothing about her looks dangerous—until you see the stillness in her stance. The patience. Like stone waiting to shape itself.

Across from her, Vihar prowls forward, a tempest incarnate, his hair tossing around like ocean surf during a storm. His coat snaps sharply at his knees as he steps forward, eyes flashing. There is no patience or kindness in his gaze—only determination.

No one has forgotten what Jin Feng did to Teo. And no one is expecting Vihar to hold back.

Professor Bram Graves, the earth Magick dueling professor, raises his hand. "Begin."

Vihar doesn't wait. A surge of wind bursts through the grove, flattening herbs, snapping stalks, tossing petals like confetti. Beatrice braces low, sliding backward as the first wave of wind hits. But she doesn't panic—she moves with purpose, trailing her fingers through the sand.

A mound of earth rises to meet the next blast. It doesn't stop the wind, but it bends it—sending it sideways in a burst of thyme and dust.

Vihar scowls, lip curling in disgust. "I thought Whittaker trained warriors. All I see is a gardener."

Beatrice shifts left, toward the cracked herb bed. Her fingers curl, and beneath the sand, root systems begin to stir.

Vihar strikes again, wind slicing a clean arc toward her torso. But Beatrice drops—and the ground drops with her. A hidden trench splits open beneath him. He stumbles mid-lunge and crashes sideways, half his momentum lost.

Gasps echo from the students lining the grove's stone walls.

Beatrice rises slowly, the earth closing behind her. "You're loud, like the wind you control. You're used to everything bending to you," she says. "But you aren't careful. There is a time for action and a time for patience."

Vihar sneers, cold, calculating. "Let's see how careful you are after I destroy you *and* your garden."

He lifts both arms—and the wind howls. It tears across the grove like an invisible beast, shredding leaves, snapping vines off their trellises. One blast shatters a large glass pane in the greenhouse. Another sends a raised bed crashing sideways.

The glass.

A cruel gust sends the broken shards slicing through the air, hurling them around like wild knives, uncontrolled and indiscriminate.

Beatrice barely has time to react. A wall of stone surges between her and the attack, the wind exploding against it. The glass flings sideways.

And then—

A scream.

My heart stops.

Because I know, even before I turn to look, who it is.

Amelia.

She was standing near the aqueduct edge. Too close. The wind slammed her against a lattice frame, crumpling her like a broken doll. Shards of glass piercing her body, her limbs flailing at different angles, a sick image of a marionette with strings tangled around her in violence.

Beatrice cries out, running to her. Vihar sees but doesn't care. His hands rise again, wind already spiraling for another blow.

Time seems to freeze.

And something inside me *snaps.*

The broken aqueduct's runoff swirls around my boots.

I don't think. The water obeys me before I even tell it to.

It licks upward, coiling into the air like breath made liquid, wrapping my arms in a shimmer that catches the sun and fractures it.

The next strike isn't wind. It's water.

The current screams as it moves, a whip of heated water that hisses through the broken grove and slams into Vihar, knocking him off his feet. He catches himself in midair—but I don't give him time to recover.

I raise my arms, the water following—coiling upward, lashing forward like something hunting.

He throws a gale toward me. I don't even try to move.

The water swallows it and him completely. It wraps his arms, his chest. Freezing to ice in a single breath.

He thrashes—and I squeeze tighter.

A thread of water finds his mouth just as he begins to shout. The sound cuts off. The water surges in. And down. His body jerks, eyes wide, bubbles shattering against the cold.

I stand there and watch, my pulse a steady drum, my fingers trembling—not from weakness but from choice.

Part of me wants to stop it. To ease my grip, to let him breathe.

But part of me doesn't.

Because it isn't just him anymore. It's every Magick who took things from me. Every hand that hurt my father. Every blade raised against those like my family.

The water isn't just drowning him—it's drowning *them*. All of them. And gods help me, for one terrible heartbeat, I want it to.

"Enough!" Headmaster Thorne's voice cracks across the courtyard like a thunderclap.

Professors Graves and Ashar are already moving. Shields form in a flash, severing the magick before I can respond. Vihar collapses, coughing, sputtering, drenched and shivering in the sunlit sand. He looks shaken. The brush with death clings to him in the form of thin icicles still hanging from his coat.

The water hisses as it falls away, not satisfied. Or maybe it's me that's not.

The grove is silent except for the broken trickle of the aqueduct. Professor Ashar is staring at me as if I'm a piece of a puzzle he wasn't aware he was missing. His head is tilted to the side, his eyes cold, a question in them.

Amelia groans from where she lies, half sheltered beneath a

lattice beam. Rozsen and Elliot are already with her. Peter crouches beside them, anxious and worried as he holds Amelia's small hand in his. Ian stands over Vihar, fists clenched, vibrating with fury.

"She's okay," Elliot says, her voice shaking. "We've got her."

"She's not okay," Ian snaps, anger bristling, fire magick sparking at his knuckles. "He could have killed her!" But Professor Kael is there, holding a hand up to Ian, a command to stand down.

Then the whispers start. Everywhere. All around me. I can hear them beneath the buzzing of the crowd.

"Did you see what she did?"

"The water—did you see how it moved?"

"Did she mean to do that?"

I can feel my squad's eyes flicking between Amelia, Vihar, and me. A mixture of awe and disbelief and something else... Fear.

At the power I just displayed.

Rozsen's look is sharp, almost accusatory. Not anger, exactly, but hurt. That I didn't trust her to know this part of me. But even through the sting of her gaze, I feel the pride behind it. Of watching me finally let go and show what I'm capable of. Like she's always known it was there, under the surface.

I stare at my hands. They're still wet, still vibrating faintly with residual magick. Water shimmers on my wrists like silver veins. The sapphire of my ring glistens, the water clinging to it like a veil. Water didn't just come when I called—it surged, with more force than I meant. More instinct than control.

I feel Gavrail before I see him, standing next to me, shoulders squared. His gaze is focused, a lethal stillness echoing in the space he takes—eyes fixed on Vihar like he's already planning the next move if mine didn't land hard enough.

Noa moves through the crowd in seconds, silent until he's standing in front of me. "Celeste."

I flinch. I don't look away from my hands.

"You almost..." He touches my wrist, his voice quiet, gentle—but edged. "Are you okay?"

I shake my head. "I don't know." My shoulders tense, shame suddenly curling cold in my chest.

"She nearly drowned a student," Professor Graves barks, stepping into the ring. "In front of half the school."

"Because you let it get that far," Gavrail says coldly, taking up a defensive stance next to me. "Maybe don't lecture the one who stepped in when you should have."

Graves stiffens, but doesn't respond.

Gavrail doesn't move. He just stands there, an immovable force. Vihar won't meet his eyes—neither will anyone else.

The whispers continue. Students around the grove watch the scene unfold with wide eyes. Some are pale. Some look thrilled. One girl from Vikhrostrum mutters something in a different tongue before backing slowly toward the archway.

"Celeste Farris." Thorne's voice rings out. Clear. Authoritative. "My office. Thirty minutes."

I turn, slowly. The water is already evaporating from my arms, but the mark it leaves is unmistakable.

The Garden Grove, once vibrant with the new life of spring, now stands bruised and broken—flower beds overturned, trellises cracked, petals scattered like ashes.

And in the center of it all—me.

Thorne is standing there, arms at his sides, looking at me with a mixture of curiosity and something else, something darker—and there it is, just behind his eyes: a flicker of something that almost looks like... satisfaction. Like I've just proven a point I didn't know he wanted me to make.

Wet footprints follow me as I walk away, the whispers still rising like wind in my wake.

CHAPTER 47

Not all serpents strike. Some simply wait for prey to step close enough before swallowing it whole.

—"The Coil Beneath the Rock," from *Tales from the Breath of Stone*

I head to the ancient Administration building, nestled between the infirmary and the gymnasium. The building stands like a sentinel—quiet, watchful, and out of place among the newer architecture.

Built in the early 1700s, it's one of the oldest—and most quietly beautiful—structures on campus. Its exterior is carved from weather-darkened stone. Shimmers of light from the arched stained-glass windows color the fortress-like facade. Three stories tall and narrow with a slightly crooked silhouette, the building leans with age, but never falls. It has been said—never officially confirmed—that beneath it lie the stone dungeons, sealed off generations ago—a remnant from an era when punishment was law and mercy was still learning to speak. The building predates the school's more enlightened governance, back when Magick Councils ruled with iron fists and dissent was chained, not debated.

The lower levels no longer appear on architectural schematics, and no faculty member will acknowledge their existence out loud. But the signs remain: a bricked-over stairwell behind the eastern records room. Doors that lead nowhere. Some say the dungeons weren't just cells, but places of magickal nullification, where a specific type of stone was built into the bones of the building itself to suppress elemental magick. Once used to hold people too dangerous to kill, but too powerful to release. There are even rumors of a door in Thorne's office, hidden behind centuries-old tapestries, that leads straight down into the past.

I take the polished stone steps to the top floor. The marble hallway outside the headmaster's study is unusually quiet, the stained glass overhead casting fractured light patterns across the floor. The air feels dense—like the corridor is holding its breath. A place of judgment, not passage.

The headmaster's door looms at the far end—taller than any of the others along the hall, made of heavy, dark-stained ironwood, veined with shadowy grain that catches the light. Carved into its surface are curling glyphs in an old dialect of elemental magick—they seem to pulse faintly when I get too close.

The lock on the door involves no simple turn of a key; it's a layered mechanism of shifting metal rings nested within each other, each one etched with impossibly fine runes. It looks more like a puzzle box than a lock, designed to rebuff intrusion, not just mechanically. A subtle hum rises from it—faint, like wind trapped behind stone. The silver handle is wrought in the shape of a serpent devouring its own tail, and looks cool to the touch.

The door opens before I reach for it. And my ring burns cold.

"Miss Farris," Thorne says. His voice is calm, smooth. Almost disinterested. "Come in."

I freeze. "It's—Celeste, sir. I'm not—"

"Of course." A faint smile touches his lips, but it doesn't fully reach his eyes. "Celeste. You've become quite the topic around campus lately, the show you just put on only furthering that."

He steps aside, a silent invitation.

I hesitate, then step inside reluctantly. The water in my veins is immediately on edge.

His study is lined with tall shelves full of Service medals and old globes, maps with curling edges and tomes bound in cracked leather. The windows are slightly ajar, a breeze curling through the room despite the chill outside. It smells like aged paper and fresh ink, but underneath, a cold metallic tang rides the air, laced with ozone.

He leads me toward the desk—a broad, time-darkened slab of walnut worn smooth at the edges, cluttered with parchment stacks, a heavy glass paperweight, and an open scheduler lined with neat, slanted handwriting.

To the left stand three tall file cabinets. The first two are metal and stand out in this room of ancient books and gleaming wood—deliberately modern. The last one is carved of some ancient wood, its paint scuffed and dull with age. I note that its drawers have locks.

Behind the desk, a wide window overlooks the quad. From this height, I can just make out students crossing the lawn below, blurred by the glass, their voices faint.

He rounds the desk, folding his hands behind his back. "Your professors tell me you are on track to be ranked first in your year. A remarkable feat for one with such a late start in magick."

"Thank you, sir."

He nods, almost to himself, before looking at me again. "I knew your father. Did you know that?"

I hesitate before nodding. "My mother told me as much."

"A brilliant man," Thorne murmurs. "Troubled, perhaps. But brilliant."

There's something wrong with the way he says it. Like he's memorized the phrase. Practiced it.

"I pulled strings to make sure you had a place here, once I saw your name on the admissions list."

"That was... kind of you."

A silence stretches between us. The breeze shifts, unsettling a sheaf of parchment on the edge of his desk.

"You remind me of him in some ways," he says, almost absently. "Though not so much in others."

I study his face. There's something too careful in the way he's talking to me—something slinking behind the stillness.

A sharp knock interrupts.

Thorne's gaze flicks to the door. "One moment," he says, moving to answer it.

He leaves the door ajar as he steps into the hallway, voice low, speaking to someone just out of view. A staff member, maybe. I can't make out the words.

My eyes drift to the corner of the room.

Propped beside an unused reading chair, a stack of maps is laid out on a side table, with more rolled maps leaning against the wall beside them. Most of them are old—thick parchment edged in gold, detailing fault lines and ancient borderlands. I'm drawn to the one on top showing Whittaker's grounds in delicate inkwork, drawn before the Logistics building was even built.

I almost fail to notice the one beneath it.

A plain map. Folded once. Faded topography shaped in a way that's instantly familiar.

I shift my weight subtly for a better angle, just enough to catch the outline of mountains along one edge and a wide body of water curving like a sickle near the bottom.

I know that curve.

The lake.

My lake.

And just beyond it—though the names are too small to read —I'm almost certain I see the ridgeline that cuts above my farm in Virginia.

No marks. No ink. No indication of why it's here.

Just the wrong map in the wrong place.

But what the hell is it doing here?

The floor creaks softly as Thorne returns, smoothing the cuffs of his sleeves. He motions for me to sit in one of the two high-back tufted-leather chairs across from his desk. "Apologies," he says, as if nothing's shifted at all. "Where were we?"

"You were saying I remind you of my father?" I sit down.

He waves the question off. "He too had a way of hiding things in plain sight. You—" He stops, watching me intently now, as if trying to read me. "Your power. It's… untempered. Curious." He walks to the window, looking out over the quad. "When he died…" A shadow crosses his face in that moment, gone in the next. "The world will not be the same because of it," he says finally, searching my face.

I nod, slow and guarded. "Were you able to connect with him… before he—?"

"Your father was a complicated man. Always chasing shadows. Never content with the world as it was."

A chill drifts across the floor. He didn't answer the question.

"I do remember the last time I saw him, though," Thorne says, his voice quiet now. "He was wearing that awful blue shirt he always favored—I always told him to throw it away; too many holes." He shakes his head as he looks out toward the quad again. "But he was asking for my help regarding you, as a matter of fact."

He glances at me, something flickering behind his eyes. A shift, like a mask slipping.

"He had written a letter expressing concern about your powers that were emerging. He wanted my advice. He came here to meet with me, to discuss what could be done."

My breath catches.

"He came to Whittaker?" I ask, confused. He never told me that. In fact, he almost never left the farm in the months before he died. And definitely not long enough to get to Whittaker and back.

"Never mind this talk of sad things," Thorne says briskly. "I always believe tragedy has a purpose. Sometimes... it's the beginning of something greater."

"What possible purpose could there be for my father dying?" The words escape before I can stop them. My eyes are narrowed, ice sharpening my voice. My hands clench at my sides, but I don't let him see.

"Only what was inevitable," he says cryptically. His face is unreadable.

A breeze slips through an open window somewhere, sudden and biting—too cold for spring. The papers on his desk flutter in response.

"Your mother always worried about him," Thorne murmurs, not quite facing me. "Said he kept too many secrets. Couldn't let go of his obsession with Magicks. With his hatred of them." A pause. "She was right, of course. In the end, the weight of it all was too much."

The words hang in the air like embers on the verge of catching flame.

I heard the rumors—that it wasn't an accident at all, that he possibly killed himself. But I know better. I knew my father, and while he might have been capable of a lot of things, things I wasn't even aware of until recently, he would *never* have done that.

Thorne steps toward the door, already ending the conversation. "You have great potential, Celeste. More than any student I've seen in a long time. I do hope you'll use it... wisely."

I stand up and follow him.

The door clicks shut behind me before it dawns on me that

he never gave me the punishment I thought I'd been sent for. No detention. No warning. Just dismissal.

But as I walk back through the hall, the water in my blood pulls tight—like a current yanked against the tide.

Intuition and observation collide, sharp and cold as ice in my blood.

The map.

The evasiveness.

The perfectly timed conversation meant to charm, to disarm.

And the feeling I can't shake—the way my elemental sense recoiled, the way my ring still burns. Like the water in my veins recognized something older, fouler, more hidden than polished words could mask.

My father's past. What happened to him on the lake that day...

Thorne knows more than he's letting on.

CHAPTER 48

It is the nature of shadow to slip past what other magick cannot.
—Veil and Void: Advanced Theory of Shadow Manipulation

"What is his connection to your dad? I don't buy the childhood friend bullshit your mother seems to think." Gavrail sits in the common area of the Spanish Steps, posture loose but eyes sharp as he, Noa, and I go over our latest fusion findings. "Why the map of your farm?" he presses, drumming his fingers on the wood of the bar behind us. The motion is casual. The question is not.

"He's the headmaster of Whittaker with ties to the Service," Noa replies without looking up from his notes. "I'm sure he has maps of every territory we control. Doesn't mean anything."

"Doesn't it?" Gavrail tilts his head toward me. "You said it was tucked behind the others, folded. Not cataloged. Not part of the continent or Whittaker's history. Just… there."

I nod. "It wasn't labeled or marked, but I saw the lake. The lake he died in. My hometown. He also mentioned a blue shirt;

the same one my dad happened to be wearing the day he died. That can't be just coincidence."

Noa finally looks up, brows drawn, tension already in his jaw. "You don't know what it means. You're grasping at shadows."

Gavrail leans forward. His voice drops and I swear the room seems to shrink. "Maybe," he says. "But sometimes shadows are cast by something real. I don't like him. He's hiding something —I can feel it. The way he talks around everything. The way he brought her here. To this school. *His* school. That kind of care is not benign."

Noa scoffs, rising from his stool. "You want to what, break into his office? Tear through his files and hope he's left behind a signed confession?"

Silence settles for a beat too long.

Gavrail looks at me the way someone reads a map: slowly, cataloging every weakness and every strength. "We could do it."

"I never said I would—" I begin, but he cuts me off cleanly.

"But you're thinking it." The certainty in his voice leaves no room for debate. "You want answers."

My pulse ticks upward. Not just because he's right, but because I hate that he knows me so well.

"If there's something in those file cabinets… records, correspondence, anything. Maybe the letter he said my father wrote to him. At least just to know that it wasn't a lie. I need to know what happened on the lake that day. What their history is. Why Thorne knew so much and said so little. If he knows the truth about me and my family's history."

Noa pushes back from the bar, standing now. "You're both insane. Thorne is dangerous. He's protected, powerful, and he's watching you already. You think you can sneak past him without consequences?"

"I think," Gavrail says slowly, rising with the deliberate grace of someone who *wants* to be underestimated, "that the risk of not knowing is starting to outweigh the risk of getting caught."

"No," Noa says, jaw tight. "You're not dragging her into this."

"She's already in it," Gavrail snaps. "Her family's buried in secrets and the one man who might know the truth is playing mind games. She deserves answers."

"I'm right here, by the way," I say, sharper than I intend to. "And I'll decide for myself."

They both fall silent. The tension crackles, like a storm about to break.

"I'm not saying we go in blind," Gavrail says after a moment, quieter now, controlled. "We plan it. Timing. Entry. You know the office now, Celeste—what's inside, maybe even ideas of where to look."

Noa runs a hand through his hair. "This is a mistake."

"Maybe," I say, voice steady. "But it might be the only way to get answers."

Gavrail meets my eyes, then nods once. "Then we do it."

Noa turns away, pacing once before stopping, his back to us. "You'd better not get caught," he says, low and frustrated. "Because if you do—"

"We won't," Gavrail says—less a promise than a verdict. His voice is smooth and dangerous, like a storm banked beneath clouds. Hidden. Waiting. Final.

I don't say anything. But somewhere deep beneath the silence, I know: the choice has already been made.

* * *

WE SETTLE on the following week, a Wednesday night. The Administration building closes early, and Headmaster Thorne starts late on Thursdays, giving us a buffer if anything goes sideways.

Noa is still not totally on board with our plan, but he doesn't try to stop us either. Having spent the most time in the Admin building out of the three of us, he tells us what he knows and manages to "borrow" a keycard from Madame Vanderwall, the office secretary.

Gavrail, meanwhile, catalogs any security measures with a glance—cameras, locked doors, wards. Everything is inventory. He corroborates with Noa, the two of them going over every detail like they're calibrating a weapon—angles, timing, sight lines—until everything clicks into place with a cold, perfect certainty.

We plan and re-plan: entry, egress, contingencies, safe windows, fallback signals. Every potential failure is a vector Gavrail quiets before it can breathe.

I want to look at the map, maybe Thorne's scheduler to see where he was that day in August. Look through the file cabinets too—letters, records, anything that might tie Thorne to my father.

At some point between the maps and the watch rotations, I realize precisely how dangerous Gavrail is. Clandestine missions are not improvisation for him—they're choreography. When he moves, the air seems to hold still for him. He doesn't just anticipate risk; he dismantles it.

Secrets and shadows aren't just things he uses.

They're a *religion.*

And he's their god.

I should be focused on the plan, the timing, the risks—but I find myself watching him instead. The way he leans over the desk, one hand braced on the building blueprint, the other tracing invisible lines over it with shadow. A book about rune warding sits next to it. The lamplight spills across his profile, gilding the edges of his jaw, catching on a faint scar at his temple, one I've never noticed before. His focus is absolute; a kind of stillness that makes the world feel narrowed down to breath and pulse.

He senses my stare before I can look away.

Of course he does.

"You'd make a great spy," I tease.

He smirks—that damned dimple flickering. "Well, if I ever decide to disappear into the world of espionage..." His gaze flicks to mine, lingering just long enough for my stomach to tighten. "I know exactly who I'd want as my partner."

I roll my eyes, but the warmth in my chest betrays me. "Right, because that time we took your dad's car for an unauthorized spin went so well for us?"

He shrugs. "At least life would never be boring," he counters.

I open my mouth to say something—but the sound doesn't make it out.

His gaze lingers a beat longer, unreadable, before he turns back to the table, shadows folding close around him like they belong there.

And maybe they do.

That afternoon, he moves alone across the top floor, slipping through the building's edges like a shadow with purpose. He studies the headmaster's door as a locksmith studies a vault—its pins, its tension, wards, magickal barriers. He returns with a small glint in his eye, the kind that says a problem is only a series of smaller problems waiting for a hand willing to solve them.

Confident, not cocky. Certain, not careless. A look that tells me that the lock-picking days of his youth, the same skills he taught me, will be more than adequate. And not far from us, a door sits silent and inert, my past sealed behind it—holding truths to be torn open and secrets drenched in blood.

CHAPTER 49

In every age of tyranny, a veil is woven. In every age of rebellion, it is torn.

—A History of Elemental Conflict: The Magickal Wars and Rebellions of the Last Millennium

When Wednesday arrives, we're ready. Noa doesn't come—he paces the Spanish Steps like a caged flame, giving us a few hours of distance and an alibi should we need it.

Night folds over the campus, cloaking it in shadow. Above, only the thinnest sliver of moon cuts through the dark, like the last remnants of the Cheshire Cat, smirking at us from above.

Gavrail's shadows blind the camera and swipe the keycard while ushering us inside the building under their silken dark cover. It's easy. Almost too easy.

We tiptoe to the third floor. The office door stands like a sentinel—iron-reinforced oak carved with runes so old they've nearly worn away. Layers of mundane security conceal deeper ones.

Somewhere below us, a floorboard sighs, like the building is shifting its weight. We pause, listening hard enough to hear our own breath. But no sounds follow.

Gavrail crouches beside the door, his hands moving like clockwork, elegant and spare. "Start with the top," he murmurs. His voice is so low it feels like thought more than sound.

I raise a brow. "You want *me* to do it?"

A flicker of his mouth—half amusement, half challenge. Shadows curl at his coat like they want to answer for him, but he tips his chin toward the lock.

I focus. A narrow thread of water coils from my fingertips, slipping into the keyhole. The pins tremble, yielding one by one. The click is soft but certain. I glance back at him, proud despite myself.

He doesn't praise. He just watches—silver eyes bright, as though he's cataloging the way I move, the way I listen. Like he's storing me in memory the way he stores weaknesses in an enemy. But I see the corners of his lips tip up despite himself.

The second lock resists more fiercely. My water stalls. This one's not just mechanical. Gavrail's hand covers mine as he whispers some words in old Umbric, a dead language I didn't even know he could speak. Shadows begin pouring like smoke into the seams. Not fusing—pressing. Their force slides over mine until it feels inevitable, like his magick is teaching mine how to finish the job. Pushing.

Another click.

"Rune warded," he says without looking at me, his hand still on mine. "The third is a pressure enchantment," he mutters. No hesitation, just certainty. He moves his palm and presses it flat to the wooden door, right over a symbol that looks like three concentric rings. Darkness ripples outward, mimicking a hand in various sizes and with different pressure points until something clicks.

The ward shudders, then releases with a metallic sigh.

The door unlatches. A hushed silence follows as we slip inside.

Thorne's study yawns before us—dim, cold, cavernous. The fireplace sits empty, untouched. Bookshelves climb the walls like battlements. Artifacts gleam beneath dusty glass—things that seem to pulse faintly in the dark with a magick all their own.

Nothing is out of place. Not a quill left at rest. Not a single piece of parchment unfiled.

Even in absence, Thorne feels present. Watching.

My boots make no sound on the rug as I move to the file cabinets—the polished metal ones first, dull under the moonlight. I pull open the student drawer. Files hum with whispered histories—names I know, lives measured in awards and write-ups. I flip through until my own name appears.

I hesitate, then pull it free. The information is clean. Sanitized. The world's version of my life: grades, class ranking, dormitory assignment. As if nothing unusual shadows my days. But it's a mask. I know it, and I'm pretty sure Thorne knows it too.

Rozsen. Nate. Finn. Amelia. All here. Labeled. Documented.

My fingers drift to the next cabinet. The staff files. Professors, teaching assistants, the delegates from Vikhrostrum.

The last cabinet bears no label. Its surface is smooth, dark wood—ancient, unlike the others. And locked.

I reach out, my water testing its edges, but the moment it touches the cabinet, a low hum begins to vibrate beneath my fingers.

Another ward.

I pull my hand back, frowning. "This one's different."

Gavrail crouches beside me, already fishing through the

inner pocket of his coat. "That's because it's not just locked and warded. It's protected by something else."

He draws out a small glass vial, stoppered with wax. The liquid inside is a dense black, almost violet when caught by the moonlight spilling through the window. It swirls slowly, like smoke trapped in oil.

I inhale sharply. "Is that—?"

Shadowmire.

From our last fusion—bottled and saved, just in case.

The air changes the second he uncorks the vial: cold and sharp, the way the sky tastes before a storm breaks.

With a surgeon's care, he tips it. A single drop falls into the cabinet's top-drawer keyhole. It doesn't burn—it seeps. Intelligent. Deliberate. Like it's testing the ward before it decides to devour it.

"I've been experimenting," he murmurs. His mouth tilts into a smirk. "Turns out it's good for more than just hiding from our parents." He watches the keyhole like it's a pulse point. "Shadowmire doesn't just break barriers. It learns them—takes their shape—then unravels them from the inside." His gaze flicks to mine. "Locks aren't built for that kind of pressure."

A faint hiss. No flash. No heat. Just a subtle shift in the room—like the world exhales.

The shadowmire threads inward, thick and oily. It moves like ink over paper, slipping along the wards' seams, finding every rule the lock is trying to enforce, then loosening them.

I feel it. The same way I felt it in the Grotto. Not his and not mine—*ours.*

The cabinet groans, a low, unnatural sound, like a bone shifting out of socket.

A long beat of silence.

Then—*click.*

The drawer slides open an inch on its own.

I release the breath I was holding.

Inside are carefully organized folders—heavier, older than anything else in the room. Some are stamped with wax, others lined with silk.

Ancient lines. Lineages. Tracked, cataloged, and watched.

Ashander

Caelstrom

Emberlain

Ferruskai

Hassan

Morvaine

Shaedryn

Terravanth

Thalrien

My hand hovers over the folder bearing my own name.

Celeste Thalrien.

My next breath comes uneven.

I pull it free. The folder practically vibrates in my hands.

This one is thicker than the rest. Inside: photographs. My mother when she was younger, radiant, a protective curve to her body. A baby wrapped in her father's arms. Another of a little girl outside a villa in Italy—me at six, eyes too wise. Another still—me and Gavrail, arm in arm in Bulgaria, cheeks flushed from snow and mischief. Then my graduation in Virginia. My mother. My father. So much joy. So much history.

But none of this I gave.

Thorne has been tracking me.

Page after page—addresses. Medical records. School names. Functions attended. The cat I adored when I was ten. The time I broke my wrist falling out of a tree.

He hasn't just watched me.

He's studied me.

My pulse hammers. This isn't curiosity. This is preparation. Strategy. Like he's been assembling the parts of a puzzle since long before I even knew I was on the board. Thorne mapped my past. My home. Not just where I live now, but where I came from, where I was shaped. The idea of him knowing those places—studying them—feels invasive. Like a predator tracking prey.

My hand trembles slightly as I lift the next photograph. Something shifts beneath it.

A square of blue velvet, wrapped like a present.

Carefully, I unfold it. A folio—thick parchment edged in faded gold thread. The parchment is aged but well-preserved, covered with blue ink that has not faded. The old script of the water clans—elegant, formal, deliberate.

A lineage record.

At the top: *House Thalrien.*

Some names are familiar, but most are not.

And then, my father's name is listed cleanly—*Selric Thalrien* —and beside it, in dark, precise handwriting: *Rosalind Staten Farris.*

Below them, a single line descends.

Celeste Thalrien.

A hand-drawn eight-pointed star is next to my name.

I stare at it, my pulse echoing in my ears. The parchment crackles faintly as I turn the page.

A second branch. This one drawn from *Selric Thalrien* to a different name:

Valarie Normandy Thalrien.

Below it:

Orren Thalrien.

My chest tightens. A name I never knew. A brother. *My* brother.

Next to Valarie's name is a birthdate, and a death date—twenty-seven years ago. But for Orren, there is only the date of his birth, five years before mine.

No death. Just a blank space. Waiting…

The room tilts off center for a breathless moment as I try to make sense of what that blank space could mean.

Metal clinks faintly as I adjust the velvet. Something is hidden beneath the parchment.

I lift it carefully—and gasp.

A crest. Silver-blue, old as tide and salt. A mermaid engraved in profile, soft and smooth from generations of touch. Concentric ripples fan outward from her figure.

I stare. I remember it, vividly. Hidden in my father's drawer, long ago.

The moment my fingers brush it, warmth pools in my chest, like stepping into a deep, still lake. Water stirs inside me—not conjured, not summoned, but remembered. *Ancient. Familiar.*

I know, instinctively, that this crest carries more than just lineage. It holds *memory*. Power. And it calls to my blood like a song buried under centuries.

From the shadows, Gavrail murmurs, "Find anything?"

I grab the ledger and the crest, replacing the file carefully, tucking the blue velvet back. My fingers are trembling. The truth I found is too quiet to scream, but too loud to ignore.

Whatever Thorne wants with me… it didn't begin at Whittaker.

It began long before I even knew Whittaker existed.

We slip back into the hallway, shadows curling like smoke around our shoulders—Gavrail's work. We vanish together into the building's hush.

I glance at him as we rush through the hallway and down the stairs in silence. His mouth is grim, his shoulders tense.

Once we're outside, cloaked by the cool night air, I take my first real breath.

He looks at me and the items I hold. "I looked at his planner." His lips are pressed tight, barely controlled anger beneath the calm mask he always wears. Shadows twitch across the ground

like they want answers, and they want them written in blood.
"The day your father died," Gavrail says slowly, eyes never leaving mine, "his planner was blank. No meetings. No classes. Just two initials—S.T.—and an address." He pauses. "Your address."

S.T.

Selric Thalrien.

* * *

GAVRAIL'S ROOM in the Ivy House is sparse but not sterile—each detail intentional. A burnished metal lamp casts amber light over books on fusion theory and mythic inheritance, all lying in organized stacks.

One wall is covered in maps of magickal territories marked with cryptic symbols and small, handwritten notes—strategic, surgically precise. Another is draped with dark velvet banners from Vikhrostrum, their sigils not just proud but ominous, reminders of oaths kept and blood spilled.

A single plant sits in the window, leaves green and waxy, a gift from Amelia he hasn't had the heart to kill. The space smells faintly of cedarwood and ink. And him.

The Thalrien crest lies between us on a folded linen square, half glinting in a narrow shaft of moonlight. Its edges have been softened by age, but the mermaid etched in profile is unmistakable. Gavrail keeps glancing at it out of the corner of his eye, a muscle ticking in his jaw.

Not just curiosity. Something unreadable settles into his expression.

A thought comes quietly—and doesn't leave. That somehow, he knew of its existence. But maybe just didn't expect to find it here.

His gaze lingers a fraction too long before sliding away again, his shoulders going slightly too still. His fingers flex once at his sides—but he doesn't ask about the crest. Just watches it like it's shifted something beneath the surface and he's decided, in the same breath, not to say why.

I reach out, brushing my fingertips over the worn silver-blue surface. The hum is instant, low and slow, and it stirs something in me like an ancient current dredging some silt of memory. My breath catches.

"I think—" I swallow, blinking hard. "I think this crest is the result of elemental fusion."

Gavrail looks up sharply from his desk where he's been inspecting the Thalrien ledger we took. For a long moment, he studies me, then the crest. He picks it up and turns it over in his palm.

Nothing happens.

His expression flickers with disappointment. "It doesn't respond to me," he says quietly. He examines the crest like it's a lock he hasn't yet found the key for. Like he's already figuring out *why* it won't yield to him—and what that means for the world that tries to use me to unlock it instead.

"It would make sense," I murmur, heart beating too fast in my chest. "If the Thalriens were one of the great lines that were capable of true elemental fusion—maybe they fused their magick into the one thing they knew would be passed down through generations. Their crest."

"Not just a symbol," Gavrail says. "But a vessel."

He holds it out to me again, and the moment it touches my palm, that pulse flares, echoing in my ears, my chest.

Then—a pull. Gentle, but insistent, like the tide pulling at the shore. I feel the shift behind my eyes first, then in my head: fragments of memories that aren't mine. A woman standing knee-deep in the surf, arms raised to call a storm. A man kneeling in fog, blood in the water around him, whispering my name—not Celeste. *Thalrien.*

The air tastes of salt. My vision swims.

I feel Gavrail's hands at my elbows, steadying me.

And then the cold rushes in—not empty, but full of something: sorrow, strength, love, legacy, and water.

Water remembers.

Magick is definitely infused into the crest, ancient, deep, filled with the water of the many hands that came before me.

I nod, words spilling. "They imbued it. Each generation adding something—grief, power, memory. Pieces of themselves."

"Something that would survive," Gavrail adds softly, "even if they didn't."

I turn it over, where a motto is inscribed in a crescent arc on the back.

"*To know the depth, one must first dive in,*" Gavrail reads aloud.

"What does it mean?" I ask, confused.

"I don't know," he replies. "But I might know where to look."

* * *

Back at the Blue Dahlia, I tiptoe into my bedroom so as not to wake Rozsen, who's snoring softly as dreams drift heavy around her. I grab the book and walk back into the living room. It's well after midnight now.

The pages of my elemental fusion tome crackle softly as Gavrail turns them, the firelight catching in the gold-veined script. Outside the bay window, wind whispers against the glass, the hush of a world trying to press close.

I lean over his shoulder, an elbow planted on the coffee table, the weight of the Thalrien crest like a pulse in my pocket. I haven't been able to stop touching it since I found it—my fingers drawn again and again to the carved lines of the mermaid, the ridged edge worn smooth with time.

"There," Gavrail murmurs, tapping a page near the bottom. "Read that."

I narrow my eyes. The passage is dense and lyrical, but one line catches:

AND WHEN THE *sea's heir forgets the tide, she must return the sigil to a sacred source, where memory sleeps in stillness.*

I READ IT TWICE MORE, my mouth dry. "You think...?"

Gavrail leans back, arms folded. "It doesn't say crest. But 'sigil'? 'Sea's heir'? Zvez, that's you."

I frown. "You don't think it just means, like... metaphorically returning to your roots?"

He flips the page. "That's what I thought too—until this."

The opposite page holds a hand-drawn ink illustration. It's faded and weathered, but clear: a hand held out over a still pool of water, something glinting between the fingers—a coin, or medallion, etched with a faint design too smudged to fully see, but unmistakably round. Concentric ripples flow outward from where it's poised over the surface.

I pull the crest from my pocket. Without a word, I line it up beside the drawing.

The shape, the size—it matches. The ripple pattern engraved behind the mermaid mirrors the illustrated water, the same rings spreading from the center.

"It wants to be returned," I whisper. "Not to a person. To the element. To sacred waters."

Gavrail straightens slowly, brow furrowing in thought.

My breath leaves me in a rush as I close my eyes, hearing the whisper of it even now. "I know where we need to go."

CHAPTER 50

To seek what is hidden beneath still water is to risk drowning in what it remembers.

—Bloodlines of the Deep and the Art of Water Magick

We walk in silence, fear and hope clashing together in my chest. I want the truth, but I'm also afraid of what I might find. Gavrail is just ahead, his shadows cloaking us as they did earlier. We don't even leave footprints behind.

I've never been to the Cavern this late at night. It's dark. Quiet. The cave opening looks like a silent scream, with a depthless pool beyond that's been swallowed by the night. Besides our torches, the only other light comes from the slight glow of my ring as it reflects the stars above.

We step into the second chamber—the Crystal Cavern. Our torches flicker against the walls, casting iridescent glints across the room where semi-precious stones gleam faintly like frozen stars. Gavrail moves to light the rest of the torches.

The pool in the center whispers to me, the way it always does. Its surface is smooth and mirror-like, reflecting nothing and everything. Above it, the crumbled rock wall bears the three ancient crests carved in stone: Thalrien, Virellan, and Morvaine—marks of the old water families. My blood. My inheritance.

I kneel at the edge, heart pounding as I hold the Thalrien crest in my hands. A tremor of awareness ripples through me. This pool isn't just a spring. It's an archive. A test. A vault.

And now, I have the key.

The pool pulses with an ancient, bittersweet warmth, something almost like—*sentience*. Watching. Waiting. *For me.*

The Thalrien crest warms slightly in my palm, its silver filigree catching the light like veins pulsing beneath skin—glowing faintly, as if it too has waited a long time for this.

I glance at Gavrail, fear pressing tight in my lungs. He's watching the pool like it's a threat. His shadows curl slightly closer as he takes my hand in his, his warmth and strength steadying me, my breathing syncing with his. His heartbeat matches my own. I know without a doubt that he would be the one to enter the pool if he could. That he would drown beside me if it meant I wouldn't have to be alone.

With a deep, steadying breath, I step into the pool.

I feel a sense of déjà vu as the water climbs around me, cool but welcoming. I lower myself beneath the surface, the crest cradled in my hands.

The moment it hits the water—the pool reacts.

Light blooms from the center of the spring, soft blue radiating outward: eight spires, almost like a star, with me at its center—the same symbol I saw when I touched the water the first time back in December. The sacred water carries whispers of long-forgotten memories, cold, vivid, ancient.

Ripples begin to unfold outward like roots under ice, curling around me, caressing me. Accepting me as one of its own.

The air pulls taut in the cave above me, and under the water, the crest glows as the past begins to unfold before my eyes.

* * *

MY FATHER STANDS at the edge of a wooden dock, wind tearing at his coat. Rain slashes the lake, the water behind him churning—but the vision remains sharp. His hazel eyes are fierce, tired, set with a refusal unyielding as iron, ringing clear in his gaze.

Thorne stands across from him, hands loose at his sides, but power coiled tight around his body—air magick shimmering like heat.

They are arguing.

The wooden dock creaks under their weight as my father stands there, shoulders hunched in defiance, soaked to the bone. In his outstretched hand, the Thalrien crest catches the flickering light. "Take it," he says, holding the crest out between them like it's poison. "I want no part of this. I'm not a Thalrien. Not anymore."

Thorne doesn't move. His jaw tightens, his face impassive as he regards him. "You can pretend, Selric," he says, "but that blood is still in you, and in her. You think you can hide her from the world? From what she is?"

"She's not a weapon!" my father growls.

"She's not a child anymore."

My father's hand trembles, just once, then he scoffs and shoves the crest back into his coat. "Then you're a fool," he mutters. "I should've never trusted you." He looks out toward the lake.

Thorne takes a single step forward, something clinking in his hands. "No, you shouldn't have."

The air shifts.

It happens in less than a second. A strange sort of chain now wrapped around my father's wrist. He looks down, surprised. Eyes wide with shock and the pain of betrayal.

I can feel it even here under the water—like the memory itself is holding its breath.

The rain drums a mournful cadence on the dock as my father's voice drops to a whisper. "Why?" is all he says.

Thorne's reply cuts like ice, slicing through the windswept rain. "Because the world needs her," he says coldly. "And because you were too weak to even try."

Thorne raises his hand—and the wind collapses inward, oxygen ripped from the air with surgical precision. My father staggers, choking. No water. No blood. Just silence and drowning in open air.

Then he falls. Face still fixed in disbelief, hands reaching toward his throat for air that isn't there.

The water in the lake convulses once—violent and distressed—before becoming totally, utterly still.

Thorne stands over the body for a long moment.

Then, almost gently, he removes the chain from my father's wrist and reaches into his coat, pocketing the crest.

He walks to the edge of the dock and uses his air magick to pull the body into the boat, unmooring it and sending it silently out into the water.

When it is far enough, he tips the boat with a flick of his hand.

And the lake swallows everything.

* * *

THE VISION SHATTERS like broken glass, and I gasp—breathless, shivering—as I struggle toward the surface. The glowing pool around me dims as its light retreats. The Thalrien crest is still clutched in my hand. Its surface is warm, even underwater, humming with the echoes of a final unspeakable act.

But then—

A ripple. Subtle. Strange. The water beneath me stirs like breath.

My legs won't move. The liquid tugs—not with force, but with familiarity. Like an invitation I don't remember accepting. Like coming home—except not a home I know.

The water holds me, slick and silken, curling around every inch of skin like recognition.

And then it begins to take me.

My fingers blur—all except one, the one with my ring, now burning hot in the cold water. My skin turns glassy, blue-lit, dissolving at the edges. Panic claws at my lungs as they start to burn for air. The crest slips from my grasp, sinking just beyond reach, drifting downward like a falling star.

I try to cry out—but it's too late. I have no voice. No breath. My body unravels. I am water. I am memory. I am magick unbound.

I am gone, and I don't know how to return.

And still, the water holds me. Too long. Too deep. Too much.

Then—

A shift. Not water. Something warmer. Sharper. It slides in like smoke through a crack in stone. It's not gentle. It's desperate.

Shadow.

It coils around the edges—reaching, both furious and frantic, like it's tearing the dark apart to find me. The two forces twist, water and shadow braiding together, not fighting but fusing. A cocoon of midnight and moonlight—*shadowmire.*

I feel him through it. His panic. His presence, seeping into me. I lean into it without thinking. Into him. Into the only dark that's ever felt like home. Like mine.

And slowly, I start to remember.

My chest spasms. My heart kicks once, then again. The ring

still burns on my hand, the sapphire flaring blue against the white.

Hands. Strong. Familiar.

They pull me up and out of the water.

"I've got you," he growls, and I don't know if he means my body or my soul, but I'm pretty sure in this moment, it's both.

Air slams into me like a blow. My body collapses against stone, skin intact once more—but trembling, brittle with cold and something deeper. Terror.

Rigid arms are around me, my face pressed against his chest, no space, no air—like distance is a risk he's not willing to take. A towel he must have grabbed on the way is held tight in his hands as he tries to warm my chilled skin. His body is solid heat, his breath harsh against my temple, jaw flexed. He looks at me like he's not sure I'm all the way here.

"What the hell just happened?" he demands, voice low, the force of it cracking like thunder through the Cavern walls.

I open my mouth, but the words won't come. I'm still trembling. Still tasting salt and fear. Sorrow and resolve. Tears now flow freely, both from the panic and from what was just revealed about the past.

I feel his hands on me, pressing into me—whispers of shadow leaking warmth into my core—until my breathing starts to settle. Until my hands finally come up to cover his. My fingers curl around him like instinct. Like memory. Like need. And he finally exhales the breath he was holding.

"I couldn't see you," he says, barely audible over my gasping breaths. "You were just—gone." The words scrape out of him. He reaches out, brushing the wet hair from my face. A flash of fear, for me. And something deeper. Absolute. Unyielding. "Celeste," he says, gentler now. "That wasn't just water memory."

I nod, or try to. "I didn't mean to. I didn't know it could—"

"Keep you?" He stares at me, soaked and speechless for a

long moment. Then finally, voice rough: "It almost didn't let you go."

His arms stay around me like armor. But I'm not cold. Not anymore. I think back to the vision in the pool.

Thorne killed my father not out of simple malice, but because he wanted *me*.

Now, with the legacy of Thalrien in my hands, I see the path laid before me: either embrace the very power my father sought to reject and protect me from, or decide, once and for all, what kind of future I want to forge.

The Thalrien crest still waits at the bottom of the water, glinting like a secret yet to be claimed. Gavrail fishes it out with a flick of shadow—sharp and quick—not willing to let me near the water again.

Because the water *wanted* me.

And next time, it might not let me go.

CHAPTER 51

Some rivers run forward. Some run back. And some run beneath us—their current carrying what was once lost.

—Waters of the Deep

I can't sleep.

Not after what just happened.

Not after what I saw in the pool.

Gavrail doesn't ask. He just bundles me in soft blankets and locks the door.

"You're staying here tonight." No room for argument. Not with that look in his eyes—like he'd cover the whole world in darkness if it meant he could keep me safe.

He gives me the bed. I lie stiffly beneath the covers, staring at the ceiling while his restless breathing rises and falls from the floor beside me.

My thoughts loop, jagged and breathless.

Thorne killed my father.

The Thalriens were fusion masters.

Thorne killed my father.

I'm not just powerful. I'm some kind of *weapon.*

Thorne killed my father.

I have a brother who might still be alive.

Water remembers.

Water remembers *me.*

Somewhere between night and dawn, I must fall asleep, because my dream is waiting. I'm back in the Cavern, but this time, its walls glimmer faintly with crystals. The pool lies still at the center, black and endless, stars trembling across its surface in silver ripples.

My reflection looks back at me—small, wide-eyed. A child.

Figures hover at the water's edge, hooded and faceless. Their shadows stretch long and silent in the dark.

And then the voice, soft and coaxing as a hand is held out toward me.

"Come here, Celeste."

Only this time, it's not a stranger. Not a nightmare.

My father.

He reaches for me, trembling. The pool shivers. The stars fracture. Cold silk slides over my skin—too real, too familiar—

I jolt upright with a strangled gasp.

The room spins. My hands fly to my throat. *No air.* No air—

"Celeste."

Gavrail is there, his arms around me in an instant.

"Breathe, love," he says at my ear.

I cling to him without meaning to.

His grip tightens—too tight—then he loosens it, as if he realizes what he's doing. He starts to pull away.

I shake again, a small involuntary shudder, and he freezes—then swears under his breath like he's losing a fight.

"*Fuck,*" he mutters, more to himself, and it's not surrender. It's a decision.

He gathers the blanket around both of us and moves fully

onto the bed, keeping me pinned to his heat. Like if he lets go, the water might remember where to find me.

"Sleep," he orders softly, moving my head to his chest, his arms wrapped tight around me. "I'll be right here when you wake up."

And he doesn't let go.

His scent fills my lungs—amber-dark and dusk-deep, a bite of smoke and grounding leather—and the Cavern slips away.

Sleep takes me, soft and warm. And this time when I dream, it's of shadowed woods, dark paths, and whispering leaves, the air thick with damp earth and night-blooming sap. Creatures watch from the trees, their silver eyes reflecting the starlight like pools of mercury.

I walk deeper. The forest shifts around me, subtle as breath. A path opening where there wasn't one a heartbeat ago. Guiding. Guarding.

The dark gathers at my back. Not threatening. *Claiming.* It curls around my ankles like a vow, cool and steady, as if it's always known the shape of me.

Then the sky splits.

Rain slams down in sudden sheets, cold and electric, thunder rolling so close it rattles my bones. Lightning zigzags across the canopy—once, twice—until one spear of white-blue fire strikes the ground at my feet.

Heat blooms. Violent. Alive.

Flames lick through the brush, racing up the trunks, devouring the world in a golden roar. The fire pulls—steady, bright, and full of hunger. And I know if I step forward, I'll be consumed.

The darkness tightens behind me just as fire surges in front.

And I'm caught between them, trembling—not from fear, but from the terrible truth of wanting both.

Choose, the fire seems to say.

Stay, the dark pleads.

The flames suddenly soar, blindingly bright, and the shadows lunge to meet them.

I try to move—

A floorboard gives a soft complaint somewhere next to me and the dream rips apart.

The air changes—heat, spice, and something achingly familiar. I wake to warmth: a cup pressed gently into my hands, arms folding around me from behind, tucking me into cedar, clove, and mint.

Noa.

My breath catches, and for one disorienting, fractured second, I don't understand.

I was—

I was just—

My gaze snaps across the room. Searching. Needing—

Gavrail's eyes lock on mine.

He's there, sitting in a chair in the corner of his room. Something unreadable flickers across his face—too fast to catch, too sharp to mistake.

Only then do I feel Noa's arms around me.

I turn. His face is drawn, turquoise eyes hooded in shadow.

"Gavrail came and got me," he murmurs. "Told me what happened. The pool. What you found." His voice is soft but caught at the edges, like it can't quite hold the weight of everything he's thinking. "You must have been terrified. If someone hadn't been there to pull you out..." His gaze flicks across the room before coming back to me. "What you saw in the vision." His jaw tenses. "Thorne... Cel, he's the headmaster."

I pull back and stare up at him. "You don't believe me?" My voice slices too sharp, too fast. A blade I can't sheathe, its edge cutting me and at the same time sharpening in preparation for others to bleed.

Noa flinches, guilt flashing in his eyes. "No—it's not that. I believe you. I do."

"Then why do you sound like you're trying to convince yourself?"

The edge hasn't dulled. I don't want it to.

He exhales, visibly trying to steady himself. "I'm trying to stay calm here. Because from the sounds of it, you nearly just drowned in your own magick. Because if what you saw in that vision about Thorne is true... everything changes." His knuckles are clenched and his mouth is set. Determined. "If Thorne really killed your father—if he's behind all of it... Cel, we can't just storm in after him. He's powerful. Connected. If we charge in, he'll destroy us before we even speak."

Gavrail leans back in the chair, one leg stretched out, posture loose—almost bored. His eyes are anything but. They narrow, dark and cutting, as his head tilts with quiet, dangerous interest. "Then tell me, *soldier*," he says, the words low and razor-edged. "What do you suggest?" His knuckles drum against the desk in a slow, deliberate tap. "What's your plan—beg the system that bred monsters to rescue us from one?"

Noa meets his gaze without flinching. "We be smart. Strategic. I'm in the Service now—I can reach out to General Vaylor. Tell him everything. He'll want to help."

"And how do you know he's not part of this?" Gavrail's eyes turn dark and lethal, piercing through Noa like a sword of shadow. "Men like Thorne don't move in isolation."

Noa stiffens. "He wouldn't be. I cannot believe he would have anything to do with what happened to Celeste's father."

"You sound sure." Gavrail's tone cuts. "But you're still new to war. Faith is a luxury it burns out of you."

Noa's eyes darken. "Not everyone's a liar, Gavrail. Not everyone's the enemy." His eyes flash with fire. "Maybe you've walked in darkness so long, you've started to think everyone's a shadow."

Gavrail doesn't blink, his silence colder than words.

Their stares clash like flint and steel. I can almost feel the spark catch. One still trying to believe in the system. The other already scorched by it.

I press the mug to my lips, the warmth of the tea a lie.

I rise. "Enough." My voice lands like a stone in the silence—final. Cold. Measured. "We write to the general," I say, meeting Noa's eyes first—because strategy matters. Then I turn to Gavrail—because so does fear. "But we also watch the shadows."

Water remembers.

And I'm ready to make the world remember too.

* * *

THE REST of the week is excruciating—pretending nothing is wrong, going about our days like nothing has changed.

When the truth is—everything has.

Noa wrote to Vaylor. He didn't claim discoveries. He didn't mention conversations. He positioned it as a routine review that raised flags: my father's record didn't align with the narrative Thorne was pushing. He asked Vaylor for clarification the way soldiers do when they suspect rot in the chain of command—calm on paper, alarm underneath. My name barely appeared, and only where it had to: next-of-kin. Context. Nothing more. Noa didn't make me the source of anything. He made himself the witness. Just an officer watching the edges of a system fray, and choosing the one person dangerous enough to pull on that thread and snap it without the whole thing unraveling.

Thursday passes in a blur.

I visit Amelia in the infirmary—her wounds are healing faster now that all the glass has been removed. Her breathing is steadier. The cuts are clean.

Professor Ching and I brew a fresh batch of Eir's Shadowbark, steeped with the frostbloom thistle Amelia and I gathered earlier this year in the grove. The potion dulls her pain, slows the bleeding, and lets her finally rest. Our Weldver Salt does its job too, mending the worst of the damage.

I feel like a ghost wearing skin. A shell going through the motions.

Friday brings Elemental Mastery with Professor Neris at the Lakehouse. After my display in the Garden Grove, she's taken to working with me privately—teaching me the finer threads of water magick that Noa and Gavrail cannot.

Her pale eyes are too knowing.

She watches me as I shift water between its three states: solid, liquid, vapor. Later, she shows me how to shape a ribbon of water into something separate, almost sentient, yet still tethered to its maker. It weaves around her in a graceful dance, taking the shape of a sea otter—mesmerizing. Enchanting. Like my water horses when they play.

I try to shape one to match hers, but something in me falters. My hand hovers above the surface of the lake, but a memory surges up: drowning in the dark, the way the water held me. I nearly pull back.

But then I feel it—her water. Calming, soft, intertwining with mine. Like an embrace.

She steps beside me as we watch our magick dance. "The water knows you now. Truly. It doesn't speak names lightly," she says, her voice a quiet lilt. "Do not be afraid of what you are. What you are capable of. Water gives, and water takes. But it doesn't just sing." She eyes me thoughtfully now. "You can also make it *listen*."

There's a pause. Then carefully—

"The Thalrien line was once the current beneath the tides—the quiet force that shaped the shorelines of power. Now, it's a name nearly washed from memory." She catches my gaze. "Or deliberately drowned."

A single tear slips down my cheek. I look away toward the lake.

"Why?" is all my broken heart can whisper.

"Because water remembers. And some fear what it refuses to forget. Remember, those who seek to rewrite the rules are never the ones written into them."

I turn to her, startled. Realization dawns like sunlight hitting the back of a wave. "You knew him… My father?"

She smiles softly, her ribbon of water still twining with mine. "I knew *of* him. We may be different, you and I—but we're still part of the same ocean."

She begins to walk away, and I see it then: the small water lily inked beneath her upper arm. Her ribbon dissolves into the lake as she stands at its edge, eyes on the horizon.

"Celeste," she says, not turning back, "you must learn to wield what you are without letting it wield you. Not just for yourself. There are those who would bind your power to their ends—call it duty, or loyalty, or the good of the realm."

I nod, heart aching with understanding. With warning.

"Some currents run deep," she says. "But not all waters are clean."

And with that, she walks away—leaving me to face the lake. To face the truth.

Alone.

CHAPTER 52

Fusion is not a joining—it is surrender. One must choose: to flow, or to shatter.

—Elemental Fusion: The Art and Origin of Convergence

I head out early to our bay on Friday for duel training with Gavrail and Noa. We stick to our usual schedule, though none of it feels normal. We're just waiting now—for General Vaylor's reply, for something to snap.

The water whispers to me the entire time as I weave my way around the now-dry path blooming with life and change. The late-afternoon sun bleeds gold across the surface of the lake, casting long shadows through the red maples as I step onto the familiar shore. The bay has changed since March—it's softer now, alive in a way that makes the silence feel heavier. Insects hum low in the underbrush, and somewhere, a heron takes flight, startled by my presence. The rock-strewn beach is empty save for a few creatures watching me from the shadows.

The water stirs at my arrival, whispering against the rocks as I kneel beside it, threading my fingers through its cool surface. I feel it too—something shifting. The air tastes of metal and ozone, storm-charged, like the world has teeth today.

A twig snaps behind me.

And my ring burns cold.

I turn.

"You're a hard woman to catch alone," says a voice I know so well now that it's been haunting my nightmares.

Thorne steps from the trees, his coat billowing as if lifted by an invisible breeze, hands tucked into his pockets. He looks calm. Cool. Collected. Like he owns the very wind around him.

It makes me want to scream.

My magick rises before I do. The lake water behind me begins to shift, pushing forward in slow ripples. My hands clench into fists and a predatory stillness comes over me as I stare at him while he moves closer.

"I feel like the time has come for some truth between us," he says, hands facing upward in supplication.

I continue to stare at him, feeling the lake surge quietly against my boots, drawn to me like a shield, a guard, an assassin. Maybe all three.

"Celeste," he says, smiling faintly, kindly even. "I'm not upset. I would have given you your family crest once I felt you were ready."

So… he knows what I took.

He looks at me again, hands casually placed back in his pockets. Trying to make sure I don't see him as the threat that he is. "I think you know why I'm here."

"Do I?"

The lake answers for me, lifting in small tendrils that lick around my ankles. He watches them with curiosity, like a man admiring something he already believes he owns.

"You've grown stronger. Just like your father." He pauses, gauging me. "But not quite like him, are you?" He cocks his head, as if he's assessing a future opponent.

"Why don't you come a little closer and find out." Scratch that—*current opponent.* I glare at him.

He stares at me, and I wonder if he sees the daughter of the friend he murdered in cold blood or only the weapon he wants to possess.

"I have his eyes, you know," I say in a voice that sounds nothing like mine—cold, detached, a dagger sheathed in silk. "Do you see him when you look at me?"

I catch a flash of regret, but he holds my gaze, unflinching. "I did what I had to, and I think you know that now."

"You mean killing him?" I want him to admit it. I want him to look me in the eyes and admit that he killed my father.

"If it weren't for me, you would still be locked in that glass prison of his. Being eaten away from the inside by a power that has always been yours to claim." He looks at me with something close to reverence. It sickens me.

The water quietly draws up the backs of my legs and into my hands, then moves to coat my body in a shield so clear it's almost invisible.

Thorne's expression doesn't change. "He made his choice."

"Say it."

He tilts his head. "Why?"

I raise my hand. The water rises, lifting in suspended orbs, bright with a strange shimmer—like glass ready to break.

"Say it."

A pause. Then—

"Yes."

I don't just see my father's death anymore. I see my whole life rewritten by his hands.

It detonates something inside me.

A wave explodes from the lake, roaring as it crashes toward him. Thorne raises a hand and slices it with a blade of wind, splitting the water down the center. The air hisses where his magick touches mine.

I don't stop. I summon the lake again, my fury climbing with the tide. A cresting wall surges up behind me—taller than the trees—before I slam it down on top of him with all the force of a broken heart.

The forest groans with the impact. Water surges around us as I slam my hand to the ground. Thorne disappears beneath the now-frozen water.

But not for long.

A cyclone explodes outward. Thorne steps through the vapor, dry, untouched, the water spiraling around him as if afraid to touch him. "You don't want to do this, Celeste."

"Wrong again." I grit my teeth as I raise a spear of ice and fling it. He deflects it with a twist of his hand, sending it careening into a tree, bark exploding.

Thorne moves in a blink. One moment he's at the forest edge—the next, he's at my side, windstepping, as if time and space have no rules. I guess not when you control the air in which it exists.

A blade appears at my throat, invisible but sharp enough to draw blood. I hiss at the sting as a bead of red slides down my neck.

"Celeste, you have no idea how long we have waited for someone like you—someone with your potential. You could change everything."

"I will not be your weapon," I say through clenched teeth.

"With you, we could fuse what the world has so far kept separate. We could end rebellions in a single season."

"Fusion is not yours to keep," I snarl. "*I'm* not yours to keep. To *force* into submission." Hot, angry tears fill my eyes.

Madness, collapse, death—the old stories snap through my head like warning bells. The fates of those Magicks who came before me. The fate that could be mine if Thorne has his way.

He shakes his head, almost mournful. "You don't have a choice."

"There is always a choice." My teeth bare on the words.

A pause. A breath. His voice turns deathly quiet against my ear. "Don't play games you can't win." He says it like the outcome's already been decided. Like I'm some foregone conclusion. My future already written down in a file somewhere.

My skin prickles.

The air changes—pressure dropping, light bending—

Not Thorne's air. Not my water.

I watch as the shadows around me start to stretch like they've been holding their breath. A smile tugs at my mouth, sharp and involuntary, not because I'm safe… but because I know, in this moment, that Thorne no longer is.

And somewhere in the trees, darkness explodes.

"Let. Her. Go." The growl comes from the shadows of the woods, from the boulders by the lake. Everywhere around us. Mist snakes in as darkness tightens its vise-like grip.

Gavrail.

He emerges slowly, hands at his sides, face carved from stone. The dark around him writhes and twitches. Two creatures—black, spined, and low to the ground—glide beside him, their eyes glowing violet.

"You're not part of this," Thorne says, tightening his grip.

"Wrong again."

Gavrail sends the beasts forward in a surge of shadow. Thorne releases me to face them, sending out a whirlwind so sharp it howls. One of the shadows is shredded in midair; the other melts into smoke and reforms behind Gavrail.

"The prodigal son here to do what his father could not?" Thorne shouts into the darkness. "Gavrail, you know as well as I do what Neron would do with her if he had her." The shadows still. "She's *safer* here with us. With me. If I were you, I'd be *thanking* me for reuniting you two and keeping her out of his hands."

Gavrail appears in the shadow of the boulder to my right, catching my eye for just a heartbeat before giving me the slightest nod.

I drop to my knees and sweep my arms wide. The water answers like it's been waiting for centuries.

Thorne races toward Gavrail, compressing the air into a landing, stepping over my water and unleashing a needlestorm: thin spears of wind coming from every direction, all headed for the same target. But none reach it—the second shadow monster swallows them all with an angry breath. Thorne backtracks, this time waving an arm overhead, kicking up plumes of dirt and jagged rocks, forming a cloud of compressed dark air—but it's not aimed at Gavrail.

This one is headed straight for me, and I don't have enough time to react.

I close my eyes, bracing for impact, only to find myself encased in shadow—a soft, velvet shield, covering me completely.

Gavrail's eyes are on me. Only me.

It's exactly what Thorne wanted.

A distraction for just a breath, because that one second is all Thorne needs. He's already windstepped to Gavrail's side, clenching his fist—Gavrail grasping at his throat, the air being stolen from his lungs.

I scream as I run toward him. *No, not like this.* First my father. Now Gavrail. This will *not* be the end to our story.

Thorne holds up a hand toward me, stopping me with a gust of wind as he speaks. "Work with us willingly, let us train you to reach your full potential, and no harm will come to either of you. You will have my protection. I promise you."

Tears are falling now, ice crystals cutting tracks down my cheeks, mixing my blood with water. He holds Gavrail off the ground, an impenetrable shield of air around him as Gavrail struggles to breathe. He tries to wave me off, but even the most powerful shadow magick still needs air to live. Thorne has us.

He has *me.*

I lower my hands, walking toward them, an unexplained tether panicked and fluttering in my chest.

But something catches my eye. An orange glow glinting off the reflection of water behind them.

A warmth starts crawling up my skin.

I can feel him before I see him.

Thorne's voice is pure ice. "You think you know power?" Gone is the pretense of the concerned family friend. "This"—he gestures to Gavrail still suspended—"is nothing. I haven't even started yet."

"Neither have I."

The voice comes from behind. Quiet. Deadly.

Noa.

He's walking across the field of jagged ice, his fire already lit across his knuckles, tracing molten lines in the air as he moves —orange and gold, blinding.

He meets my eyes. I nod once.

We move together.

Noa flings fire as I summon water—our magick meeting and spinning outward in spiraling loops, catching in the air like a cyclone laced with flame and frost.

Maelflare.

The explosion knocks Thorne back. My feet brace against the ground, sliding across ice as I try to contain the storm and aim it at him. Gavrail drops from his encased prison of wind and crawls to his knees, taking deep gasps of air as he gets to his feet.

Thorne snarls and stands—burned, soaked, furious. But I can see the first crack, the uncertainty and awe on his face.

Noa raises his hand. I raise mine. Gavrail's shadows move forward. The three of us merge without speaking.

Water. Fire. Shadow.

We strike.

Noa's fire forms a cage, Gavrail's shadows anchor it in place, and I fill it with a tide that hardens into something heavier—shadowmire, viscous and writhing, dragging Thorne down. The tar-like magick flickers with shapes—faces, maybe, or memories.

Thorne roars and lashes out—wind slicing, slashing, raining rocks and debris in gusts around us. I hear Gavrail grunt as a small pile of boulders slams into his back and shoulder, but it isn't enough to knock him down. My arms drip with small rivulets of blood from tiny cuts my water isn't able to shield from, but still I hold my hands steady.

Thorne drops to his knees, sinking further into the shadowmire, which lapses around him like quicksand, the maelflare still encircling him, his wind magick snuffed out in the eye of the storm. *My* storm. *Our* storm.

Noa's chains snap forward—freeze-fire locking Thorne's limbs to the ground. The frost-rimmed blue flames bite into muscle without burning skin.

"Impossible," he gasps, his eyes on all three of us working in tandem.

And then—

"Stand down!"

The voice booms from the ridge above the bay.

Uniformed figures appear beyond the trees—Service agents, weapons drawn. Moving with practiced and lethal precision.

At their center—General Vaylor.

"Easy," he calls, already striding toward us. His gaze flicks to Noa, measured and approving. "Good work, Officer Gallegher." A beat. "We'll take it from here."

My knees buckle.

I pull back, my magick ebbing like the tide returning home to the sea. The air loses its razor edge, softening into a breeze that brushes my skin like an afterthought. The world around me begins to sway out of focus. I feel emptied. Hollowed out.

But alive.

Gavrail drops to a knee, his body a shield in front of mine, shadows curling tight as if they alone can hold me together.

Noa crosses the distance in two strides, hands still glowing. He hooks an arm around my waist and hauls me upright, pulling me into his chest like he can anchor me there.

Gavrail rises beside us. Noa reaches out, clasping his forearm—firm, deliberate. A nod passes between them.

Trust. Truth. And me.

I taste salt, but I don't know if it's blood or tears, or both.

The current is still there. Raging inside me.

And I see him. My father. A memory—

Sun, sea, and my bare feet in the sand. I was six, maybe seven. I hadn't meant to go that close to the shoreline. I watched as a monstrous wave crested toward me, mesmerized by the way the light fractured off its surface—the tide sucking back like a breath before the bite. Suddenly, arms were around me as he grabbed me, pulling me back, his voice raw, warning me to run. The wave crashed around us anyway. Cold and furious. We came up sputtering in the surf, and I saw pure fear in his eyes. Not for himself.

For me.

But I didn't run. And now that wave isn't outside me—it's in my blood, roaring and endless. And I don't know who I am now that I'm not holding it all back.

But still.

I don't run.

* * *

I STAND OUTSIDE the Admin building, the questioning in the council chamber finally behind me. Vaylor and his team were already inbound after Noa's intel—only to arrive moments too late, after Thorne had already made his move.

The unburied truths now press into every silence. The general's normally aloof presence softens—just slightly—when he speaks of my father.

Justice, at last, being served.

He's already called my mother. Her voice cracks when she reaches me on the phone, frantic and thick with grief. The pain of losing him fresh and raw all over again.

I watch as they lead Thorne away, flanked by two Service soldiers. That unshakable mask of his is firmly back in place. He doesn't look at me.

Noa is still inside with Vaylor, already being inducted into the Service. They walk out together. The general clasps Noa's shoulder with a firm hand—half comfort, half pride—before moving on. Noa catches my eye, a sad smile brushing his lips before he turns to speak with Finn.

The school buzzes with whispers and theories. Stories spreading like wildfire.

My squadmates find me. Rozsen says nothing—just pulls me into a bone-crushing hug. The tears come without warning, spilling into the crook of her shoulder. The others circle around us, cradling us both with their love.

I spend the next hour retelling everything, carefully repeating the story Noa, Gavrail, and I agreed upon. Secrets, lies, and buried truths all spill out in a tangled web. This is my life now—a delicate balance between trust and truth, protection and deception.

General Vaylor wants my lineage kept classified. The boys agree it's safer that way.

Two names. Two legacies. Two halves of the same coin.

But some truths are meant to be protected. Some lies are born of love. I carry both now—and walk the line between them, no longer afraid of what it might cost.

My name is Celeste Thalrien.

And I don't run.

CHAPTER 53

The veil lifts for no one. But in the darkest moments, some slip beneath.

—Magick Conflicts and Rebellions: Teachings of the Silver Veil

I close my bedroom door and lean against it with a heavy sigh. The weight of the last few hours, weeks—months—settles into my bones like lead.

I head to the shower to scrub off the touch of Thorne's wind against my skin. The anger, the pain, the helplessness—still there, just below the surface.

A soft knock on my bathroom door.

He doesn't wait for a reply before stepping inside.

Noa.

His expression is caught somewhere between uncertainty and something deeper—concern, love. He reaches for me, his fingers brushing along my cheek. I turn into his palm, his thumb catching the tear that slips free.

Wordlessly, he leads me to the bench beside the shower.

With a tenderness that undoes me, he undresses me like I'm something breakable.

Shoes. Socks. Shirt. Leggings. Everything I'm wearing is soaked in blood, dirt, tears, and grief—the dark aftertaste of rage and revenge.

I hear the water start to run, the sound soft, like the patter of rain on a still summer lake. The steam ghosts through the air as the warm water condenses against the cool glass.

He undresses, too, and I let him lead me into the shower. The water is a balm against my fractured soul.

He washes me—my hair, my skin, careful with the cuts on my arm, mostly healed now thanks to Madame Ching's tending. The foamy lather of lavender soap mingles with the scent that is so unmistakably him—cedar, mint, clove. Safety and love wrapped into one.

He treats me like I'm made of spun glass, delicate and fragile. Places a soft kiss on a bruise on my shoulder as he continues washing me.

I turn around, facing him. The warm water splashes between us as he pauses, holding a washcloth in his hands. He has a small cut on his cheek and the purple undertones of a bruise starting to form on his chest.

I reach for him. He looks at me, his eyes flickering with a question. Desire brims beneath the surface of duty, of love, of wanting to make sure I'm alright.

I answer him with my lips on his.

I back him against the tile wall of the shower, cold against the enveloping warmth. He stumbles, hesitates for just a moment—before crashing into me with a kiss of his own. Hard. Desperate. Pulling me to him with a force like gravity before wrapping his arms around me as he deepens the kiss. His tongue lashes against mine, claiming, devouring.

I don't want slow. I don't want careful.

I want to feel.

To burn.

To be reminded that I'm still alive. And I know he feels it too.

He pushes me against the corner of the shower so he can angle me just slightly above him on the tile lip as he wraps my leg around him while he enters me—fast and deep.

The mix of soap and water makes us slide against each other, friction turned fire. Every movement, every sound, is a crescendo both delicious and dangerous as we move with each thrust.

It's intense, guttural, consuming. Exactly what I want. What I need.

His lips find my throat—soft, reverent—and for a heartbeat, I feel the sharp edge of Thorne's invisible blade, cold against my skin. My body seizes, memory flooding in. Until I force my eyes open and see him—Noa. Concern is etched across his face. He kisses me again, slower this time, coaxing me back. To him. To this moment. And I let go. Melting into the heat of us.

His hand finds me, thumb circling with steady pressure, strumming me into a rhythm that sends sparks racing behind my eyes. The charged air hums around us with the makings of a storm.

Fire and water. Chaos lashing itself together with memory and truth.

We combust as one.

Sparks of lightning flash as we crash back down, gasping, panting. Hearts racing like the water that's still rushing over us.

It's not just ecstasy—it's defiance. Proof I can still choose this, choose *him*, even with ghosts pressing against my skin.

His fingers brush my lips, that crooked smile blooming on his face. "I didn't expect *that* when I came to check on you."

I smile, breathless. Sated. Whole in a way only he makes me feel.

"Thank you for checking on me."

* * *

WE GET DRESSED in fresh clothes, finding some of his sleepwear tucked away in my dresser—a quiet, familiar comfort that makes my chest ache.

I pack a small bag for the walk to the Spanish Steps, not wanting to waste what little time we have left before his graduation next week. As I gather my things, I notice Gavrail's book still sitting on my desk. I slide it into my bag, planning to return it to him along the way.

The walk across campus feels suspended in amber—everything changing, everything ending, too soon. I tell Noa I'll meet him at his dorm, but I need to stop at the Ivy House first. He kisses me, long and lingering, before releasing me at the gate—his warmth still haunting my lips as I climb the stairs.

I knock once before pushing Gavrail's door open.

He's shirtless, sitting before a mirror, shadows curling around him like the tired wings of some fallen angel. The light cuts across the room in uneven gold, catching on the blood drying at his temple, the bruised edge of his shoulder, an open gash on his back.

"Gavrail?"

He doesn't answer right away, only glances up. His gaze meets mine in the mirror, eyes dulled with exhaustion but burning faintly beneath, like embers refusing to die.

I take in his wounds and something in me goes feral—violent—at the marks on his skin. That strange tether draws me closer once again.

"You should go to the infirmary. Madame Ching can help—"

"I've got it," he says through clenched teeth. He's trying to clean the wound on his back, but he can't quite reach.

Before I can think better of it, I cross the room and take the cloth from his hand. "Here," I murmur. "Let me."

The moment my fingers brush his skin, the air shifts. His breath catches, almost imperceptibly.

I clean the gash along his back, dragging the cloth gently along the length of the wound, clearing away the blood and debris in careful strokes. His warmth hums under my palms; the muscles at his spine twitch, reacting to my touch. My fingers trace the line of the injury, mapping it, as if knowing its shape might somehow help me mend it faster. When the blood finally stops welling, I reach for the bandage, securing it to his skin with strips of tape. My palms flatten briefly against his back when I finish—feeling the rise and fall of his breath, matching my own.

When I move in front of him, our knees brush. I reach up, dabbing at the cut by his temple, and he just watches—body still, face unreadable, eyes brighter than before.

"You shouldn't be here," he says finally, voice quiet enough that it barely crosses the space between us. His hand catches mine as I lower it, fingers closing over my wrist, anchoring me.

"I'm already here," I whisper. "And I came to return your book."

He exhales, a sound that's half defeat, half something else entirely. The tension in his shoulders fractures. For a heartbeat, he just breathes me in—as if my presence might keep him upright a little longer.

The silence stretches, thick with everything we won't name.

His thumb moves absently over the inside of my wrist, tracing the pulse there. "You're shaking," he murmurs.

"I'm just glad it's all over."

His mouth tilts—but not into a smile. "I almost cost you everything," he says, the words rough, splintering in his throat. "If I hadn't hesitated—if Noa hadn't..." He doesn't finish. His control slips, and his forehead drops against my shoulder. The movement is small, but it shatters me.

For a breath, I forget the world. Thorne. The Service. The

lake. There's only this—his weight against me, his hair damp against my skin, his breath trembling through my collarbone.

The world doesn't end—but something in me does.

I rest my cheek against his head, fingers tracing the hard line of his spine, careful where the skin breaks. His scent—dark amber, smoke, leather—wraps around me, threaded with the clean warmth of his shampoo. Shadows coil close, hesitant, possessive, as if guarding what they can't quite claim.

Time stops.

Then, reluctantly, he draws away.

The loss is sharp. It leaves a hollow place that echoes as he stands. He drags air back into his lungs and offers me his hand. When he pulls me to my feet, the space between us feels like a wound we both keep reopening.

He looks at me then—not through me, not past me, but *at me*. And for a heartbeat, the world narrows again to the space between our breaths.

Something in his expression shifts—grief, hope, want—and I know if either of us moves, even an inch, a line will be crossed and something far more dangerous will break.

So I don't move.

Neither does he.

Because if I breathe in too deeply, I'll drown.

"Oh—right." I break the spell as I fumble for the book in my bag. "I came to give this back."

He takes it, but something catches my eye—a sliver of parchment tucked inside the spine. He catches my stare and his eyes narrow as I ease it free, heart stuttering as I unfold the fragile paper.

He watches, wary, as if the smallest thing could undo him again.

"It's an address," I breathe. "Paris."

He takes it from me, fingers brushing mine. His eyes flick over the line, then still.

14 Rue des Fossés Saint-Jacques, 75005 Paris, France.

Beneath it, one sentence, written in looping script:

For when you and Celeste are ready for answers. —M.S.

A strange rune is drawn beneath it in silver ink. A vertical line with three tick marks crossing the top half, almost like a key.

My throat goes dry as I try to swallow.

M.S.

Minka Senkova.

Gavrail's mother.

CHAPTER 54

The four years at Whittaker will be an unprecedented time in your lives. The person who arrived here is not the same person who will leave. No one leaves these halls unchanged.

—Whittaker School of Magick Handbook for New Students,
"Founder's Note"

The golden light of late afternoon spills over the quad, catching on the white banners fluttering overhead. Rows of chairs stretch across the lawn, filling with fourth-years in ash-gray robes stitched with silver thread as they move through, finding their seats. The mood is electric, charged with beginnings and endings, excitement and sorrow, anticipation of celebrations to be had—and the heavy silence of goodbyes waiting to be said.

I look across the quad and startle when I see a familiar face.

Blonde. Bright. All sun and spark, just like I remember—Alissa. She's laughing at something a man next to her says—a tall, bookish guy with a too-tight blazer and nervous hands. That must be her boyfriend, Greg.

I freeze. Just for a breath. My past in human form.

Alissa turns. Our eyes lock across the crowd.

A beat.

Then—she runs.

"Cel!" she calls, and suddenly, she's hugging me like nothing has changed. Like it's still us. "Oh my gods, look at you! You're literally glowing. Are you doing that on purpose? Is that a Magick thing? Wait—don't tell me. I don't care. I'm just… Hi."

I can't breathe for a second. My throat tightens and the tears threaten to hit too fast to fully blink away. But I hug her back, arms full of ache and memory. "Hi," I whisper. "You're here."

She pulls away just enough to hold me at arm's length. "Of course I'm here. You didn't think we'd miss Noa's graduation, did you? Mom would've set the school on fire."

"Almost did," Brigid chimes in, walking up with that same warm-laugh-laced-with-chaos energy. "Someone told me we weren't all on the list, so I burned a hole in the air to make a point."

"She did," Blake confirms, appearing at her side. "It was a very expensive point. They almost kicked us out until we told them we were Noa's parents." The pride in his voice is unmistakable.

Alissa grins and grabs the hand of the man standing next to her, tugging him forward. "This is Greg. We met in New York. He's basically made of stress and soy lattes. But I love him."

Greg offers a sheepish wave. "Hi. You're Celeste."

I smile. "The one and only."

Then I feel it, before I even turn.

Noa.

His presence radiates strength and safety; heat pressed to my bones—comfort with a pulse of flame beneath it. I glance over my shoulder and find him watching us, eyes full of something I can't quite name. Something like peace. Or maybe hope.

Brigid loops her arm through mine and kisses my cheek. "It's good to see you again, sweetheart. You're family, whether you like it or not."

And just like that, I let myself have it. The warmth. The laughter that feels like home, even though everything has changed.

The world may still be burning at the edges, but this—this moment—is something whole.

* * *

THE CHAIRS FILL up with soon-to-be graduates, all students poised and ready. Professors are now sitting on the raised dais at the front, all except for one empty seat—Thorne's.

In his place stands Professor Gideon Barrows, now interim headmaster. His voice is calm and steady as he stands at the podium and welcomes the future.

"To our fourth-years: you stood at the edge of chaos and did not break. You proved that tradition must bow to truth, that courage can rise from anyone—whether born to power or forged by it." He pauses, eyes sweeping the crowd. "Let it be known that Whittaker does not simply send out students. We release guardians. Scholars. Warriors. Leaders." He lets the words hang for a moment. "And you—each of you—carry that legacy forward today."

A ripple of warm applause fills the air, genuine and heartfelt.

Names are called, one by one, and students cross the dais—there is cheering, crying, some watchers holding each other too tightly for it to just be joy.

"Finn Rourke."

A loud whoop rises from the Blue Dahlia section as Finn saunters up, all cocky grin as he gives an exaggerated bow. He flashes a wink toward the crowd, drawing laughter and eye rolls in equal measure. But when Barrows clasps his hand, Finn's face softens—just for a moment—as if the weight of it all finally lands.

"Ryan Halloway."

Ryan moves with quiet determination, each step steady. His friends cheer, but he doesn't break stride—grounded, composed, utterly himself. When he accepts his diploma, his eyes flick to Finn, to Noa, and then to the crowd. His expression is stoic, but his jaw is tight with emotion.

Then:

"Noa Gallegher."

Noa stands in uniform, not as a student, but as the first of General Vaylor's elite squad to be named directly from Whittaker. The quad quiets. He walks to the front, where the general himself pins a silver insignia over his chest—a windswept flame surrounded by stars.

"For valor in defense of this school. For strength, for sacrifice, for duty."

The applause swells, Noa's family cheering the loudest next to me, but Noa barely seems to hear it. He searches the crowd until he finds what he's looking for.

Our eyes lock, just as they did that night at the bonfire, when firelight painted his face in gold and shadow, him up there and me in the crowd. Back then, we didn't know what we were stepping into—what we'd become to each other. I smile at him, even though tears are blurring everything now.

After the rest of the graduates are called on stage, Barrows returns to the podium, eyes gleaming. "Go forward," he says, his voice carrying, steady and strong, "not without fear—but with it. Fear means you are awake. Fear means you are paying attention. That you understand the weight of what you wield."

He closes the scroll in his hand and looks up at the crowd, voice brightening to the expected ceremonial tone.

"Congratulations, graduates. May you all follow the righteous path of balance, and may the world hereby tremble at your feet."

The quad erupts in cheers and laughter. Caps and robes and blasts of magick are flung into the air. Hug after hug ripples through the crowd like aftershocks. The quad is no longer solemn—now it's alive, ringing with the joy of freedom, and the ache of change.

* * *

GAVRAIL

Gideon Barrows approaches like he knows how to move through predators—unexpectedly quiet, unhurried, footsteps lost beneath the old oaks of the quad. Graduation is unraveling into noise and celebratory chaos: laughter, shouted names, diplomas clutched as proof of survival.

I stay at the edge where the crowd can't trap me. My gaze drifts—involuntarily, inevitably—toward Celeste, who is talking softly with a few friends. She stands near the dais with her squad, head tipped back as she laughs. The sound hits me, sharp as glass piercing under ribs. Like my body doesn't know what to do with joy that isn't paid for in blood.

"Gavrail. A moment?" Barrows's voice is low. Measured.

I turn toward him, wary. Respectful enough to keep my face blank. "Sir."

"You've done remarkable things here this year," he says, eyes steady. "Not just with your power—but with your restraint. Your sense of honor. Of purpose."

Praise. A lure, dressed as recognition.

I don't answer. I let silence do what it's always done for me—make people fill it with what they want.

Barrows follows my line of sight anyway, as if he can't help himself. As if she is a gravitational force and we're all just pretending otherwise.

"I'll be honest," he continues. "The transition ahead will be difficult. This school—this legacy—is at a crossroads." His gaze returns to mine. "I was hoping you might consider returning. Joining us as a fourth-year. With my support." He pauses, watching for the crack. "You'd help shape what this school becomes. And I'd make sure you have the freedom to grow. Not just follow orders."

Freedom. Another word people offer when they want ownership with better optics.

Something in me shifts anyway—raw and unwanted. Because the only freedom I've ever cared about has a name.

My eyes cut back to Celeste. She's framed by the late light, hair catching fire at the edges, expression soft. For a second, the urge to go to her is so violent it feels like hunger.

Barrows's voice drops, almost gentle. "Just... consider it an open invitation," he says, pausing, and then—"I always find that the choices that challenge us the most often bring the deepest purpose." He looks out over the quad again, gaze catching on Celeste—then back to me, like a man setting a hook. "And the ones who matter most... the ones who change everything... they're always worth waiting for. Don't you think?"

His hand taps my shoulder once, before he walks away.

I don't move. Not at first.

I just watch Celeste as she turns, swallowed by bodies and sunlight and noise. My fingers twitch once—an old reflex, like shadows answering a call.

Then I curl them into a fist and force myself to stay where I am.

Because wanting her has always been the most dangerous thing about me.

* * *

NOA

Students spill from the quad in every direction—some wiping tears from their eyes, others laughing freely, a few still tossing flickers of magick into the air as they celebrate.

I've only just extricated myself from my mother's hugs and tears. My sister is practically bouncing with contained energy, while my father—solemn and sturdy—offers a few quiet words about what to expect at the Iron Wing training grounds. There's a shine in his eyes when he looks at my new uniform.

Just beyond the edge of the crowd, I slip away, needing a moment to breathe. Needing Celeste, who said she'd meet me back at the Steps.

Finn and Ryan are right behind me.

"Well, well," Finn says, a wide grin tugging at his lips. "Look who's official now—government badge, shiny title. 'Echo Squad,' the brave, the proud, the personally recruited soldier—sounds very cloak-and-dagger. Should I start saluting now?"

Ryan's voice is deadpan. "I think you're supposed to bow. Or offer him a blood oath. Something dramatic."

I laugh, rubbing the back of my neck. "Please don't. I barely know what I'm doing. Honestly? I feel like I'm standing on the edge of something, and I can't see the ground."

"Welcome to adulthood, my friend," Finn says, his grin softening.

"Or government service," Ryan adds dryly. "Same thing."

We all laugh, but it's a quiet kind of laughter, weighted with the unspoken truth of what lies ahead. Something is shifting, and we can all feel it.

Finn's voice drops a notch. "You earned it, Noa. After everything with Thorne… most people wouldn't have made it out of that bay alive. But you? You led."

My smile falters. "I didn't have a choice."

Because there is never a choice, not when it comes to *her*.

We fall silent, our eyes drifting back toward the quad. The dais stands empty now, white banners still catching the last rays of golden sunlight.

Finn holds his graduation cap to his heart, mock-serious. "Come summer, when you're off saving the realm or whatever, try to remember the little people."

I smirk. "You two will be joining me come fall, remember?"

Finn chuckles. "Definitely. Can't let you have all the fun and adventures by yourself."

We start to walk slowly back toward the Spanish Steps, a comfortable silence between us, forged of friendship, love, and duty.

I glance toward where the willow tree sways softly in the evening breeze. Beneath its weeping branches, Celeste is waiting.

My voice drops to a whisper. "I'll catch up with you guys later."

Finn and Ryan nod, reading the moment clearly. Finn squeezes my shoulder, and they leave me standing alone, the weight of goodbye pressing down as I head toward the willow tree and the woman I love.

CHAPTER 55

Some tides retreat to gather strength, only to return with the force to shape the shore.

—Traces in the Tide: Water in Elemental Practice

CELESTE

The willow stands like a mythic creature, its green-and-silver arms drooping in sorrow. Fairy lights blink gold against the dusk, casting soft halos of light beneath it. I sit on the stone bench, arms folded, but my eyes flick toward the path at the sound of footsteps.

Noa emerges from the shadows—hands in pockets, posture easy. Too easy. Like this is just a regular day.

I don't smile. Not fully. Just a flicker that dies before it can grow.

He sees it anyway. Because he sees *me*—especially the parts I try to hide away.

"So." His voice is careful, casual on purpose. "Gavrail. You. Europe this summer?"

I nod slowly.

"Old ruins, fancy food, mopey guys in long coats." A hint of laughter ghosts at the edge of his words, trying to keep it light. "Right up your alley."

"And you?" I push off the bench and take a step toward him. "Running headfirst into danger with a bunch of glorified Service soldiers? That's your idea of a good time?"

"Please." He flashes that cocky grin I love so much. "*I'm* the danger."

I make it two steps before my voice catches. "Noa..."

He closes the distance first, cutting me off. "Hey." His shoulders lift with a breath he tries to play off. "You're not losing me. You're just... putting me in storage for a bit."

"And what if that bit becomes more than a while? Or close to forever?" I ask, biting my bottom lip. Saying the words I fear out loud.

His grin fades. He keeps his hands in his pockets like he's afraid they'll betray him if they move. His voice drops—low, steady, honest. "Then forever's going to be real pissed when I come back to ruin its timeline."

I let out a shaky laugh that breaks into something dangerously close to a sob.

He finally pulls his hands free and cups my face. His thumbs brush beneath my eyes before the tears can fall. He tucks a strand of hair behind my ear, looking at me like he's memorizing every part of me. "I don't want to hold you back, Cel," he says slowly, like the words weigh more than the world itself. "These next few years—I'll be gone more than I'm here. Probably off-grid. You deserve something... steadier."

His shoulders are drawn, jaw tense. Like it's taking all his willpower to force himself to speak.

"I want you building your life so big I have to fight to fit back into it," he says, voice roughening, "not counting your days by my absence."

Then he drops his hands and steps back—the decision carved into the set of his mouth.

"I can't be selfish," he whispers. "Not about this. Not about you."

His eyes go glassy. Mine do too.

"You are my beginning," he says, and his voice cracks on the truth of it. "And—you'll be my end." A swallow. A breath he has to earn. "Because when all this is done, when I can be here in the way you deserve…" His gaze locks on mine, terrified and certain at once. "If you still choose me, I will spend the rest of my life earning that choice."

The way he's looking at me cracks something open inside.

I step into him again, because I can't not. I pull him to me, pressing my forehead to his. We breathe together for a moment, the world narrowing to just this—warmth, heartbeat, the fragile space between yes and goodbye.

Then he kisses me. Soft and slow.

When he pulls back, my voice is shaking. "Don't you dare die out there," I say, smacking his chest lightly.

One eyebrow lifts, the ghost of a smirk on his beautiful face. "Try not to start any wars without me, Farris."

A laugh trembles out of me and dies quickly. The air stills, suddenly too quiet.

"You can ask me to wait," I whisper.

"You can ask me to stay," he replies, just as softly.

The words hang between us—easy to say, impossible to live with.

He closes his eyes for a beat. When he opens them, there's wreckage and resolve.

"I won't ask that of you," he whispers, his voice breaking slightly. "Not like that."

Because if either of us said yes, we'd have to watch the slow way it would drown us both.

He kisses me again. It's heat and ache and goodbye, dressed

up as "See you later." When he finally pulls back, his eyes are wet. So are mine.

"You're going to be brilliant," he says, voice steadier than it has any right to be. "Burning through Whittaker next year with that terrifying brain and that impossible heart."

I swallow hard.

"I know you and Gavrail will find more answers in Europe." His mouth twitches—regret, maybe, or pain. Possibly both. "He told me about the note from his mom. I think it's the right call. To go there. To find out what she knows." He pauses then, a slight smile on his lips as he tugs at my hair, teasing. "Although Europe might not survive the two of you."

"I'll try not to break too many ancient monuments."

"Leave a few standing. Just in case I visit."

I lean into him again and he wraps his arms around me, pulling me close. The quiet seeps back into the air, heavy with things unsaid.

"This part sucks," I murmur into his chest.

"I know." He strokes my hair as I breathe him in. Cedar and clove and mint. *Home.* Even if it's a home I'm going to have to rebuild.

A soft cough sounds behind us.

The moment snaps.

Gavrail.

"Barrows says your car arrives in two hours to take you to base camp." His voice is low, edged with steel.

Noa's arms tighten around me once before he releases me.

We draw apart reluctantly.

"See you at the carriage house?" Noa asks. He kisses me once more—a brush of lips against my forehead. But I feel it like a knife slicing through my heart.

I nod, and walk away before he can see the tears start to fall.

* * *

NOA

The sky bleeds into slate, the last traces of sunlight lost to the horizon.

I stand beneath the willow's sweeping branches, eyes locked on the path where Celeste just vanished. My fists are clenched, shoulders rigid with restraint. The ache hasn't hit yet—not fully—but I feel it coiling in my chest, waiting.

Behind me: footfalls. A pause. Gavrail hasn't left.

My voice rings out, too loud and sharp, even to my own ears. "Take care of her for me."

The words cost me. As I knew they would. Asking *him* of all people to take care of what's most precious to me. And yet begrudgingly, there is no one I'd trust her with more.

I turn. Gavrail stands in the half-light, a shadow drawn from the edge of the world.

"She's the best of both of us. *Better* than both of us." There's no challenge in my tone—just truth, shaped by pain.

Gavrail doesn't look away. Shadows drape across his features, concealing what stirs beneath, but something passes between us. An acknowledgment. Maybe even respect.

"I know," he says, steady.

I step closer. My voice sharpens further—not with anger, but the desperate clarity of someone who'd burn the world to keep a promise. "If you hurt her… I'll come for you," I say. "Across realms, through shadow and storm. I'll drag you back by your throat if I have to."

Gavrail holds my gaze, unflinching. "I'd expect nothing less." But there is a flicker that crosses his face—approval. Calculation. Match met.

The air shifts. The space where she stood still feels full, still feels like her.

Gavrail's voice quiets, just slightly. Not soft, but something close. "From someone who already made the mistake once... don't walk away from her."

I stiffen, then drag a hand through my hair, exhaling like I'm trying to keep the words down. They rise anyway. "That is *not* what I'm doing," I snap. "And I already told you once—I won't be the one to walk away."

Gavrail's posture shifts. Not surrender exactly, but more like.... understanding.

Because if anyone can understand what protection looks like when it costs you everything, it's him.

He nods once. Sharp. Clean. A soldier's nod. He turns to walk back toward the path—but after a few steps, pauses and looks back over one shoulder.

"Take care of yourself, Noa. Remember—the Service isn't your family. It's a leash. Don't trade your soul for their orders."

I don't respond. But my breath is heavy in the air.

Gavrail's cutting gaze lingers a moment longer. Then: "Don't lose the part of you that still belongs to her."

With that, he walks into the dark without looking back.

I stay, alone beneath the whispering willow. The ache is heavier now. Real. I tilt my head to the dark sky, breathing in the evening air.

The wind moves through the leaves above.

This isn't goodbye.

She is gravity—relentless, inescapable.

Even if war swallows me whole, I will gladly spend the rest of my life finding my way back—to her.

* * *

CELESTE

Later that evening, beneath the glow of a rising moon, an unmarked black car pulls up along the outer lane of campus.

Its windows are tinted. Its engine hums—low, smooth, and final.

Finn stands by the trunk, loading the last of the bags. Noa lingers near the open door, duffle slung over one shoulder, body tight with restraint.

I stand a few feet away, arms crossed over my chest, trying to hold myself together by force alone. My eyes water, but no tears fall.

Noa hesitates, hand on the doorframe. Then, slowly, he turns to me.

Neither of us speaks.

I take a step. Then another. And suddenly, I'm in his arms.

Noa drops the bag. One hand tangles in my hair while the other grabs my waist, like he's desperate to memorize the shape of me one last time. He kisses me—hard and aching and alive. Tasting of salt and breath and every unspoken word we've run out of time to say. His teeth graze my lower lip; my gasp is the opening he needs to take the kiss deeper—until the world falls away and all that's left is lips, and tongues, and breath, and the taste of him searing through me.

Not a goodbye. A promise.

His hand slides to the back of my neck, pulling me closer until I can feel his heartbeat pounding against mine. My fingers clutch his collar like I can anchor him there. Like I can stop time.

But time is merciless.

He pulls back, just enough to rest his forehead against mine. Breathless. Shaking. "I love you," he whispers.

My hand lifts as he steps away, brushing the air between us —as if it could somehow tether me to him. "I love you," I manage, but my voice breaks, thin as glass.

Noa nods once. Sharp. Controlled. Like it's all he can give without falling apart.

He steps into the car. The door shuts with a dull finality.

The vehicle pulls away, headlights slicing through shadow as it disappears into the night.

I don't move for a long time. I just stand there, watching the darkness that swallowed him and took him away.

Summer is here. But it hasn't come with warmth. It came with fire, licking at the seams of fate. With shadow curling at its heels. With water rising—silent and certain—through the cracks in the world.

Because lines have shifted.

And somewhere deep beneath it all…

War has begun to whisper my name.

EPILOGUE

THORNE

The containment ward hums low, almost like a breath. Ancient stone pulses along the outside of the walls, locking me in a cage woven of light and silence.

But silence never lasts.

Bootsteps echo.

General Vaylor steps into the viewing window, long coat sweeping behind him, expression unflinching beneath the flickering glow. He stops just outside the perimeter of the nullifying stone and wards, hands clasped behind his back.

"Come to gloat, General?" I ask. "Or just making sure the mess you created doesn't bleed too far?"

He doesn't blink—only his mouth moves, curling with contempt. "You really fucked this up, Thorne."

I chuckle—a low, charged sound—as I lean back against the cold stone wall, chains rasping faintly when I move.

Vaylor's ice-blue eyes flick to the ward-stone. Then to the containment lattice. Then—finally—to my face.

"You failed," he says, without heat. "You were supposed to bring her in willingly."

I don't give him the satisfaction of a reaction.

He sighs, almost bored. Like I'm just paperwork, a form that needs filing. He flicks a speck of dust off his otherwise pristine uniform. "It doesn't matter now," he says, smoothing his cuff. "The contingency plan is already in place."

My hands clench into fists, but I don't let him see. Because I know what kind of man he is. What he is capable of.

Celeste still believes love is a choice. But that is exactly the lie that will break her—because love makes people walk straight into a cage if it means keeping someone else out of it.

Vaylor leans in closer to the glass, voice dropping to something almost gentle. "You were right about one thing," he says. "She wasn't ready." His smile is small. Controlled. "It was a good idea to give her someone she *could* trust," he murmurs. "Someone who could train her, steady her, and steer her straight to me when the time is right."

The air thins—oxygen siphoned with the same quiet precision that I used to kill Selric on that dock. The general's doing, since my magick is all but dead within these walls. Vaylor reminding me that everything, even the air I breathe, now belongs to him.

She thinks I am the monster in her story.

Turns out I was only the gate.

And Vaylor has already found the key.

ACKNOWLEDGMENTS

No story is ever written alone—and *Shadowmire* is no exception.

What began as monthly dinner filled with romantasy discussions with some of the funniest, most brilliant, and beautiful women I know... I cannot thank my "Fairy Porn Bookclub" enough for the support, inspiration, and wonderfully unhinged commentary on the books we've all come to know and love.

To my beta readers and early supporters—thank you so much for your honesty, your enthusiasm, and your relentless demand for more. Your insight has helped to shape not just this story, but all the ones to follow.

A huge thank you to my editors, Jessica Mckelden and Claire Bradshaw, who combed through every page with incredible care, giving this book the polish and refinement it needed to become what it is today.

To the readers who took a chance on this world... your excitement, your theories, and your love for these characters have meant more to me than I can ever fully put into words.

And finally, to the story itself.

This began with a single dream—a cavern, a pull I couldn't ignore, and a story that refused to let me go. I wrote it down, not knowing what it would become. There were moments I doubted it. Moments I thought I was in over my head...

But somehow, the characters always led me back.

Back to the beginning.

So remember fellow writers and readers, if you ever find that you are lost, whether in a story or in life...

Return to the beginning—to wonder—and you will find your way home.

ABOUT THE AUTHOR

Reaghan Quinn fell in love with magick at a very young age.

Drawn to stories where power comes at a cost and love refuses to stay simple, she loves to enter worlds with ancient magick, rival loyalties, and where characters are forced to choose between what's right... and what will ruin them.

Her debut novel, Shadowmire, is a dark academia romantasy woven with elemental magick, hidden agendas, and a love triangle that refuses to follow the rules. It's for readers who crave slow-burn tension but want fast-burn devotion, and the kind of chemistry that feels like it might combust at any moment.

When she's not writing, Reaghan can usually be found chasing inspiration under stormy skies, quiet beaches, or anywhere that feels like it might be hiding secrets.

She believes that the best stories always leave a mark—that they make you ache a little, haunt a little, and make you wonder what you would have chosen if the magick called to you.

And if it did...

Would you answer?

AUTHOR'S NOTE

Thank you for reading

SHADOWMIRE

Did you like it? Love it?
Want to tell your friends about it?

If you enjoyed Shadowmire, I would be forever grateful if you would leave a review on Amazon. Reviews help indie authors reach new readers and help other readers decide if this book is for them.

For a bonus Gavrail chapter, join my newsletter at:

www.ReaghanQuinn.com

I hope to see you soon for book 2 of the Starweaver series, the SILVER VEIL!

Love,
Reaghan

instagram.com/reaghanquinn
facebook.com/reaghanmquinn
tiktok.com/@reaghan.quinn

Made in the USA
Middletown, DE
10 August 2026

30663709R00262